THE GUILTY ONE

THE GUILTY ONE

LISA BALLANTYNE

WILLIAM MORROW
An Imprint of HarperCollinsPublishers

Designed by Jamie Lynn Kerner

First published in 2012 in Great Britain by Piatkus Books, an imprint of Little, Brown Book Group, a Hachette UK Company, London.

ISBN 978-1-62490-290-1

To my family

The soul in darkness sins, but the real sinner is he who caused the darkness.

—Victor Hugo, *Les Misérables*

CRIMES

1

A LITTLE BOY WAS FOUND DEAD IN BARNARD PARK.

THE AIR SMELLED OF GUNPOWDER WHEN DANIEL EMERGED from the Angel tube stop and headed for Islington Police Station. It was midsummer and airless, the moon slipping unseen into a bright, troubled sky. The day was gravid, ready to burst.

As he started up Liverpool Road, the thunder came and then thick drops of rain, reprimanding, chastening. He turned up his collar and ran past the Waitrose and the Sainsbury's, dodging last-minute shoppers. Daniel was a runner and so he did not feel the strain in his chest or his legs, even when the rain fell heavier, soaking the shoulders and the back of his jacket, causing him to run faster, and faster.

Inside the police station, he shook the water from his hair and wiped his face with one hand. He brushed the water off his briefcase. When he said his name, he steamed up the glass that separated him from the receptionist.

The duty officer, Sergeant Turner, was waiting for him and pressed a dry hand into his. In his office, Daniel took off his jacket and hung it over the back of the chair.

"You got here quickly," Turner began.

Instinctively, Daniel slid his business card onto the sergeant's desk. Daniel frequented police stations in London, but had not been in this one in Islington before.

"Partner at Harvey, Hunter and Steele?" the sergeant said, smiling.

"I understand he's a juvenile?"

"Sebastian is eleven years old."

The sergeant looked at Daniel as if searching for a response in his face. Daniel had spent a lifetime perfecting reflection and knew that he gave nothing away in his dark brown eyes as he stared back at the detective.

Daniel was an experienced defender of juveniles: as a solicitor he had defended fifteen-year-olds accused of shooting fellow gang members, and several other teenagers who robbed for drugs. But never an actual child—never a little boy. In fact he had had very little contact with children at all. His own experience of being a child was his only reference point.

"He's not under arrest, is he?" Daniel asked Turner.

"Not at the moment, but there's something not right. You'll see for yourself. He knows exactly what happened to that little boy. I can tell he does. It wasn't until after we called you that we found the mother. She arrived about twenty minutes ago. Mother says she was in all this time, but poorly, and only just got the messages. We've applied for a warrant to search the family home."

Daniel watched as Turner's reddish cheeks sagged in emphasis.

"So he's a suspect for the actual murder?"

"You're damn right he is."

Daniel sighed and took a pad out of his briefcase. Chilling a little in his damp clothes, he took notes as the police officer briefly described the crime and the witnesses and details of the interview with the child so far.

Sebastian was being questioned in relation to the discovery of another child's body. The little boy who had been found dead was called Ben Stokes. He appeared to have been beaten to death in a leafy corner of the adventure playground in Barnard Park on Sunday afternoon. A brick had been smashed against his face, fracturing his eye socket. This brick, and branches and leaves, had been used by the attacker to cover his broken face. His body had been hidden underneath the wooden playhouse in the corner of the park, and it was here, on Monday morning, that he was found by one of the youths who worked in the adventure playground.

"Ben's mother reported him missing early Sunday evening," said Turner. "She said the boy had gone outside to ride his bike along the pavement of Richmond Crescent that afternoon. He wasn't allowed to leave the crescent, but when she looked out to check, there was no sign."

"And you've taken this boy in for questioning because . . ."

"After the body was found, we set up an incident van on the Barnsbury Road. A local man reported that he had seen two small boys fighting in Barnard Park. One of the boys matched Ben's description. He said he shouted at the boys to stop, and the other child had smiled at him—said they were only playing. When we approached Ben's mother with the description of the other boy, she named Sebastian Croll—your boy in there—only a few doors down from the Stokeses' house.

"Sebastian was home alone on Richmond Crescent—or so we thought—when two officers stopped by at four o'clock this afternoon. Sebastian told the officers that his mother was out, that his father was overseas on business. We arranged an appropriate adult and took him down to the station just after that. It's been obvious since we started that he's hiding something—the social worker insisted that a solicitor be called."

Daniel nodded and flipped his pad shut.

"I'll take you through," said Turner.

As he was led to the interview room, Daniel felt the familiar claustrophobia of police stations engulf him. The walls were papered with public authority notices about drunk driving, drugs, and domestic abuse. All the blinds were closed and dirty.

The interview room was windowless. The walls were painted pale green and were completely blank. Straight ahead of him sat Sebastian. The police had taken the boy's clothes and so he was dressed in a white paper suit, which crackled as Sebastian shifted in his chair. The oversize suit made the boy seem even smaller and more vulnerable—younger than eleven. He was strikingly beautiful, almost like a little girl, with a wide heart-shaped face, small red lips, and large green eyes that sparkled with intelligence. His very pale skin was sprinkled with freckles over the nose. His hair was dark brown, and neatly cut. He smiled at Daniel, who smiled back. Daniel did his best to conceal his shock. The child seemed so young that Daniel almost did not know how to speak to him.

Sergeant Turner began introductions. He was a tall man—
even taller than Daniel—and seemed too large for the small
room. He hunched as he introduced Daniel to Sebastian's
mother, Charlotte.

"Thank you so much for coming," said Charlotte. "We
really appreciate it."

Daniel nodded at Charlotte and then turned toward her
son.

"You must be Sebastian?" he said, sitting down and opening his briefcase.

"Yes, that's right. You can call me Seb if you like."

Daniel was relieved that the boy seemed so open.

"All right, Seb. Pleased to meet you."

"Pleased to meet you too. You're my solicitor, aren't you?"
Sebastian grinned and Daniel raised an eyebrow. The boy
would be his youngest client, yet his words made him seem
more confident than teenagers he had defended. Sebastian's
desperate green eyes and lilting, proper voice disarmed him.
The mother's jewelry seemed heavier than she was, the cut of
her clothes expensive. The fine bones of her hand moved bird-
like as she stroked Sebastian's leg.

This little boy must be innocent, Daniel thought as he
opened his folder.

Coffee and teas and chocolate biscuits were brought in. Sergeant Turner then left them alone so that Daniel could meet
privately with his young client and his mother.

"Please may I have one?" asked Sebastian, his clean slender
fingers, so similar to his mother's, hovering over the biscuits.

Daniel nodded, smiling at the boy's politeness. He remembered being a child in trouble, navigating an adult world, and

suddenly felt responsible for the boy. He slung his still-damp jacket on the back of the chair and loosened his tie.

Charlotte was combing her fingers through her hair. She paused to examine her manicured nails before clasping her hands. Daniel's own mother had had very long nails and he paused for a moment, distracted by them.

"Excuse me," she said, raising her heavily made-up eyelids and then lowering them again. "Will this take long? I must pop out to call Seb's father, to let him know that you're here. He's in Hong Kong, but he asked for an update. I'm going to run home quickly in a minute. They said I could bring him some clothes before they start questioning again. I just can't believe that they took *all of his clothes*. They even took a DNA sample—I mean, I wasn't even here . . ."

The air was thick with the wet leather of the briefcase and the heavy musk of Charlotte's perfume. Sebastian rubbed his hands together and sat up straight, as if strangely excited by Daniel's presence. He took one of Daniel's business cards from their slot in his folder and sat back in his seat, admiring it.

"It's a nice card. Are you a partner?"

"I am."

"So you'll be able to get me off then?"

"You've not been charged with anything. We'll just have a quick chat to go over your story and then the police have some more questions for you."

"They think I hurt that boy, but I never."

"You mean, you *didn't*," whispered Charlotte, "what have I told you about that . . . ?"

Daniel frowned in private acknowledgment of Charlotte's out-of-place reproof.

"Okay, so do you want to tell me what *did* happen on Sunday afternoon?" said Daniel. He took notes as the boy told his side of the story, about going out to play with his neighbor Ben Stokes.

"The Stokeses are just a few doors down," added Charlotte. "Just now and again they'll play together. Ben's a nice little boy, quite bright, but he's a little young for Sebastian."

"He's only eight," said Sebastian, smiling at Daniel and nodding, looking him full in the eye. He put a hand over his mouth as if to suppress a laugh. "Or should I say he *was* eight. He's dead now, isn't he?"

Daniel made an effort not to start at Sebastian's words.

"Is that funny?" Daniel asked. He glanced at Sebastian's mother, but she was distracted, looking at her nails, as if she hadn't heard. "Do you know what happened to him?"

Sebastian looked away. "I think somebody might have attacked him. Maybe a pedophile."

"Why do you say that?"

"Well, they've been asking me all these questions. They think something's happened to him since I saw him last and I suppose if he's dead it must have been a pedophile or a serial killer or something like that . . ."

Daniel frowned at the boy, but he seemed calm, considering Ben's fate as if it were merely an intellectual question. Daniel pressed on, quizzing Sebastian on his actions before and after he returned home the day before. The boy was clear and consistent.

"Fine," Daniel said. He felt as if the boy might trust him. He believed him. "Mrs. Croll?"

"Please call me Charlotte. I've never liked my married name."

"Fine, Charlotte, I just wanted to ask you a couple of things too, if that's okay?"

"Of course."

Daniel could see that she had a spot of lipstick on her teeth and, as he turned to her, noticed the strain in her small frame. Despite the careful curls and the precise eyeliner, the skin around her eyes was tired. Her smile was an effort.

"When the police found Sebastian today, he was home alone?"

"No, I was at home, but I was asleep. I'd had a migraine and taken a couple of tablets for it. I was just dead to the world."

"When Sebastian was taken away, according to the police report, he said that he didn't know where you were."

"Oh, he'd just be kidding. He does that. He likes winding people up, you know."

"I was just winding them up," echoed Sebastian eagerly.

"The police had no idea where you were; that was why they asked for a social worker . . ."

"Like I said," said Charlotte quietly, "I was having a lie-down."

Daniel pressed his teeth together. He wondered what Charlotte was hiding. He felt surer of the boy than he did of his mother.

"And on Sunday, when Sebastian came home, were you there?"

"Yes, when he came in from playing with Ben I was in the house. I'm in all the time . . ."

"And you didn't notice anything strange when Sebastian returned home?"

"No, not in the slightest. He just came in and . . . watched some telly I think."

"And what time did he come home?"

"About three."

"All right," Daniel said. "How do you feel, Seb? Can you go on with the police questioning for a little longer?"

Charlotte turned to Sebastian and put her arm around him. "Well, it is late. We're very happy to help, but maybe we should leave it until tomorrow."

"I'll ask," said Daniel. "I can tell them he needs rest, but they might not agree. And if they do allow it, they might not give him bail."

"Bail? What on earth?" said Charlotte.

"I will request it, but it is unusual where there's been a murder."

"Sebastian has *nothing* to do with this business," said Charlotte, the tendons in her neck straining as she raised her voice.

"It's all right. Wait here."

It was nearly nine o'clock in the evening, but the police were intent on continuing questioning. Charlotte ran back to Richmond Crescent for clothes for her son, and so Sebastian was able to change out of his white paper suit into blue jogging bottoms and a gray sweatshirt. He was led again to the interview room.

Sebastian sat beside Daniel, with his mother on the other side—at the end of the table. Sergeant Turner sat opposite Daniel. He was accompanied by a second police officer, the long-faced Inspector Black, who sat opposite Sebastian.

"Sebastian, you do not have to say anything, but it may

harm your defense if you do not mention now something which you later rely on in court. Anything you do say may be given in evidence . . ."

Sebastian sniffed, looking up at Daniel, and pulled the cuffs of his sweatshirt over his hands as he listened to the formal words.

"You all cozy now in your nice clean clothes?" said the police officer. "You know why we took your clothes, don't you, Seb?"

"Yes, you want to check for forensic evidence."

Sebastian's words were measured, clear and cool.

"That's right, what kind of evidence do you think we'll find?"

"I'm not sure."

"When we picked you up this afternoon, you had some spots on your trainers. The marks appeared to be blood, Seb. Can you explain what the marks were?"

"I'm not sure. I might have cut myself when I was playing, I can't remember. Or it might've been dirt. . . ."

Sergeant Turner cleared his throat.

"Don't you think you might remember if you'd cut yourself bad enough to leave blood spots on your shoes?"

"It would all depend."

"So you think that it is blood on your shoes, but you believe the blood to be your own?" continued the inspector in a cigarette-ravaged voice.

"No, I've no idea what the marks are. If I'm out playing, quite often I get a little dirty. I was just saying that if it is blood, then probably I cut myself playing."

"How would you have cut yourself?"

"Maybe falling on a rock or jumping out of a tree. A branch could have scratched me."

"Were you doing a lot of jumping out of trees yesterday or today?"

"No, I was mostly watching television."

"You didn't go to school today?"

"No, I wasn't feeling very well in the morning. I had a sore tummy, so I stayed home."

"Did your teacher know you were off ill today?"

"Well, what usually happens is that you take in a note the next time you go in . . ."

"If you were inside all day today, Sebastian, how did your trainers get like that? How did the blood get onto them?" Sergeant Turner asked the question leaning forward. Daniel could smell the stale coffee on his breath.

"Could it have been blood from yesterday?"

"We don't know that it's blood on his shoes, Sergeant. Maybe you could rephrase your question?" said Daniel, raising one eyebrow at the police officer. He knew that they would try to trap the boy in this way.

Angrily, Turner said, "Were those the same shoes you were wearing on Sunday, Sebastian?"

"Maybe. I might have put them back on again. I don't remember. I have a lot of shoes. I suppose we'll have to wait and see."

Daniel glanced at Sebastian and tried to remember being eleven years old. He remembered being shy to meet adults' eyes. He remembered nettle stings and feeling badly dressed. He remembered anger. But Sebastian was confident and articulate. A spark in the boy's eyes suggested he was enjoying being questioned, despite the detective's harshness.

"Yes, we shall. We'll soon find out what the marks on your shoes are, and if it's blood, exactly whose blood it is."

"Did you take some of Ben's blood?"

The dead boy's name sounded so primitive, so hallowed, in the windowless room, like a transient bubble, oily and colorful and floating before everyone. Daniel held his breath, but the bubble burst anyway.

"We'll know pretty soon whether any of his blood is on your shoes." Turner whispered the response.

"When you're dead," said Sebastian, his voice clear, quizzical, "does your blood still flow? Is it still a liquid? I thought it might turn solid or something."

Daniel felt the hairs on his arms rise. He could see the eyes of the police officers narrowing at the macabre turn of the conversation. Daniel could sense what they were thinking, but he still believed in the boy. He recalled being judged by adults as a child and how unfair that judgment had been. Sebastian was obviously bright, and some part of Daniel understood his curious mind.

It was well after ten when the interview ended. Daniel felt sapped as he watched Sebastian being put to bed in his cell. Charlotte was leaning over the boy, stroking his hair.

"I don't want to sleep here," Sebastian said, turning to Daniel. "Can't you make them let me go home?"

"It'll be okay, Seb," Daniel tried to reassure him. "You're being very brave. Just need to get started on the questions early tomorrow. It's as easy to sleep here. At least you'll be safe."

Sebastian looked up and smiled.

"Will you go and see the body now?" said Sebastian.

Daniel shook his head quickly. He hoped the police officer near the cells had not overheard. He reminded himself that children interpret the world differently from adults. Even the older juveniles he had defended had been impulsive in their speech and Daniel had had to counsel them to consider before they spoke or acted. He put on his jacket, shivering under its still-damp skin. With tight lips, he said good-bye to Charlotte and Sebastian and said that he would see them in the morning.

WHEN DANIEL SURFACED AT THE MILE END TUBE STATION, IT was after eleven thirty and the summer sky was navy blue. He had been lucky to catch the tube. The rain had stopped but the air still felt charged.

He took a deep breath and walked with his tie in his shirt pocket, his sleeves rolled up and his jacket hooked over one shoulder. Normally he would take the bus home, jump on the 339 if he could catch it, but tonight he walked straight down the Grove Road, past the old-fashioned barber's and the take-out places, past the Baptist church and pubs he never entered, and modern flats standing back from the road. When he saw Victoria Park ahead of him, he was nearly home.

The day felt heavy and he hoped that the boy would not be charged, that the forensic evidence would clear him. The system was hard enough on adults let alone children. He needed to be alone now—time to think—and felt glad that his last girlfriend had moved out of his flat only two months before.

Inside, he took a beer from the fridge and sipped it as he opened his mail. At the bottom of the pile was a letter. It was written on pale blue notepaper with the address handwritten in ink. The rain had wet the letter and part of Daniel's name and address had become blurred, yet he recognized the hand-writing.

He took a deep swill of beer before he slipped his little finger inside the fold of the envelope and ripped.

Dearest Danny,

    This is a hard letter to write.

    I've not been well, and I know now that I don't have much longer. I can't be sure to have my strength later, so I want to write to you now. I've asked the nurse to post this when it's my time. I can't say I'm looking forward to the last bit, but I'm not frightened about dying. I don't want you to worry.

    I wish I could see you one more time, is all. I wish you were with me. I feel far from home, and far from you.

    So many regrets and bless you, love, you are one of them—if not the biggest regret that I have. I wish I'd done more for you; I wish I'd fought harder.

    I've said it to you often enough over the years, but know that all I ever wanted was to protect you. I wanted you to be free and happy and strong, and do you know what?—I think you are.

    Although I know it was wrong to do what I did, I think of you now, working in London, and it brings me a strange peace. I miss you, but that is my own selfishness. In my heart I know that you are doing grand. I am fit to burst with pride at the fact that you're a lawyer, but I am not a bit surprised.

    I have left you the farm, for what it's worth. You could probably buy the old place with a week's wages, but maybe for a time it was home to you. At the very least, I wish that.

*I always knew you'd be successful. I just hope that you
are happy. Happiness is harder to achieve. I know that you
probably still don't understand, but your happiness was all
I ever wished for. I love you. You are my son whether you
like it or not. Try not to hate me for what I did. Release
me from that and I will rest easy.*

All my love,
Mam

He folded the letter and replaced it in its envelope. He finished his beer and stood for a moment with the back of his
hand pressed to his lips. His fingers were trembling.

2

H E'S A RUNNER," THE SOCIAL WORKER SAID TO MINNIE.
Daniel was standing in Minnie's kitchen next to a suitcase
that contained everything he owned. Her kitchen smelled
funny: of animals and fruit and burned wood. The house was
cramped and dark and Daniel didn't want to stay.

Minnie looked at him, with her hands on her hips. Daniel
could tell right away that she was kind. Her cheeks were red
and her eyes moved about a lot. She wore a skirt that hung
right down to her ankles, a man's boots, and a long gray cardigan that she kept pulling closer around her body. She had big
boobs and a big stomach and lots of curly gray hair that was
piled on top of her head.

"Runs away any chance he gets," said the social worker in a
tired voice to Minnie, and then, louder, to Daniel, "You've nowhere to run to now, though, eh, pet? Yer mam's poorly, isn't she?"

Tricia reached out to squeeze Daniel's shoulder. He twisted away from her and sat down at the kitchen table.

Minnie's old sheepdog, Blitz, began to lick his knuckles. The social worker whispered *overdose* to Minnie, but Daniel still heard her. Minnie winked at him to let him know that she knew he had heard.

In his pocket, Daniel pressed his mother's necklace in his fingers. She had given it to him three years ago, when she was between boyfriends and sober. It was the last time he had been *allowed* to see her. Social work finally stopped all but supervised visits, but Daniel always ran back to her. Wherever she was, he could always find his mother. She needed him.

In his pocket, with his forefinger and thumb, he could feel the letter of her first name: *S.*

In the car, the social worker had told Daniel that she was taking him to Brampton because no one else would have him in the Newcastle area.

"It's a bit far out, but I think you'll like Minnie," she had said.

Daniel looked away. Tricia looked like all the other social workers who had been entrusted with him: piss-colored hair and ugly clothes. Daniel hated her, like he hated all the others.

"She's got a farm, and she's on her own. *No men.* You should be all right if there's no men, eh, pet? No need for all your carrying on. You're lucky Minnie said yes. Yer proper hard to place now. Nob'dy wants boys with all your nonsense. See how you get on an' I'll see you end of the month."

"I want to see me mam."

"She's not well, pet, that's why you can't see her. It's in your best interests. She needs time to get better, doesn't she? You want her to get better, don't you?"

After she was gone, Minnie showed him to his room. She heaved herself up the stairs and he watched her hips knock back and forth. He thought about a bass drum strapped to the chest of a band boy and the furred beaters that thump time. The bedroom was in the eaves of the house: a single bed looking out onto the backyard, where she kept the chickens and her goat, Hector. This yard was Flynn Farm.

He felt like he always did when he was shown his new room. Cold. Out of place. He wanted to leave, but instead he put his suitcase on the bed. The bedspread was pink and the wallpaper was covered in tiny rosebuds.

"Sorry about the color scheme in here. They usually send me girls."

They looked at each other. Minnie opened her eyes wide at Daniel and smiled. "If it all goes well, we can change it, like. You can choose the color you want."

He looked at his fingernails.

"You can put your underwear in there, love. Hang the rest up in there," she said as she moved her weight around the restricted space. A pigeon was cooing at the window and she knocked the windowpane to shoo it.

"Hate pigeons," she said. "Nothing but vermin, if you ask me."

Minnie asked him what he wanted for tea and he shrugged his shoulders. She told him he could choose between cottage pie and corned beef and he chose cottage pie. She asked him to wash up for dinner.

When she left him, he took his switchblade out of his pocket and put it under his pillow. He also had a pocketknife in his jeans pocket. He put his clothes away as she had asked, his socks and clean T-shirt sitting to one side of the otherwise empty drawer. They looked awkward on their own, so he pushed them up close to each other. The drawer was lined with flowery paper that smelled funny and he worried that his clothes would smell like that too.

Daniel locked the door in Minnie's long thin bathroom and sat on the edge of the bath. The bath was bright yellow and the wallpaper was blue. There was dirt and mold all round the taps and the floor was covered in dog hair. He stood up and began to wash his hands, standing on his tiptoes so he could look in the mirror.

You're an evil little bastard.

Daniel remembered these words as he stared at his face, his short dark hair, his dark eyes, his square chin. It had been Malcolm, his last foster father, who had said that to him. Daniel had slashed his tires and poured his vodka into his fish tank. The fish had died.

There was a little porcelain butterfly on a shelf in the bathroom. It looked old and cheap, painted in bright colors that were yellow and blue like her bathroom. Daniel put it in his pocket, wiped his hands on his trousers, and went downstairs.

The kitchen floor was dirty, with crumbs and muddy footprints. The dog lay in its basket, licking its balls. The kitchen table, the fridge, and the counters were cluttered. Daniel bit his lip and took it all in. Plant pots and pens, a small gardening fork. A bag of dog biscuits; enormous boxes of tinfoil stacked; cookery books; jars with spaghetti sticking out of them; three different-size teapots; empty jam jars; dirty, oily-looking oven gloves; cloths and bottles of disinfectant. The bin was full and stacked beside it were two empty bottles of gin. He could hear the cluck of her chickens outside.

"You don't say much, do you?" she said, looking over her shoulder at him as she ripped the leaves off a lettuce. "Come over here and help me make the salad."

"I don't like salad."

"That's fine. We'll make a small one just for me. This is my lettuce and my tomatoes, you know. You haven't tasted salad until you've grown it yourself. Come on, help me do these."

Daniel got up. His head was level with her shoulders and he felt tall beside her. She placed a chopping board in front of him and gave him a knife, then washed three tomatoes and placed them on the board in front of him, next to the bowl of lettuce leaves. She showed him how to slice the tomatoes into wedges.

"Don't you want to try one?" She held a wedge out to his lips.

He shook his head and she popped the slice of tomato into her own mouth.

He sliced the first tomato, watching her as she put ice into a tall glass, squeezed lemon juice over it, then emptied the remainder of a bottle of gin over it. When she added the tonic the ice cracked and fizzed. She stooped to place the gin bottle with the others then returned to his side.

"Well done," she said. "They are perfectly sliced."

He had thought about doing it since she'd given him the knife. He didn't want to hurt her, but he wanted to frighten her. He wanted her to know the truth about him right away. He turned and held the knife up to her face, the point about an inch from her nose. Tomato seeds bloodied its blade. He wanted to see her mouth turn down in fear. He wanted her to scream. He had tried it before with others and it had made him feel powerful to see them flinch and recoil. He didn't care if she was his last chance. He didn't want to be in her stinking house.

The dog sat up in its basket and barked. The sudden noise made Daniel flinch, but Minnie didn't move away from him. She pressed her lips together and sighed down her nose. "You've only done one tomato, love," she said.

Her eyes had changed; they were not as friendly as they had been when Daniel arrived.

"Aren't you scared?" he asked, tightening his grip on the knife so it shook a little before her face.

"No, love, and if you'd lived my life you wouldn't be scared either. Now get those tomatoes chopped."

"I could stab you."

"Could you, now . . ."

Daniel stabbed the knife into the chopping board once, twice, then turned away from her and began to slice the other tomato. His forearm ached a little. It had twisted when he stabbed the knife into the wood. Minnie turned her back on him and took a sip of her drink. Blitz came to her side and she dropped a hand so that he could lick her knuckles.

By the time she served dinner he was starved, but he pretended not to be. He ate with his elbow on the table and a hand supporting his face.

She was chatty, talking about the farm and the vegetables that she grew.

"Where are you from?" he asked her, with his mouth full.

"Well, Cork originally, but I've been here for longer than I was there. I was in London for a while too . . ."

"Where's Cork?"

"Where's Cork? My goodness, don't you know Cork's in Ireland?"

Daniel lowered his eyes.

"Cork is the real capital of Ireland. It's about half the size of Newcastle, mind you," she said, not looking at him as she cut up her salad. She paused, then said: "I'm sorry to hear about your mum. Sounds like she's not very well right now."

Daniel stopped eating for a moment. He tightened his fist around his fork and stabbed it gently into the table. He saw that she wore a gold cross around her neck. He marveled for a moment at the tiny suffering that had been carved onto it.

"Why'd you come 'ere then?" he said, pointing his fork at her. "Why leave a city for 'ere? Middle of nowhere."

"My husband wanted to live here. We met down in London. I worked as a psychiatric nurse down there, after I left Ireland. He was an electrician, among other things. He grew up here, in Brampton. It was as good a place as any to me at the time. He wanted to be here and that was grand with me." She finished her drink and the ice rattled. She had that same look in her eye that she had when he held the knife at her.

"What's a psychiatric nurse?"

"Well, it's a nurse who looks after people with mental illness."

Daniel met Minnie's gaze for a moment and then looked away.

"Are you divorced then?"

"No, my husband died," she said, getting up and washing her plate. Daniel watched her back as he finished his tea. He scraped the plate a little.

"There's more if you want it," she said, still with her back to him. He did want more, but said he was fine. He took the plate to her and she said thank you, and he noticed that her eyes had changed, and were warm again.

When she was finished with the washing up, she came up to his room with some towels and asked if there was anything he was needing, like toothpaste, or a toothbrush.

He sat on the bed, looking at the red swirls on the carpet.

"I'll leave one out for you in the bathroom. I have a couple of new ones. Anything else you need?"

He shook his head.

"You've not got much stuff, have you? We'll maybe need to get you clothes for school." She was opening the wardrobe and touching the hem of the one pair of trousers he had hung there.

Daniel let himself fall back on the bed. He put his hands in his pockets and pulled out the little porcelain butterfly. He lay back examining it. She was talking at him, bending down and picking things up from the floor, closing the windows. When she bent down she made little grunts and sighs.

"What've you got there?" she said suddenly.

Daniel put it back in his pocket, but she had seen it. He smiled. He liked the look on her face. It was wobbly with concern. Her lips were tight and she was standing at the foot of the bed, frowning at him.

"That doesn't belong to you."

He looked up at her. Strange that she did not flinch with the knife but would lose it over a stupid porcelain butterfly. Her voice was so quiet he had to sit up a little on the bed to hear her. He had to try not to breathe.

"Daniel, I know we don't know each other very well. I know you've had a hard time and I'll do what I can to make things easier for you. I expect a certain amount of trouble. I wouldn't be in this game otherwise. But there are some things that you have to respect. It is the only way that this will work.

The ornament's not yours for taking. It's important to me. When you brush your teeth, I want you to put it back on the shelf."

"I won't," he said. "I want to keep it. I like it."

"Well, I can understand that. If you're careful, you can look after it for a couple of days, but then I would like you to return it to the shelf in the bathroom, where we can both appreciate it. Mind you, that is two days only, a special treat for you because this is your new home and I want you to settle in. But in two days I will ask for it back, if you have not yet returned it."

Daniel had not been spoken to in this way before. He was not sure if she was angry, or indulging him. His elbows were hurting a little from the strain of sitting up.

She pulled her cardigan around her, and left the room. The scent of lemon juice followed her.

3

DANIEL GOT UP AT HALF PAST FIVE IN THE MORNING AND RAN a ten-mile circuit of Victoria Park and South Hackney. Normally he wouldn't do a long run like this during the week, but today he needed it. The run used to take him an hour and five, but now he could do it in sixty minutes if he pushed himself. He strove to get at least a minute faster every year. There was something death defying in that achievement.

Running came more naturally to Daniel than most other things; flight often seemed the most logical course.

He had not slept, but he pushed himself to keep to time. As he ran, he concentrated on different muscles. He tightened his torso and felt it twist from side to side. As he ran uphill, he concentrated on his thighs and the push in them as he maintained the pace. He had lived in this area of the East End for nearly eight years and now knew every inch of the park, which he could see from his bedroom window. He knew every tree root that prized bumps in the paths, like fingers awaking from the dead. He knew the places that would be cool in the summer and the parts that could be icy in winter. He knew the areas that flooded when the rains came.

Every now and again thoughts came to him. When he brushed them aside, Daniel realized that they had slowed him down.

Now, as he turned toward home, his thoughts returned to the letter. He couldn't believe that she was really dead.

Dead. His foot caught on a rock and he lunged forward. Unable to catch himself, he fell his full length, scraping the skin off his knee and grazing his forearm and the heel of his hand, drawing blood.

"Fuck," he said out loud, picking himself up.

An old man, with an overweight Labrador, tipped his cap at him. "You all right, son? You fell hard. The light's always funny at this time."

He was breathing too hard to reply, but he tried to smile at the man and held up one hand to let him know that he was fine. He tried to continue with the run, but blood from his hand was running down his arm. Reluctantly, he jogged along Old Ford Road and up the cream stone steps in front of his flat.

Daniel showered and bandaged his hand, then dressed in a pink shirt with white collar and cuffs. The wound on his hand throbbed when he fastened his cuff links. He took a deep breath. Since meeting the boy and receiving the letter, the hours had been assaulting him. Looking at himself in the mirror he pulled his shoulders back in an attempt to clear his mind. He didn't want to think about the letter today. He felt the way he had when he was a child: confused, forgetful, not sure how it had all started or why it had fallen apart.

DANIEL HAD ARRANGED TO MEET CHARLOTTE AT THE CROLL family home and take her to the police station. It seemed strange that she had slept through her young son being taken by the police and he wanted to take this opportunity to speak to her.

Richmond Crescent was resplendent in the August sunshine: smart sash-and-case windows gleaming above stark white ledges. Daniel climbed the steps to their door and loosened his tie. The bell was embedded in porcelain, decorated with painted flowers. Daniel pressed once, and cleared his throat, looking over his shoulder at an antique Bentley parked on the curb. He was about to press again when the door opened to reveal an older woman in an apron, holding a duster.

"Please come in," she said with an accent that could have been Polish. She dipped her head and moved toward the living room, pointing with her duster to the stairs. "Mrs. Croll in kitchen."

Alone in the hall, Daniel took in the fresh flag irises, the Chinese vases and silks, the dark antique furniture. He put one hand in his pocket, not sure where the kitchen was. He followed the smell of toast down a staircase covered in thick cream carpet, worrying that his shoes would mark it.

Charlotte was wearing sunglasses. She was slumped over a coffee and the paper. Sun streamed into the basement kitchen and reflected off its white surfaces.

"Daniel," exclaimed Charlotte, turning round. "Help yourself to coffee. I'll be ready in a minute. Forgive me, I have a headache and it's just so bloody bright in here even at this godawful hour!"

"It's gonna be a hot one today," Daniel said and nodded, standing in the middle of the kitchen and holding his briefcase in both hands.

"Sit down, have a coffee."

"Thanks. I just had one."

"My husband called at the crack of dawn. It was two in the afternoon in Hong Kong." She put two fingers to her temples as she sipped her orange juice. "He was asking me if Sebastian had actually been arrested or not. He got terribly annoyed with me. I told him I didn't think so, is that correct? I mean . . . it's just because Sebastian knew Ben . . . but then they do seem to be terribly serious . . ."

"He has been arrested, but he's not been charged. He's been formally cautioned, and he's being questioned for murder, and this might go on for a few days. Better prepare yourself. At this stage, I think you're right to be helpful. We'll see how today goes. . . ."

Charlotte's face froze for a second. In the bright sunlight, Daniel noticed the heavy makeup clogged in the wrinkles around her mouth.

"We just have to help him deal with this in the right way. We don't want him to incriminate himself, but we want to make sure he answers the questions as fully as he can. If he doesn't say something now that's relevant later, it can go against him in court . . . ," Daniel said.

"God, how utterly ridiculous . . . the poor child being put through all this. The case won't go to court, will it?"

"Only if the police have enough evidence to charge him. He's a suspect at the moment, nothing else. They don't have any evidence, really, but the forensic evidence is key. We might get that report back today, and hopefully that will discount him."

Daniel cleared his throat. He wanted to believe his own comforting words.

"Sebastian's never been in any trouble like this before?" Daniel asked.

"No, of course not. This is all just a terrible mistake."

"And he gets on fine at school—no problems with the other kids, or . . . academic issues?"

"Well, I mean, he doesn't *adore* school. My husband says it's because he's too bright. They don't challenge him enough, you know."

"So he does have problems, then?" said Daniel, raising one eyebrow at Charlotte and noticing the strain on her throat as she defended her son.

"He gets frustrated. He really is quite brilliant. He takes after his father, or so Ken keeps telling me. They just don't know how to deal with him at school, how to . . . release his potential.

"Do you . . ." Charlotte paused, removing her sunglasses. Daniel saw that her eyes were suddenly bright with expectation. "Shall I show you some of the work he's done? He really is quite an exceptional child. I really don't know how I produced him."

Charlotte wiped her palms on her trousers and skipped up the stairs. Daniel followed. He made an effort to keep up with her, up to the ground floor and then up again to Sebastian's bedroom.

On the first floor, Charlotte turned the brass handle and opened Sebastian's bedroom door. Daniel felt wary about entering, but Charlotte beckoned him inside.

The room was small. Daniel took in the Spider-Man bedspread and the powder blue walls. It seemed quieter than the kitchen and was darker, the window facing north. It was a private space disturbed, and Daniel felt as if he was intruding.

"Look at that picture," said Charlotte, pointing to a charcoal drawing pinned to the wall. Daniel saw an old woman, with a hooked nose. The charcoal had smudged in places, and the woman's eyes seemed full of warning. "Possibly you can tell that it's me. He did that for me at Christmas. One of our artist friends says it displays quite a precocious talent. I don't think there's much of a likeness, but apparently it conveys a sense of character . . ."

Daniel nodded. There were stuffed toys lined up on the bed. Charlotte bent and picked up Sebastian's schoolbag, pulling small notebooks from the satchel and leafing through the pages where the boy had been commended before thrusting them at Daniel. He glanced at the pages before putting the notebooks down onto the chest of drawers.

Charlotte stooped, then, to pick up a packet of coloring pens that were scattered on the floor. As Daniel watched her he noticed the neat position of Sebastian's slippers by his bedside, and the way that his books were stacked with the largest on the bottom and the smallest on the top.

"He's an exceptional boy," said Charlotte. "In math, he almost never gets anything wrong, and he already plays piano very well. It is just that his fingers are too small."

Daniel took a breath, remembering his own childhood and being shown how to play the piano. He remembered the almost painful stretch of his young hands to find the chords.

In the hall, getting ready to leave, Charlotte took time to tie a silk scarf around her neck. Again, Daniel was aware of how fragile she was. He watched as the beads of her spine appeared as she bent to pick up her bag.

He thought of Sebastian waiting in the cell for Charlotte. Again, he was reminded of his own mother: he remembered waiting for her in social work offices and police stations, wondering when she would appear. Only as an adult had he managed any bitterness about those years. As a child he had been grateful that she came at all.

They walked to Islington Police Station, on the opposite side of the road from Barnard Park. It was an exposed stretch of park, with paths and a football field. The only place to hide violence was the adventure playground that ran alongside Copenhagen Street, rimmed by bushes and trees. Daniel knew that the police had already obtained CCTV footage from Islington Borough Council. He wondered what that would reveal. The corner of Copenhagen Street, just past the incident van, was strewn with flower tributes to Ben. Daniel had stopped to read some of the messages on his way to the Stokeses' house.

The warmth and brightness of the morning was forbidden in the interview room. Sebastian sat at the top of the table, with Daniel and his mother facing the police officers. Sergeant

Turner was accompanied this time by PC Brown, a thin expectant man whose knees banged against the desk when he
moved. Daniel knew that there was another roomful of police
officers listening to the conversation. The interview was video-
recorded and watched from another room.

"Okay, Sebastian," said Sergeant Turner, " . . . what time do
you think it was when you saw Ben out playing on his bike?"

"I don't know."

"Can you remember if it was before your lunch or after?"

"It was after lunch."

"It was definitely after lunch," Charlotte commented. "I
made him lunch before he went out."

The police officer frowned at Charlotte's interruption and
made notes.

"Whose idea was it to go to the park?"

Sebastian put four fingers into his mouth. He turned his
mint eyes up to the ceiling and rolled them back and forth. "I
don't remember."

"Surely you can remember whose idea it was. He was on
his bike and you didn't have a bike. Was it your idea?"

"*I just said* I don't remember."

Daniel watched the smallest spasm of rage flame in the boy's
lips. He wondered if it was this which he understood when he
looked at Sebastian. Anger was what Daniel remembered most
from his childhood: anger and fear. Daniel had never owned
Sebastian's confidence, but there was still something about the
boy that made Daniel remember himself as a child.

"What happened to your hand?" Sebastian asked Daniel
suddenly.

At first Daniel wondered if the boy was seeking refuge from

the police officer's questioning, or distraction from his own anger. Daniel shot a look at the police sergeant, then answered, "I fell . . . running."

"Did it hurt?"

"Not much."

"Okay, Seb, so to get back to your story," said Sergeant Turner, "one of you decided to go to the park, then what happened?"

Sebastian slumped down in his chair, chin into his chest.

Charlotte began to stroke Sebastian's leg. "He's very sorry, Sergeant, he's just tired. This is all so intense, isn't it, darling?

"I think it's just the detail that's a bit wearing . . ."

"Forgive me, Mrs. Croll, but detail is my job. Can I ask you to be quiet and try not to answer for him?"

Mrs. Croll nodded.

"So how did you get into the park, Seb?"

"From the top gate . . ."

"I see. Did you start having an argument with Ben when you were inside the park?"

Sebastian shook his head violently, as if to shake away a fly.

"You're shaking your head, but there was a witness who said he saw two boys of your age fighting at the top of the park. Did anyone speak to you when you were with Ben—tell you to stop fighting?"

"I'm so sorry, Sergeant," said Charlotte. "He just said that he and Ben didn't have a falling-out. Seb's just not the type for fighting, are you?"

The sergeant took a deep breath then asked Sebastian if he wanted a break and a drink of juice. When the boy left to go to the bathroom, accompanied by PC Brown, the sergeant folded his arms on the table. Daniel noticed the fleshy softness of the man's hands.

"I know it's hard, Mrs. Croll, but if you could *try* not to answer for him?"

"I know, I will—I can, I suppose it's just second nature. I can see he's not being as articulate as he could and I just want to help clear things up."

"That's what we all want—to clear things up. Do you think you might step out for a little bit—have a cup of coffee maybe, just while I go through the rest of the questions?"

Charlotte sat up in her seat and looked at Daniel.

"It's up to you," said Daniel. "Or you could agree to stay, but remain silent. You're entitled to be here."

"You'll make sure he's okay?" Charlotte asked.

"Of course."

She seemed pained to leave and gave Daniel a strained look before being shown out.

When Sebastian was brought back in, without his mother, he chose to sit closer to Daniel. He seemed fidgety and Daniel felt the occasional brush of the boy's arm against his, a foot against his trouser leg.

"So, you say there was no argument between you and Ben?"

"No, we were play-fighting for a little bit. We were playing hide-and-seek and chasing each other, then when he caught up with me we were rolling in the grass and play-fighting."

"Sometimes play-fighting can get out of hand. Is that what happened? Did you take it too far?"

Again, Sebastian's cheeks colored with anger. "No," he said. "*I* didn't, but Ben hit me a couple of times and it hurt— maybe he didn't mean to and so I shoved him off me."

"I see. You shoved Ben. What were you doing when the man with the dog called on you to stop? Were you hitting him?"

"No." Sebastian was beginning to look pained. "Sergeant, this is getting very repetitive," said Daniel. "I think you'll find he's answered these questions already. Can we move on?"

Sebastian sighed deeply and Daniel caught his eye and winked at him. The boy smiled broadly and then tried to wink back, scrunching up both his eyes.

"I can't do that, look," he said, his eyes tightly shut. "I need to practice."

"Never mind that now," said the sergeant. "After your fight, did you go to the adventure playground?"

Sebastian was grinning with his eyes tight shut and the sergeant gave Daniel a look of exasperation. Daniel cleared his throat and then gently touched Sebastian's arm.

"I know it's hard, but just a little longer, okay, Seb?"

"Is your hand sore?"

"Not anymore, thanks, it's getting better."

"Was it bleeding?"

"Not anymore."

"Was it *gushing* with blood?" Again the mint eyes wide before Daniel.

Daniel was surprised to feel his heart beating faster. He shook his head once—straightening his shoulders—and watched the police officers wetting their lips as they studied the boy.

"What happened once you were at the adventure playground?"

"We climbed up high and played on the tires, then I said I wanted to go home 'cause I was hungry."

"I've got a picture here of the playground; where were you climbing?"

"I want to see my mum," said Sebastian.

"Just a little longer, Sebastian. We've asked your mum to wait outside and you can see her as soon as you're able to tell us what happened," said the sergeant.

Daniel understood being a boy Sebastian's age and being denied his mother—the desperation he'd felt at the forced distance between them. He imagined that Sebastian too felt this.

"If you can, point out to me where you were climbing," said the sergeant.

"I don't know," Sebastian whimpered. "I want my mum . . ."

Daniel exhaled and placed the palm of his hand gently on the table. "It's clear my client wants his mother to be asked back."

"She agreed to step out to let us talk to him without her."

"He's entitled to have his mum here if he wants her to be. Unless she comes back in, he won't be answering any more questions."

The interview was paused while an officer went to fetch Sebastian's mother. Daniel stepped out to use the bathroom, and the sergeant joined him in the corridor. "Look, son, I know you have a job to do, but we both know what the score is here. I won't tell you your job. I know you want to show him in the best light—get the best angle on whatever he did—but the kid wants to tell the truth. He's a little boy and he wants to tell the truth about what he did—you have to let him. He did it; he just has to say he did it. You didn't see that little battered body in the flesh, I did. You didn't have to console the—"

"Can I stop you right there? Bring his mum in and then we can continue questioning. If it means all this takes longer, then it's just going to have to take longer."

"The super has just agreed to another twelve hours."

Daniel nodded and put his hands into his pockets.

"That'll take us to four A.M. on Tuesday, but we're also applying to the magistrate's court for more time. We have all the time in the world, you mark my words on that."

DANIEL ENTERED THE INTERVIEW ROOM AND TURNED ANother leaf in his pad. The eye of the camera stared at them from the corner of the room.

"They're sending your mum in."

"Did you tell them off? You're a good lawyer, I think."

"You've got a right to see your mum if you want to. My job is to make sure you know your rights."

Charlotte's perfume assumed the room before she did. She sat on the other side of Sergeant Turner. Daniel felt sure she had been asked to sit apart from her son and to keep quiet.

As the sergeant continued to question Sebastian she said nothing, seldom even looking at Sebastian. She fixed her attention on her bracelet and then her skirt and then her cuticles and then Daniel. He felt her watching as he noted down the sergeant's questions and Sebastian's taciturn replies.

Sergeant Turner crossed out something on his own notepad and underlined something else. "Right. Let's get back to where we were. Let's go back to the adventure playground. Tell me again about the argument you were having with Ben."

"I told you already," said Sebastian, his lower teeth showing again. "It wasn't an argument; it was a *discussion*. I said I wanted to go home, but he didn't want me to."

"Tell me again about your *discussion*."

Daniel nodded at Sebastian, to urge him to answer the questions. He wanted the boy to calm down. Losing his temper made him seem guilty, and Daniel didn't want the boy to incriminate himself. Like the police, he too wondered about the boy's sudden temper, yet he wanted the boy to remain consistent in his story. Daniel made a decision to ask for a break if the boy became more upset.

"We climbed up the tires right to the very top of the wooden climbing frame," Sebastian continued. "It's really high up there. I was getting tired and I was thinking about my mum and her headache. I said I wanted to go home, but Ben didn't want me to. He tried to make me stay out. Then he got annoyed and he was shoving me and I told him to stop it."

"*He* was shoving you?"

"Yes, he wanted me to stay out and play."

"Did that annoy you when he pushed you? Did you push him back?"

"No."

"Did you maybe push him off the climbing frame?"

"You had your answer, Sergeant," said Daniel, his voice sounding loud in the small interview room.

"*I didn't push him off*, but Ben said he was going to jump. He wanted to impress me, you see. I was going home and he wanted me to stay and watch him jump."

"Ben was a little boy, not a big boy like you. You were really high up. You sure he decided to jump?"

"Where are we going with this, Sergeant?" said Daniel.

The sergeant cleared his throat and put down his pen.

"Is that what really happened, Sebastian?"

"Yes, it is." He was petulant now, slumped in the chair.

"Are you sure you didn't push him off? Did you push him off and then maybe start fighting with him?"

"No!" Again rage seemed to flash in the boy's lips and cheeks.

"Are you getting angry, Seb?"

Sebastian folded his arms and narrowed his eyes.

"Are you angry at me because I figured it out? Did you push Ben down?"

"I never."

"Sometimes, when people get angry, it's because they're trying to cover something up. Do you understand?"

Sebastian slid off his chair and dropped to the ground suddenly. He lay on his back on the interview room floor and started to scream. It made Daniel jump. Sebastian cried and wailed and when he turned his face toward Daniel, it was contorted and streaked with tears.

"I didn't push him. I didn't push him."

"How do you think he got down there then?"

"I don't know, I didn't hurt him. I . . . I never . . ." Sebastian's screams were so sharp that Turner put a hand to his ear.

It was a few moments before Daniel realized that his mouth was open, staring at the boy. He felt suddenly very cold in the airless room—out of his depth, despite his experience.

Turner paused the interview so that Sebastian could compose himself. Charlotte approached her son gingerly, her elbows sticking out. The boy's face was red with rage and streaked with tears.

"Darling, *please*," said Charlotte, her nails hovering above her son. Her hands were red, the capillaries showing, and her fingers trembled. "Darling, *what on earth*? Please can you calm down? Mummy doesn't like to see you so upset. Please don't let yourself get so upset."

Daniel wanted to run, to lengthen his muscles and dispel the taut screams of the boy and the cramped solemnity of the interrogation room. He went to the men's room again and splashed cold water onto his face and studied himself in the small mirror, leaning on the sink.

He wanted to give the case up, not because of what it was, but because of what it promised to be. He guessed from the way the police were hounding Sebastian that they had some positive results from the lab. If the boy was charged, the media would be all over it. Daniel didn't feel ready. Just over a year ago he had taken on a juvenile case—a boy accused of shooting another gang member. It had gone to the Old Bailey and the boy had been sent down. He had been a vulnerable client, softly spoken, with bitten-down nails. Even now Daniel hated to think of him being inside. And now here was another child about to enter the system, only he was even younger.

Daniel was standing at the front desk when the detective superintendent came up and took him by the elbow. He was a tall man, heavyset, with gray cropped hair and despairing hazel eyes.

"It's all right," he said, slapping Daniel on the shoulder. "We all feel it."

"M'all right," he said. His breaths were there in his throat, like butterflies. He coughed as they escaped him.

"Are you from Newcastle?"

Daniel nodded. "You?"

"Hull. You can't tell with you sometimes, yer accent's got London through it, hasn't it?"

"Been here awhile."

Sergeant Turner said that the superintendent wanted to see Daniel. He was shown into the office, which was cramped and dark, the light of the day splashing down from a small window above.

"Bit tense in there," said the superintendent as he came into the room.

Daniel didn't mean to sigh, but when McCrum heard it, he laughed quietly in acknowledgment.

"All we go through, but still we're not used to this."

Daniel coughed and nodded. For the first time he felt an affinity for the man.

"The hardest thing I ever had to do. Watch that poor woman when she saw that little 'un—murdered in that way. Hard . . . do you have children, Daniel?"

He shook his head.

"I have two. Doesn't bear bloody thinkin' about, does it?"

"The situation—"

"The situation has changed. We're probably going to charge him with little Ben's murder."

"On what grounds? From what I have—"

"He was witnessed fighting Ben, and we found him dead shortly afterward. We now have an oral report from forensics confirming little Ben's blood on Sebastian's shoes and clothes. There was more blood-stained clothing in the house. We'll be asking him about this over the next few hours. We'll be applying to a magistrate for more time if we don't get a confession by two. We got the warrant for Richmond Crescent this morning and the forensics team is still there . . . who knows what else they'll throw up."

"What about the CCTV footage?"

"We're still going through it. Nothing yet. You know how long that takes . . ."

4

DANIEL GOT UP IN THE MORNING, DRESSED, AND WENT downstairs. Minnie was not there and he hung around in the kitchen for a few moments wondering what to do. He had not really slept. He had not returned the china butterfly when he brushed his teeth. He had hidden it in the room. He had decided that he was never going to give it back. He wanted to keep it only because she wanted him to return it. He didn't even know why he had picked it up, but now it had value to him.

"There you are, pet. You hungry?"

She was dragging a pail of animal feed into the hall.

"I'll make us some porridge and then I'll show you round. Show you your jobs. We all have jobs to do around here."

Daniel frowned at her. She talked as if she had a large family, but it was only her and the animals.

Minnie made porridge and cleared a space on the table so they could eat. She made a strange sound when she was eating, as if she was breathing it in. After she swallowed, she would make a tutting sound in appreciation of the taste. The noise distracted Daniel and so she finished first.

"There's more if you want it, pet."

Again, he said that he was full.

"Fine then. Let's go to it. You don't have wellies, do you?"

He shook his head.

"It's all right. I have pretty much all sizes. Come on."

Outside, she opened the shed and he stepped inside. It smelled of damp earth. Along one wall was a row of rubber boots, large and small, just as she had said. There were ten or twelve pairs all in a row. Some were baby size and then there was a pair of giant, man-size, green Wellington boots.

"Are these all the kids you've taken in?" he asked as he tried a pair on.

"And then some," she said, bending over to tidy up one or two that had fallen on their sides. When she bent over, her skirt rode up at the back to expose her white calves.

"How long have you been fostering then?"

"Oh, I don't know, love. Must be more than ten years now."

"D'you get sad when the kids leave?"

"Not if they're going to happy places. One or two've gotten adopted by nice families . . ."

"Sometimes you get to go back to yer mam, though . . ."

"That's right. Sometimes, if it's for the best."

His boots were a little too big, but they would do. He followed Minnie as she opened the door of the chicken coop and stepped inside. The coop smelled of pee. Birds clucked at his feet and he thought of kicking them away, as he did with pigeons in the park, but he stopped himself.

"I look after Hector," she said. "He's old and he can be a bit bad tempered. I do him as soon as I get up. Your job is to feed the chickens and to look for eggs. It's the most important job here. Hector's there just 'cause I love 'im, but I make money from the chickens. I'll show you how to feed them and then we can look for eggs. It's easy, you'll catch on and then you can do that every morning before school. That'll be your job."

The coop stretched back for fifty yards. Some of it was covered, but then the rest was open. Daniel watched her as she took handfuls of feed and sprinkled it in the open part of the coop. She told him to try and so he copied her, scattering the feed.

"That's corn," she said. "The farmer two over gives it to me for a box of eggs. Not too much of it mind. One or two handfuls is enough. They get the kitchen scraps and then there's the grass and weeds that they like too. How many do we have here, do you think?"

"'Bout forty," he said.

She turned and looked at Daniel in a strange way, her mouth open a little.

"Well done, smarty-pants. We have thirty-nine. How could you tell that?"

"Looks to be that many."

"All right, now while they're busy eating, we go and look for the eggs. Take this . . ." She handed Daniel a cardboard tray and they stepped into the covered space. "You can see where they've been sitting," she said, "see, look. I got one here. Lovely big one that is."

Daniel didn't like the farm and her house, but he found that he liked this task. He felt a brisk thump of joy as he searched for and found the eggs. They were dirty, splattered with hen shit and stuck with feathers, but he liked the eggs. He didn't want to break them, as he wanted to break the porcelain butterfly and kick the chickens. He kept one, secreting it inside his pocket. It was a small brown one, and he felt it, still warm.

When they were finished, they counted the eggs. There were twenty-six. Minnie started to move about the yard, preparing Hector's feed and talking to the chickens that clucked around her ankles. There was a fork against the wall and Daniel picked it up. It was almost too heavy for him, but he lifted it above his head like a weight lifter. It fell to the side.

"Careful, love," she said.

Daniel bent and picked it up again. She was bent over, her massive skirted bottom in the air. Holding the fork near his head, he stepped forward and pricked her on the backside with it.

"Here," she said, standing up suddenly. "Put that down." Her accent was funny, especially when she said words like *down*.

Daniel grinned back at her and wielded the fork, taking one step toward her and then another, the tip of the fork raised toward her face. Again, she didn't back away from him.

Daniel felt a sudden jolt as his pelvis was smacked into his spinal column. He dropped the fork and then it came again. The goat rammed him a second time in the lower back and he went forward, falling on top of the fork, face into the mud. He got up right away and spun around, fists tight and ready for a fight. The goat lowered his head, so that Daniel could see the fine brown horns.

"No, Danny," she said, taking him by the elbow and pulling him back. "Don't! He'll go through you like you wouldn't believe. The old goat's got a soft spot for me. He wouldn't have liked what you did there. Just leave him, now. You get gored with one of those horns and that'll be you."

Daniel allowed himself to be pulled away. He walked toward the house, walking sideways so that he was facing the goat. As he reached the doorstep, he stuck his tongue out at Hector. The goat charged again and Daniel ran into the house.

Minnie told Daniel to get washed and get ready to go out. He did as she asked, while she stood in the kitchen, washing the eggs and repacking them.

He washed his face in the bathroom and brushed his teeth, then crept upstairs. The egg was still whole in his pocket and he put it in the drawer by his bedside. He sat it on a glove and placed three socks around it, like a nest, to warm it, closed the drawer and was about to start downstairs when, as an afterthought, he went back into the room and took his mother's necklace from under his pillow and placed that in the nest too, right beside the egg. He checked his back and buttocks for scratches from the goat's horns. He had two grazes on either palm from when he fell.

Minnie was winding a pink woolen scarf around her neck. She was still wearing the same gray skirt and boots that she had worn the day before. On top of her long cardigan, she put on a green coat. It was too tight for her to button up, and so she went out like that, with it open and the pink scarf swinging.

Minnie said they were going to register Daniel at the local school and then they would buy him some new school clothes.

"We'll walk," she said, as they walked past her car. It was a dark red Renault with spiderwebs strung across the right-hand rearview mirror. "Need to show you the way to school anyway, don't I?"

Daniel shrugged and followed her.

"I hate school," he told her. "I'll only get kicked out. I always get kicked out."

"Well, I don't wonder if you have that attitude."

"What do you mean?"

"Think positively. If you do, you might just be surprised."

"Like think about me mam getting better and then she will?"

Minnie didn't say anything. He was a pace behind her.

"I wished that for years anyway and it never 'appened."

"Being positive's different to wishing. What you're talking about is just wishing."

It was fifty feet from her house before they reached a proper path. Minnie told him it was a twenty-minute walk to school.

First they walked through estates, then a park, then a field with cows in it. As they walked, Minnie told Daniel about Brampton, although he told her he didn't care. He wouldn't be staying long.

Brampton was just two miles south of Hadrian's Wall, she told him. When he said he had never heard of the wall, she said she would take him one day. It was ten miles to Carlisle and fifty-five miles to Newcastle.

Fifty-five miles, Daniel thought as he walked behind her.

"You all right there, pet?" she asked. "You're looking right down in the mouth today."

"M'all right."

"What is it you like to do? Not used to boys, so I'm not. You'll need to keep me up to date. What is it you like, eh? Football?"

"I dunno," he said.

They passed the park and Daniel turned to look at the swings. There was a heavyset man alone on one of them, letting his foot gently rock him.

"Want to have a shot? We've got time, you know."

"That bloke's there," he said, squinting at the sun, which was now high in the sky.

"That's just Billy Harper. Billy'll not bother you. He loves them swings. Always has. He's all right. Wouldn't hurt a fly. Around here, pet, everyone knows everyone else. It's the worst thing about the place, you'll find out. But the good thing is, once you have everyone's measure you've nothing to fear. There's no secrets in Brampton."

Daniel thought about that: no secrets and everyone knowing your measure. He knew small places. He'd been put in a few of them, when his mam was sick. He didn't like small places. He liked Newcastle. He wanted to live in London. He didn't like people knowing his measure.

As if she had heard his thoughts, she said, "So you like Newcastle then?"

"Aye," he said.

"Would you like to live there again?"

"I want to live in London."

"My, really? London, I think that's a fine idea. I loved it there. If you grow up and move to London, what do you think you'll be?"

"I'll be a pickpocket."

Daniel thought she might tell him off then, but she turned and gave him a little push with her elbow. "Like Fagin, you mean?"

"What's that?"

"Haven't you seen *Oliver Twist*?"

"Maybe. Aye, I think so."

"There's an old man in that—pickpocket—comes to a bad end."

Daniel kicked at some stones. A cow turned in her path and moved toward him. Daniel jumped a little and skipped behind Minnie.

She laughed. "Och, lad, cows'll not 'arm you. It's the bulls you got to watch for. You'll learn."

"How can you tell if it's a cow or a bull?"

"Well, lucky you. You're here in Brampton. A town full of farmers—you can find out the answer."

"But that's a cow, is it?"

"It is."

"An old cow like you."

She turned to him on the path, stopped walking and looked at him. She was out of breath a little and her cheeks were red. The light in her eyes had gone again. Daniel's heart began to beat very fast, the way it did when he used to come home to his mam's after being away. His heart would thump as he touched the door handle, not knowing what he would find behind the door.

"Have I insulted you since you've been here?"

He looked at her, with his lips just parted.

"Have I?"

He shook his head.

"Speak up."

"You haven't."

"All I ask is a similar courtesy. Do you understand?"

He nodded.

"And while we're at it, you know your time is soon up with that butterfly."

"What do you mean?"

"I said you could have it for a few days, but now I need it back. This evening, when you wash your face and brush your teeth, I want you to return it, do you understand?"

He nodded again, but her back was turned.

"I said, do you understand?"

"Yes," he said, louder than he had meant.

"Good," she said. "I'm glad we understand each other. Now let's forget it."

He followed her along the path, watching her boots in the grass and noticing that the back of her skirt was splashed with mud. His arms felt funny and he shook them to get the bad feeling out of them.

"Look!" she said to him, stopping and pointing at the sky. "Do you see it?"

"What?"

"A kestrel! See it, with the pointed wings and long tail?"

The bird sculpted a wide arc in the sky and then perched on a high treetop. Daniel saw it, and raised his hand to see more clearly.

"They're beauties. We have to watch them from getting the chickens when they're small, but I think they're elegant, don't you?"

Daniel shrugged.

When they got there, the school was an old building surrounded by run-down huts. He didn't like the look of it, but followed Minnie up the steps. She hadn't made an appointment and so they had to sit and wait. He didn't like schools and he felt the ceiling of the place pressing down on him. Again, she seemed aware of how he felt.

"It's all right, pet," she said. "You don't have to start here today. We just need to get you enrolled. After you're all booked in, we'll get you some new togs. You can choose them yourself. Within reason, mind you, I'm not made of money, like," she said, leaning into him.

She smelled almost floral. The definite smell of last night's gin, but then the lemon and the damp smell of her wool, the chickens, and somehow the whiff of the summer grass they had brushed through as they walked to the school. For a moment, smelling her, he felt close to her.

The principal was ready to see them. Daniel expected Minnie to ask him to sit outside, but she pulled him up by the elbow and together they stepped inside the principal's office. He was a middle-aged man, with thick glasses. Daniel hated him before he had even sat down.

Minnie took ages to get into the chair beside Daniel, in front of the principal's desk. She wound off her scarf and took off her coat and then spent time rearranging her cardigan and skirt. Daniel noticed that she had left muddy footprints that trailed from the waiting room into the office.

"Minnie," said the principal. "Always a pleasure."

Daniel could see from a triangular nameplate on his desk that his name was MR. F. V. HART.

Minnie coughed and turned toward Daniel.

"Yes," said Hart. "And whom do you have for us today?"

"This is Daniel," said Minnie. "Daniel Hunter."

"I see, and how old are you, Daniel?"

"Eleven," he said. His voice sounded strange in the room, like a girl's. Daniel looked again at the carpet and Minnie's muddy boots.

Mr. Hart's eyes narrowed as he regarded Daniel. Minnie opened her bag and put a piece of paper in front of Mr. Hart. It was paperwork from social work. Mr. Hart took it and lit his pipe at the same time, biting hard onto the stem of the pipe and sucking until the dirty, heavy smoke drifted over Minnie and Daniel.

"It seems we don't have his papers in from the last school he was at. What was the last school he was at?"

"Maybe you could ask him? He's sitting right there."

"Well, Daniel?"

"Graves School in Newcastle, sir."

"I see. We'll request it. What kind of pupil were you there, Daniel, would you say?"

"Dunno," he said. He heard Minnie breathe, and thought she might be smiling at him, but when he turned she wasn't looking at him. Hart raised his eyebrows and so Daniel added, "Not the best."

"Why do I sense that to be an understatement?" said Hart, relighting his pipe and sucking until smoke blew down his nose.

"This is your new start," said Minnie, looking at Daniel. "Isn't it? You plan on being proper exemplary from here on in."

He turned to her and smiled, then turned to Hart and nodded.

~

THE NEXT MORNING, DANIEL AWOKE WITH THE THOUGHT OF the new school pressing on him, heavier than the blankets of his bed. So many new schools. He listened to the chickens in the yard outside and the pigeons cooing in the gutters. He had dreamed about his mother again. She was lying on the couch in the old flat and he couldn't wake her up. He called an ambulance but the ambulance wasn't there yet and so he was trying to wake her, trying to give her the kiss of life as he had seen on television.

The dream was close to something that Daniel had actually experienced. Gary, his mum's boyfriend, had beaten up Daniel and his mum and then left, taking most of the money and a bottle of vodka with him. Daniel's mother had spent what was left of her dole money on a hit because she said she wanted to feel better. When Daniel woke in the middle of the night, she was hanging off the couch with her eyes half open. Daniel had been unable to wake her and had called an ambulance. In real life the ambulance came quickly and they revived his mother. Daniel had been five.

Again and again he dreamed of her. Each time he could not save her.

Daniel lay on his side and reached into the bedside drawer. His hands closed on the egg, which was cold as a stone now. He warmed it in the palm of his hand. Again he reached into the drawer, his fingers searching for the cheap gold necklace that she had worn around her neck and given to him one day when he was good. *When he was good.*

It was gone.

Daniel sat up and took the drawer out. He placed the egg

on his pillow and searched through the drawer for the neck-lace. He upturned the drawer, and shook out the sock and the children's books, the pens and old stamps torn from envelopes that had been left in the drawer by her other children. The necklace was not there.

"I can't go to school," he told her. He was dressed in the clothes she had laid out for him: white vest and pants, gray trousers and a white shirt. He had done the shirt up in a hurry and the buttons were mismatched. He stood before her frown-ing, with his hair sticking up.

Minnie was spooning out porridge for him and dropping aspirin into a glass for herself.

"'Course you can, love. I've made your lunch." She pushed a bag of sandwiches toward him.

He stood before her trembling, the egg in his right hand. His clean socks were getting all mucky from her kitchen floor.

"Did you steal my necklace?" He could only whisper it.

Minnie raised an eyebrow at him.

"It was in a drawer with the egg and now it's gone. Give it back, now."

Daniel threw the egg onto the kitchen floor and it smashed with a splat that sent Blitz skipping back to his basket.

Minnie bent and put the sandwiches into his schoolbag. He ripped the bag from her and threw it across the floor after the egg. She stood up very straight and clasped her hands in front of her.

"You have to go to school. If you replace the butterfly, I'll replace the necklace."

"I'll smash yer fuckin' bu'erfly if you don't gimme my neck-lace, you thieving old cow."

She turned her back on him. He thought about getting the

knife out of his pocket but the knife hadn't worried her before. He turned and ran upstairs. He had hidden the butterfly under his mattress.

"Here," he said, putting it onto the work surface. "Here's your stupid bu'erfly, now give me the necklace."

She was wearing his necklace. He couldn't believe it. She took it off and handed it to Daniel, then put the butterfly in her pocket.

"So, what have we learned from that, Danny?" she said as he got his breath back.

"That you're a fat thieving slag."

"I think we've learned that the both of us have precious things. If you respect mine, I'll respect yours. Do you remember the way to school?"

"Fuck off."

He slipped on his shoes and slammed the door, dragging his schoolbag behind him. On the way he kicked at the nettles and dandelions that grew. He picked up stones as he went and threw them at the cows, but they were too far away. Billy Harper wasn't on the swings, so Daniel stopped and swung them right round so that none of the other children could play on them. He was late for school but he didn't care.

He didn't care about last chances or new starts. He just wanted everyone to fuck off and leave him alone.

He got lines on his first day for being late.

His teacher was called Miss Pringle and she reminded him of the butterfly. She wore a pale blue sweater and had blond hair that hung below her shoulder blades. Her tight jeans had a rose embroidered on the pocket. She was the youngest teacher he had ever had.

"Would you like to sit at the blue table, Daniel?" Miss Pringle said, bending over a little to talk to him with her palms pressed together between her knees.

He nodded and sat down at the table, which was beside her desk. There were two other boys and three girls at the table. There was a piece of blue paper taped onto the middle of the table. Daniel sat with his hands under the table, looking at a space on the floor beside Miss Pringle's desk.

"Girls and boys, we're happy to welcome Daniel to the class. Would you like to say welcome to our class?"

Welcome to our class, Daniel.

He felt his shoulders hunch, feeling their eyes on him.

"Daniel moved here from Newcastle. We all like Newcastle, don't we?"

There was a sputter of comment and a scraping of chairs. Daniel glanced up at his teacher. She seemed about to ask him a question, but then decided against it. He was grateful.

All throughout the morning, Miss Pringle kept rubbing his back then hunkering down beside him to find out if everything was all right. He wasn't doing the work that she had asked them to do, and she thought he didn't understand.

The lads at his table were called Gordon and Brian. Gordon said that he liked Daniel's motorbike pencil case, which Minnie had bought for him. Daniel leaned across the table and whispered to Gordon that if he touched it, he would stab him. Daniel told him he had a knife. The girls at the table laughed and he promised to show them.

The girls were Sylvia and Beth.

"Me mam told me you're the new Flynn foster kid," said Sylvia.

Daniel slumped down into the desk, over the notebook that he had covered in pictures of guns, although Miss Pringle had asked them to write about their favorite hobby.

Beth leaned over and pulled Daniel's notebook away from him.

"Give it back," he told her.

"How long have you lived here then?" Beth asked, her eyes wide with glee, holding his notebook beyond his grasp.

"Four days. Give me back my notebook or I'll pull your hair."

"If you touch me, I'll kick you in the balls. Me dad showed me how. You know Old Flynn's an Irish witch, don't you? Have you seen her broomstick yet?"

Daniel pulled Beth's hair, but not so hard that she would cry out. He reached across the table and snatched back his notebook.

"You should be careful. She makes all the kids into stew. She ate her own daughter and then she killed her husband with a poker from the fire. Left him bleeding in the back garden, with the blood pouring all over the grass . . ."

"What's going on here?" Miss Pringle was standing with her hands on her hips.

"Daniel pulled my hair, miss."

"We don't tell tales, Sylvia."

Outside in the playground at lunchtime, Daniel ate the cheese and pickle sandwiches that Minnie had prepared, watching the lads play football. He sat on the wall to watch, sniffing in the wind, trying to catch someone's eye. When he'd finished his lunch he tossed the bag onto the ground. The wind caught it and swept it to the gutters of the playing field, near the wire fence. He put his hands in his pockets and hunched over. It was cold, but he had nowhere else to go until it was time to go back. He liked watching them play.

"Wanna game, man? One down, like."

The lad who asked him was short with red hair and mud splattered down his gray trousers. He wiped his nose with his sleeve as he waited for Daniel to reply.

Daniel jumped off the wall and walked toward him, hands in his pockets.

"Wae'aye, man."

"Can you play, like?"

"Aye."

The game made him feel good. He had had a dark, heavy feeling in his stomach since the fight with Minnie over the necklace and he felt it lift for a moment as he ran the length of the muddy field. He wanted to score, to prove himself, but there wasn't a chance. He played hard and was out of breath when the bell rang.

The boy who had asked him to play came up at the end. He walked beside Daniel with the ball hooked under his arm.

"You play all right. You can play again tomorrow, if Kev isn't back."

"Aye."

"What's your name?"

"Danny."

"I'm Derek. Are you the new lad?"

"Aye."

A boy with black hair tried to punch the ball out of Derek's hands.

"Give over. It's mine. This is Danny."

"I know," said the boy with the black hair. "You're the new foster kid at Flynn Farm, aren't you? We're the next farm down. Me mam told me that Minnie the Witch had a new one, like."

"Why d'you call her a witch?"

"'Cause she is one," said Derek. "You better watch, like. She killed her daughter and then killed her husband on the grass outside the house. Everybody knows."

No secrets, Daniel remembered. *Everyone knows your measure.*

"Me mam saw her husband dying and called the ambulance, but it was too late," said the boy with the black hair. He was grinning at Daniel and showing the gaps between his teeth.

"Why's she 'ave to be a witch? She might just be a murderer?"

"Why she never get arrested then? Me dad says you only 'ave to look at her to see she's not right. You could end up like her last one."

"What d'you mean?"

"She was only at Minnie's for about a month. Nob'dy at school even knew her name. Right quiet lass. She went into this crazy fit in the playground and died."

The boy with the black hair dropped to the ground in imitation of the child having fits. He lay with his legs open and sent his arms flailing, palsied and electrified.

Daniel watched. He felt an urge to kick him suddenly, but did not. He shrugged his shoulders and followed them back to the school.

5

DANIEL FELT COLD AFTER HIS RUN. HE APPRECIATED THE rare chill, knowing that the tube would be stifling on a day like this. Fixing his tie, he viewed the room behind him in the mirror, early sun streaming through the bedroom window. He had to be at the police station by eight thirty so that questioning could begin again, but took the time, as he always did, to get the knot just right. He bit down on a yawn.

Last night, with a beer after midnight, he had checked the number for City General Hospital in Carlisle. He had decided not to call, but had taken note of the number anyway. If Minnie really was sick, he knew she would have been taken there. Just the thought of her being ill and dying brought a pain to his breastbone, causing him to take a deep breath. Then it would be replaced with the burn of his anger at her, dry in his gullet—still there after all this time. He would not call her. She had been dead to him for years anyway.

Back in the interview room, Daniel inhaled the stale air of yesterday's questions as he waited for Sebastian. Sergeant Turner's eyes were bleary. The older man pulled gently at his collar and straightened his cuffs. Daniel knew that the police had been given a verbal report from forensics confirming blood on Sebastian's clothes, which had been positively identified as belonging to Ben Stokes. The CCTV film had been scrutinized by police who had yet to confirm a sighting of the boys.

Sebastian was tired when the officer brought him in. Charlotte followed, removing her shades only when she sat down, her fingertips trembling.

Sergeant Turner went through the routine of identifying himself, stating the date and the time. Daniel took the lid off his pen and waited for the questioning to begin.

"How do you feel this morning, Sebastian?" said Sergeant Turner.

"Fine thanks," said Sebastian. "I had French toast for breakfast. It wasn't as good as Olga's though."

"Olga will make you some when you come home," said Charlotte, her voice rough, almost hoarse.

"You remember we took your clothes, Sebastian, to send them to the lab for testing?"

"Of course I remember."

"Well, we have a verbal report from the lab that says the red marks on your shirt were actually blood."

Sebastian pursed his lips, as if he might kiss someone. He sat back in his chair with one eyebrow raised.

"Do you know whose blood might have been on your shirt, Sebastian?"

"A bird's."

"Why, did you hurt a bird?"

"No, but I saw a dead one once and I picked it up. It was still warm and its blood was all sticky."

"Did you see the dead bird on the day that Ben was killed?"

"I can't remember exactly."

"Well, as it turns out, the blood that was on your shirt didn't belong to a bird. It was human blood. It was Ben Stokes's blood."

Sebastian surveyed the corners of the room and Daniel was sure he saw the boy smile. It wasn't a large smile, but a small curving of his lips. Daniel could feel his heart beating.

"Do you know how Ben's blood might've gotten onto your shirt, Sebastian?"

"Maybe he had cut himself, and when we were playing it kind of rubbed onto me."

"Well, the special doctors who looked at your shirt are able to tell a lot of things about the kind of blood that's on your shirt. It turns out that the blood that is on your shirt is what's called expired blood. That's blood that was blown out of Ben's mouth or nose . . ."

Charlotte covered her face with her hands. Her long nails reached up her forehead into the roots of her hair.

"There's also aerial splatter of blood on your trousers and your shoes. That's blood that's been dispersed as a result of force . . ."

Now both of Sebastian's eyebrows were raised. He looked up into the camera. For a moment, Daniel was transfixed. It was the sight of the pretty young boy looking upward into the eye of authority; all the unseen watching him, upstairs, looking at his childlike expressions and trying to find cause to blame. Daniel remembered the saints that Minnie had prayed to, her soft, full fingers twirling the beads of her rosary. There had been arrows to assail St. Sebastian, yet he had lived. Daniel could not remember how he had died, but it had been a violent death. Even as the police officers produced further evidence of Sebastian's guilt, Daniel felt a stronger need to defend him. The witness had come forward to say that he had also seen Sebastian fighting with Ben much later in the day, in the adventure playground, after Sebastian's mother said he returned home, although the sighting was not confirmed on CCTV. Daniel was not intimidated by this, nor the forensics. He had undermined such evidence often enough.

Daniel could sense the police officers' excitement as they persisted with their questions. He was waiting for them to step over the line—almost wanting them to go too far so that he could put a stop to it.

"Can you explain how Ben's blood might've gotten onto your clothes, Seb?" Turner asked again, his jowls heavy. "The scientists tell us that this kind of blood on your clothes might suggest that you had hurt Ben and made him bleed in this way."

"Might suggest," said Sebastian.

"Excuse me?"

"The blood *might suggest* that I had hurt him. Suggest means you don't know for sure . . ."

Daniel watched a ripple of anger cross Turner's face. They

wanted to break the boy—that was the point of the lengthy questioning—but Sebastian was proving stronger than they were.

"*You* know for sure, don't you, Sebastian. Tell us what you did to Ben."

"I told you," Sebastian said, lower teeth protruding above his lower lip. "I didn't hurt him. He hurt himself."

"How did he hurt himself, Sebastian?"

"He wanted to impress me, so he jumped off the climbing frame and hurt himself. He banged his head and his nose was bleeding. I went to see if he was all right, so I suppose that would have been when his blood got onto me."

Despite the temper, this new information seemed to please Sebastian. He sat up straighter and nodded a little, as if to confirm its authenticity.

At seven o'clock on Wednesday, they brought dinner to Sebastian and his mother, which they ate in the cells. It depressed Daniel to watch them. Charlotte ate little. Daniel followed her when she stepped outside for a cigarette. It was still raining. He turned up the collar on his jacket and put his hands in his pockets. The smell of her cigarette smoke turned his stomach.

"They just said they're going to charge him," said Daniel.

"He's innocent, you know." Her large eyes were imploring.

"But they're going to charge him."

Charlotte turned from him slightly and he could see her shoulders shaking. Only when she sniffed did he realize that she was crying.

"C'mon," said Daniel, feeling almost protective of her. "Shall we tell him together? He needs you to be strong right now." Daniel was not sure why he said that—he kept a distance from his clients—but part of him kept on remembering being a young boy in trouble, with a mother who was unable to protect him.

Charlotte was still shaking, but Daniel watched her straighten her shoulders and take a deep breath. Her rib cage became visible through the V of her sweater. She turned and smiled at him, the skin around her eyes still wet with tears.

"How old are you?" she said, her long nails on Daniel's forearm suddenly.

"Thirty-five."

"You look younger. I'm not trying to flatter you, but I thought you were in your twenties still. You look good; I wondered if you were old enough for this . . . to know your stuff, I mean."

Daniel laughed and shrugged his shoulders. He looked at his feet. When he looked up he saw that her cigarette was getting damp. Warm raindrops clung to the stoic, lacquered curls of her hair.

"I like a man who looks after himself." She wrinkled her nose at the rain. "So they charge him and then what?" She sucked hard on her cigarette and her cheeks hollowed. Her words were harsh but Daniel could still see her trembling. He wondered about the husband in Hong Kong, and how he could leave her to deal with this on her own.

"He'll appear in youth court first thing tomorrow morning. The case itself'll probably go to the Crown Court, so there'll be a plea and case management hearing in about two weeks . . ."

"Plea hearing? Well, he's not guilty of course."

"The only thing is that they'll ask for him to be taken into custody through all of this, probably a secure unit. It will be a few months until the trial. We'll obviously ask that he be granted bail, but in murder cases the judge tends to rule for custody, even for a child."

"Murder. Cases. Murder. We can pay, you know? Whatever it costs."

"Like I said, I'll get a good barrister for you and they'll argue, but we have to prepare ourselves for him being in custody for some time before the trial."

"When will the trial be?"

"It all depends. I would think by November . . ."

Charlotte covered her mouth as she gulped. "And his defense?"

"We'll be contacting potential witnesses for the defense, and instructing expert witnesses, in this case psychiatrists, psychologists . . ."

"Why on earth?"

"Well, they'll assess Sebastian—whether he's fit or sane enough to stand trial."

"Don't be ridiculous. He's perfectly sane."

"But they will also talk about the crime itself and assess whether Sebastian is mature enough to understand the offense he is charged with committing . . ."

She sucked hard at the last of her cigarette. It was a stub tweezered in her manicured nails and yet she sucked at it. Daniel saw the lipstick stains on the butt and the cigarette stains on her fingertips. He remembered his own mother's yellow fingertips and the line of her skull appearing when she inhaled. He remembered the bite of hunger, watching as she swapped a ten-pound note for drugs. He remembered lollipops for dinner, crunching them too fast.

He closed his eyes and took a breath. It was the letter, he knew, not Charlotte, which had provoked these memories. He shook his head as if to release them.

It was seven o'clock in the evening. The interview room was calmed by the sweet smell wafting from Sebastian's hot chocolate.

Sergeant Turner cleared his throat. Written notice of the charge was given to Charlotte and Daniel as Sebastian's appropriate adult representatives.

"Sebastian Croll, you are charged with the offense stated below: murdering Benjamin Tyler Stokes on Sunday the eighth, August 2010."

"That's all right with me," Sebastian answered. He held his breath, as if he was about to take a dive.

Daniel felt his throat tighten as he watched the boy. Part of him admired the boy's gall but another part of him wondered what it was masking. He glanced at Charlotte and she was rocking gently, holding on to her elbows. It was as if she was to be charged instead of her son.

Turner faltered for a moment at the boy's response. The boy turned to his mother. "I didn't do it, Mummy!"

Charlotte put a hand on his leg to calm him. He began to pick at his fingernails, his lower lip out.

"You do not have to say anything, but it may harm your defense if you do not mention now something that you later rely on in court. Anything you do say may be given in evidence."

"I didn't do it, you know. Mum, I didn't," said Sebastian.

He began to cry.

⌇

DANIEL WAS THERE AT 8:55 THE NEXT MORNING WHEN THE security van drew up and opened its doors to receive Sebastian. Daniel stood with his arms folded as the boy was led from his cell, his thin wrists cuffed, into the cage in the back of the van. Shades on, Charlotte cried. She gripped Daniel's forearm as the cage doors were closed and locked.

"Mummy," Sebastian called from inside. "Mummy!" His screams were like a nail coursing along the metal casing of the van. Daniel held his breath. He had watched this happen to so many clients, people he was willing to fight for, people he admired, people he despised. This moment had always been calm for him. It signaled the beginning. The beginning of his case, the beginning of the defense.

Watching the doors close on Sebastian, Daniel felt different than he had before. He still couldn't put his finger on it, but there was something about Sebastian that he connected with and he kept hearing his own childhood cries in the boy's desperate pleas. He remembered being Sebastian's age. He had been troubled. He had been capable of violence. What was it that saved him from this fate?

When the doors were locked, Daniel and Charlotte could still hear Sebastian crying inside. Daniel didn't know if the little boy was innocent or guilty. Part of him believed that Sebastian had told him the truth, another part of him was concerned about the boy's strange interest in blood and his tantrums that seemed worthy of a younger child. But Sebastian's innocence or guilt was inconsequential. Daniel did not judge his clients. They were all entitled to a defense and he worked as hard for those he hated as those he admired. But juveniles were always difficult. Even when they were guilty, as Tyrel had been, he wanted to keep them out of the prison system. He had seen what happened to juveniles inside—drug dependency and reoffending. The help that Daniel felt they needed was considered too expensive by politicians who used the criminal justice system to try and win political points.

DANIEL SAT IN HIS OFFICE OVERLOOKING LIVERPOOL STREET. He had the radio on low as he made notes on Sebastian's case.

He had placed the letter in the front pocket of his briefcase; the paper was crumpled now, from being read and reread. Now he took it out and read it again. He still had not called the hospital. He refused to believe Minnie was dead, but read the letter again as if he had missed something. It was a cruel ploy, he decided. All her phone calls over the years asking for forgiveness, and then tiring of that and just asking to see him one more time.

Daniel wondered if the letter was another attempt to have him back in her life. She might well be sick, but trying to manipulate. He folded the letter and pushed it away from him. Just thinking about her made his stomach tight with anger.

The office was warm; delicate rays of sunshine shot through the sash windows and illuminated dust. He picked up the telephone.

After all the things he had said to her, she would still call every year on his birthday and sometimes at Christmas. He would avoid her calls, but then lie awake at night arguing with her in his head. It seemed that the years did nothing to calm the anger he felt toward her. The few times that they had spoken, Daniel had been clipped and distant, not allowing her to tempt

him into conversation when she asked how he was enjoying
work or if he had a girlfriend. He had mastered detachment
long ago, but Minnie had helped him to perfect it. It was because of her that he didn't want to let anyone in. She would
talk to him about the farm and the animals, as if to remind
him of home. He was only reminded of how she had let him
down. Sometimes she would say again that she was sorry, and
he would cut her off. He would hang up the phone. He hated
her justifications even more than what she had done. She said
it had been for his own good. He didn't like to remember, and
mostly he did not, but the pain of that still took his breath away.

He had not called *her* for more than fifteen years.

Not since their disagreement, when he told her that he
wished she was dead.

It hadn't seemed enough. He remembered wanting to hurt
her more.

Nevertheless, he dialed without checking her number or
struggling to recall. The phone rang and Daniel took a deep
breath. He cleared his throat and leaned forward on the desk,
eye on the door of his office.

He imagined her prising herself out of the chair in the
living room as her latest pound mongrel raised its eyebrows
at her. He could almost smell her gin and hear her sighs. *Hold
yer horses, I'm comin', I'm comin',* she would say. The phone
switched to answer phone. Daniel put the receiver to his chin
for a moment, thinking. He didn't have time for this. He
hung up.

Outside the window, he saw a runner, lean and wiry.
Daniel watched him navigating the traffic and the pedestrians.
He could see from his style and the length of his stride that he

was making a good pace, but from this distance it seemed as if
the man was running slowly. The trees shimmered at Daniel
from behind the glass. He had been at the office since early
morning and had not yet stepped outside to feel the grace of
the sun on his skin.

"You busy?" said Veronica Steele, Daniel's senior partner,
popping her head round the door.

"What's up?"

Veronica sat on the arm of the couch, facing him. "Just
wondering how you're holding up."

Daniel threw a pencil down onto a pad that was covered
with scribbles. He spun to face her, hands behind his head.

"I'm all right." Daniel sat back in his chair.

"You've decided to stay with it?"

"Yes." He ran a hand through his hair. "Not the best career
decision, I'm sure. I know it'll get messy. Half of me feels totally out of my depth and the other half wants to try and . . .
save him?"

"He's pleading not guilty . . . ?"

"Yes, sticking hard to his story. The mother is backing him
up."

"Was it Highbury Corner you were at on Thursday?"

"Yup, bail refused as predicted, so he's been sent to the
Parklands House secure unit."

"God that's bleak. He'll be the youngest one in there."

Daniel nodded, rubbing a hand across his jaw.

"Who's your Queen's Counsel—did you say Irene took it?"

"Yes, she got the nod. Did you hear? Made the QC list in
March."

"Yes, I wrote to congratulate her."

"I was surprised she took this on, but she was even at the youth court. I'm so glad she did, though. We have a chance."

The telephone rang and Daniel picked it up, hand over the receiver, apologizing to Veronica.

"Steph," he said, "I asked you not to put through any calls."

"I know, Danny, I'm sorry. It's just, it's a personal call for you. He says it's urgent. I thought I'd ask if you wanted to take it?"

"Who is it?"

"A lawyer from the north. He said it's about a family member."

"Put him through." Daniel sighed and shrugged at Veronica, who smiled and left the room.

Daniel cleared his throat again. The muscles in his body were suddenly sprung.

"Hello, is that Daniel Hunter?"

"It is. Can I help you?"

"My name's John Cunningham, solicitor for Mrs. Flynn. Daniel, I'm sorry. I have some bad news for you. Your mother has passed away. I don't know if you've heard . . . but she has left instructions—"

"She's not my mother."

Daniel couldn't keep the anger out of his voice.

There was silence on the line for a minute. Daniel could only hear his heart beating.

"I understand Minnie . . . adopted you in 1988."

"Look, what is it? I'm actually about to go into a meeting."

"I'm sorry to disturb you. Possibly I could call another time? It's just about the funeral and then there's the matter of the will."

"I don't want anything of hers."

"She has left her entire estate."

"Her *estate*." Daniel stood up. He tried to laugh, but he only managed to open his mouth.

"A simple funeral is being held on Tuesday the eighteenth, if you wish to attend."

The breath almost didn't carry his words, but he said, "I don't have the time."

"I see, but the inheritance—"

"Like I said, I don't want anything."

"All right, well, there's no rush. I expect it'll take a while to settle the house. I'll be in touch again when—"

"Look, I really don't have time just now."

"Fine. Shall I call again on Wednesday, after the funeral? I have left my details with your colleague, should you wish to get in . . . "

"Very well. Good-bye."

Daniel hung up. He rubbed his eyes with forefinger and thumb then took a deep breath.

DANIEL HAD TO CHANGE AT WHITECHAPEL AND TAKE THE London Overground to Parklands House. When he emerged at Anerley, the street smelled of exhaust fumes and evaporated rain. Daniel could feel the sweat forming at his hairline and between his shoulder blades. The sky was low, pressing on him. It was Friday morning, just a day since the first hearing at Highbury Corner, and he was going to meet Sebastian and his parents. Sebastian's father had returned from Hong Kong and this was the first time Daniel would meet him.

He felt strangely apprehensive about meeting the boy again, and meeting his family. Daniel had not slept well. His morning run had been slow because he had been tired before he began. Two nights in a row he had woken up dreaming of Brampton, her house with the dirty floors and the chickens in the coop outside.

Her funeral would be held in a few days, but he did not yet feel her loss.

When he arrived at the secure unit, the Crolls were waiting. Daniel had asked to meet with them first before he spoke to Sebastian. They sat at a table in a bright room with high, small windows.

"Good to meet you, Daniel," said Sebastian's father, striding across the room to squeeze his hand. He was an inch or so taller than Daniel and so he stretched his spine and pushed his shoulders back as he accepted the older man's hand. His hand was dry and warm and yet the strength of it caused Daniel to inhale slightly.

Kenneth King Croll was a powerful man. He was heavy: stomach and jowls, reddened brown skin and thick, dark hair. He stood with his hands on his hips, allowing his pelvis to tilt, as if to assert he was a better man than Daniel. The spider veins on his cheeks had been formed by the best wines and whiskey. He possessed a seismic arrogance and wealth. All the energy in the room was drawn to him, like a whirlpool. Charlotte sat near him, eyes always finding him whenever he spoke or lifted his hands. Daniel took the lid from his fountain pen and slid his business card across the table. Kenneth studied it with a slight curl in his full lips.

Charlotte brought watery coffee from the machine. She

was still immaculate; her long nails a different color every time Daniel saw her. Her hands shook slightly as she placed each cup on the table.

"I just *hate* him being in here," she said. "This place is quite vile. One of the kids committed suicide in here last week, did you hear? Hanged himself. It doesn't bear *thinking* about. Did you know about that, Daniel?"

Daniel nodded. His own client, Tyrel, had tried to kill himself soon after the sentence. The boy had recently been moved to adult prison and Daniel worried that he would try again. Even secure units didn't provide the kind of care that Daniel felt juveniles needed.

Charlotte's trembling fingers touched her lips as she thought about it.

"He'll survive," said Kenneth. "Daniel, go on, what's the score now?"

"I just don't want him to be here," Charlotte whispered as Daniel flicked through his notes. Kenneth tutted at her.

Before the Crolls, Daniel's muscles contracted with tension. He sensed that beneath the colored lacquer, silk, and fine Italian wool there was something terrible about this family.

"I just wanted to go over a few things with you before we see Sebastian. I wanted to talk to . . . warn you, I suppose, that there might be substantial media attention. We need to be careful of that, work out a strategy and try to stick to it so that we can keep that intrusion to a minimum. It will, of course, be automatic that his identity is not disclosed . . . We're still waiting on the indictment bundle from the CPS and when we get that, probably in the next day or so, we can properly instruct counsel. There will be a chance for you and Sebastian to meet the barrister—Irene Clarke QC. She came to the youth court hearing, but I don't think you saw her."

"How old are you, son?" said Kenneth Croll. He was holding Daniel's business card between finger and thumb and tapping it on the table.

"Is that relevant?"

"You'll forgive me, but you look like you're just out of university."

"I'm a partner in my firm. I've been working in criminal law for nearly fifteen years."

Croll blinked at him to indicate that he understood. He began to tap the card on the table again.

"We expect to get the bundle from the CPS in the next few days. From what we know so far the case is based on the blood found on Sebastian's clothes, coupled with the witness who saw the boys fighting both before and after the time when Charlotte says Seb was home. We know they also have neighbor and teacher witnesses . . . these are less important. There is also the fact that the body was found in the playground, which Sebastian has admitted visiting with Ben on the day of the murder . . ."

"He's an eleven-year-old," boomed Croll, "where else would he go except a bloody playground? This is a joke."

"I think there's a strong case to be made here. Most of the evidence is circumstantial. It rests on the forensics, but Sebastian has a legitimate reason for having the victim's blood on his clothes. We'll know more after speaking to the pathologist and forensic scientists, but right now it looks like the kids fought, and the victim subsequently had a nosebleed that caused blood transferral onto Sebastian's clothes. Sebastian had an alibi—

you, Charlotte—from three P.M. that afternoon, and the later sighting of the boys is questionable. The police didn't find any CCTV images to back up their case against him. This was a bloody murder, but Sebastian *didn't* come home covered in blood. He didn't do it."

"It's all just a mistake, you see," Charlotte offered, her voice cracking. "Even with forensic things, the police often make mistakes."

"What would you know?" said Croll, his voice a whisper. "Leave the country for two weeks and you let him get arrested. I think you'd best stay out of it, don't you?"

Charlotte exhaled suddenly, her fragile shoulders rising almost to her ears. She reddened under her brown foundation at Croll's criticism. Daniel caught her eye.

"Daniel," said Croll, his voice now so loud that Daniel could almost feel its vibrations in the table on which they leaned, "Umm . . . You've done a fine job and we thank you for stepping in like this. Thank you for your help at the police station and for taking things this far, but I've got some contacts of my own. I think we'll want the case passed to another defense team. We don't want to take any chances. I don't mean to be rude, but I feel the need to cut to the chase here. I don't think you've got the experience we need . . . You understand?"

Daniel opened his mouth to speak. He thought about telling Croll that Harvey, Hunter and Steele was one of London's leading law practices. Instead he said nothing. He stood up. "That's your decision," he said quietly, trying to smile. "It is entirely up to you. You're entitled to choose the defense team best suited to you. Good luck, and you know where I am if you need anything."

Back out on the street, Daniel took off his jacket and rolled up his sleeves, squinting in the sunshine. He hadn't been let go for years and tried to remember if he had ever been let go so quickly. He felt injured by Kenneth Croll's dismissal, but he didn't know if it was his pride or the lost chance to defend the boy that hurt. Daniel stood in the street and looked up at Parklands House. It was a cruel name for a prison.

He started to walk toward the train, telling himself that the case would have been difficult, especially because of the media attention it was bound to generate, but he was reeling. It was hard to walk away. The day was still and warm and yet it felt like walking into the wind. He felt it tug and pull at him, taking him off course. He had not felt like this in a while, but it was familiar; it felt like leaving, and losing.

6

AFTER SCHOOL HE MADE HIS WAY BACK TO MINNIE'S HOUSE. He walked slowly, his satchel hanging off his shoulders and his tie loose. He picked up a stick to beat the grass on either side of his path. He was tired and thinking about his mam. He remembered her sitting in front of the mirror in her bedroom and putting her eyeliner on and asking him if he thought she looked like Twiggy. She looked pretty with her makeup on.

He blinked twice as he remembered the eyeliner running down her cheek and the lopsided smile when she injected. She didn't look pretty then.

He looked up and saw the kestrel again, hovering over the moor. Daniel stood and watched as it snatched a field mouse from the grass and carried it off.

He didn't hear them come up behind him, but someone

pushed his right shoulder, hard, and he lurched forward. He turned and there were three boys.

"Oi, new lad!"

"Fuck off an' leave me alone."

He turned but they pushed him again. He tightened his fist but he knew he would get beaten up if he went for them. There were too many of them. He stood before them and let his satchel fall to the ground.

"Like living with the old witch, do ya?"

He shrugged his shoulders.

"What you doin' that for? You a fag? Oooo!" The biggest lad wiggled his hips and rubbed his palms against his chest. Daniel's knife was in his bag but there was no time to get it out. He charged the big lad instead and hit him in the stomach with his head.

He hurt him.

The lad retched, as if he might throw up, but the other two boys pulled Daniel down. They kicked his body, legs, arms, and face. Daniel put his elbows over his face but the boy who had called him a fag grabbed his hair and pulled his head right back. Daniel felt his chin lifted and his neck stretch. The boy's fist smashed into Daniel's nose. Daniel heard the crack and tasted the blood, felt his body snap against the blow.

They left him bleeding in the grass.

Daniel stayed curled up in a ball until he heard their voices fade. He could taste blood in his mouth and his body hurt all over. His arms started to tingle and itch. When he squinted at his forearm he saw that it was covered in white spots. He was lying in a bed of nettles. He rolled over and onto his knees. He wasn't crying, but his eyes were watering and he wiped them with the raised nettle sting on his forearm. The tears seemed to help the sting for a moment and then the itch returned.

An older man walked past with his dog. It was a Rottweiler and it snarled at him, saliva and wrinkled nose. The bark and snap of its chain made Daniel jump. He got to his feet.

"You all right there, lad?" the man asked, looking backward at Daniel as he walked on.

Daniel turned and ran.

He ran across the Dandy to Brampton station. He didn't have money for the bus or the train, but he knew the way to Newcastle. He ran holding his side where he had been kicked, and then walked for a few strides before trying to run again.

Cars growled past with such speed that it affected his balance. His mind was blank, reduced to the pain in his nose, the ache in his side, the blood in his throat, the angry sting on his arm, and the lightness of himself, burned out and lifted up like papers in a chimney. The blood from his nose had dried on his chin and he rubbed it off. He couldn't breathe through his nose but he didn't want to touch it in case it bled again. He was cold. He rolled down the sleeves of his shirt and buttoned the cuffs. His nettle skin rubbed, swollen, against the cotton of his shirt.

Home. He wanted to be with her, wherever she was. The social worker had told him that she was out of the hospital. He would be home when she welcomed him, when she took him into her arms. He almost turned back, but then he pictured her again. He forgot the cars and the hard road and the blood in his throat. He remembered his mam putting her makeup on and the smell of her, all talcum powder after her bath. It made him forget the cold.

He was thirsty. His tongue stuck to the roof of his mouth. He tried to forget his thirst and remember instead the tingle of her fingers through his hair. How long was it, he tried to remember, since she had done that? His hair had been cut several times. Had she even touched this hair that now grew on his head?

He was walking along, counting months on his fingers, when a van drew up beside him.

Daniel stood well back. The driver was a man with long hair and tattoos on his forearm. He rolled down the window and leaned over to shout to him.

"Where you headed, lad?"

"Newcastle."

"Hop in then."

Daniel knew the man could be a nut but he climbed up beside him anyway. He wanted to see his mam again. The man was listening to the radio and it was loud enough that Daniel didn't feel the need to talk. The man drove with his hands folded over the steering wheel. The muscles in his arms flexed when he turned the wheel. He smelled of old sweat, and the van was dirty, full of crushed cans and empty cigarette packets.

"Eeeh, man, better put your seat belt on, eh?"

Daniel did as he asked him.

The man bit a cigarette out of the packet that was on the dashboard and asked Daniel to hand him the lighter that was by his feet. Daniel watched the man light his cigarette. He had a tattoo of a naked lady on his arm and a scar like a burn on his neck.

The man rolled the window down and exhaled smoke out into the air that rushed behind them.

"You want one?"

Biting his lip, Daniel took a cigarette. He lit it and rolled his window down as the man had done. He put one knee up on the seat and let his left arm rest on the open window. Daniel smoked like that, feeling free and bitter and wild and alone. The cigarette made his eyes water. He laid his head back as the rush hit him. He felt sick, as he always did when he had a cigarette, but he knew he wouldn't throw up.

"What you up to in Newcastle, then?"

"Just going to see me mam."

"Got yerself in a scrap, did ye?"

Daniel shrugged and took another drag.

"You'll be able to clean yerself up when you get home, like."

"Aye."

"What would you've done if I hadn't stopped?"

"Just walked."

"Eeeh, that's a long way, lad. Take you all night."

"I'm not bothered, but thanks for the lift all the same."

The man laughed and Daniel didn't know why he was laughing. The man's front teeth were broken. He finished his cigarette and then flicked it out of the window. Daniel watched the red sparks of the discarded cigarette leave them. He too wanted to toss his cigarette but it was only smoked halfway. Daniel thought he might get in trouble for wasting it. He took another few drags then flicked it out of the window when the man leaned out of his truck to hawk and spit.

"Will yer mam have your tea on, then?"

"Aye."

"What does she make for you?"

"She makes . . . roast beef and Yorkshire pudding."

His mother had only ever made him toast. She made good cheese on toast.

"Roast beef on a Tuesday? My, I need to come live with you. That's not bad, that is. Where am I dropping you?"

"Just the center. Wherever's easier."

"I can take you home, like, man? I'm overnight in New-castle. I want you home in time for your roast beef, don't I? Where are you?"

"The Cowgate, it's—"

The man laughed again, and Daniel frowned at him. "Yer a'right, man. I know the Cowgate, like. I'll take you there."

Daniel felt cold when he was dropped off. The man left him at the roundabout and tooted his horn as he drove away.

Daniel pulled his shoulders up against the cold and ran the rest of the way: down Ponteland Road and along Chestnut Avenue onto Whitehorn Crescent. His mam had been living there for the past two years. He hadn't lived with her there. It was a white house on the end of a row, next to two redbrick houses that were boarded up. He ran toward it. His nose was starting to bleed again and it hurt when he ran, so he slowed down. He put his hand up to touch it. It felt too big, like some-one else's nose. Even with his nose blocked with blood, he could still smell the cigarette off his fingers. His satchel was jumping up and down on his shoulders, so he let it fall off and ran with it in one hand.

He stopped at the path to the house. The glass was broken in all the windows, and the upstairs window was gone; every-thing inside was black. He frowned up at her window. It was getting dark, but the window looked blacker than all the other unlit windows. The grass in the garden was tall as his knees and growing all over the path. He took giant steps through the grass to the side door. The grass was littered with objects: a flattened traffic cone, an upturned baby's carriage, an old shoe. He could hear a dog barking. He was breathing hard.

He paused at the door before he turned the handle. His heart was beating hard and he bit his lip. There would be no roast beef. Still, he thought about her throwing open the door and holding him. Maybe she didn't have a boyfriend just now. Maybe her friends weren't round. Maybe she was clean. Maybe she would make him toast and they would sit on the couch together watching *Crown Court*. He felt a strange burning in his chest. He held his breath.

When he opened the door and stepped into the hall, it smelled damp and charred. He peered inside the living room but everything was black. He didn't cry. He walked inside. The kitchen was gone. He placed a hand on the wall and then looked at his black palm. The air was still damp with smoke and it caught the back of his throat. In the living room, the couch was scorched to a spring skeleton. He climbed upstairs. The carpet squelched with water and the banister was charred. The bath and the sink were black with soot. In one of the bedrooms, the glass of the mirrored wardrobe was broken, but he managed to slide the door open a little. Her clothes were still inside, unburned. Daniel slipped inside the wardrobe and pressed her dresses against his face. He slid down to crouch among her shoes and sandals. He put his forehead against his knees.

He didn't know how long he was crouched in the wardrobe, but after a while he heard someone on the stairs. They were walking from room to room, shouting, "Is anyone in here?"

Daniel wanted to find out where his mother had gone, but when he walked into the hall a man grabbed him by the collar and pushed him against the wall. The man was only a little taller than Daniel was. He was wearing a white vest. Daniel could smell the man's salt sweat over the charred smell of the flat. The man's stomach pressed against Daniel as he held him to the wall.

"What the hell are you doin' in 'ere?" the man said. "Scram, go on."

"Where did me mam go?"

"Yer mam? Who's yer mam?"

"She lived here, her clothes're still here."

"The junkies burned the place down, didn't they? Out of it, all of them. They didn't even know the place was on fire. I had to call the fire brigade. The whole bloody row could've gone up."

"What about me mam?"

"I don't know anything about yer mam. They took them all out on stretchers—still bloody out of it probably. One of 'em were burned to a crisp. It were right disgusting. Couldn't tell if it were man or woman."

Daniel twisted away from him and started to run down the stairs. He could hear the man calling after him. He started to cry on the way down and then he slipped and fell down a few of the steps. He scraped his arm, but he didn't really feel it. He got up and ran out of the door and through the grass, stumbling on the traffic cone. His feet slapped on the pavement. He didn't know where he was running, but he was running as fast as he could. His bag must have fallen off somewhere, in the wardrobe or on the stairs, and he felt light and fast without its uneven weight on his shoulders. He ran right down Ponteland Road.

It was dark and he was sitting on the curb on the West Road when a policewoman came up to him. He didn't look at her, but when she asked him to go with her he went because he was tired out. At the station they called his social worker and she drove him back to Minnie's house.

It was after ten by the time they arrived in Brampton. The town seemed so dark, the green of the fields black against the night sky. Daniel's eyelids felt thick and he tried to keep them open as he looked out of the car window. Tricia was talking to him about running away and about the reformatory and how he would be going there if he couldn't stay put. He didn't turn to look at her as she spoke. The smell of her perfume hurt his nose and his head.

Minnie was standing outside her front door, with her big cardigan wrapped round her. Blitz ran up to Daniel when he got out of the car. Minnie reached out to him but he twisted away from her and walked into the house. The dog followed him. Daniel sat at the bottom of the stairs waiting for them to come in, playing with the dog's ears, which were like squares of velvet. Blitz lay on his back so that Daniel could scratch his stomach, and even though he was tired, he got down on his knees to do it. The white hair on the dog's stomach was dirty from the yard.

He could hear Minnie and Tricia outside the door. They were whispering. *School. Mother. Police. Fire. Decision.* Although he was straining, he could hear only these words clearly. He had asked the police and his social worker about his mother. The police didn't bother to try and find out, but Tricia told him in the car that she would look into what happened to her and that she would tell Minnie if she heard anything.

"Why are you going to tell Minnie, why won't you just tell me?" Daniel had shouted at her.

"If you don't behave yourself, you're going to be in a reformatory next year and that'll be you until you're eighteen."

MINNIE CLOSED THE DOOR AND STOOD LOOKING AT HIM with her hands on her hips.

"What?"

"You look like you've had a hard day. Let me run you a bath."

He thought she was going to say something else. He had prepared himself for harsh words. He went into the bathroom and sat on the toilet seat as she agitated bubbles in the bath. The mirror steamed up and the air smelled clean.

She took a washcloth and soaked it in the hot bathwater.

"Your nose is looking pretty nasty. Let me wash away some of that blood before you get in. Bit late, but we'll put some ice on it. We don't want you to have a squashed boxer's nose, do we? Not a good-lookin' lad like you; wouldn't be right."

He let her tend to his nose. She was gentle and the cloth was warm. She rubbed away the dried blood and then washed around his nose.

"Does it hurt, love?"

"Not really."

"You're a brave soul."

He could smell the gin on her breath when she leaned close to him.

When she was finished, she ran her hand through his hair and rested her palm on his cheek.

"Do you want to talk about it?"

He shrugged.

"You went to find your mother?"

"She wasn't there." His voice thickened.

She pulled him into her gently, and he felt the rough wool of her cardigan against his cheek. He started to cry again, but he didn't know why.

"There," she said, rubbing his back. "Better out than in. Tricia'll let me know if they find out about your mum. You're going to be all right. I know it doesn't seem like it, but I could tell from the first minute I met you that you're a very special boy. You're strong and you're bright. You'll not be little forever. Whatever anyone else tells you, being grown up's a lot better. You get to make your own decisions and live where you like and with whom you want and you'll be grand."

The bathroom was wet with steam. Daniel felt so tired. He laid his head against her stomach and cried. He put his hands on her hips. His hands couldn't meet in the middle, but it felt good resting on her stomach and feeling the rise and fall as she breathed.

He sat up and wiped his eyes with his sleeve.

"Come on. Get in there, and get warmed up while I make you some supper. Just leave those dirty clothes on the floor. I'll bring your pajamas down."

When she left, he undressed and stepped into the bath. It was too hot and he took some time lowering himself down into it. The bubbles whispered at him. His arms were a real mess: grazed from the stairs and bruised from the kicking. He had bruises on his side and his ribs too. It felt better once he was in the bath. He laid right back and let his head slip under the water, wondering if this was what it felt like to be dead: warmth and silence and the lap of water. He felt the pressure in his lungs and sat up. He was wiping the bubbles off his face when Minnie came in again.

She put a towel on the toilet seat for him and then placed his pajamas on top. There was a stool by the side of the bath and she leaned on the sink and lowered herself down onto it.

"How's your bath? Are you feeling any better?"

He nodded.

"You look better, I have to say. What a fright you gave me with all that blood. What happened to you? Look at your arms. You're covered in bruises."

"Got in a fight at school."

"Who was it? I know them all in Brampton. They buy my eggs. I can talk to their mothers."

He inhaled. He was about to tell her that he got a kicking because of her, but he decided against it. He was too tired to fight with her, and he liked her, just a little bit—just right then, for fixing his nose and running him the bath.

"You'll be hungry."

He nodded.

"I had stew for dinner. I still have yours in the fridge. If you want I'll heat it up for you."

He nodded again, touching his nose to check if it was bleeding again.

"Or do you just want cheese on toast since it's so late? Cup of cocoa."

"Cheese on toast."

"Right you are then. You should start getting out soon. Stay in too long, you'll get a chill."

"Minnie?" He put one hand on the edge of the bath as she passed. "You know the butterfly—why do you like it so much? Is it worth a lot of money?"

She pulled her cardigan around her. He wasn't being cheeky. He wanted to know, yet he could sense her withdraw.

"It's worth a lot to me," she said. She started to leave, but then she turned at the door. "My daughter gave it to me."

Daniel leaned on the side of the bath so that he could see her face. She looked sad for a moment but then she was gone and he heard her sighing as she made her way down the stairs.

Later, in his bedroom, listening to the creaks as the house fell asleep, he checked that his mam's necklace was still there and his knife was still under his pillow.

7

DANIEL PUSHED HIS SHOULDER BLADES BACK INTO THE driver's seat as he drove up the M6. He drove with the window down and his elbow out. The noise of the wind almost drowned out the radio, but he needed the air. Driving north he felt an almost magnetic pull. He had not planned to go up for the funeral, but had spent a restless weekend, his mind alternately tormented by thoughts of Sebastian and Minnie. He had woken up with a headache at six o'clock in the morning, showered, dressed, and gotten straight into the car. He had been on the road for nearly four hours, driving in a mindless way, looking forward and remembering, letting his foot fall heavily on the accelerator.

He imagined arriving in Brampton and being slowed by the unrepentant green, the smell of manure threading the air. He imagined pulling up at her house and listening to the barks of her latest pound dog. It would come running toward him: a boxer, or a mongrel, or a collie. Whatever trauma the dog had experienced, it would still stop in its tracks and heed her when she called for it to stop barking. She would tell the dog that Daniel was family and there was no need for the racket.

Family. The kitchen floor would be unwashed and the putty around the windows would be pecked by the chickens. She would be half drunk and offer him one and he would accept and they would drink gin in the afternoon, until she cried at the sight of him, and wept for his loss. She would kiss him with her lemon lips and tell him that she loved him. *Loved him.* What would he feel? So long since he had been close to her and yet the smell of her would be familiar. Even though he was angry enough to hit her, the smell of her would bring him comfort and he would sit down with her in the living room. He would enjoy her company and watching the way her face flushed when she spoke. He would feel relief to be near her, listening to her lilting Irish voice. It would be baptismal and deliverance would flood him, soak him like the northern rain, and leave him clean before her and ready to accept all that he had done, and all that she had done. He would forgive them both.

He pulled into the service area.

I'll never forgive you, he had screamed at her once, so long ago.

I've never been able to forgive myself, lad. How could I expect you to, she had said, later, years later, over the phone—trying to make him understand. She had called often after he moved down to London, less as the years went by, as if she had lost hope that he could forgive her.

I only wanted to protect you, she would try to explain. But he would never hear of it. He had never allowed her to explain, no matter how hard she tried. Some things could never be forgiven.

Daniel bought a coffee and stretched his legs. He was only twenty miles from Brampton now. The air was cooler and he thought he could already smell the farms. He set his coffee cup on the roof of his car and put his hands into his pockets, pushing his shoulders up to his ears. His eyes were hot from the effort of concentrating on the road. It was nearly lunchtime and the coffee was like mercury in his stomach. He had driven halfway up the country and now that seemed inexplicable. If he had not come so far already, he would have turned back.

He drove the last twenty miles slowly, keeping to the inside lane, listening to the friction of the air against his open window. At the Rosehill roundabout he took the third exit, wincing at the turning signposted Hexam, Newcastle.

After the trout farm he saw Brampton ahead of him, set among the tilled fields like a crude gem. A kestrel hovered by the side of the road and then disappeared from view. The warm smell of manure came, as he had expected, and was instantly calming. After London, the air tasted so fresh. The redbrick council houses and neat gardens seemed smaller than he remembered. Brampton was primitive and quiet as Daniel checked his speed and drove right through the town to the farm he had grown up on, high on the Carlisle Road.

He parked outside Minnie's farm, and sat for a few minutes, his hands on the wheel, listening to the sound of his breath. He might have driven away again, but instead he got out of the car.

He walked very slowly toward Minnie's door. His fingers

were trembling and his throat was dry. There was no mongrel barking, no hoarse cockerel or clucking chickens. The farm was locked, although Daniel thought he could still see the impressions of her men's boots in the yard. Daniel looked up at the window that had been his bedroom. He made fists with his hands in his pockets.

He walked around the back of the house. The chicken coop was still there, but empty. The door of the coop swayed in the wind; scant white feathers still clung to the mesh. There was no goat, but Daniel could still see the impressions of hooves in the mud. Could it be that the old goats had outlived her? Daniel sighed as he thought of the animals leaving her and being replaced, like the foster children she had raised and then let go, time and again.

Daniel pulled out his house keys. Alongside the key to his London flat, he still had Minnie's house key. The same brass key that she had given Daniel when he was a boy.

The house smelled damp and was quiet when he opened the door. From its depths, the cold reached out to him like elderly hands. He slipped inside, pulling the sleeves of his sweater over his hands to warm them. The house still smelled of her. Daniel stood in the kitchen letting his fingers move from the crowded work surface to the sewing kit, to the boxes of animal feed and the jars of coins, buttons, and spaghetti. The kitchen table was piled high with newspapers. Mindful spiders scuttled from the floorboards.

He opened the fridge. There wasn't much food, but it had not been emptied. The tomatoes were shrunken, wearing furred gray hats. The half bottle of milk was yellow and sour. Lettuce was wilted to seaweed. Daniel closed the door.

He went into the living room, where the last newspaper she had read was lying open on the couch. It had been a Tuesday then, when she had last been in the house. He could picture her with her feet up, reading *The Guardian*. He touched the paper and felt a chill. He felt both close to her and distant, as if she were a reflection he could see in a window or a lake.

Her old piano was open by the window. Daniel pulled out the stool and sat down, listening to the wood strain under his weight. He pumped one of the pedals gently with his foot, letting his fingers fall heavy on the keys, the notes discordant under his touch. He remembered nights as a child when he would creep downstairs and sit on the stairs, the toes of one foot warming the other as he listened to her play. She played slow, sad, classical pieces that he did not recognize at the time but which he had learned to name as he got older: Rachmaninov, Elgar, Beethoven, Ravel, Shostakovich. The drunker she became, the louder she would play and the more notes she would miss.

He remembered standing in the cold of the hall, watching her through the ajar living room door. She was heavy on the keys, so that the piano itself seemed to protest beneath her. Her calloused, bare feet pumped the pedals as strands of her gray curls fell in her face.

Daniel smiled, sounding single notes on the piano. He could not play. She had tried to teach him once or twice. His forefinger found the notes and then listened to the sound of them: cold, shuddering, lonely. He closed his eyes, remembering; the room was still thick and heavy with the scent of dog. What had happened to the dog when Minnie died? he wondered.

Every year he had known her, on the eighth of August, she

drank herself into a stupor listening to one record over and over again. It was a record she wouldn't let him touch. She kept it tight in its sleeve except for that one day of the year when she would let it spin and allow the fine needle of the stylus to find its fingerprint threads. She would sit in the half dark, the living room lit only by the fire, and listen to Ravel's Piano Concerto in G Major. Daniel had been at university before he knew the name of the track, although he had memorized every note well before then.

Once, she had let him sit with her. He had been thirteen or fourteen and still trying to understand her. She had made him sit quietly, turned from her and facing the record that scratched its way into the music as she waited, her chin bobbing up and down slightly in expectation of the notes and the pathos that would find her.

When the music started, he had turned to watch her face, surprised by the effect the music had on her. It reminded him of his mother injecting heroin. The same rapture, the same devout attention, the same bewilderment—although she would seek it out again and again.

At first Minnie would seem to follow the notes with her eyes, her breath deepening and her chest rising. Her eyes would water, and from across the room, Daniel would see the sheen of them. She was like a painting: a Rembrandt—lucent, rustic, there. Her fingers on the armchair would mime the notes, although he had never heard her play this song. She would listen but never, not even once, did she play that song.

And then the discordant notes, the A sharp and B. As they continued to sound and sound again, a rare tear would form and fall, flashing across her cheek. Dissonant but somehow right: sounding out what she felt.

She seemed to seek out the discord, as a finger finds a wound.

How many nights in August had he woken to the sound of piano music and crept downstairs to realize that she was weeping. The sobs were robbed from her. It was as if she was being hit in the stomach, again and again. Daniel remembered pulling himself into a ball as he listened, frightened for her, not understanding what was wrong, feeling unable to comfort her. He had been frightened to go inside the room and face her like that. Already he had come to see her as strong, impervious— braver, harder than his own mother. As a child he could not fathom her sorrow. He never fully understood *why*. He had come to love her strong calves and muscular hands and loud, strong laugh. He couldn't bear to see her broken, at a loss.

But in the morning, *to be sure*, she would be fine again. Two aspirins and an omelet after the chickens were fed, and it was over for another year. The next summer it would happen again. Her pain never seemed to lessen. Each year it would return with the same ferocity, like a perennial frost.

Daniel thought about it. Minnie must have died on the ninth or the tenth of August. Was it the grief that had finally killed her?

He looked around the room. He was surprised to feel the weight of the house. The memories that it held leaned on him and brushed against him. He remembered both her tears and her laughter: the easy lilt of it that had once charmed him. Then he remembered again what she had done to him. Gone, but still he could not forgive her. Understanding her was something, but it was not enough.

Daniel closed the lid of the piano. He looked at Minnie's chair, remembering the sight of her, sitting with her feet up, telling stories with the light of the fire in her eyes and her cheeks pink with mirth. Beside the chair was an open box file. Daniel picked it up and sat down in Minnie's chair to examine the contents. Newspaper clippings from the *Brampton News* and the *Newcastle Evening Times* fluttered into his lap like anxious moths.

> ***Tragedy of Child Death Age Six—****A serious car crash involving a woman and two children resulted in the death of six-year-old Delia Flynn, from Brampton, in Cumbria. The other child passenger sustained minor injuries but was released from the hospital on Thursday evening. Delia was taken to Carlisle General Hospital where she died two days later from serious internal injuries.*
>
>   *The mother of the child, who was driving the car and who escaped with minor injuries, refused to comment.*

There were another two articles on the car accident, and then another piece drew Daniel's attention. It was partially torn and had been ripped from near the fold of the newspaper.

> ***Farmer Found Dead in Possible Suicide—****A local man and Brampton farmer was found dead on Tuesday night following a shooting accident. An investigation is under way, but police are not treating the death as suspicious.*

Daniel sat in silence in the cold living room. As a child he had tried to ask her about her family, but she would always change the subject. The rest of the box file was filled with paintings that Delia had done: finger paintings, leaf rubbings, and mosaics of lentil and macaroni. Not knowing why, Daniel folded up the two newspaper clippings and slipped them into his back pocket.

It was cold, and he stamped his feet as he walked around. He picked up the telephone. The line was now dead. The answer phone was flashing and he played the messages.

There was a breathy female voice that whispered, "Minnie, it's Agnes. I heard you're not able to come on Sunday. I just wanted to say I'm happy to take the stall. I hope you're not feeling too bad. Talk t'you later, I think . . ."

The machine moved to the next message:

"Mrs. Flynn, this is Dr. Hardgreaves. I hope you can call me back. I have the results from the consultant. You missed your last appointment. They certainly warrant discussion and I hope that you are able to reschedule. Thank you."

End of messages, the machine proclaimed.

There were letters piled on the chair next to the telephone in the hall. Daniel flicked through them. There were red letters from the electricity board and the telephone company, letters from the RSPCA and PDSA, copies of *Farmers Weekly*. Daniel swept them to the floor and sat down, a hand covering his mouth.

The chill tone of the discordant notes sounded in his head. *Dead. Dead. Dead.*

Daniel was unable to stay the night in Minnie's aching house. He found a room in a local hotel, where he ate a too-rare steak and drank a bottle of red wine. He fell asleep with his clothes on, on top of the nylon covers in a damp room that smelled as if someone had died in it. He had phoned Cunningham, Minnie's lawyer, from the road. As he had expected, the funeral was to be held at the crematorium on Crawhall.

It was a Tuesday. Brampton was cooler than London, the sun banished by cloud. Daniel could smell the trees in the air and the unyielding green of them was oppressive. It was too quiet and people seemed to turn to look when they heard his footsteps. He longed for the anonymity, urgency, and noise of London.

The doors to the memorial hall were open when he arrived and he was shown inside. The hall was just over half full. The mourners were men and women Minnie's age. Daniel sat near the back, in the middle of one of the empty pews. A tall, thin, balding man in gray approached him.

"Are you . . . Danny?" the man whispered, although the service had not begun.

Daniel nodded.

"John Cunningham, pleased to meet you."

His hand was dry and hard. Daniel felt his own damp with sweat.

"I'm so glad you decided to come. Come forward. Makes it look better."

Daniel wanted to hide at the back, but he got up and followed Cunningham to the front. Women he recognized from his childhood: farmers who had worked market stalls with Minnie nodded at him as he sat down.

"There're no drinks or anything afterward," Cunningham

whispered in Daniel's ear. His breath smelled of milky coffee. "But if you have time for a chat after . . . ?"

Daniel nodded once.

"I'm going to say a few words for her. I wonder if you want to also? I can speak to the minister?"

"You're all right," said Daniel, turning away.

He sat through the short ceremony with his teeth pressed so hard together that the muscles in his right cheek began to ache. There were hymns and then the minister's practiced words of kindness delivered in a rounded Carlisle accent. Daniel found himself staring at the coffin, still disbelieving that she was actually inside. He swallowed as the minister called on John Cunningham to deliver the eulogy.

At the podium, Cunningham cleared his throat loudly and read from a piece of paper.

"I am proud to be one member of the gathering of people here today in honor of a wonderful woman who brightened up all of our lives and the lives of many more beyond these four walls. Minnie is an example to us all, and I hope she felt proud of everything she achieved in her life.

"I got to know Minnie in a professional capacity after the tragic deaths of her husband and daughter, Norman Flynn and Cordelia Rae Flynn—may they rest in peace."

Daniel sat up and took a deep breath. *Cordelia Rae.* He had never known her full name. The rare times that Minnie mentioned her, she was Delia.

"Through the years, I came to value her friendship and to respect her as someone who served others in a manner to which we should all aspire.

"Minnie . . . was a rebel."

There was a sputtering of teary laughter. Daniel frowned. His breaths were shallow in his chest.

"She didn't care what anyone thought of her. She wore what she wanted, she did what she wanted, and she said what she wanted and you could like it . . . or just lump it." Again laughter, like a carpet being beaten. "But she was honest and kind, and it was those qualities that led her to be a foster mother to dozens of damaged children and to become a mother again, in the eighties, when she adopted her dear son, Danny, who thankfully is able to join us here today . . ."

The women seated to Daniel's right turned to him. He felt the color rising on his cheeks. He leaned forward onto his elbows.

"Most of us here today know Minnie as a farmer—we've either worked alongside her or bought her produce. Here again, she showed her care and attention in the way she looked after her livestock. The small farm wasn't just a living, the animals were her children too and she nurtured them as she nurtured all others who needed her.

"As a friend, that is my final impression of her. She was independent, she was rebellious, she was her own woman, but more than all of that she was a caring person and the world is so much poorer for the loss of her. God love you, Minnie Flynn, may you rest in peace."

Daniel watched as the women who sat beside him bowed their heads. He did the same, still feeling the burn in his cheeks. One of the women began to cry.

Cunningham sat down and was patted on the shoulder by

the woman who sat to his right. The minister leaned on the podium with two hands.

"As we come to the committal, Minnie has asked that we listen to this piece of music that was special to her. The earthly life of Minnie has come to an end, and we now commit her body to the elements. Earth to earth, ashes to ashes, and dust to dust, trusting in the infinite mercy of God . . ."

Daniel held his breath. He looked around, wondering where the sound would come from. He knew before he heard the piano chords what piece she would have chosen.

Despite himself, when the music started, he felt the tension that his body held release. The lilting, insistent steps of the music took him forward as he watched the curtains draw slowly over her coffin. Time seemed to linger and lag, and sitting there with strangers listening to the music that was so intimate to her and so intimate to Daniel, he began to remember.

Moments in his life were pressed into being and vanished again, like the notes themselves. The A sharp note, and then the B note: He opened his mouth in shock as he felt his cheeks flush. His throat hurt.

How long it had been since he had heard the full concerto. He must have been a teenager when he heard it last: it was more painful in his memory, the discord sharper. Now he was surprised by the tranquil serenity of the piece, and how—in its entirety, finished, complete—both its harmony and its dissonance seemed exactly right.

The feelings that the music ushered in were strange to him. He pressed his teeth hard together, right to the end, not wanting to admit to his grief. He remembered her warm, strong fingers and her soft, gray curls. His skin remembered the roughness of her hands. It was this that brought the tension to his body and the flush to his cheek. He wouldn't cry, she didn't deserve it, but some small part of him was yielding and asking to mourn for her.

In the parking lot, the sun had come out. Daniel took off his jacket as he walked to his car. He felt exhausted suddenly, no longer fit for the seven-hour drive back to London. He felt a hand on his arm and turned. It was an old woman, her face pinched and sunken. It took Daniel a moment, but finally he recognized her as Minnie's sister, Harriet.

"Do you know who I am?" she said, her lips turning down, contorting her whole face.

"Of course. How are you?"

"Who am I then? Say my name, who am I?"

Daniel took a breath and then said, "You're Harriet, Aunt Harriet."

"Made it up, did you? Found the bloody time, now that she's dead?"

"I . . . I didn't . . ."

"I hope you're ashamed of yourself, lad. I hope that's why you're here. God forgive you."

Harriet walked away, stabbing her way across the parking lot with her stick. Daniel turned toward his car and leaned on the roof. The leaves and the funeral and the quiet countryside had set his head spinning. He exhaled, rubbing the moistness of his fingertips. He heard Cunningham calling him and turned.

"Danny—we've not had a chance. Would you have time for lunch then, or a cup of tea?"

He would have liked to refuse Cunningham, to be on

his way, but all he wanted to do was lie down, and so Daniel agreed.

In the café, Daniel hung his head and put a hand across his face. Cunningham had ordered a pot of tea for them both and a bowl of soup for himself. Daniel was not eating.

"It must be hard for you," said Cunningham, folding his arms.

Daniel cleared his throat and looked away, embarrassed by his own confused feelings for Minnie and chastened by Harriet's harsh words. He was not sure why he felt so emotional. He had said good-bye to Minnie long ago.

"She was a gem. A pure gem. She touched so many people."

"She was a tough old boot. Think she made as many enemies as she did friends . . ."

"We'd've had it at the chapel, but she specifically requested a nonreligious committal and a cremation. A cremation, would you ever believe it?"

"She gave up on God," said Daniel.

"I know she didn't practice for many years. I don't have the time myself, if truth be told, but I always thought that her faith was still important to her."

"She told me once that the rituals and the charms were the hardest to let go of—she didn't hold store in them, but she couldn't stop. She told me once that Christianity was just another of her bad habits. If you knew her, she did a rosary when she was drunk. Bad habits go together . . . Your speech was good. It was right. She was a rebel."

"I think she should have gone back to Cork after Norman died. Her sister said as much; did you speak to her? She was the one at the end of the row."

"I know her sister. She used to visit us. I said a few words."
Again Daniel looked away, but Cunningham did not notice
and continued talking.

"She was a woman before her time, she was, Minnie. She
needed to be in a city, somewhere cosmopolitan . . ."

"Nah, she loved the country. That's what she lived for . . ."

"But her ideas were all city ideas, she'd've been better off."

"Maybe. It was her choice. Like you said, she loved her
animals."

Cunningham's soup came and there were a few moments
when he busied himself with napkin and buttered roll. Daniel
sipped his tea and watched, still unsure what Cunningham
needed to talk about so urgently. He was content to be quiet.

"It'll be some time before the estate is settled. I need to get
a firm to clear the house and then get it on the market. In its
condition, I'm not expecting a quick sale, but you never know.
I just want you to be prepared for it being a few months before
we can settle up, as it were."

"Like I said on the phone, I don't want anything."

Cunningham took a wary mouthful of soup. He dabbed his
mouth with a napkin and then said, "I thought you might have
changed your mind, coming to the funeral and all."

"I don't know why I came. I suppose I had to . . . ," Daniel
said and rubbed his hands over his face, " . . . see for myself she
was really dead. We've not been in touch for a while."

"She told me . . . There's no rush about the estate. Like I
said, it'll be months before it's finalized. I'll contact you nearer
the time and you can see how you feel then."

"Fine, but I can tell you now I won't change my mind. You
can give it to the dogs' home. I'm sure that'd please her."

"Well, like I said, there's no rush. We can sort that out in due course."

Silence stretched out before them, like a dog asking to be petted.

Cunningham looked out of the window. "Minnie was a gem, eh? Good laugh. Great sense of humor, eh?"

"I don't remember."

The man frowned at Daniel then turned his attention to his soup.

"So, was it cancer then?" said Daniel, taking a deep breath.

Cunningham swallowed, nodding. "But she didn't fight it, you know. She could have had chemotherapy; there were surgery options but she refused them all."

"Of course—she would have."

"She told me that she'd been unhappy. I know you had a falling-out a few years ago."

"She was unhappy long before that," said Daniel.

Cunningham's spoon sounded against the bowl as he scraped it clean. "You were one of her foster kids originally, weren't you?"

Daniel nodded once. His shoulders and upper arms were suddenly tight and he shifted to release the tension.

"You were special to her. She told me that. You were like her own," said Cunningham.

Daniel looked at him. He had a spot of soup on his mustache and his eyes were open and searching. Daniel felt a surprising anger toward the man. The café was suddenly too warm.

"I'm sorry," said Cunningham, motioning for the bill, as if realizing that he had crossed a line. "She gave me a box of things for you. They are trinkets and photographs mostly—

nothing of any great value—but she wanted you to have them. Best you take them now. We'll be clearing the house and then the will'll be a while in settling. They're in the car."

Cunningham drained his cup. "I know this must be hard on you. I know you had your differences, but still . . ."

Daniel shook his head, unsure what to say. The pain had returned to his throat again. He felt as he had in the funeral parlor, fighting back tears and angry with himself because of that.

"Did you want to deal with the house yourself? As family, you're entitled . . ."

"No, just get a firm in, there's nothing . . . I really don't have time for it." It felt better saying that. The words were like fresh air. He felt squared by them, braced.

"Feel free to go and take any personal items from the property while you're up, but like I said, there are a few things she's set aside."

They stood up to leave; Cunningham paid the bill. Before he opened the door, Daniel asked, "She didn't suffer, did she?"

They stepped out into the early autumn sun. The sharp clarity of it caused Daniel to squint.

"She did suffer, but she knew that was unavoidable. I think she'd had enough really and she just wanted everything to end."

They shook hands. Daniel felt Cunningham's short, hard grip as conflicted, communicating the unsaid. It reminded him of handshakes he had given to clients after the judge had sent them down. Kindness delivered with quick violence.

Daniel was about to turn from him, excused, expelled, but then Cunningham threw up his hands.

"Your box! Your box is in my car. One minute."

Daniel waited while Cunningham retrieved the cardboard box from the trunk of his car. The smell of the fields and the farms did not calm him. It seemed raw.

"There you go," said Cunningham. "Not worth a lot, but like I said, she wanted you to have it."

To avoid a second handshake, Cunningham saluted Daniel in the funeral home parking lot. Daniel was confused by the gesture, but nodded good-bye.

The box was light. He placed it in the trunk of his car without looking inside.

8

HE SLIPPED HIS FEET INTO THE TOO-BIG RUBBER BOOTS. Through his socks they felt cold, like jelly gone hard. He scattered kitchen slops for the chickens as she had asked. He tried not to touch the cold vegetables with his fingers but some corn got stuck on his nails. He flicked it off like snot. Minnie had told him she thought his nose was broken. He found it hard to breathe as he fed the chickens. He didn't mind so much as he hated the smell of them: ammonia and rotting vegetables and damp feathers.

It was Saturday and she was making sausage and eggs for him. He could see her at the kitchen window. She was always quiet in the mornings. He knew it was the other side of the gin. He was eleven years old and knew about hangovers of the drug and drink kind, although he had never had one. He had

been drunk, though. He had taken two cans of beer to bed
with him one night and drank them watching *Dallas* on the
portable black and white in his mother's room. He had been
sick all down his pajamas.

He wore his mother's necklace as he fed the scraps to the
birds—didn't care if it made him look like a girl. He wanted
to know the necklace was safe. He wanted to know she was
safe. He wondered what the social worker had told Minnie the
night before. In the car on the way back, Tricia had told him
that she didn't know anything about his mother and the fire
and that she would have to look into it. But he felt there was
something she was holding back.

Daniel put his back against the wall and sidestepped back
into the house as Hector the goat watched him ruefully. His
goat face reminded Daniel of Tricia, his social worker. He
slipped off his wellies in the hall. Blitz was lying right in front
of the door. He lifted his head when Daniel entered but did not
move and so Daniel had to step over him. The kitchen smelled
of fat and pork and onions.

Minnie served up. The sausages were so slick they slid over
the plate when she placed them on it. He took his fork and
pierced their skin. That was what he liked best: piercing the
skin and watching the juices ooze.

"Are you feeling better this morning?" she asked.

He shrugged his shoulders, looking at his food.

"How's your nose? Could you sleep okay?"

He nodded.

"I need to talk to you."

He looked up at her face, his fork paused on his plate. Her

eyes were opened a little wider than they usually were. Daniel felt his appetite fade, felt the oil from the sausages slick in his throat.

"Sometimes when bad things happen to you, it probably seems easier just to run away, but I want you to try not running, to face the things you don't like instead. It seems harder but in the long run you're better off. Trust me."

"I wasn't running away."

"What were you doing, then?"

"I was going to visit me mam."

Minnie sighed and pushed her plate away. He watched as she bit her lip and then leaned forward, reaching out for his hand. He pulled away from her slowly, but she stayed like that, with her hand stretched out toward him across the table.

"We're going to find out what happened to your mum. I want you to know that I am on the phone to them every day about it. I promise I'll find out for you. . . ."

"She'll be all right. She's always all right, like."

"I believe that too. I just want you to trust me. I'm on your side, love. You don't need to do everything on your own anymore."

Promise. Trust. On your own. The words hammered inside his chest. It was as if he hadn't heard her or as if the words were stones, hitting him. *Love. Trust. Own.* Daniel was not sure why they bruised.

"Shut up about it."

"Danny, I know you want to see your mum. I understand it. I'm going to help you find out where she is, and within reason we can talk to your social worker about visits. But you have to watch out, Danny. I can't have you running off all the time. They'll take you away from me, you know, and that is the last thing I want on this earth."

Daniel was not sure if the thought of not seeing his mother or being taken from Minnie was what frightened him. He was tired of going to new places and then being sent away, yet he didn't expect to stay here. He knew the leaving would be soon. It was best that he should initiate it.

First he became aware of his fingers, still sticky from the corn, sticking together as if they were webbed, then his heart began to beat hard and he couldn't breathe. He stood up from the table and his chair fell back onto the floor. The bang of it startled Blitz, who jumped to his feet. Daniel ran out of the kitchen and straight upstairs to his room.

"Danny!" he heard her call.

He stood at the bedroom window, looking down at the yard. His eyes were hot and his hands were trembling. He heard her on the stairs, pulling on the banister to heave herself up. He turned round and the dizzy rosebuds on the wallpaper swarmed at him.

He put his hands into his hair and pulled it until tears came to his eyes. He screamed long and hard, until he was out of breath. As soon as she entered the bedroom, he took the jewelry box from the dresser and smashed it into the mirror on the wardrobe. When she moved toward him, he took the dresser and toppled it in her path. He saw her climb onto the bed to get to him and he started to bang on the glass of the window with his fist and then his head. He wanted out, away from her. He wanted his mam.

He couldn't hear what she was saying but her lips were moving and her eyes were turned down in distress. As soon as he felt her hands on him he spun and smacked her across the mouth. He turned away from her then. He didn't want to see the reproach in her eyes. He started to bang on the window again, with his fist and then his head, and it cracked, but then he felt her hands on his shoulders. He swung round with his fists tight, but she pulled him into her and down onto the floor.

She had her arms around him. His face was pressed against her chest and he could feel her arms around him like rope and the sheer weight of her. He fought it. He kicked and he tried to get free, but it was no use. He tried to scream again, but she only held him tighter.

"That's it, lad, you're okay. You're going to be okay. Let it out now. Let it all out. You're all right."

He didn't mean to cry. He didn't even try to stop it. He was so tired. It just came out of him, the tears and the breaths. He couldn't stop. She sat up and leaned against the broken mirror of the wardrobe, all the time keeping him close to her. She stopped pinning his arms, but she pulled him tighter. He felt her lips on his forehead. He was aware of the noise that he was making: his stolen, broken breaths and the smell of her. The damp wool of her was suddenly soothing and he breathed her in.

Daniel didn't know how long they stayed like that, but it was a long time. The weather changed outside and the damp morning was replaced with bright sun thrown onto the doused house and farm. He had stopped crying, but he kept breathing in sighs and sucked breaths, as if he was tasting something very hot. He was spent as a coin. He didn't know where he was going next.

"There now, hush, my love," she whispered to him as he tried to breathe evenly. "You're all right. I'm not your mum. I can never be your mum, but I'm here all the same. I'll always be here if you need me."

He was too tired to sit up or reply to her, but part of him was glad she was there and he tightened his grip around her waist. She held him a little tighter in response.

After a while, he could breathe properly again. Slowly, she let him go. Later, in bed early, he tried to remember if anyone else had held him like that. Most people didn't get that close to him. His mother had kissed him. Yes, she had run her fingers through his hair. She had comforted him once or twice when he'd been hurt.

Daniel helped Minnie to her feet and then they tried to put the room back together. The window was cracked and the mirror was smashed. Minnie sighed when she surveyed the destruction.

"I'm sorry. I didn't mean to break them," he said. "I'll get them fixed for you, like."

"Didn't know you had that kind of money," she said, laughing.

"I could get some."

"That you on about your pickpocket career again? I don't think so." She bent to pick up the jewelry box from the floor. She bent at the hip with her bottom sticking up and her skirt riding up at the back, so you could see her white legs and her man's socks that came up to the knee. He could see that he had wearied her. Her cheeks were red and she had sweat on her lip.

"I'd get a paper round, like."

"Paper round? Who has time for papers? You can help me on the stall at weekends. Help me deliver the eggs. I'll get you pocket money for that."

"All right then."

"Aye, but mind you, I need someone careful. Can you be careful with the eggs?"

"I'll be careful. I promise."

"Well, we'll see then. We'll have to see."

9

IN THE CAR, DANIEL DROVE ABOVE THE SPEED LIMIT, THE
windows open again, enjoying the fresh air and taking deep
breaths that stretched his diaphragm. He frowned at the
road, trying to understand why he had been so upset at the
funeral, and then so angry at Cunningham. It had been childish and emotional. He berated himself, gently cursing under
his breath as he drove.

Now that he was on the road again, he felt better, relaxed
but tired. Brampton was a downer; the distractions of work
still seemed far away. He took another deep breath and wondered if it was the scent of manure doping him. He should
have taken the M6 straight down to London—he wanted to be
home before dark—but he found himself just driving with the
window open, smelling the fields, observing the small houses
and remembering places he had visited as a child.

He found himself on the A69, almost by accident, and then he was trapped in traffic, with Newcastle ahead of him. Daniel had not intended a detour, but there was something that he wanted to see again; something he needed to do, today of all days.

Daniel drove into the city and past the university, out onto the Jesmond Road. He drove much slower here, almost in fear of arrival.

When he got out of the car, the sun was hidden behind clouds. He was mindful of the long drive ahead of him, yet he wanted to stay and see her one more time.

The entrance to the cemetery was a maternal arch of red sandstone and he found himself drawn into its depths. He knew where to go; he had followed the path with teenage footsteps, finding the place where she was laid to rest.

Daniel was surprised by how quickly he found her gravestone. Its white marble was now discolored and stained. The black-painted letters of her name had almost entirely flaked away, so that from a distance her name read: SAM GERALD HUNT, instead of Samantha Geraldine Hunter. Daniel sighed with his hands in his pockets.

It was a simple cross, with gravel at its foot to negate the need for flowers, upkeep, protestations of love.

Rocking on his heels before the grave, Daniel thought about the words from Minnie's ceremony: *Commit. Body. Elements. Earthly. Dust. Ashes. Trust. Mercy.* He remembered standing before this grave as a younger man, feeling wounded because his own name was not engraved on the cheap marble. He had wanted it to read: LOVING MOTHER TO DANIEL HUNTER. Had she been a loving mother? Had she loved him at all?

He had been angry about this death for a long time, but now he couldn't understand why he had felt that way. Now, he stood unmoved by the fact that his name was not on the gravestone. He knew that he shared DNA with the bones below his feet, but he had no need for these bones any longer.

He thought of Minnie, immolated and cast on the wind. In his mind he could smell her, feel the chuff of her cardigan on his cheek, and see the glee in her watery blue eyes. Like the present itself he would chase her now, ephemeral, like the ever unsnatchable *now*. For years he had shunned her, but now she was gone: not in the old house, not in the farm, not in the cemetery, not in her sister's eyes. Minnie had disappeared from the earth without so much as a piece of marble sitting dumbly to tell of her passing.

Daniel remembered crying at this grave. Now he stood with eyes dry and hands in pockets. He could remember Minnie more easily than he could recall his own mother. He had been so little when he'd last lived with his mother. For years their meetings had been fraught and brief. He had run to her and been dragged away.

He had stayed with Minnie. She had been with him as a child, a teenager, and a young adult. Now that she was gone he felt strangely calm, but alone: more alone than he had felt before he knew of her death. It was this that he could not fathom. She had been lost to him years before, but now he felt her loss.

Losses should not be weighed, he thought. And yet now, considering the loss of both his mothers, he felt Minnie's loss the greater.

≈

DRIVING BACK TO LONDON, DANIEL STOPPED AT THE SERVICE station at Donnington Park. He bought petrol and a coffee and then checked his phone for the first time since he had left.

There were three missed calls from work. Sipping lukewarm coffee and inhaling petrol fumes, Daniel called Veronica. He sat in the driver's seat with the door open, listening to the hoarse whisper of the motorway behind him.

"Are you all right?" said Veronica. "We've been trying to get in touch with you. You are *not going to believe this* . . . How was your funeral, by the way, not someone close, was it?"

Daniel cleared his throat. "No . . . no, what happened?"

"You've not been answering your phone!"

"Yeah, I . . . turned it off. I had stuff to deal with . . ."

"You have the Sebastian Croll case back if you want it. Will you take it?"

"What do you mean?"

"Kenneth King Croll *is* well connected."

Daniel rubbed a hand across his jaw. He hadn't shaved and he felt the stubble against his palm.

"The case ended up with McMann Walkers, but . . . believe it or not, Sebastian wouldn't work with them. He had a massive tantrum and said he would *only have you* as his solicitor!"

"Why wouldn't Seb work with them—what did they do?"

"Well, the solicitor from McMann Walkers went to see Sebastian the day after you left. I know him, Doug Brown, apparently he's an old school pal of Croll's . . .

"Anyway, I don't have all the details, but Sebastian was *very* rude to him. His parents stepped in but then Sebastian starting screaming and shouting and saying that he wanted you back. He actually asked for you—for his lawyer, Daniel." Veronica twittered with laughter. "In the end it was so bad that McMann Walkers turned it down. I've had that King Kong bloke, whatever you call him . . . calling me nonstop. They want you back to keep Sebastian happy."

Daniel finished his coffee and bit his lip. He *had* felt an urge to protect the boy, to save him. Sebastian was the same age that Daniel had been when he stood in Minnie's kitchen for the first time. But now Minnie was gone and Daniel felt drained. He wasn't sure that he was ready for the case any longer.

"So, will you take it back?" asked Veronica. Her clear voice was insistent. "I looked at the brief and it seems strong."

"Of course I'll take it," said Daniel, but the words were robbed from his lips. The motorway growled behind him and he turned from its callous, aberrant noise.

"Great. Will you call Irene's chambers tomorrow? Make sure she and her Queen's Counsel are still available? I would have approached her, but I wanted to check with you first."

Daniel drove fast, leaving the north behind him. He stopped off at the office to pick up Sebastian's brief. It was late, and as he walked through the office's surreally quiet spaces, he felt relieved that none of his colleagues was there.

The day was waning when Daniel finally returned to Bow. He picked up takeout in South Hackney and then found a parking space not far from his flat on Old Ford Road. The sun was setting on Victoria Park, the pond with its fountain like a watery sundial reflecting the bloodied sky. He could smell the vestiges of barbecues in the air. Opening the trunk of his car, he lifted out the box that Cunningham had given him and walked to the flat chin down, the box in one hand and the takeout and his keys in another.

He felt strangely deflated, the empty farmhouse inside him still, creaking with her loss. He heard notes again, painful as exposed bone. They chimed cold and hard.

He put the box on the kitchen table but still did not open it to see what it contained. Instead, he ate his curry quickly, hunched over the table in the box's shadow, then had a shower. He made the shower too hot and leaned into the jet, holding on to the nozzle with both hands. His skin stung as he toweled himself dry. He stood naked in the bathroom, looking at his face in the mirror as his skin chilled, and thought of the kestrel he had seen hovering over the Brampton moors. He remembered the bird, stiffening its wings and rising on a thermal. He felt himself as alone as unyielding.

The last two days had left him cowed, but he didn't know if it was fear of the boy's case and all that it implied, or fear of her loss—fear of life knowing that she was gone; he didn't need to ignore her anymore.

Loss. Daniel considered as he rubbed a hand across his chin and chose not to shave. *Loss.* He wrapped a towel around his waist and exhaled. *Loss.* It was like everything else. It could be practiced. He almost did not feel it anymore. His mother was gone and now Minnie was gone; he would be fine.

Daniel changed and began to leaf through Sebastian's case. He hoped that Irene would still be free and willing to take the case back. He would call her clerk first thing. He and Irene had worked closely on several cases but particularly on Tyrel's gang-shooting case the previous year. They had both been devastated when Tyrel was convicted.

The last time he had seen her was at her party to celebrate her promotion to Queen's Counsel in March, although he had barely managed to say two words to her. She was a Londoner, born in Barnes, and nearly five years older than Daniel, but she had read law in Newcastle. She liked to try and impress him with her Newcastle accent. Daniel couldn't bear to think of anyone else defending Sebastian.

Alone in the flat, Daniel found that he couldn't sleep, so he settled down to work. His clerk had already watched the CCTV tapes, which had been released to the defense through disclosure. Daniel watched them again, in case they had missed something. During the day, the cameras were mostly facing Copenhagen Street and Barnaby Road, turning to focus on the park after seven P.M. Daniel fast-forwarded to flashes of the park, but there were no unaccompanied children, no one else who seemed suspicious.

It was after one o'clock in the morning when he finished writing notes on Sebastian's defense and only then did he open the lip of the cardboard box that Minnie had left for him. It contained what he expected: his school photographs, photos of picnics on the beach at Tynemouth. There were his medals from primary school and prizes from secondary school, drawings and paintings that he had done for her as a child, an old address book of Minnie's.

There was the framed photograph that had sat on her mantelpiece, showing Minnie with her daughter and her husband. Her husband was holding the little girl in his arms and she was blowing bubbles that drifted over Minnie's face. As a child Daniel had marveled at this picture because of Minnie's youth. She was slimmer, with short, dark hair and a large white smile. He had to look carefully at the photograph to find her features as he knew them.

At the bottom of the box, Daniel's fingers found something cold and hard. He finished his beer as he liberated the object from the depths of the box.

It was the porcelain butterfly, its blue and yellow brighter than he remembered it. It seemed cheap. There was a chip on the wing but it was otherwise undamaged. Daniel held it in his palm.

He thought about her gathering up these things and putting them aside for him, about her illness and how that would have manifested. He imagined her asking the nurse to help her sit up in her hospital bed, so that she could write to him. He could almost see her, making small sighs at the effort, the shine of her blue eyes as she signed the letter, *Mam*. She had known then she was dying. She had known that she would never see him again.

He tried hard to remember the last time that he had spoken to her. All these years but never a birthday or a Christmas passed without her cards and phone calls. Last Christmas he had gone skiing in France. She had left two messages and sent a card with a twenty-pound check inside. As he always did, he deleted the message, ripped up the check, and put the card straight into the trash. He felt a twinge of guilt at the aggression implied in these acts.

It would have been his birthday in April, when he had spoken to her last. He had been in a rush; otherwise he would have checked and seen her number before he picked up the telephone. He had been late home from work and was now late for dinner.

"It's me, love," she had said. Always she spoke with the

same familiarity, as if they had seen each other only last week. "I just wanted to wish you happy birthday."

"Thanks," he had said, the muscle in his jaw throbbing. "I can't talk now, I'm trying to go out."

"Of course. Going somewhere nice I hope."

"No, it's a work thing."

"Oh, I see. And how is your work? Are you still enjoying it?"

"Look, when are you going to stop?" he had shouted. She had said nothing. "I don't want to speak to you."

Daniel remembered waiting for a response before he hung up. She might have known already about the cancer by then. He had hung up but then thought about her for the rest of the night, his stomach tight with anger. Or had it been guilt?

The music from the funeral was still lilting in his mind. He remembered Harriet's accusing tones, as if it had been his fault, as if Minnie had been blameless. Daniel doubted that she would have told Harriet what she had done. Harriet thought he was ungrateful, but he was the one who had been *wronged*.

Now, Daniel held the butterfly up to look at it. He remembered standing in Minnie's kitchen for the first time, and holding a knife up to her face, the hard, unflinching look in her eyes. It was that he had first loved about her: her fearlessness.

Daniel's thoughts turned to Sebastian. He wondered what the boy had seen in him, why he had insisted on him as his lawyer. He stroked the butterfly one more time with his thumb and then placed it gently onto the coffee table.

10

"LOOK," SAID DANIEL, WAVING TO MINNIE FROM THE YARD. "I'm feeding him!"

He stood with both feet together, feeding a carrot to Hector the goat. He had been at Minnie's nearly a year now and felt a strange comfort in the muddy backyard and cluttered kitchen. He liked his jobs and he liked the animals, although Hector was only just starting to accept him.

She knocked on the window. "You be careful! He can be crafty."

The small Brampton school was better for him too. He had been given lines a few times and the strap once—for knocking over a desk—but he had also been given a gold medal for English and a silver one for math. Minnie was good at math and liked to help him with his homework. Pretty Miss Pringle, his teacher, liked him, and he was on the football team.

Minnie banged her fingers on the glass again. "Watch your fingers."

Daniel heard the telephone ring and Minnie disappeared from the window. It was May and the yard was scattered with buttercups and daisies amid the long grass that edged the house. Dizzy butterflies floated from bloom to bloom and Danny watched them as the carrot became shorter. Heeding Minnie, he pulled his hand away when the stump became too small. Hector lowered his head and finished the carrot, stalk and all. Gently, Danny stroked the goat's warm short hair, withdrawing his hand and backing away every time the goat lowered its head.

"I'll get you another one later," he said.

He was getting on well with Minnie now. On the weekends they would have a laugh together. One day after market they had made a tent in the living room using her foldaway table and a bundle of sheets. She had brought her old jewelry box down to use as treasure and crawled inside with him, pretending they were wealthy bedouins. She made him fish fingers for tea and they ate them in the tent with their hands, dipping them into ketchup.

Another day they had played pirates and she had made him walk the plank blindfolded off the footstool in her living room. He liked her laugh, which always began with three big booms and then turned into a cackle and a giggle and would go on for several minutes. Just watching her laugh made him smile now.

Last weekend, they had decorated his bedroom, and Minnie had let him pick the color. He chose a pale blue for the walls and bright blue for his door and the baseboards. She had let him paint with her and they had spent the whole weekend with the radio on stripping away the rosebuds and painting the walls.

The door to the house slammed and Minnie stood there with one hand on her forehead.

"What's up?" Daniel asked.

He now understood Minnie's face. Often she would frown when she was perfectly happy going about her work. When she was worried or angry, her frown would vanish and her lips would turn down slightly.

"Come in, lad, come in. Tricia's just off the phone. She's coming to get you."

Despite the warm summer breeze and the fact that he had been sweating going about his afternoon chores, Daniel felt suddenly chilled. The sun was still high in a sky of aching blue, but he felt the shadows creep as if cast from his own mind over the yard, darkening the hue of the butterflies as they toyed with petal and bud.

Daniel rested one hand on Hector again, and the old goat started away, skipping to the length of its rope in the dried-mud yard.

"No, I'm not going. M'not leaving . . . I'll—"

"Hold yer horses, will ye. I don't think she's going to move you, but there's a meeting set up with your mum. . . ."

Minnie stood in the doorway and clasped her arms. She looked at Daniel with her lips pressed together.

The air seemed noisy to Daniel suddenly, the bees roared and the chickens screamed. He pressed his hands over his ears for a few moments. Minnie came to him but he twisted away from her and into the house. She found him curled behind the piano in the living room, which was where he went when he felt like this. He didn't feel like this a lot now.

He watched her feet as she approached, fat in dirty slippers, and then saw her ankles appear as she sat in the chair nearest the piano.

"You don't have to go, love, it's your choice, but I think it might be best. I know it's unsettling. Long time since you saw her, isn't it?"

Daniel shifted slightly and kicked the piano a little; it sounded, a hollow moan, as if wounded by him. Daniel sniffed. In his position, he could smell the unvarnished wood of the piano and breathed it in. The smell comforted him.

"C'mere."

Normally Daniel would not go to her. He would stay where he was and she would either wait near him if he was upset, or go next door to wait if he was quiet. Today, not wanting her to go, he got up and sat on the arm of her chair. She pressed him into her. He liked the fact that she was so big. Even when he was a small child, his own mother had seemed fragile. When she held him the bones of her sometimes hurt him, needled him with their insistent pressing.

Daniel felt the round edge of Minnie's chin on the top of his head. "I think they just want to have a chat with you, okay? Then you can come back and I'll make you roast beef for tea. When you're out I'll buy it 'specially. We'll have Sunday roast on Saturday, just for you."

"With Yorkshire pudding?"

"But *of course*, and gravy, and some of your carrots that you've grown yourself. They're the tastiest that the earth's ever produced. You've got a knack, so you do."

She eased him up off the chair. "All right then, go clean yourself up. Tricia'll be here soon."

〜

DANIEL LOOKED OVER HIS SHOULDER AT MINNIE AS TRICIA LED him toward her car. He was wearing a checked, short-sleeved shirt and blue jeans. He had a familiar feeling in his stomach, as if his insides had been taken out and replaced with pieces of crushed paper or dried leaves. He felt stuffed, but empty and light. He had put on his mother's necklace and he now rubbed it between finger and thumb as he sat next to Tricia in the car.

"You've been doing a lot better, Danny. You keep it up."

"Am I going to live with me mam?" he asked, looking out of his side window as if a passerby might answer.

"No, you're not."

"Are you putting me someplace else?"

"Not for now; I'll take you back to Minnie's tonight."

Still looking out of the window, Daniel bit his lip.

"Will I get to be on me own with her?"

"Yer mam? No, Danny, it's a supervised meeting, I'm afraid. Do you want to listen to the radio?"

Daniel shrugged and Tricia twiddled the dial until she found a song she liked. Daniel tried to think about collecting eggs, or planting carrots or playing football, but his mind was dark and blank. He remembered sitting in the wardrobe in his mother's smoke-blackened flat.

"What you sticking out your tongue for?" said Tricia suddenly.

Daniel withdrew his tongue. He could taste the charcoal.

"Eeeh, wee man, look at the size of ye."

The bones of her were still painful to him. He tensed even before she embraced him, in expectation of rib and elbow. She looked the same, but her eyes were black underneath. Daniel was shocked that he didn't want to touch her.

Tricia stood holding her handbag in two hands. "I'll go get us something to drink, give you a few moments to catch up, then I'll come back and help you through it."

Daniel was not sure who she was talking to. He didn't know what they needed helped through.

Daniel saw that his mother was about to cry. He stood up and stroked her hair in the way that she liked. "It's all right, mam, don't cry."

"You're always my hero, aren't ye? How you been? You living somewhere nice?"

"S'all right."

"You been playing football?"

"Bit."

Daniel watched as she wiped her eyes with her bitten nails. She had bruises on her forearms, and he tried not to look at these.

Tricia came back with two cups of coffee and a can of juice for Daniel. She sat down on the sofa and placed one cup of coffee in front of Daniel's mother.

"There you go. How you getting on, eh?"

"I can't do it. I need a cig first. Have you got one?" She was standing up, looking down at Tricia with her hands in her hair. He hated when she did that; it made her face seem thinner. "Have you got one, Danny? I need a cigarette."

"I'll go get you one," said Daniel, but Tricia stood up.

"No, stay here. I'll . . . I'll get some cigarettes."

They were in the social work office in Newcastle. Daniel had been there before. He hated the sloped-back, orange and green chairs and gray linoleum floor. He slumped back in one of the chairs now and watched his mother pace. She was wear-

ing jeans and a tight white T-shirt. He could see her spine and
the sharp angles of her hip bones.

With her back to him, she said, "I won't say this in front of
her, but I'm sorry, Danny. Sorry I've been rubbish. You'll be
better off, I know that, but I just feel shit, like . . ."

"You're not rubbish—," Daniel started.

Tricia came in and handed cigarettes and a lighter to his
mother. "Managed to scrounge half a pack from a colleague.
He says you can keep them."

Daniel's mother leaned over the table and lit her cigarette
with her hand cupped around it, as if she were outside in a
wind. She sucked hard and Daniel watched as the skin of her
face clung to her skull.

"Yer mam and I were at court this week, Danny," Tricia
prompted.

Daniel watched Tricia's face. She was looking at his mother
with too-wide eyes. His mother was looking at the table and
rocking slightly. The hairs on her arms were sticking up.

"I had my last chance, Danny. This is the last time I get to
see you, like. No more visits ever; they're putting you up for
adoption."

Daniel did not hear the words in the right order. They
swarmed at him like bees. His mother didn't look at him. She
looked at the table, elbows on her knees, inhaling twice before
she finished what she had to say.

Daniel was still slumped in the chair. The dry leaves inside
him shifted.

Tricia cleared her throat. "When you're eighteen, you will
have the right to resume contact if you choose to . . ."

It felt as if the leaves had suddenly ignited in the sparks from his mother's cigarette. Daniel tightened his stomach muscles. He jumped up and grabbed the cigarettes and threw them in Tricia's face. He tried to punch her but she had his wrists. He managed to kick her on the shin before she pinned him to the chair.

"Don't, Danny," he heard his mother say. "You're just making it harder on everybody. It's for the best, you'll see."

"No," he screamed, feeling the heat in his cheeks and the roots of his hair. "No!"

"Stop it, stop it," Tricia was shouting. Daniel could smell the milky coffee on her breath.

He felt his mother's fingers through his hair, the gentle tingle of her nails on his scalp. He relaxed under Tricia's weight, and she stood up and then lifted him up to sit on the chair.

"That's it," said Tricia. "Just behave yourself. Remember you're on your last chance too."

Daniel's mother stubbed out her cigarette in the foil ashtray on the table. "C'mere," she said, and he fell into her. He smelled the cigarettes on the fingers that touched his face. The bones of her yielded for him again, and he felt the pain of them.

Daniel let his head roll from side to side as Tricia drove him back to Minnie's. He felt the vibration of the tires on the road. Tricia had the radio off and every now and again she would talk to him, as if he had asked for an explanation.

"So, you'll be at Minnie's for now, but we're applying to have you adopted. It's a great opportunity, really. No more moving around—your own home, a new mum and dad, maybe even brothers or sisters, imagine that . . . of course you're going to have to keep behaving yourself. Nobody wants to adopt a boy with be'avioral problems, do they? No new mum and dad is going to want to get kicked or punched . . . Like your mum said, it's for the best. Older boys are 'ard to place, but if you're good, we might be in luck."

She was silent as they drove down the Carlisle Road and Daniel closed his eyes. He opened them when the car jolted to a stop. He saw Blitz approaching the car, his tail wagging and his tongue hanging out.

Daniel swallowed. "If nobody else wants me, do I get to stay here then?"

"No, love . . . Minnie's a foster parent. There'll be another little boy or girl needing to come here. But don't you worry. I'll find you a great new—"

Daniel had slammed the door before he heard Tricia utter the word *home*.

11

ONCE INSIDE PARKLANDS HOUSE, DANIEL WAS SEARCHED and scanned. Dogs sniffed his clothes and briefcase for drugs.

An attendant brought him coffee and said that Sebastian would be along soon. Charlotte had called Daniel to say that she was running a little late, but to begin without her. He felt apprehensive in the small room. It had to be kept locked at all times, he had been advised, but there was a panic alarm to call for attention if he needed anything. He felt the paper-and-leaves sensation in his stomach, dry and shifting; it made him feel uneasy.

Sebastian was brought in by a care worker.

"Good to see you again, Seb," Daniel said. "Are you all right?"

"Not really. I hate it in here."

"Do you want something to drink?"

"I'm all right, thanks. I just had some orange juice. Can you get me out of here? I hate it. It's horrible. I want to go home."

"Have your mum and dad been to see you a lot?"

"My mum's been a few times, but I want to go home . . . can't you sort it out? I just want to go home."

Sebastian's head fell suddenly into the crook of his elbow. He curled his other arm around him.

Daniel stood up and leaned over Sebastian, putting a hand on the boy's shoulder. He rubbed and patted. "Come on, you're all right. I'm on your side, remember? I know you want home, but we have to work with the law. I can't get you home just now. The judge wants you here as much to protect you as anything else."

"I don't want to be protected. I just want to go home."

Again, Daniel felt a prickle of understanding for the boy. It came to him like a nettle sting: heat and itch, lurching him into his memory. He remembered arriving at Minnie's for the first time, and the social worker telling him that, for his own good, he should be kept away from his mother.

"What I can do is work to get you home after your trial. How about that? You ready to work with me on it? I need your help. I can't do it on my own."

Sebastian sniffed and wiped his eyes on his sleeve. When he looked up, his eyelashes were wet and separated.

"Mum's late," said Sebastian, "She'll be in bed. My dad flew out last night. It's better if I'm there. That's why you need to get me out."

"What'll be better if you're there?" Daniel asked. Although he was sure he knew what Sebastian was going to say, he wondered if he was projecting on to the boy.

"Do *you* like *your* father?" said Sebastian, as if he hadn't heard Daniel's question.

"I don't have a father."

"Everybody has a father, silly. Don't you know that?"

Daniel smiled at the boy. "Well, I never knew him. That's what I meant. He left before I was born."

"Was he nice to your mum?"

Daniel returned Sebastian's gaze. He knew what the boy was trying to say. He had watched the boy's parents and had witnessed Kenneth's aggression toward the boy's mother. Daniel blinked to remember his own mother thrown across a room so hard that she broke the arm of the armchair onto which she fell. He remembered standing between her and the man who wanted to hurt her again. He remembered his leg trembling and the smell of urine.

"Listen, we need to get down to work. Now that we're back working together, is there anything you've remembered that you need to tell me?"

Sebastian looked at Daniel and shook his head.

"We're on our own now. I'm your lawyer and you're my client. You can tell me anything. I won't judge you. I have to act in your best interests. Is there anything about the Sunday you were playing with Ben that you want to tell me? If you do, now is the time. We don't like surprises later on."

"I've told you everything, *absolutely* everything."

"Good, well, I'm going to try my best to get you out of here."

There was a magnetic sound of metal smacking cleanly together as the electronic door unlocked. Charlotte came into the room in a flurry of apologies and tinkling bangles. She twisted Sebastian's face toward her gently and kissed him on the side of his forehead.

"I'm so sorry, traffic was a nightmare!" she exclaimed, loosening her lilac silk scarf and slipping off her jacket. "And then those bloody dogs at security. They terrify me. It seemed like an age before I was through."

"Mum doesn't like dogs," said Sebastian.

"It's all right," said Daniel. "I just wanted to run through with Sebastian what's going to happen now."

"Great, fire away," said Charlotte with a strange, fraught enthusiasm. She was wearing a turtleneck and kept pulling the sleeves over her hands.

"Well, we have a lot of work to do over the next few months to prepare you for trial and there are a number of other people that you'll need to meet and talk to . . . we're going to make an appointment for a psychologist to come and see you, and then in a week or so you can meet again with your barrister, who will present your story in court. Does that make sense?"

"I think so. But what will the psychologist do?"

"You're not to worry about that. It's just to see how you might cope with the trial. He's our witness, remember, so you're not to worry, okay?

"What I wanted to try and explain to you today was the prosecution's case against you—that is, the arguments that they will put forward to try to prove that you killed Ben. We have only recently received these documents, and I'm working on building your defense based on what the prosecution has against you . . . If you don't understand anything, let me know."

"It's crystal clear," said Sebastian.

Daniel paused as he watched Sebastian. As a child he had

come close to being in Sebastian's position—but he had never owned Sebastian's confidence.

"The main evidence against you is that although you say you were only playing with Ben, and that he did fall and hurt himself while he was with you, your clothes and shoes have Ben's blood on them . . ."

"It's not a big problem," said Sebastian, his eyes bright and alert suddenly.

"Why's that?"

"Well, because you can say the blood and stuff got onto me because he got himself hurt. . . ."

There was a pause. Sebastian met Daniel's eyes, then nodded once.

"We'll be arguing that Ben fell and hurt himself, and we have your mum as an alibi from three P.M. in the afternoon onward, which throws into question the witness's assertion that he saw you fighting with Ben again later in the day. But the prosecution will argue that the blood and DNA on your clothes is evidence that you murdered him."

Daniel glanced at Charlotte. The ring finger on each of her hands was trembling. Her attention seemed to drift, so that Daniel wondered if she had heard.

"I didn't hurt Ben like that, I was just playing with him . . ."

"I know, but someone did hurt him, you know—hurt him very badly—someone murdered him . . ."

"Murder's not *that* bad."

In the silence of the room, Daniel could hear Charlotte swallow.

"We all die, you know," said Sebastian, smiling faintly.

"Are you telling me you know how Ben died? You can tell

me now, if you want." Daniel winced in expectation of what the boy would say.

Sebastian tilted his head to one side and smiled again.

Daniel raised his eyebrows to prompt him. After a few moments, the small boy shook his head.

On his legal pad Daniel wrote down for Sebastian the sequence of events that would follow: from the first conference with the barrister to the preparation for trial.

"After the committal hearing, there will be a period of waiting for the trial. I want you to know that you and your parents can still see me or talk to me during that period if you have any questions."

"Cool," said Sebastian. "But . . . when will the trial be?"

"Not for a few months yet, Seb. We have a lot of work to do before then, but I promise we will take you to see the court before your trial."

"Noooooo," Sebastian whined, slapping a hand on the desk. "I want to go sooner. I don't want to stay here."

Charlotte sat up and took a breath, as if someone had thrown a cup of water in her face. "There, darling, there," she said, her fingers fluttering to Sebastian's hair.

Sebastian's eyes shone as if he might cry.

"Look, Seb, I've got an idea," said Daniel. "How about I run and get us some sandwiches. How does that sound?"

"I'll go," said Charlotte, on her feet. Daniel noticed a purple bruise on her wrist as she reached for her bag. "I really need some air anyway. I'll be right back."

When the heavy door clunked shut, Sebastian rose to his feet and began to walk around the room. The boy was thin, with delicate wrists, and elbows that protruded. Daniel thought that apart from anything else he was too small to be capable of Ben's brutal murder.

"Seb, did anyone else speak to you that day in the park, apart from the man who called on you both to stop fighting?" The chairs were fixed, so Daniel had to stand up to face Sebastian. The boy stood just taller than Daniel's waist. Ben Stokes had been three years younger than Sebastian, but was only two inches shorter.

Sebastian shrugged. He shook his head, not looking at Daniel. He was leaning against the wall, examining his nails and then turning forefinger on thumb as if miming a nursery rhyme: *Incy wincy spider.*

"Were you aware of anyone acting strangely in the park— did you see anyone watching you play?"

Again Sebastian shrugged.

"Do you know why she's wearing *that* sweater?" said Sebastian. He held his hand up to his face, thumb and forefingers touching, and looked at Daniel through the rectangle of his fingers.

"What, do you mean, your mum?"

"Yes, when she wears *that* jumper it means that she has strangle marks on her neck." Sebastian was still looking at Daniel through his fingers.

"Strangle marks?"

Sebastian put both hands to his throat and squeezed until his face started to turn red.

"Stop it, Seb," said Daniel. He reached out and pulled gently at the child's elbow.

Sebastian fell against the wall laughing.

"Were you scared?" he asked, smiling so broadly that Daniel could see one of the child's missing teeth.

"I don't want you to hurt yourself," said Daniel.

"I was just trying to show you," said Sebastian. He returned to sit at the table. He seemed tired, reflective. "Sometimes if he gets annoyed he squeezes her throat. You can get dead that way too, you know? If you squeeze too hard."

"Are you talking about your mum and your dad?"

There was the sound of the door unlocking. Sebastian leaned over the table, one hand held up to cover his mouth, and whispered, "If you pull down the neck of her jumper you'll see the marks."

Charlotte came in with the sandwiches and Daniel found himself watching her more closely as she unpacked the bag of food and drinks. He looked at Sebastian, who was choosing a sandwich. *Better when I'm there,* he remembered the boy saying. Daniel felt another sudden flush of empathy for the child. He remembered his own mother with a man's hands around her throat. He remembered how desperate he had felt as a child, separated from her, unable to protect her. It had driven him to terrible things.

12

EARLY DAWN AND DANIEL WAS IN THE COOP.

The first ground frost of autumn, and his fingers were stiff with the cold. The day opened lazily to him as he inhaled the smell of the coop, chill with frost but warmed by feather and straw. Minnie was asleep. He had heard her snoring above the sound of her alarm as he made his way downstairs. In the living room, a drink had toppled on the piano top. It had dried to a white stain, like a large blister on the wood.

Now he was outside as she lay unconscious, carefully going about his chores. He felt strange: bereft, alone, cruel—like a falcon he had seen on his way to school one day, intent on a post, dismembering a field mouse.

He didn't know where his mother was. It felt as if she had been stolen.

Daniel picked up a warm brown egg. He was about to

place it in the cardboard tray that she had left out for him, as always, on the kitchen counter. He felt it hard inside his palm. His palm sensed the vulnerability of the egg. His palm knew the shell skin and the liquid yolk it contained, the suspended promise of chick.

Without meaning to, almost so that his palm could feel the sharp nip of broken shell and the cloying run of albumen, Daniel squeezed the egg and crushed it. The yolk ran through his fingers like blood.

Daniel felt a flush of heat suddenly: nape of his neck and small of his back. He picked up one egg after another and squeezed. His fingertips dripped clear drops of this small violence into the straw.

As if in protest, the hens ran from him, squawking displeasure. Daniel kicked at one hen but it flew in his face, a mad red flutter. Daniel lunged at the hen, his fingers still slick with the eggs. He pinned the animal to the ground and smiled as he felt its wing snap under his weight. He sat up on his knees. The bird clucked and stumbled, in a circle, trailing its broken wing. Its beak opened and shut, without voice.

Daniel waited for a moment, breathing hard. The shriek of the chickens behind him made the hairs stand up on his arms. Slowly, methodically, as if he was folding socks, Daniel tried to tear one wing from the chicken. Its open beak and frantic tongue appalled him and so he broke its neck. He leaned on the chicken and pulled its head away from its body.

The chicken was still, blood in its bead eye.

Daniel tripped as he left the coop. He fell on his elbows and the chicken blood on his hands touched his face. He got up and walked into the house with the blood on his cheek and the feathers of the bird he had killed still clinging to his trainers and fingers.

She was awake and filling the kettle when he entered. She was standing with her back to him, her dirty dressing gown hanging to her calves. She had the radio on and was humming to a pop song. He first thought to start up the stairs to the bathroom but found himself rooted to the spot. He wanted her to turn and see him, soiled with his violence.

"What on earth?" she said, with a smile on her face, when she turned.

Maybe it was the feather that clung to his trainer or the bright yellow of the yolk that was now smeared on his cheek with the chicken's blood. Minnie's lips tightened and she pushed past him out into the yard. He watched her from the back door as she stood with one hand over her mouth at the entrance to the coop.

She came back in the house and he watched her face for rage, horror, disappointment. She wouldn't look at him. She thumped up the stairs and appeared moments later in her gray skirt and her man's boots and the old sweatshirt that she wore when she was cleaning. He stood right at the bottom of the stairs, the egg and blood drying on his hands, making the skin tight and dry. He stood in her path, expecting punishment, wanting punishment.

She stopped at the foot of the stairs and looked at him for the first time.

"Clean yourself up," was all she said.

She pushed past him again and out into the yard.

From the bathroom window, he watched her collecting the broken shells and soiled straw. He scrubbed his hands and face then stood watching her work. He took the feather from his trainer and stood looking out of the window, holding it between finger and thumb. He let the feather fall, dizzy but trusting, into the wind, as he saw her making her way back to the house. She carried the dead chicken by its feet. The neck of the chicken swung loose with every step she took.

He stayed upstairs, under the bedcovers, then in the cupboard as she worked downstairs. His stomach began to rumble as the heat and energy of the morning left him. He felt cold and pulled his cuffs over his hands. He stepped out of the cupboard and stood looking at himself in the mirror he had cracked only a week before.

Evil little bastard, he remembered again. He looked at his face, the fragments of it mismatched. He felt his heart beat harder. He stood at the top of the stairs and then sat down there, listening to the sounds she was making in the kitchen. Blitz made his way upstairs and stood panting, looking at him. Daniel reached up to stroke the dog's velvet ears. Blitz allowed it for a moment, then turned and made his way back downstairs. Daniel edged forward, onto the middle step, then to the bottom where he stood holding on to the post of the banister. It was ten minutes before he mustered the courage to stand at the door of the kitchen.

"I don't even want to look at you," she said, still with her back turned to him.

"Are you angry?"

"No, Danny," she said, turning round to face him. She stood with tight lips and her chest puffed out. "But I feel very sad. Very sad indeed."

Her eyes were fierce, intense blue and watery and too wide. Her face seemed to loom before him, even though she was standing on the other side of the kitchen. Daniel sighed and hung his head.

She pulled out a chair for him.

"Sit there. I have a job for you."

He sat where she asked. She brought a large chopping board with the dead chicken on it and placed it before him.

"Here's what you do," she said, holding the chicken roughly and ripping the feathers from it. She tore and tore again and soon there was a bare patch of skin, pimpled and white.

"This murdered bird is our dinner," she said. "We need it plucked before we can gut it and roast it."

Minnie stood over him and watched as he grasped the soft feathers, the red of them giving way to gray at the root as he pulled them into his fist.

"Rip," she said. "Rip hard."

Daniel pulled too hard and the skin came away with the feathers, leaving a scalded mark on the flesh.

"Like this," she said, pushing his hand away and tearing off a clutch of feathers, leaving the soft white pimpled skin beneath. "Can you do that?"

Daniel was embarrassed to feel his throat tighten and his eyes moisten. He nodded and opened his mouth to speak to her.

"I don't want to," he said, in a whisper.

"She didn't want to die, but you crippled her and then killed her. Do it, do it right now."

She had her back to him and as she spoke she slammed a glass onto the wooden work surface. Daniel heard the chink, klink of her ice cubes and the weak peeing sound of the plastic lemon, which she added when she didn't have money or mind for real lemons. The sobering heaviness of the gin bottle being uncapped caused Daniel to shiver and he did as she asked. More gently this time, he gripped the feathers of the bird and ripped. The sudden baldness of the bird was startling.

When the bird was plucked, Daniel sat with feathers sticking to his fingers and the pimpled chicken before him. He wanted to leave, to run outside and across the Dandy and twirl the swings away from the little children. He wanted to return to the wardrobe, to feel its close, dark embrace. The smell of the plucked dead chicken made him feel sick.

Minnie took the bird and cut it from between its thighs. It was a rough, hard slit and Daniel could feel the strength that she put into it. She reached inside and Daniel watched her thick, red hand disappear.

"You have to reach up inside, as far as you can until you can feel the solid lump—the gizzard. Get a firm grip on that and pull, gently and slowly. Everything should come out together mind. Here! You try, I don't want to do it for you."

"I don't want to." Daniel heard his own voice as whining.

"Don't be a baby." She had never scorned him before, but he heard that in her voice now.

Leaning over the sink, the basin trembling beneath him, Daniel inserted his hand into the bloody insides of the chicken.

"Don't worry too much about the lungs," Minnie said. "They tend to stay stuck to the carcass."

Daniel felt sick but he tried to grab the warm entrails and pull them. With each pull his own stomach tightened and bile rose in his throat. When finally he was able to pull forth the dark red slime, he stepped back as his own guts spewed onto the floor along with the bird's.

Daniel bent over and vomited onto the kitchen floor. He had not eaten, and so his vomit was thin, yellow-colored liquid that splashed onto the guts of the bird.

"It's all right," said Minnie. "I'll sort it. You go and clean yourself up."

In the bathroom, Daniel dry-heaved into the bowl, then sat slumped against the wall. The butterfly smiled at him from the shelf. He felt wretched. He felt like a snail cut from its shell. He washed his face in cool water and dried it with a washcloth, then brushed his teeth until the taste of the sick was gone.

He waited a few minutes before going back into the kitchen. He felt strange, as if he didn't want to leave the bathroom. He felt like he did in the bathroom at home when one of them was hurting his mother. He had the same dark soup of scared in his stomach and the same itch in his muscles.

Carefully, Daniel unlocked the door and stood at the top of the stairs. He went to bed with his clothes on, but didn't sleep. He listened intently to the sounds of her in the kitchen. The sound of the oven opening and closing, her footsteps crossing the floor, her words to Blitz and then the sound of Blitz's food being poured into his bowl.

"You were up there for ages," Minnie said when she saw him. "I was almost coming up after you. It's after two, and you haven't had any breakfast. Are you hungry now?"

Daniel shook his head.

"But you'll eat. Sit down."

Daniel sat at the table and looked at the dumb place mat with a Cheshire pony on it.

She had roasted the chicken and carved it. Slices of breast sat on his plate next to the tinned sweet corn and boiled potatoes.

"Eat it."

"Don't want it."

"You'll eat it."

"I don't want it." He pushed his plate away.

"You can murder it, so you'll take responsibility. You'll eat it. You'll know it's dead and its goodness is inside you."

"I won't eat it."

"You'll sit here and I'll sit here until you've eaten it." Minnie placed her drink hard onto the table. The ice shuddered in protest.

They sat until her drink was finished. He thought she would get up and refill and that would have been his cue to leave, but she let the glass lie dry before her. She looked at him and blinked slowly. Time started to grow on them, like moss on the stones in the yard. Daniel looked at the cold chicken and vegetables on the plate and wondered if he could swallow them like pills.

"What if I eat the vegetables, like?"

"You're a bright lad, so why do you ask that? You know I don't care if you touch the vegetables, but I'll have you eat every morsel of the bird that you killed. Those birds are my living, but that's not why I'm angry. You know I eat the birds when it's their time. I care for them and love them and yes, we do eat them, but they are killed in a proper way, not out of violence, not out of hate or anger. This one's dead and we won't waste it, but I want you to know it's dead because of you, because of what you did. If it weren't we would have its eggs tomorrow. I know that you've had a hard time, Danny, and anytime you like you can talk to me about it. I know you're angry and you've a right to be. I'll do my best to help you, but I can't have you killing my birds every time you feel bad."

Daniel began to cry. He cried like a child smaller than he was, slumped in the chair and quietly humming his sadness over wet lip. He put a hand over his eyes so that he didn't have to look at her.

When he stopped crying, he opened his eyes and took breath after new clean breath. She was still before him with her empty glass, and her steel blue eyes fixed on him.

"Calm down, that's it. Get your breath back and eat it up."

Defeated, Daniel sat up and began to cut the chicken. He cut a very small piece and set it on his fork. He let the meat touch his tongue and then took it into his mouth.

GUILT

13

DANIEL LOOKED AT THE CLOCK AND SAW THAT IT WAS nearly three. A cool blue light filtered into the room. He couldn't tell if it was the moon or the streetlamps below that caused the chill, austere glow. He had worked until ten, eaten at his desk, and then gone to the Crown for a pint on his way home. Casual strips of desire whipped him, but the stress of the day had left him empty and he felt light as he turned and turned again in its wake.

In the near dark, he lay on his back with his hands behind his head. He thought about the years of anger toward Minnie that had folded into years of disregard. This had been his defense against her, he realized: anger and disregard. Now that she was dead his anger was still there, but set adrift. Half asleep he watched it float and turn.

He had chosen to leave her all those years ago and now it was hard for him to grieve for her. To grieve he had to remember, and remembering was grief. In the half dark he blinked as he remembered graduating and his first few years as a lawyer in London. All this had been without her. He had felt proud of his self-sufficiency. After he cut her off, he had paid his own way through university and then got a job at a firm in London, only three months after graduating. He had taken credit for this, but now, in the near dark, he was honest enough to wonder if he would have gone to a university at all had it not been for Minnie.

He felt darkness circling around him and alighting on his chest, hooded, wicked, shining black like a raven. Daniel put a palm to his bare chest, as if to relieve the sting of the claws.

He had left *her*, yet her leaving still seemed the greater. As he turned and turned again he felt the death beyond the loss that he had created. Her death was heavier, dark, like a bird of prey against the night sky.

Ten past three.

With his mouth and eyes open, Daniel remembered killing the chicken. He remembered his child's hands throttling the bird that she held dear. He sat up and swung his legs out of the bed. He sat there in the half dark, his body curved over his knees. Because there was nothing else that would stop it, he pulled on his shorts, stepped into his trainers, and went running.

Four o'clock when he checked his watch. The early autumn morning was warm and fresh against his face. He could smell the water from the fountain when he ran past it, and then the dewy leaves of the trees. The pounding of his feet on the path and the warming of his muscles energized him and he ran faster than he usually would, lengthening his stride and allowing his torso to drive him forward. Even at this pace, images came to him, causing him to lose concentration: he saw again her coffin; Minnie with her wellies on and her hands on her hips, cheeks reddened by the wind; Blitz bowing his head deferentially when she entered the room; the market stall stacked with fresh eggs; his childhood bedroom with the rosebud wallpaper.

He had been wild. Who else but Minnie would have taken on such a child? His social worker had warned him. Minnie had cared for him when no one else would.

Although he was already breathing hard, Daniel ran faster. He felt heat in his stomach muscles and his thighs. A stitch seared along his side and he slowed to accommodate it, but didn't stop. He took longer, slower breaths, as he had been taught, yet the stitch remained. In the darkness of the park, indigents shifted on cold benches, newspaper fluttering over their faces. His mind was torn between the pain in his side and the reluctant ache that came whenever he thought of Minnie. She had been the guilty one, but, accused at her funeral, he now considered his part in her death. He had intended to hurt her after all. He had been aware of punishing her. She had deserved it.

Deserved. Daniel staggered, then slowed to a walk. He was still a mile from home. The night acquiesced to a shameful, reluctant glow in the west. Daybreak. It seemed appropriate to Daniel, that the new day should be a small violence. The dark blue sky was beginning to bloody. He walked with his hands on his hips, breathing hard, sweat coursing between his shoulder blades. He wasn't ready for the day. He was exhausted before it had even begun.

When he arrived back at the flat, he was sweating hard. He drank a pint of water and had a shower, staying under the jet for longer than usual, letting the water pour onto his face. He could feel the slow pulse in his veins from the exercise, and yet for once he did not feel calmed by it. All his life he had been running. He had run away from his mother's home and her boyfriends. He had run away from foster homes, back to his mother; he had run away from Minnie, to university, to London. Now he still wanted to run—he still felt the need for it, an angry hunger in his muscles—but there was no longer any place to run to. And there was nothing left to run away from. His mother was dead, and now Minnie too; the one he had loved, and the one who had loved him were both gone, and with it his love and his proof that he could be loved.

Dressing, he opened the box that she had left him and took out the photograph of Minnie and her family. Why had she left him this photo? he wondered. He understood the photographs of him and Minnie at the beach, the photos from the market stall or working on the farm. This photograph he had always been drawn to, but only because it depicted a youthful Minnie—a good mother and her perfect family. Perfect families had obsessed Daniel when he was a child. He used to watch them on buses and in parks, hungrily studying the interactions between parents and children, and between the parents themselves. He liked to see what he had missed out on as a child.

Frowning, Daniel put the photograph on the mantelpiece beside his Newcastle United tankard.

He buttoned his shirt and ate his breakfast and was ready to leave at five thirty. He would be at work at six. As an afterthought, brushing his teeth and throwing files into his briefcase, he went back to the box and retrieved the butterfly. He didn't know why, but he put it into his briefcase also.

Daniel bought a paper when he exited the tube at Liverpool Street. Rarely was he at work this early. Even the paper felt fresh, warm as bread. He knew a coffee shop that would be open by the station. He bought a coffee and instead of taking it straight to his office, he lingered and allowed himself the luxury of reading the paper while he sipped the hot liquid.

On page four of the *Daily Mail*, Daniel saw the headline "Angel of Death" and sighed.

> *Boy of eleven held over horrific Angel Islington murder of eight-year-old Ben Stokes, who was found beaten to death in Barnard Park over a week ago.*
>
> *The Crown Prosecution Service (CPS) said it had advised Islington Borough Police to charge the boy, who is reportedly from the area, with murder. Ben Stokes was found dead with his skull smashed with bricks, hidden in a children's play area.*
>
> *Jim Smith, head of the service's Crown Court unit, said: "We authorized the police to charge a boy age eleven for the murder of eight-year-old Ben Stokes."*
>
> *The boy, who cannot be named for legal reasons, appeared at a youth court hearing at Highbury Corner Magistrates Court on Friday morning and stood in the dock with a security officer. The boy wore a shirt and tie and green pullover as the charges were read to him. He did not show any emotion during the hearing. The boy has been remanded in custody and will appear in court again on August 23.*
>
> *The boy, who lives with professional parents in an affluent area of Angel, was well known at his Islington primary school for violent and disruptive behavior. The boy's*

*mother refused to answer her door to reporters yesterday. Ben
Stokes's parents were also too distressed to speak to reporters,
but released a statement that said, "We are overcome by grief
on the death of our beloved Ben. We will not be able to rest
until the person responsible is brought to justice."*

*The assault—which bears similarities to the murder of
toddler James Bulger by two ten-year-olds in 1993—has
horrified the nation. Prime Minister David Cameron and
newly appointed Home Secretary Jacqui Smith called it "ap-
palling."*

Daniel walked with his tie loosened and the paper under his
arm. The coffee was now cooling and he sipped it as he walked
to his office. There had been other articles, small paragraphs in
the local press at the time of the bail hearing. This article was
different. It was a headline.

It's starting, he thought. *It is starting already*. It was bright
daylight now, but the day still smelled young. His stomach was
curdled with tiredness and he felt as if he could lie down on the
pavement, press his cheek to the dirty stone, and sleep.

Daniel was first to arrive at work. The cleaners were still
there, emptying trash cans and wiping desktops. In his office,
Daniel finished his coffee reading through Sebastian's prosecution papers. There were several photographs of Ben's battered
body. The first showed the crime scene itself, with Ben's face
buried under the brick and sticks that had been used to assault
him, as if the killer wanted to make a shrine of his small body.
Other pictures had been taken at the autopsy and showed the
full extent of injuries to the face: the broken nose and fractured

eye socket. It did not look like a child's face, but rather a doll that had been broken, squeezed out of shape. Daniel frowned as he looked at the photographs.

His phone rang and Daniel picked it up.

"It's Irene Clarke," said Stephanie.

"Fine, put her through."

Daniel waited to hear her voice. Apart from a glimpse of her at her QC party in March, it had been nearly a year since he had seen her. They had gone out the night of Tyrel's sentence. He remembered her small sarcastic mouth and her arched brows.

"Hello, Danny, how are you?"

"More to the point, how are you? How's life as a QC?"

Irene laughed.

"You coming with me to see the pathologist tomorrow?" Daniel asked. "Just looking through the reports now."

"Yes, definitely. I was just calling to say we should meet at Green Park or something—go together."

"Sure," said Daniel. "And afterward I might even buy you a drink—toast your success, like." He deliberately allowed his accent to broaden. He smiled, expecting her to tease him, to lapse into her best *wae'aye, man.*

"I've been working so bloody hard," she said. "I've almost forgotten all about it. Be good to see you though. Been a while."

"I can't tell you how glad I am that you took this." The honesty brought a brief warmth to his face.

"I had to. It touches a chord . . . ," she said.

"I know. Me too."

⁓

SHE WAS WAITING FOR HIM AT GREEN PARK WHEN HE AR-
rived, late afternoon. She looked pale and tired, her hair flattened on top and at the sides as if she had just taken her wig off,
but her face lit up when she saw him. He kissed her on both
cheeks and she squeezed his upper arm, running her hand right
down his arm to his wrist, which she held for a second before
letting go. "Danny boy, eh. You look good."

"So do you," he said, meaning it. Despite her wig-flattened
blond hair and tired eyes, she stood out on the street, with her
chin tilted to one side to admire him. Irene always made him
want to stand up straight and pull back his shoulders.

They made their way down Piccadilly, past the Ritz and then
to Carlton House Terrace where they were to meet the pathologist, Jill Gault, in her office overlooking St. James's Park.

Daniel could smell Irene's perfume as he walked, even as
buses passed contributing warm gusts of smog to the air. Their
strides matched and Daniel was distracted for a moment by the
easy rhythm of their paces.

It was late afternoon but the sun was merciless, high in the
sky, like a critical eye. The pathologist's office was a relief: not
air-conditioned but cool, the heat of the day forbidden by the
thick, stone walls. She sat behind an expansive desk with tortoiseshell glasses pushed up into her curly red hair.

"Can I get you tea or coffee?" said Dr. Gault.

Daniel and Irene both declined.

Dr. Gault opened a brown file, and lowered her glasses to
the end of her nose, to allow her to review Ben Stokes's pathol-
ogy report.

"Your report was very interesting, Dr. Gault," Daniel said.
"You're clear that the cause of death was acute subdural he-

matoma caused by a blow to the front-right side of the head?"

Dr. Gault slid an X-ray onto the desk in front of them. With her pen, she indicated the extent of the hemorrhaging.

"You are quite sure that the murder weapon was the brick found at the scene?" Irene asked.

"Yes, the contours match exactly."

"I see. Correct me if I'm wrong," Irene continued, "but you have identified the time of death as approximately six forty-five in the evening, but you have been unable to state the time of the assault—that's the case with this type of injury?"

"That's correct," said Dr. Gault, letting her pen fall to the desk before sitting back in her chair and letting her hands rest on her stomach. "With this type of injury, it is quite impossible to determine the time of the assault. Hemorrhaging causes pressure on the brain, but it can be anything from minutes to ten hours or more before it becomes fatal."

"So that means that the attack could conceivably have happened around six o'clock at night?" said Daniel, with one eyebrow raised.

"That's correct, or it could have happened some hours before."

Daniel and Irene looked at each other. Already Daniel could see Irene presenting this in court.

It was cooler when they emerged from the doctor's office, but the London streets still felt dirty and noisy and hot. It was just after five o'clock and crowded, people navigating each other like fish; cars honked at cyclists; people talked on invisible cell phones; taxi doors slammed; buses breathed in and up from the road, out and down toward it; jets coursed soundlessly through the blue sky above it all.

"Well, that was useful," said Irene, putting on her sunglasses and taking off her jacket.

She had strong, square shoulders, like a tennis player, and Daniel admired them. He pulled off his tie and put it into his pocket. "Let me buy the QC a drink, then?"

They were early enough to get one of the tables on the street. They sat opposite each other, sipping ale as the shadows lengthened and tired summer wasps floated lazily around empty glasses.

"To you," Daniel said, clinking glasses with her.

"So," Irene said, leaning back, observing him. "Do you think Sebastian did it?"

Daniel shrugged. He could feel the sun on his brow. "He's adamant that he didn't do it. He's a weird little kid, but I think he's telling the truth. He's just messed up."

"I found him unsettling, but I . . . barely spoke to him."

"He's bright. Only child. I think . . . probably quite isolated. He's said some stuff to me about his father attacking his mother. They're wealthy, but I don't think it's a happy home."

"I could believe that. The father seems like a misogynist—he didn't want us on the case because I'm a woman."

"No!" said Daniel. "It was me. He thought I was too young and inexperienced."

Irene sighed and shrugged, and then looked more serious: "With what we heard from Gault, there could easily have been another attacker, you know. Sebastian has an alibi from . . ."

" . . . three o'clock . . . and it's arguable that the statement from the man who said he saw Sebastian fighting after that time sounds like he was led on by the police or just confused. There's nothing distinctive about his description of Sebastian . . . and what with the distance and the foliage—I mean I've been to the park—I'm sure we can undermine it. If only we could get something on tape confirming it."

"I even watched the tape myself in case we missed something. Typical, of course, that the police only requested the council tapes . . ."

"You found others?"

"Well, two pubs in the area have CCTV. We're still going through those tapes, looking for the boys, but also this second sighting, supposedly of Sebastian . . ."

"I know, if only we could have something on tape that put someone else, not Sebastian, in the adventure playground at the time . . ."

She rested her chin on her hand and looked into the distance, across the street at the buses and cyclists that passed. Daniel liked her face, which was shaped like a melon seed. He watched as she pushed strands of her hair behind her ears.

"I'm still bruised from the last time," she said finally. "Do you ever think of it?"

Daniel sighed and nodded, running a hand through his hair.

They had avoided each other after Tyrel's trial, both stung by a guilty verdict that saw the teenager returned to the system that had raised him. He had been on trial for shooting a fellow gang member. They had both warmed to the tall boy, who had skin taut and brown as the skin of chestnuts, and a smile bright and quick as innocence. He had been born in prison to a crack-addicted mother and brought up in foster care. They had fought hard for him, but he was guilty and he had been found guilty.

"If I'm honest, one of the reasons I wanted this was because of losing for Tyrel," she said.

"He's in adult prison now. I went to see him a month or so ago. He's waiting for an appeal, y'know . . . I went to tell him there wasn't going to be one. He's really thin . . ." Daniel looked away.

"And *this one*," Irene continued. "I mean I know he's supposed to be eleven, but . . . he's tiny . . . or is that what eleven-year-olds look like these days? I'm out of touch . . . I mean at least Tyrel looked like a young man."

Daniel took a long drink and then looked away.

"You need to let it go," said Daniel. "I'm sure QCs aren't supposed to worry about all this stuff." He winked at her and smiled, but she did not return his smile. She was looking away again, remembering.

"God, we got so drunk last time."

They had gone out after the verdict. Toward the end of the night Irene had put beer caps into her eyes to impersonate the judge who sentenced Tyrel.

"My sister couldn't understand why I was so down afterward," Irene continued. "She kept saying to me, *but he was guilty*—as if that mattered, as if that negated what we were trying to do. I remember that terrible look of fear he had when he was sent down. He just looked so young. I felt strongly then, and I still do, that he needed help not punishment."

Daniel ran two hands through his hair. "Maybe we're in the wrong job," Daniel said, laughing lightly, "maybe we should go into social work."

"Or politics and just sort it all out." Irene smiled and shook her head.

"You're a great barrister, but you'd be a rubbish politician.

They'd never shut you up. Can you imagine you on *Newsnight*? You'd be ranting. You'd never be asked back."

She laughed, but then her smile fell. "God help Sebastian if he's innocent. Three months in custody until trial is hard enough on an adult."

"Even if he's guilty, it's hard," said Daniel, finishing his pint.

"I know," said Irene. "It doesn't bear thinking about. Most of the time I appreciate the justice system. You have to, don't you, in our line of work. But when it comes to kids—even kids as old and streetwise as Tyrel—you just think, God, there must be another way."

"But there is, England and Wales are out of step with much of Europe. In most other European countries children under the age of fourteen don't even appear before a criminal court." Daniel laid his palms flat on the table as he spoke. "Kids are dealt with in civil proceedings by family courts, usually in private. I mean the outcome can often be the same with violent crime . . . y'know, long-term detention in secure units, but all that's done as part of a care order, not as . . . custodial punishment."

"Compared with Europe we seem medieval . . ."

"I know, ten years old. I mean . . . ten years old! It seems ludicrous. Scotland was *eight* until earlier this year. God, I can remember being eight, ten years old . . . the confusion, the fact that you're so small, and so . . . unformed as a person . . . how can you be held criminally responsible at that age?"

Irene sighed, nodding.

"Do you know the age of criminal responsibility in Belgium?"

"Fourteen?"

"Eighteen years old. *Eighteen years old*. Scandinavian countries?"

"Fifteen."

"Exactly, fifteen years old. And we're ten! But what really
makes me angry is the fact that it's not about money or re-
sources or any of that crap. Roughly what percent of the people
you defend are from troubled backgrounds: drugs, domestic
violence . . ."

"I don't know. I would say eighty percent, easily."

"Me too. The vast majority of clients have had really difficult
upbringings . . . D'you know how much a damaged child in the
care system will cost the state throughout the course of its life?"

Irene narrowed her eyes, considering, then shrugged.

"Over *half a million* pounds. A year of one-to-one therapy
would cost a tenth of that at most. Incarceration's old fashioned
but it's bloody expensive too. The math alone should persuade
them."

"Now who's ranting? I think I'd get on *Newsnight* before
you would." Irene looked warmly at him and took a sip of beer.
"You like defense, don't you? It comes naturally to you."

"Yeah, I like being on this side of it," Daniel said, leaning
on his elbows. "Even if I dislike the person I'm defending, I
force myself to see it from their side. There has to be a pre-
sumption of innocence. I like the fairness of that . . . "

"I know; fairness is why we all got into this game. It's a
shame it doesn't always seem fair."

They watched the traffic and the scores of people rushing
home from the day, and were silent for a few moments.

"The press're gonna go crazy over this one. It'll be much worse than Tyrel. You know that, don't you?" said Irene.

Daniel nodded.

"Have you had hassle already?" she asked.

"No, have you?"

Irene shrugged and waved her hand, as if there had been hassle but she didn't want to talk about it. "It's him I worry about. The child's being vilified in the press, unnamed or not . . . where's the fairness in that? He's not even on trial yet."

"You'll raise that though, won't you?"

Irene sighed. "Yes, we can apply for a stay and say the jury has been influenced by the pretrial publicity, but we both know it's pointless. The publicity *is* prejudicial, but it will always be so. And God knows what use a stay will be to us when the child's inside anyway . . ."

She looked into the distance, as if imagining the arguments in live court. He watched her cool, blue stare.

"You must be one of the youngest female QCs now, are you not?"

"No, don't be silly, Baroness Scotland was thirty-five."

"Will you be forty this year?"

"No, I'll be thirty-nine, you sod!"

Daniel colored and looked away. She narrowed her eyes at him.

"Irene," he said to the passing traffic. "*Irene*. It seems too old fashioned for you."

"My father named me," she said, chin down. "After Irene of Rome, would you believe?"

"I would believe."

"Most of my family calls me Rene. It's only work people who call me Irene."

"Is that what I am, then? Work people?"

She laughed, and finished her beer. "No," she said, eyes sparkling but coy, "you're the lovely solicitor from Newcastle."

He hoped that she had blushed, but it could have been the beer.

"How is your Newcastle accent these days?" he asked.

"All reet, like," she managed, smiling.

He laughed at her home counties voice struggling with the consonants. She sounded Liverpudlian.

"I'm glad to be working with you again," he said quietly, no longer smiling.

"Me too," she said.

14

Y, AREN'T YOU A PROPER CHARMER. ALL RIGHT, I'LL TAKE a dozen."

Daniel sensed Minnie smiling at him as he counted out the change for Margaret Wilkes, who worked in the sweets shop. Mrs. Wilkes had told Daniel off a few weeks ago for swearing in her shop. She took her eggs and walked off while Daniel counted the takings in the ice-cream tub. Thirty-three pounds fifty.

Minnie smiled at him again and he felt rarefied by it. He was still collecting her forgiveness.

"You're good on this stall, so you are," said Minnie. "You have the patter. Only three hours in and we're making a killing. Tell you what, if we're up at the end of the day, I'll give you some commission."

"What d'ya mean?"

"Well, if we've made more than say a hundred and twenty-five, I'll give you a share."

Daniel took a breath and smiled.

"The customers seem to like you, so you're worth it. It's 'cause you're handsome. Just look at Margaret. She was all over you. I can hardly crack a smile out of her normally."

The wind blew over the sign that read FLYNN FARM—FRESH PRODUCE. Daniel straightened it, then turned to Minnie, pulling his cuffs down over his hands.

"I don't like her."

"Why ever not?" said Minnie. She was busy recording transactions in her notebook. "Old Margaret wouldn't hurt a fly."

"She says bad things about you," said Daniel, one hand in his pocket, looking up at Minnie. "You should hear her. She talks to people in the shop about you."

"Ach, let her talk if she wants to."

"They all do. All the people in the shops and the kids at school. They all say you're a witch and that you killed your husband and daughter . . ."

Daniel watched as Minnie's face went soft, relaxed and doughy, as if she were dead. Her cheeks hung heavier than they usually did. She looked older.

"Margaret says you have a broomstick and stuff and that Blitz is your familiar."

Minnie laughed then, a big belly laugh that made her stand back on her heels. She put a hand on her gut and another on the table to steady herself. She put a hand through Daniel's hair.

"They're just teasing you. Don't you know that?"

Daniel shrugged and wiped his nose with his sleeve.

"Dunno. So you didn't murder your husband then, with a poker from the fire?"

"No, love, I didn't. Some people like drama so much that they have to start inventing it because real life isn't interesting enough for them."

Daniel looked up at Minnie. She was blowing on her hands and stamping her feet. The smell of her was soothing to him now although he didn't know why. Spores of himself trusted her, but then the wind would blow again, carry them away, and he would doubt it.

The social worker had confirmed there would be no more contact with his mother. He ran back to Newcastle twice after he killed the chicken, to try to find her anyway, but new people were living in his mother's old apartment. He asked the neighbors, but no one knew where she had gone. The man he had spoken to after the fire told him that his mother was probably dead.

Tricia the social worker had told Minnie that Daniel was on the adoption register and that he could "go any time." Now, with the threat of another new home upon him, Daniel was beginning to like the farm and was trying to behave. Tricia said he would be allowed to contact his mother when he was eighteen, if he still wanted to, but until then he wasn't allowed any information about her.

"So how *did* your husband and your daughter die?" he asked, looking up at her, licking his lips, which had dried in the cold. She wouldn't look him in the eye at first, too busy straightening up the stall and pulling her coat tighter around her body. But then she met his eye. Her eyes were the hardest thing about her, Daniel thought. The watery blue of them was

so different from his own dark eyes. Sometimes it hurt to look
at her.

"An accident."

"Both of them?"

Minnie nodded.

"What happened?"

"How old are you, Danny?"

"Twelve."

"I know you've had a tough twelve years. I don't want to
presume what terrible things you've seen or done or had done
to you. I want you to know you can talk to me about *anything*
that's happened to you. I won't judge you. You can tell me
whatever you want. But when you get older maybe you'll realize there are some things people can't talk about easily. Maybe
it's good to talk about them, but good doesn't make it easy.
Maybe there are some things you don't want to talk about right
now . . . things that happened with your mum or other people.
You can talk to me about it, but if you don't want to, then I
want you to know that I respect that.

"I know you're just a boy, but already you know what it is
to lose people. You know more than most, I'm sure. I know
you miss your mum. Loss is part of life, but it's not always easy
to bear. Just know that whenever you miss your mum most, or
you feel the saddest, know that I know that pain. Sometimes
when we lose people who are precious to us, it makes the world
a dark place. It's like that person you loved was a little light
and now that they're gone it's dark. Just remember that we all
have that light, that goodness in us, and just because we're sad
doesn't mean that we can't bring happiness, and bringing happiness is being happy, that's all I know . . ."

She took a breath so deep that her breasts heaved.

"In any case, that's what I learned after Norman and Delia died, but I still can't talk about them. I hope you understand that, love, and know it's nothing against you, it's just the way I feel."

Norman and Delia. Daniel repeated the names silently. Suddenly, like the chicken he had murdered, the lives rose real and rare before him. Delia was pale as the porcelain butterfly, Norman dark as the poker that they said ended him.

Daniel nodded at Minnie and began to restack the eggs.

"Was he mean to you?" said Daniel. His nose was running and his tongue sought it out, salty and clear. He curled his tongue up his lip, but she caught him and wiped his nose roughly with a used tissue that she kept up her cardigan sleeve.

"Norman, do you mean?"

"Aye."

"Good God, no. He was the best man in the world. A proper gentleman. He was the love of my life."

Daniel frowned and wiped his nose again with his sleeve.

"Enough now. Talking about the past does nobody any good."

At the end of the day, Daniel helped Minnie to load the little produce that was left over into the car, along with the signs and the takings tin. He sat up front as she huffed into the driver's seat and started the car. She was breathing heavily, her cardigan-ensconced bosom pressing against the steering wheel. The car started on the third attempt, and Daniel began to twiddle the radio dial until he found a song. The signal was poor and fading.

"Put your seat belt on," said Minnie.

"Okay," said Daniel. "Can you fix the aerial again like last time, so we can listen to the radio on the way back?"

He liked being in the car with Minnie, but he was not sure why. She was a nervous, jerky driver and the car seemed older than she was. It was exciting when she tightened her fingers on the steering wheel and dared to go fast. There was an element of vague danger. She got out of the car and reshaped the aerial that had been fashioned from a wire coat hanger. Daniel gave her the thumbs-up when the signal was clear.

They set off driving through town. There was a hole in the exhaust and Daniel watched as pedestrians stared at their noisy car as it passed. Thinking about the commission that would be his when they counted the money this evening, Daniel started to sing along to the song on the radio. It was "Frankie Goes to Hollywood." Daniel leaned forward to tap the beat with his forefingers on the glove compartment.

Minnie glanced at him then swerved suddenly.

"What are you doing? What are you . . . what did I tell you?" she screamed, and Daniel jumped back in his seat.

She was driving along Main Street toward the Carlisle Road, past rows of cars that were parked on the footpaths. She swerved again as a delivery van pulled out from Berti's Fish and Chips, and was admonished by a loud horn. Minnie jumped at the noise and the car veered across to the other side of the road, near the junction for Longtown Road. Daniel put a hand on the dashboard as Minnie turned the wheel sharply and the car skidded to avoid the delivery van. Their car banged into the metal railings at the far side of the crossing. Daniel was thrown forward, banging his head off the dashboard.

A hand on his bump, Daniel crouched on the floor of the

car, beside the gearshift. She was staring straight ahead, breathing hard, so that her chest heaved; her hands still gripped the wheel. Daniel began to laugh. His head hurt, but it seemed funny to be thrown underneath the dashboard, and for the car to be sitting on the wrong side of the road, up against the railings.

The expansive beats of "Frankie Goes to Hollywood" now seemed too loud in the small car.

Her breathing calmed and she reached down to him. Daniel thought that she was going to rub his head and ask if he was all right. Instead she grabbed him roughly by the arms and pulled him up and into his seat.

"What on earth were you doing?" she shouted at him, shaking him. All they had been through together, but not once had she raised her voice. Daniel raised his shoulders up to his ears and turned so that he had to look at her out of the corner of his eye. Her eyes were too wide and he could see her teeth. "What did I tell you? I asked you to *put on your seat belt*. You *must* wear your seat belt. What could have happened . . . ?"

"I just forgot," whispered Daniel.

She took him by the shoulders again. Daniel could feel the pressure of her fingers through his jacket. "Well, you can't forget. You have to do what I say. You have to wear your seat belt."

"Okay," Daniel said, and then louder, "all right."

Minnie relaxed. She was still holding on to his shoulders but not squeezing him so hard. She was out of breath and her eyes were turned down in distress. "I just don't want anything to happen to you," she whispered and then pulled him into her. "I don't want *anything* to happen to you."

Daniel felt the warmth of her breath against his hair.

Minnie turned the radio off. They sat in silence for a few moments. Daniel swallowed.

"All right, put it on now," she said, and he did as she asked, clicking the seat belt into place.

She got out and inspected the bumper and the bonnet, then got back in the car. She cleared her throat and started the car. He could see her fingers trembling on the steering wheel. Daniel rubbed his arms where she had pressed. They drove in silence back to the farm.

Daniel fed the animals while Minnie started dinner. When he came back inside, stocking feet dirty on the kitchen floor, she was pouring herself a gin. Of late she would wait until after dinner, but now he scratched Blitz's stretched-out stomach as she poured herself a large glass. He heard the fizz and crack of her ice cubes and looked up. He saw that her hands were still shaking.

"I'm sorry," he said, looking at the dog.

She drank and then exhaled. "S'all right, lad. I'm sorry too. Lost it, so I did, lost it."

"Why do you drive the car when you hate it so much?"

"Well, when you're afraid of something, often the best thing you can do is do that very thing you're afraid of!"

"Why are you scared of driving anyway?"

"Well, I'm sure it's not really the driving itself. In life most things that frighten us are to do with our own heart and its flaws. You'll always be afraid of some things—never free from fear itself. But that's all right. Fear's like pain, it's there in your life to teach you about yourself."

"What d'you mean?"

"Someday you'll understand. You'll see."

Dinner was roast beef, carrots, peas, and roast potatoes. Daniel cleared a space on the table and laid out the place mats and cutlery. Chickens fluttered at the window as the day waned. By the time dinner was served, she was on her second gin and her hands had steadied. Daniel felt a familiar, fleeting sadness settle on him, light as a butterfly. He felt his skin goose-pimple. He picked up his fork.

"Minnie?"

"Hmm?" She looked up. Her face was relaxed again and her cheeks pink.

"Did Tricia call you this week?"

"No, love. Why? Do you want to speak to her?"

"Well, I was just wanting to ask her what would happen if I don't get adopted, like . . . when they'll put me in the home? I want to know when it's happening, like."

Daniel felt the warmth of her fingers on his arm. "You *will* get adopted. Eat your food."

"What if I don't though, can I stay here?"

"As long as they'll let you, yes. But you will get adopted. You want that, don't you? A new family of your own."

"I don't know. I wouldn't mind staying here with you, like." He looked at his food.

"Well, I like you here with me too, but I don't kid myself that you couldn't do better. Young parents, maybe even brothers and sisters—that's what you need—a proper new home."

"I'm well sick of new homes, like."

"This next one'll be the last, Danny. I'm sure of it."

"Why can't this be the last?"

"Eat up now, your dinner's getting cold."

They cleared up together, Daniel drying the dishes as Minnie poured herself another drink. He watched her out of the corner of his eye, noticing that her movements were slower, heavier. Minnie took the takings box through to the living room and placed it open on the coffee table next to her gin. Bending from the waist, breathing heavily, she lit the fire and the spitting smoky coals slowly began to warm the room. She put on a classic record then let herself fall into her armchair and took another sip of her drink.

"Is this when I get my commission?" asked Danny, kneeling on the floor by the coffee table.

"Well, we'll see. First I want you to count it. Can you?"

Daniel nodded. He separated all the coins and notes and began to count them, whispering the numbers. The sound of the coal fire crackling was audible above the slow movement of the symphony she had chosen. Blitz sat up straight, as he always did when a record was played. He cocked his ears and then turned three times before settling himself at her feet, nose on his paws.

"How much?" asked Minnie when Daniel had finished counting.

"One hundred and thirty-seven pounds, sixty-three pence," said Daniel.

"Well, here, put it back in the box for me, but keep a five for yourself. Thanks for all your hard work."

Daniel did as she asked. He sat cross-legged, staring at the five-pound note.

"You counted that money fast enough. Are you sure you counted it right?"

"I'm sure. You want to check?"

"I'll check later, but I believe you. You're a bright lad, aren't you? You should do better at school than you do."

Daniel shrugged and climbed onto the sofa, where he lay on his back, with his hands behind his head, facing her.

"Your teacher says as much as well, that you know the answers when she asks you but you don't ever finish an exam or a test. You don't finish your homework or do the tasks she gives you. Why is that now?"

"I can't be bothered."

Minnie was reflective. Daniel watched as she raised her chin and stared into the fire.

"Think about your mother, and your father if you can remember him," she said quietly. "Would you say they led good lives?"

Daniel waited for her to turn and look at him before he shrugged.

"When you think about growing up, what do you imagine doing?"

"I want to be in London."

"What doing? What job would you like to do, and I don't mean a pickpocket."

"I dunno."

"Well, do you want to make a lot of money, do you want to help people, do you want to work outdoors . . . ?"

"I want to make money."

"Well, you could be a banker. Work in the City, in Fleet Street . . ."

"I dunno."

She was silent and again turned to the fire. It was dark outside now, and Daniel could see the fire and her face reflected in the window.

"If we look at your life now, we see that it's controlled by the law, isn't that right? You've probably been to court more times than I have, and the law has decided that for your own safety you have to be away from your own family. I wonder if you'd be a good lawyer? Then you could have a say in all those things, and make a load of money into the bargain."

Daniel met her gaze but said nothing. No one had spoken to him like this before. No one had told him that he could choose what happened to him.

"These years coming are probably the most important in your life, Danny. You'll be going to high school next year. If you do well in your exams, the world can be your oyster. Your oyster, let me tell you! You can work in London, do anything you want, believe me. My little one, Delia, she was like you. Bright as a button. All her classes, math, English, history, she always did so well. She wanted to be a doctor. She'd've done it too . . ."

Minnie turned to the fire again. The heat from it had warmed the room, and her cheeks were red now and shining.

"What do you need to do to be a lawyer then?"

"Just do well at school, love, and then you go to a university. Think about all the people that've put you down before. That'd show them, wouldn't it? You graduating from a university and becoming a lawyer." She cackled to herself, staring at the fire, then heaved herself up to pour another drink. "Think how proud your mum would be."

Daniel lay on the couch, watching Blitz stretch: chin to the carpet and rear legs raised. He remembered his last foster father, holding him by the shoulders and whispering *evil little bastard,* and then one of his mother's boyfriends who had slapped his face and called him a *sackless nowt* when he brought back the wrong change from the shop after going to buy him cigarettes. He took a deep breath.

"So you just need to do well at school?"

"Well, yes, that's the first part. And I wouldn't bother telling you all this if I didn't think it was worth your trouble. But I know you're bright. You could show them. I know it . . ."

She left the room and Daniel heard her fixing the drink in the kitchen. The warmth of the fire was on his skin, and the words that she had said seemed to warm him from the inside too. He felt powerful, but good. It reminded him of caring for the animals.

Minnie threw herself back into the chair, spilling a little of her drink on her cardigan, which she smoothed into the wool with the palm of her hand.

"So if I was a lawyer, would I be able to help boys stay with their mum?"

"Well, there are all kinds of lawyers, love. Some work in family law, and if that was what interested you, you could do that. But some work with big companies, some work with criminals, or in the property market . . . you know, helping people to buy houses."

"So it would be like on *Crown Court*. I would stand up in front of the judge?"

"You could do that, yes. You'd be great too."

Daniel thought for a moment, listening to the chime of the ice tinkling in her glass.

"Can I put the telly on?" Daniel asked.

"All right. Turn the record off, but be careful and not scratch it. Mind how I showed you, now."

Daniel jumped up and gently lifted the stylus off the record. He lifted the record as she had shown him, two hands on the rim of the record so as not to leave fingerprints, and slid it carefully back in its sleeve.

She had an old black-and-white television with a turn dial. Daniel twisted until he found a comedy and then jumped back on the couch.

"You should get a color TV."

"Should I now? I have better things to buy with my money. Maybe when you're a rich lawyer you can buy us one."

She winked at him and Daniel smiled. He felt warm inside. It was the thought of staying here for years to come and calling this his home. He curled up on the sofa watching *Are You Being Served?* and smiling but not laughing at the jokes, only some of which he understood, still aware of the crackles of the fire and the tinkles of her ice in the background. He felt safe, he decided, that was what he felt. He felt safe with her, even if she was a drunk and a bad driver and smelled funny. He didn't want to leave.

When the show was finished, Blitz was asking to go out, and so Daniel let him out the back door. When Blitz came back in, Daniel bolted the door and took a biscuit from the tin. In the living room, Minnie's drink was empty and she had tears on her face.

The warm feeling faded as he watched her. She was staring at the television, but Daniel could tell that she didn't see it. The gray light reflected on her face. Daniel went to the fire and stood with his back to it, feeling the heat on the backs of his legs.

"Are you all right?" he asked.

Minnie swept a palm over her face, left and then right, but there were fresh tears ready to wet her cheeks.

"Sorry, love. Just ignore me," she said. "I was just thinking about today. You gave me such a fright, so you did. Promise me you'll always wear your seat belt, even if you're in another car. Promise me . . ."

She leaned forward, knuckles white on the edge of the chair, lips wet with tears or saliva.

"I promise," said Danny quietly. "I'm going to go to bed."

"All right, pet, good night." She wiped her face once, twice and then again with her right sleeve. "Remember to put the money in your piggy bank. No taking it to school and buying rubbish. C'mere . . ."

She reached out toward him and Daniel walked slowly toward her. She took his wrist and pulled him gently into her, to plant a kiss on his cheek. He lay on her for a second longer than he needed to, aware of the roughness of the wool against his right cheek and the wetness of the wool against his left.

15

IT WAS AFTER NINE AND DANIEL WAS EATING TAKEOUT THAI curry in his flat. He still had work to do, and so he sat with the laptop open on his kitchen table, drinking beer and trying not to get sauce on the keys. The radio was on low. He was due in court the next morning for a shoplifting case. Daniel had told his client, a mother of four, that he hoped she would not be given a custodial sentence. Now he sat reviewing the facts and noting down details.

Sebastian seemed to have absorbed more of his time than was necessary. Daniel always prepared well for his cases, and now took the time to go over his notes for tomorrow, but yet Sebastian's case seemed to interrupt his thoughts.

He turned his attention to his files and the notes he was making, but his mind still drifted to the lack inside him. Since he had left Minnie's as a teenager, he had become used to being alone. At the university and after, he had been known as a loner, a heartbreaker, neither a man's man nor a woman's man. His own man. A lone man. Keeping his own counsel.

Daniel remembered Minnie's sister, Harriet, standing on her tiptoes to be close to him. *I hope you're ashamed of yourself, lad,* and then the sight of her stabbing her way across the noisy gravel of the funeral home yard.

Harriet.

Daniel remembered her coming to visit, and the tense drive to pick her up in Carlisle: Minnie's knuckles white on the steering wheel as she drove, the roar of the Renault as she belted up the motorway in third gear.

Harriet was Minnie's younger sister, also a nurse, also a laugh, and also fond of the drink. Daniel remembered the taste of her sweet ginger-ale kisses when she visited, once a year, or every two years, bringing hand-knitted sweaters and jars of hard sweets.

Daniel finished his curry and pushed the plate away. Wiping his mouth, he found Minnie's box in the living room and pulled out the address book. The book was full of Brampton farmers, but then he found Harriet—*Harriet McBryde*—listed under her maiden name, although Harriet had married, had a family in Cork—he had seen the pictures. Daniel continued flicking through the book, pausing at the end, at another name he recognized: Tricia Stern.

Tricia. Daniel could still remember riding in the car with her to Minnie's farm for the first time. There was the phone number and address for Newcastle Children's Social Care Services and another number for Carlisle Social Services.

Daniel started from the beginning and went through the

book more slowly this time. *Jane Flynn*—a London number, the address somewhere in Hounslow. *Flynn* had been Minnie's married name he knew: Minnie Flynn, Norman Flynn, and Delia Flynn—the Flynns of Flynn Farm. Norman must have had family, Daniel reasoned, although Minnie had never spoken of them. She wouldn't have—she could barely mention her husband without her eyes glassing with tears.

It was late and Daniel didn't have the time. He had too much work to do and would be up until two as it was, but so many questions whirred in his mind. For years he had tried to keep her from his thoughts, but now that she was dead he found himself drawn to her. He now wanted to know why she had hurt him as she had, and why she had hurt so much. But it was too late.

Daniel took a deep breath. He flipped back through the address book, leaning forward with the heel of his hand on his forehead, so that his hair fell over his fingers.

Harriet McBryde, Middleton, Cork, 021 463532.

He picked up the telephone and dialed with his thumb, beer bottle in his other hand. He dialed all but the last number and then hung up. Harriet wouldn't want to speak to him, he reasoned. She thought he was shameful, the guilty one. He wondered what it was he wanted to know from Harriet. He wanted to know Minnie, he realized, wanted to know who she was apart from the big-hipped woman who had mothered him and saved him from himself.

Daniel ran two hands through his hair and sighed deeply.

He put the telephone down and got back to his work, steeling himself for a long night.

THE PROSECUTION HAD HIRED A PSYCHIATRIST TO ASSESS Sebastian. The report showed that he was sane and fit to plead. Daniel had also arranged a psychological assessment. The psychologist had visited Cherry Orchard House to meet with Sebastian and the report was sent to Harvey, Hunter and Steele one week later. Daniel bit his lip as he slipped the report into his briefcase. He didn't know what he had been expecting from the psychologist. Sometimes when he was with Sebastian he felt a strange affinity for him. Other times he too felt uneasy around the boy who Irene had described as *unsettling*.

In the men's room, Daniel fixed his tie and ran a hand through his hair. He was alone and he looked at himself for a second longer than he would normally, not smiling, watching his face as he imagined others saw it. He looked tired, he thought, his dark eyes shadowed underneath and his cheeks thinner than normal. He remembered his wildness as a child. He knew where it had come from, but not where it had gone. He leaned closer to the mirror and ran a finger along the bridge of his nose, feeling for the small bump that he attributed to having his nose broken when he was little.

Daniel had to be at the Old Bailey for a brief pretrial hearing and then he had made an appointment with the psychologist. He was late and so he jogged to the tube, running down the escalators and up again—excusing himself when his briefcase nudged a woman's hip. He surfaced at St. Paul's and walked to the Old Bailey.

It was after four when he escaped the Central Criminal Court and then he headed to Fulham to meet with the psychologist, Dr. Baird. Irene had been delayed, and so only Mark Gibbons, her junior counsel, made the meeting.

Baird was younger than Daniel had imagined him. His skin was pale and freckles from his nose spread up his face and onto his scalp where his strawberry blond hair was thinning. He seemed nervous.

"Can I get you tea or coffee?" said Dr. Baird, arching his thin pale eyebrows as if one of them had made an interesting remark.

Daniel refused but Mark cleared his throat and asked for tea.

His report had been detached, professional, yet offering personal insights into Sebastian's character. In terms of the defense, it could help to win sympathy for Sebastian, but Daniel and Irene had not decided how or if to use it. Dr. Baird had assessed Sebastian's suitability to stand trial in adult court, yet Daniel had wanted it to show Sebastian as the young boy he was, with minimum readiness for the rigors of courtroom drama. The psychologist had described Sebastian as intelligent and articulate and all Daniel could hope was that these positive professional opinions would help to counteract the prosecution's witnesses' statements—that Sebastian was a cruel bully—and help the jury to sympathize with him. Of course Daniel hoped that sympathy would not be needed and that facts alone would prove the boy innocent.

Dr. Baird had visited Sebastian at Parklands House, armed

with dolls and felt-tipped pens. Daniel had been absorbed by his report, not only because of its possible relevance for the trial, but because of what it revealed about Sebastian.

While Mark sipped his tea— cup trembling on its saucer— Baird sat back in his chair, hands folded over his compact stomach, and expounded on Sebastian.

"He's highly intelligent, as I note in the report—IQ of 140, and he was certainly well aware of who I was and what I was about . . ." Daniel thought that Baird sounded peeved.

"So, do you know why I am here?" the doctor had asked.

"Yes," said Sebastian. "You want to get inside my head."

"He certainly displayed an . . . uncanny maturity for a boy his age, and he was quite certain that he was innocent." Baird opened his eyes wide as he said the word. Daniel was not sure what the man intended by the expression: was he impressed or disbelieving?

"Do you know what crime you've been charged with, Sebastian?"

"Murder."

"And how do you feel about that?"

"I'm innocent."

The boy knew the difference, Baird told Daniel and Mark. He was clear about the difference between right and wrong, and knew that murder—indeed violence—was wrong.

Daniel wondered if Sebastian really understood the difference, or if he had responded according to the doctor's expectation. Daniel thought about his own childhood and his own wrongdoings—some of them criminal. He remembered no awareness of the immorality of these acts, only expediency, protection, and revenge. Minnie had helped him to understand the difference.

Daniel leafed through the report to the sections he had high-lighted before the meeting. "Dr. Baird, you've written that you have no way of knowing how Sebastian would react in a state of emotional distress, but you think that even in that state he would know what he was doing and its moral implications—forgive me for paraphrasing—what exactly does that mean?"

"Well, it means that I have met Sebastian twice and feel confident to give this assessment of him—that he knows the difference between right and wrong—but I am aware that a longer study of his behavior would be necessary in order to be conclusive about his understanding of morality and his behavior changes when under greater emotional pressure."

"I see—you say that he is . . ." Daniel turned the page and read, " '*Unable to deal with and understand strong emotions and is prone to tantrums and emotional outbursts.*' What does that mean in terms of his ability to perpetrate a violent crime?"

"Well, very little—I found him to be intellectually mature, precocious even, but as I have stated he did seem emotionally immature. We touched on some troubling subjects and he did become visibly upset, but certainly not aggressive in any way."

Daniel scanned the report again, frowning. "You ascertained there was an indication of abuse?"

"Why yes," said Baird, picking up his file and referring to his notes. "Certainly of spousal abuse in the home. You will see we did some role play with dolls, which at first Sebastian was not open to engage with . . . but eventually he did interact with the dolls. He didn't verbalize it—again an indication of emotional immaturity—but he seemed to act out scenes where his father punched and kicked his mother."

"There's been no social work engagement with the family," said Mark, finishing his tea.

"Correct," said Dr. Baird, "but medical reports do corroborate some of Sebastian's statements.

" 'I'm an only child. There was a baby but it died. I put my hand on my mum's stomach and I felt it moving. But then she fell and she gave birth to a dead thing.' "

"Sebastian described a stillbirth—quite vividly so—and Mrs. Croll did indeed suffer a third-trimester miscarriage as a result of an accident in the home," confirmed Baird.

Daniel had read in the doctor's report that Sebastian's expression had been "blank" when he provided this information to the doctor, and Baird had noted that the boy made "a short sucking sound with his mouth."

Daniel cleared his throat and glanced at Mark, who was making notes.

"Finally," said Daniel, "you dismiss the previous diagnosis of Asperger's by Sebastian's educational psychologist? This was in his school reports."

"Yes, I didn't find any evidence that he was an Asperger's sufferer, although he may have some traits related to the spectrum."

"And you are recommending regular court breaks?" said Daniel. "I think that will happen as standard, but I think we will have you testify to that effect—do you agree, Mark?"

Mark nodded eagerly, his Adam's apple bobbing nobly above his shirt collar.

"But of course—court proceedings should be altered in view of Sebastian's age and emotional state. His high intelligence means that proceedings may be understood well if properly explained, but regular breaks should be arranged so as to limit emotional strain."

Daniel said good-bye to Mark and made his way back home. He closed his eyes and sat back in his seat, feeling the rock and reel of the tube. He remembered his own powerlessness as his mother was beaten then imagined Kenneth King Croll causing Charlotte to fall and lose her baby.

Back in Bow, he unpacked his briefcase in the kitchen, scattering the Croll evidence bundle onto the table, and opened a beer. He would go through it one more time after dinner. He saw his notepad from the night before, with numbers for Harriet McBryde and Jane Flynn and sat staring at them, wondering what to do. Harriet was furious with him and Jane had never heard of him. He was family to neither.

He had a shower and changed into a T-shirt and jeans. He padded barefoot to the living room where he lifted the photograph of Minnie's first family from the mantelpiece. He carried it through to the kitchen and finished his beer staring at Minnie's face, which was gleaming with happiness, skin still unruddied by the years outdoors that were to come.

Daniel took a deep breath and picked up the telephone. He dialed Harriet's number; listening to the unusual long ring and feeling his chest tighten in expectation. He drummed his fingers gently on the table, having not thought of what he was going to say. The phone rang out and he was just about to hang up when she answered:

"Hello?" Heavy breathing, as if she had been running to the phone.

"Hi, is it . . . Harriet?"

"Yes, can I help you?" She was calm now, steeled, trying to place his voice.

"It . . . it's Danny, I saw you at . . ."

There was a long pause and then Harriet said, "What do you want?"

Daniel leaned forward on the kitchen table and reached for Minnie's photo. He spoke quietly, unaccustomed to asking for help. The room was warm and the veins on his hands were raised as he held the photo frame.

"I'm sorry about . . . when I saw you at the funeral, I was . . . anyway, I wanted to talk to you about Minnie. I've been thinking about her a lot and realize there's so much about her that I don't know—that she never told me. I wondered if you would . . ."

"Like I said to you at the funeral, Danny, this sudden interest is long overdue. She was heartbroken when you didn't speak to her or visit. *Heartbroken,* do you understand? And now she's dead, you want to find out more about the fine person that she was? I'm grieving for a sister who I loved dearly, but you said good-bye to Minnie long ago. Now, for the love of God, *leave me alone.*"

"I'm sorry," Daniel whispered, but Harriet had already hung up.

16

DANIEL WAS LOOKING AT THE COMICS IN *Brampton News* ON Front Street. He was aware of being watched and turned quickly to catch a woman in maroon overalls staring at him. When he met her gaze she smiled at him and went back to the cash desk. Daniel felt a hot flush rise on his cheek. He knew the woman as Florence MacGregor, who everyone called Flo-Mac. She bought eggs and sometimes a chicken from Minnie, and always quibbled over the price. She had very black hair and Minnie had told him that she dyed it; *some people just can't take getting older, even though there's nothing more certain in life other than dying itself,* she had told Daniel.

Daniel knew that Flo-Mac expected him to steal the comic, and was prepared to do so, just so as not to disappoint her, but just as he was rolling it up to slip down his trousers, he thought

about his career as a lawyer, and how this would look. He un-
rolled the comic and counted the change in his pocket. He had
enough.

As he was walking along the aisle to the counter, he heard Flo
whispering to her assistant. Daniel couldn't hear all the words, but
he did make out *Flynn, orphans, disgrace.*

Daniel placed the comic on the counter.

"Fourteen pence," said Flo.

Daniel threw the comic at her. "Stick it up your arse," he
said and walked out of the shop.

At school he played football at lunch and scored two goals.
In the afternoon there was a math test and Daniel finished first,
as usual, but this time he had actually filled in the answers.
He waited after class and made Miss Pringle mark his paper in
front of him. He got every answer correct and so Miss Pringle
gave him a gold star to take home to Minnie.

Daniel walked with the test paper and the gold star in front
of him as he crossed the Dandy. All of the other children were
home by now and the Dandy was quiet. Billy Harper was alone
on the swings and Daniel waved to him and the heavy man waved
back, gently swinging back and forth. He remembered the summer
before, being beaten as he crossed this piece of land. He felt different now, older. He folded the test up and put it in his pocket, then
ran home, stopping occasionally to kick the heads off daisies.

When Daniel got home, Minnie was replacing the bedding
in the goat's hut. He walked up behind her and prodded her
capacious hip.

"I was wondering where you got to. Were you malingering
as usual?"

"No, I stayed back to get my math test, look!" Daniel presented the paper to Minnie.

She frowned at the paper for a few moments, then, realizing, grabbed him and bear-hugged him, squeezing him so hard that he couldn't take a breath and his toes lifted from the ground.

"Well, that's marvelous," she said. "We'll have to celebrate. A gold star means that we definitely must have crumble and custard."

Daniel watched as she snatched at the rhubarb that grew out of control to the side of the coop. The stalks were three fingers thick and the leaves large as umbrellas. She walked into the house with three stems and then asked him if he wanted one now. While she made the crumble and heated the oil for the chips, he sat at the kitchen table dabbing a stalk of rhubarb into a bowl of sugar. The sweet-coated sourness of the rhubarb dipped in sugar reminded him of happiness and right then he was happy, with the gold star and the smell of chips cooking and the tartness of rhubarb on his tongue.

HE WAS EATING THE CRUMBLE WHEN SHE BROACHED THE SUBject. She pushed her bowl away from her as he took a custard-slicked slice of rhubarb into his mouth.

"You remember I was telling you that it is often hard for social workers to find adoptive parents for older children, like you?"

Daniel stopped eating. His arm buckled onto the table and his spoon balanced on the edge of his plate. He had food in his mouth, but could not swallow.

"Well, it seems like Tricia has found a couple who would be interested."

Minnie was watching his face for some response; Daniel could feel her eyes searching out his own. He was completely still—reflecting her.

"It's a family with older children, eighteen, twenty-two, ready to leave. They have four children of their own in total and just the one still there at home. It means you would have that family atmosphere, but get lots of attention. Better than here with just me and the animals kicking about. What do you think?"

Daniel shrugged with one shoulder and looked at his food. He did his best to swallow.

"They live in Carlisle and they have a big house. You'd have a great big bedroom, I bet . . ."

"Who cares?"

Minnie sighed. She reached out toward him, but he drew his arm away with such haste that he knocked his spoon off the table. Spots of custard landed on the wall and the table.

"They only want you to go for a tryout," she said. "They suggested this weekend, just to get to know each other."

Daniel started from the table and ran upstairs. Blitz was asleep and Daniel caught his tail a little as he fled the room. He wasn't sure if it was the yelp of the dog or Minnie's cries behind him to come back that caused the anger to whip. It cracked through his body and as soon as he was in his bedroom he was destroying it: ripping out the drawers and kicking over the bedside table, smashing yet another lamp. This time, for good measure, he stamped on the shade, once, twice, three times.

He was jammed between the wardrobe and the bed, curled up

tight, by the time Minnie entered. He steeled himself against the comforting hands that he expected on his back and his hair. He pressed tighter into himself. It reminded him of being attacked. Two of his mother's boyfriends had beaten him unconscious. He remembered sitting just like this, jammed between furniture, protecting his stomach and his head, letting his shoulders and his back take the brunt, until they pulled him out, screaming, by his hair.

Now, he resisted her comfort in the same way; he was taut to it, so that every muscle in his body was primed to recoil on her should she come near. His face was pressed into his knees so he could hear and smell his own breath, laced with a sourness, which was either the news or the rhubarb.

But Minnie didn't touch him. He heard the springs protest as she sat down on the bed. He heard her exhale and then there was silence.

He waited for a few minutes, watching the circular patterns that throbbed before his eyes when he pressed his knees into them. He felt the pain of pressure in his eyeballs, yet did not stop. The muscles in his back were straining from curving around his thighs. Slowly, he raised his head. She was sitting with her back to him. He could see her twirling the gold band on her left hand. He had begun to like her hands, the red roughness of them. He liked the feel of them against his cheek and in his hair, as if only hands as rough as hers could bring him comfort now.

Now he watched her with his chin on his knees. She was still, turned from him, watching some invisible fancy in the air. He could see the rise and fall of her chest and the dwindling sun shining in her gray hair, so that it seemed almost white, reflecting all the light.

"I just want to stay with you," he said to her finally.

"Oh, Danny," she said, with her back still to him, "I'm glad you've settled here; I wanted you to. But this is a real chance for you. This is *a family*; imagine what it would be like to have two experienced, professional parents all to yourself. Better than this mucky old farm, and nobody but old me to talk to—I'll tell you that for nothin'.."

"I like the farm . . ."

"These are real outdoor people, you know? Professional, smart people."

"So? Who cares?"

Minnie turned to him. She patted the bed beside her and said, "C'mere."

Daniel uncoiled and sat beside her. She nudged him with her shoulder and asked, "You tellin' me you're afraid of a weekend away with nice new people? Nobody's sending you anywhere. This is an opportunity for the taking."

"So I can come back if I don't like them?"

"To be sure, but who says they'll like *you*. Grumpy little bugger that you are!"

Daniel smiled then, and Minnie nudged him again. He folded into the expanse of her, tucking his arms between her hips and her bosom, his face pressed into the softness of her upper arm.

On Saturday morning, Daniel stood with his elbows on the windowsill, watching out of his bedroom window for the car. He could see Minnie's front garden with its vegetable patches and raspberry canes. The gnarled hand of the rowan tree was at the far side, reaching out of the earth with desperate sinew strewn with the blood red berries. The parents who wanted to meet him were called Jim and Val Thornton. They were not yet late, but Daniel had been waiting for an hour. With no car in sight, he stared at the rowan tree waving at him in the wind. He remembered climbing the rowan and picking the berries and Minnie telling him they were poisonous. She had said that the tree was there to keep the witches away, so how could she be a witch? Daniel watched as the sparrows and the magpies stripped the branches of their berries. He wondered why tiny birds could survive feasting on the berries that Minnie said could kill humans.

Daniel was thinking about this when a large black car pulled up in front of the farm. He hid behind the curtain, but continued to stare at the tall man with blond hair who got out of the truck and then the woman, who wore her hair up in a brightly colored scarf. When they disappeared from Daniel's view, he left the bedroom to sit at the top of the stairs. His bag was packed, at the bottom of the stairs, but Minnie had said she would have a chat with them first.

The front door was open as Minnie had gone out to meet them. Their pleasantries drifted inside like early autumn leaves. Blitz stood half inside, half out, so all Daniel could see was his wagging tail. His stomach hurt with nerves and he leaned over onto his knees in an effort to release the tension in it. He hid out of sight as Minnie showed them into the living room.

He was expecting to be called, but Blitz came for him first, panting in his face at the top of the stairs. Daniel massaged the dog's black-and-white mane and Blitz dipped his head to allow it. Then the call came.

"Danny? Do you want to come down, pet?"

Blitz started down the stairs on hearing Minnie's voice. Daniel waited a moment and took a deep breath before heading down. He

was in his stocking feet and stepped in such a way as not to make
the floorboards creek. Minnie was at the bottom of the stairs with
a strange smile on her face. He had never seen her smile like that
before—as if she was pleased with herself, or as if there was someone watching her other than him. Daniel frowned, put his hands
in his pockets and followed her into the living room.

"Well, hello there . . ."

The man tensed and threw out his arms and seemed about
to stand until the woman put her hand on his forearm. Daniel
was glad that he stayed seated. Minnie had both hands on his
shoulders and was rubbing them. Daniel nodded his hello and
scuffed his socks against the living room rug.

"I'm Val," the woman said, with a smile like the one Minnie
had been wearing, only harsher; Daniel thought her teeth were
too white, and he could see her gums. "And this is Jim, my
husband—we're both very pleased you decided to spend the
weekend with us."

Daniel nodded as Minnie steered him toward the couch.

Minnie went into the kitchen to make tea. Daniel leaned
back into the couch as Jim and Val stared at him.

"So do you want to know about us at all?" asked Val.

"I know everything already," said Daniel. "You have four
kids. There's only one kid at home and he's a boy about eighteen. You have a big house and Jim's an accountant."

Val and Jim laughed together, nervously. Daniel balanced
one foot on top of the other. He was sitting so far back into the
couch that his chin was on his chest.

"Why don't you tell us about you?" said Val. "What do you
like to do?"

"Football, feed the animals, sell stuff at the market."

"We live in Carlisle," Jim said, leaning forward, elbows on his knees. "We're always out walking or cycling, so I'm definitely up for a game of football sometime. Maybe we can do that this weekend, if you like?"

Daniel tried to shrug, but his shoulders were wedged into the couch.

Minnie brought piping-hot tea and a plate of German biscuits. Daniel remained sunk into the couch and so Minnie chatted, louder than she usually did, about the farm and how long she'd been fostering and Ireland, which she hadn't set foot on since 1968. Daniel sat still beside her, running his forefinger over a hole in the couch, which Minnie told him had been made years ago by her husband's cigarette.

"We've got your room all ready for you," said Val. "It's the biggest bedroom—the one that used to belong to our oldest boy, so you have your own TV in there."

"Is it color?" asked Daniel.

"It is."

Daniel looked at Minnie and smiled. He watched as Jim reached out for a German biscuit. He ate it all without a crumb to Blitz, who sat salivating at his feet.

"Do you have any pets?" Daniel asked, sitting up for the first time.

"No, the boys always wanted a dog, but Val's allergic . . ."

"Oh, I'm sorry," said Minnie, taking Blitz's ruff in her fist. "I'll put him out."

"No, no, a short time is fine, as long as she doesn't pet him . . . We're really so pleased you could come for the weekend though, Daniel; it'll be so nice to have a child around again." Jim's nostrils stretched when he smiled.

17

HEATHCOTE STREET CHAMBERS WAS HOLDING A PARTY—A regular September event—to allow their barristers to network with key solicitors and judges. Daniel went with Veronica, his senior partner, hoping that he would catch Irene there. He had brought a copy of confidential papers on a social work investigation into the Crolls that had been sourced by a clerk in his office.

The party was notorious—a free bar stocked with champagne; barristers and chambers clerks fawning over the big solicitors who kept them in business. Daniel had met his ex-girlfriend at the party last year, a pupil who was nearly fifteen years his junior. She had recently moved to another chambers.

When Daniel and Veronica arrived, the carpeted staircase and corridors were crammed with people pink cheeked and laughing, blocking up doorways into rooms that swelled with laughter. The air was sweet and warm and fragrant. There was no music, but the cacophony of conversations made it difficult to hear.

Daniel had to lean into Veronica. "I'll get us a drink," he said to her as she was kissed on both cheeks by one of the Crown Court judges.

He took off his jacket and put his tie in his pocket as he waited for two glasses of champagne, then carried them between the fingers of one hand as he made his way back. He spotted Irene halfway up the stairs, talking to another young QC.

Daniel reached across three judges to give Veronica her drink and then slowly made his way to the stairs. He caught Irene's eye and she turned from the man she was talking to and waved.

"Glad you made it, Danny," she said, leaning down to kiss him on the cheek.

She stayed one step above him. He felt strange standing eye to eye with her. She was still dressed for court in a knee-length pencil skirt and white blouse.

"Do you know Danny? Harvey, Hunter and Steele?" said Irene to the barrister she had been talking to.

"Oh yes, of course, Daniel Hunter, isn't it?" The barrister shook Daniel's hand and then left for the bar.

"How's Sebastian holding up at the unit?" said Irene.

Daniel smiled at the sheen on her skin and the slight flush on her exposed collarbone.

"Surviving. Listen, have you got a minute? I was sent something. We need to talk about what we're going to do with it . . ."

"I'm intrigued," said Irene, taking Daniel by the elbow and

gently maneuvering him upstairs. "Let's go to my room—don't worry—more wine in there!"

The room, like the rest of chambers, was opulently and traditionally decorated, so that even the wallpaper and the carpet seemed to emit a reassuring confidentiality. Streetlight spilled into the room from the sash windows and Irene turned on a table lamp. Voices swelled from the corridor and Daniel gently shut the door.

"Do you want more bubbly or some wine?" she asked, opening an antique cupboard by the window.

"Whatever you like," he said, finishing his champagne, enjoying its tart fizz on his tongue.

"Let's have this then," she said. The cork sounded and the bottle smoked. Irene filled Daniel's glass and her own and put the bottle of champagne on her desk. "What about the tapes? Did you find anything? Any sign of our mystery attacker?"

"Nothing," Daniel said, running a hand over his eyes.

"Here's to . . . better luck this time," said Irene, handing him a glass.

They touched glasses and Irene sat down on the edge of her desk. Daniel threw his jacket over a chair, first taking out the report that he had wanted to show her. There was laughter outside the door as a male voice shouted, "Point of law, M'lord."

Daniel unfolded the report and handed it to Irene. "This is . . . a social services report—specially convened case conference to investigate Sebastian's home life, because of the charge and the media reports," said Daniel.

"Where on earth did you get that?"

Daniel shook his head. "It was anonymously hand-posted

to my office with my name on it and 'confidential.' I got it this morning."

"Whoever did it could get hung," she said, taking the report from him and scanning it. "Who do you think it was?"

"I would think someone involved in the conference who's been following the case. Just read it."

He took a large sip of champagne as Irene read out loud: "'Reason for case conference alleged schedule-one offense by Sebastian, parents are excluded from the conference.'" Irene looked at him.

Daniel sat down on the edge of the desk beside Irene and leaned over her shoulder as she read:

> *Sustained physical violence over a number of years. Six broken ribs and a broken collarbone. Ruptured spleen. Broken nose. Diazepam, Nitrazepam, dihydracodeine. Second suicide attempt—overdose of Nitrazepam taken with alcohol. Patient offered refuge and counseling but refuses to name husband as the attacker. Doctors determined that the twenty-nine-week-old unborn baby died as a result of injuries to the amniotic sac and uterus.*

"Just like Sebastian acted out to the psychologist," said Irene, looking up and putting the report on the desk.

Daniel picked it up again and flicked to a section he had highlighted. "You read that bit, did you?"

Irene sighed and took another sip of her drink. "Charlotte tried to kill herself . . ."

"But tried to take Sebastian with her," said Daniel, frowning slightly and finishing his drink. "That's what it looks like.

He had his stomach pumped the same night that Charlotte was admitted."

"Apart from the pills, though, Sebastian has never been touched."

"Not beaten, but enough that he saw it happen to her. No wonder he's *unsettling,* as you put it."

Irene sighed. "However much you or I may want him to be, King Kong's not on trial . . . God knows who gave this to you, but there's no way we can use it."

"I know," said Daniel. "I think someone following the case and involved with the family must have naively thought that this would help explain everything."

"Very naive," said Irene, sipping her drink. "Whoever did it has jeopardized their career, but there's absolutely no way we can use this."

"You've read the school reports. Sebastian's on record as being an aggressive little bully . . . disruptive in class. We know the CPS are going to get that in," said Daniel

"We might be successful in keeping it out. We were with Tyrel. And besides, this is absolutely classified information—there's no way we can use it."

"But as you said, it only backs up what Sebastian told the psychologist. My point is that *if* the evidence of bad character is allowed, and they start to paint Sebastian as a monster, that is when we can use the domestic violence. We can get the psychologist to testify to it without this document."

Irene was shaking her head. "The judge is even less likely to allow evidence about Sebastian's violent home life than he is to allow evidence of bad character. You're right that it's good to know about, but I don't think it supports the current defense strategy or that we can use it. We're concentrating on the circumstantial evidence."

"If you see there, the same neighbor of the Crolls—Gillian Hodge—she keeps calling the police about the fighting next door. The CPS has her as a witness," Daniel said. "She has kids Sebastian's age, and she says in her statement that he's aggressive toward her kids. Now . . . the judge may not allow it and I know you'll ask for it to be excluded, but if they do try to paint Sebastian that way, we can point to the abuse as an explanation for his bullying, which is *in his school records too*, but make clear that being a bully doesn't make him a murderer."

Their eyes met. Irene's eyes were reflective.

"I see what you're saying," she said. "We can keep it in mind, but we don't want to agree with them that he is violent."

"The facts of the case are clear—they don't have fingerprints, they don't have a reliable witness who places him at the scene of the crime, the forensics are circumstantial—but I know they're going to get witnesses to testify to his bullying of other kids, even though it's irrelevant to this case. We can use the prosecution's witness against them. Gillian Hodge will admit to calling emergency services to the Croll home."

Irene nodded and put the report down. "Thanks. We can think about it." She paused, then looked seriously at Daniel.

"You look tired, Danny," she said.

"You look great," he batted back, looking her in the eye before draining his glass. She turned from the compliment.

"Didn't you seduce Carl's pupil at this party last year?" she asked. Daniel was surprised to feel his cheeks color.

"What is this, examination in chief?"

Irene laughed, arching her eyebrow and raising a finger: "Where were you on this date in September of last year?"

Daniel raised both hands palm upward toward her, letting the hair fall over his eyes.

"I heard you two split up. She moved to another set last month."

"Yeah, I heard," he said, looking at the door.

There was a pause. The relief wallpaper and thick carpet warmed and expanded the pause. Daniel felt thirsty and hot.

"What 'bout you?" said Daniel.

"Did I seduce a pupil?"

He laughed down his nose. "Weren't you seeing that magistrate's judge?"

"God, that was ages ago, keep up." She walked to him with the bottle and poured more champagne into his glass. He could smell her. She looked up into his eyes. "You really do look tired, y'know."

Daniel ran a hand over his eyes and sighed. "I know, not been getting much sleep."

"Not this case, I hope. Bloody media."

"No, well, that's part of it, but . . . a personal thing . . ." Daniel looked at her and pressed his lips together.

Irene arched her eyebrow. "A lady?"

"No, well, yeah, actually . . . my . . . mother died."

"Oh, God, Danny, I'm sorry."

There was another swell of laughter outside the door. Daniel was surprised to feel a flush on his cheek again. He didn't know why he had told Irene this truth. He looked away—*my mother, my mother*—only two months ago he had denounced her.

Minnie was gone forever, but now he could admit that she was his mother.

Irene sat down behind her desk. She took her shoes off and twirled her feet back and forth, looking at Daniel with her glass held in two hands.

"This case is going to be massive, you know, Danny."

"I know—'the Angel Killer.' Nice ring to it." He raised an eyebrow.

"I don't know if it's the sting of last year, but something about this one scares me."

"I know what you mean."

"We can't give in to it," she said, standing up suddenly and putting her shoes back on. "Bad as the publicity is now, it can only be worse at the trial."

They both reached for the report at the same time, and Daniel's hand accidentally brushed against her waist. "Sorry—that's your copy. You can keep it."

She nodded and put it into a drawer. Daniel turned the brass door handle, feeling it reassuringly cool against his palm. There was a swell of voices as he opened the door, and heat from the other side. It intruded into their quiet space.

"Thanks for the drink," he said.

"Thanks for the update."

He stood back to let her pass, but she was waiting for him and they bumped into each other again. "Sorry," he said. Her hair smelled of coconut.

In the corridor, she broke away from him. "Excuse me, will you? Got to work the room now. Duty calls!"

Daniel watched her as he descended the stairs, shaking hands and laughing with her straight, white teeth.

He walked around the party, nursing another glass of champagne. He realized that he knew almost everyone who was there, at least by sight. People shouted his name and slapped his shoulder as he passed; others waved from across the room. Daniel realized that he did not want to speak to any of them.

He wondered if it was the champagne, which he had drunk too quickly: his head felt claustrophobic. He stood on his tiptoes to let two barristers past, then pushed through the crowd to one of the big offices on the ground floor. The window was open and he could feel the cool night reaching in toward him.

As he moved toward it, Daniel was drawn into a group of solicitors. He stood with one hand in his pocket smiling intermittently at the jokes while listening to the smokers by the window.

"But you know Irene's taken that Angel Killer brief?"

"Has she? Controversial for a new QC."

"Big case though. Old Bailey. High profile."

"I know, but still, I wouldn't touch it. I hear he's pleading not guilty. Little sod's gotta be guilty as sin, doesn't he?"

"Well-heeled family. Father's a trader in Hong Kong. Do you know Giles by any chance, works for Cornells? He knows him. Apparently he's furious—says it's all a mistake."

"Well, we'll see. Irene'll sort them out."

"Safe pair of hands."

"Safe and . . . lovely to boot." The men laughed.

"You heard she made silk . . . ?"

Daniel excused himself. He drained his glass and left it on a half-moon, mahogany table beside a porcelain vase. He must have leaned too heavily on the table, because the blue and white vase rocked dangerously for a second before he steadied it.

He buttoned up his jacket and looked around for Veronica, but couldn't place her so decided to leave. He felt irritated. Perhaps Irene was right and he was just tired. He moved toward the door, feeling a trickle of sweat course down his spine.

Out on the street, the night and cool breeze were a relief. He opened another button on his shirt and walked slowly toward the tube. The momentary chill was no longer refreshing and he felt the night as thick and oppressive as the crowd had been earlier.

He felt lonely, he decided, walking, hands in pockets. It was not a feeling strange to him, and yet tonight he chose to taste it—to take it into his mouth and linger over its flavor. It was tart and surprising, like the rhubarb from Minnie's garden.

He was glad he had spoken to Irene. He remembered her turning from side to side in her chair, and then teasing him about the pupil.

He was never long between women. It was after the thrill had passed and the intimacy became real that he found it difficult. He didn't like talking about his past and he didn't trust promises. He had never told a girlfriend that he loved her, although he had loved. So many had said that they loved him, but he had never really felt it, never been able to believe them. He thought about Irene with her strong, straight shoulders. They had fought together before, and lost, and now they shared a truthfulness, an innocence. Daniel could not risk losing that. Yet despite their friendship, there was a barrier of professionalism between them that he could never imagine breaching.

Entering the tube, he passed the turnstiles and stood on the right-hand side of the escalator, passively descending into the bowels of the city. He thought about the coming trial and the press stories, which would only worsen. Sebastian—unnamed and faceless— was intrinsically evil according to the papers. Not only was the boy deemed guilty but *intrinsically evil*. The press did not presume innocence.

Sebastian's actual innocence concerned Daniel less than the boy's survival. He fully expected that the boy he and Irene had defended last year would be dead before he was twenty. He did not want Sebastian to have the same fate.

As he felt the warmth of the tube wrap around him, Daniel wondered about the line that separated adult from child. He knew the legal line: criminal responsibility from the age of ten. Daniel wondered where the real line was. He thought about himself at Sebastian's age, and how close he had come to being in the boy's position.

18

THE THORNTONS REFUSED EVEN TO DRIVE DANIEL BACK TO Minnie's. Tricia was sent to collect him at three o'clock on Sunday, even though it was a long weekend and Daniel was supposed to stay until the Monday evening.

Daniel watched from the car window as the bungalow belonging to his prospective adoptive parents grew smaller. Val and Jim went inside quickly, closing the door before the car pulled out of the drive.

"You're your own worst enemy, Danny," said Tricia. "This was your chance of a new home. Do you know how 'ard it is to place a twelve-year-old boy? Very 'ard, let me tell you, and that was a *disgraceful* thing to do."

"Didn't like 'em. I wanted back to Minnie's."

"Well, you were only there for the weekend. Couldn't you have been good for that long?"

"I just wanted back to the farm . . ." Danny was silent for a few moments and then he said, "Have you seen me mam?"

Tricia cleared her throat as she turned onto the Carlisle Road. Daniel listened to the sound of the wheels turning on the wet road. He felt a strange calmness, as after great exertion. It was the shock, the thrill, the release of being really bad again. The act had left him narcotized. He laid his head back against the seat and felt the lazy, liquid serenity seep into him.

He had won. He had wanted back to her and now he was being taken back. He had expected to be hated and so he had been hateful.

"Jim's a nice man. I know he is. You just don't give anyone a chance."

"I hate 'im."

Tricia sighed. "You're not good with men, are you, Danny? You've been getting on so well with Minnie, I thought you'd gotten over all that." Tricia talked as Danny stared out of his window at the fields and occasional trees. "I mean, you were even doing well at school . . . I told Minnie what happened and she's so upset. I'm upset too, but I can't say I'm surprised. You're damn lucky they're not pressing charges. You carry on like this you'll be in a reformatory before you're a teenager and God help you then, lad. *God help you then.* Nothing I can do for you then."

When they arrived, Minnie was standing outside her door with her cardigan pulled around her. The sight of her made Daniel's spine curl with shame. He kept his eyes to the ground, afraid of her challenging blue. Daniel walked straight past Minnie into the house and carried his bag upstairs. He took comfort from the pale blue walls he had chosen himself, the racing-car bedcover that Minnie had bought for him and the window with the view of the yard. Daniel took off his mother's necklace and placed it in the drawer beside his bed. He was home now and it would be safe. His knife had been taken off him at the Thorntons' but Daniel did not worry. He would not need it here.

Blitz came to the bedroom door, head low and panting, tail waving pleasure to see him. As soon as Daniel reached for the dog, it dropped to the floor and presented its stomach. Scratching him, Daniel could hear Tricia and Minnie talking at the foot of the stairs. The smell of the dog and the hushed voices reminded him of his first visit to Flynn Farm. Daniel felt relieved to smell the place and hear the lilting sound of Minnie's voice, yet he didn't dare go downstairs. He was pleased to be back, but the last forty-eight hours had left him uneasy. He wanted to stay upstairs with the dog, but Blitz, sensing his desperation, tired of him and slipped downstairs. Daniel heard Tricia leave and then the sounds of Minnie making dinner. He knew she was waiting for him to go downstairs, but he resisted. He could sense her disappointment waiting for him at the bottom of the stairs. He slipped under the covers of his bed and lay there, reluctantly remembering.

THE FIRST DAY HAD GONE WITHOUT INCIDENT, ALTHOUGH Daniel had felt ill at ease in the big house with its clean surfaces and cream carpets. He had to take his shoes off at the door and every glass had to be rested on a coaster. His bedroom had a double bed and a large television, but the room was too big and dark at night and he didn't sleep for fear of its strangeness and the shadows it unleashed.

Used to waking up with the cockerel, feeding the animals, and collecting the eggs, Daniel woke before the Thorntons and crept downstairs. The house was immaculate. Daniel was hungry and so went into the kitchen where he found bread and buttered a slice. When he was putting the butter back in the fridge he saw strawberry jam and so spread that onto his bread too. It was daylight, but the clock on the stove said ten past six. The jam was not as good as Minnie's, which he had helped her to make, marveling that it could all happen so quickly: from plant, to pot, to mouth.

He sat in the kitchen for a short while and then carried his plate through to the living room where he switched on the television and found some cartoons. He was laughing out loud at one of the cartoons when the bread fell from his hand and landed, jam down, onto the carpet. He attempted to wipe it with warm water, but it only drove the stain into the fabric. Daniel rested his plate on top of the stain and continued watching.

It was Jim who came down first, about half an hour later, rubbing his eyes, but still with his stretchy smile. Daniel could see from the clock on the video recorder that it was 6:47. Jim made a cup of coffee in the kitchen and came through and sat on the couch. Daniel continued to sit with his back to Jim, but he was no longer watching the cartoons; instead he was watching Jim's pale reflection on the television screen. Jim rubbed his eyes and yawned and raised his cup to his lips.

"You're an early riser, aren't you?"

Daniel half-smiled at him.

"What time did you get up?"

Daniel shrugged.

"You're all dressed and everything. I see you made yourself at home."

"I was hungry."

"It's all right. If you're hungry, you should eat. It's not a criticism."

Daniel felt a sudden unease. He felt watched by Jim in a way that made the hairs on his neck stand on end. He turned back to the television, watching the man in his peripheral vision.

"You finished with that plate, son?" said Jim.

The man was standing over him. His hand out for the plate.

"No," said Daniel.

"Beg your pardon?"

"Don't call me that."

"Call you what?"

"I'm not your son."

"Ah," said Jim. Daniel glanced up and the smile was stretching his face again. "Of course, all right. I get the message. Come on, let me take that."

"Leave it, all right?" Daniel felt his heart beating suddenly.

"We don't usually allow food in the living room, food is for the kitchen—but you weren't to know. Come on . . ."

"Leave it, all right?" Daniel's mouth was very dry.

"What is it?" Jim laughed. "I'm just going to take your empty plate."

Daniel jumped to his feet. He didn't know when or where his body had learned to be so alert to male anger, but he was now adroit. Although Jim's voice was even, Daniel could hear its strangled wrath. The vibration caused the hairs on Daniel's arms to rise.

Daniel hung his head. The words coming out of the man's mouth were assaulting him now. They were heavy clods of dirt hurled. He stopped hearing the words themselves, so that Jim's mouth was a horrible, oscillating hole that leered and yawned.

Daniel couldn't remember what came next, not in the right sequence. He lay under the duvet and took a deep breath, breathing in the smell of the dog and the farm. Daniel buried his face and felt the heat of his own breath on his face. He was almost completely under the covers now.

He was facing up to Jim. Daniel was in his bare feet and he scrunched his toes on the carpet, steeling himself. Jim's face seemed to loom before him, teeth and nose too big on his face. The man bent down toward Daniel suddenly.

Daniel jumped back and pulled his knife from his jeans pocket. He flicked it open and held it up to the man's face.

"Dear God." Jim jumped back and so Daniel stepped forward.

"What's going on?" It was Val, in her dressing gown.

"Get back, leave this to me," Jim shouted, so loud that it made Daniel jump.

"Leave me alone," said Daniel, turning with the knife in front of him so that he could back away from Jim, toward the wall.

"Put that down immediately," said Jim.

Daniel watched the startled panic in his eyes. He watched the man's Adam's apple bobbing up and down. Daniel smiled, watching the light reflecting off the blade onto Jim's T-shirt. Jim reached out toward him, trying to grab Daniel's T-shirt.

"Watch!" Val shrieked.

Daniel stabbed out. He cut Jim's forearm. The man pulled back, holding his arm with his free hand. Daniel watched as a thin line of blood ran through his fingers and onto the carpet. Daniel relaxed for a moment, but Jim turned suddenly and pushed Daniel onto the floor, stepping on his hand and twisting the knife from his grasp.

Every time he watched it in his mind it was different. Now Daniel was not sure what had actually happened. First he remembered that Jim had raised his hand and Daniel anticipated a strike. Then that seemed wrong; Jim had just turned slightly and Daniel saw an opportunity.

Daniel screamed when he was pinned to the floor. He kicked and lunged at Jim every time he managed to pull his hand free. Val took Jim by the arm and the pair of them left Daniel lying on the floor in the living room, closing the door behind them. Daniel kicked and punched at the door, his lower teeth biting into his upper lip. He smashed all the ornaments on the mantelpiece and then sat down by the side of a sofa, his knees tucked into his chest, rubbing the letter of his mother's name.

THE HEAT ON HIS FACE WAS TOO MUCH AND SO DANIEL SAT up and pushed back the covers. The day seemed fresh and good, like the milk under the cream, yet Daniel felt bad. The badness was heavy inside him. He could retch, but he would never retch it up. The badness was there inside him and there it would stay.

Daniel rolled onto his back. He could smell the chicken that Minnie was cooking in the kitchen. The smell of the bird roasting turned his stomach. He lay, staring at the ceiling, watching the scenes flicker silently on the back of his forehead.

Daniel heard his stomach rumbling. He heard the cackle of the fryer as Minnie lowered wet fingers of potato into the fat. He could feel his heart beating hard, as if it might break through his chest, although he was lying completely still. Then he heard Minnie on the stairs, heavy footsteps and the wooden handrail straining against her weight. The sighs as she climbed.

Minnie sat down on the bed, and pulled back the covers to reveal his face. Daniel felt the exposure and closed his eyes. He felt the warm tickle of her fingers on his forehead.

"What're you thinkin', Danny?" she whispered.

"What I done."

"Pardon?"

"M'thinkin' 'bout what I done."

"Why *did* you do that, can you remember?"

Daniel shook his head on the pillow.

"I don't know what I'm going to do with you, so I don't. There's no sin in not liking someone—there's loads of people I don't care for, but you just can't *stab* people. Try and think about why you would want to do something like that."

Daniel turned on his side. He turned toward her, his hands under his chin and his knees up.

"Why?" Minnie whispered. He felt her fingers comb through his hair.

"'Cause I'm bad," he murmured, but she didn't hear him.

She leaned in close, her hand heavy on his head now. "What, love?"

"'Cause I'm bad."

She pulled him up by his elbow and he swung his legs

round to sit beside her. She took his chin in her two fingers. He looked at her eyes and they were twinkling, like the first day he met her. "You are not bad," she said. He felt the pinch of her fingers on his chin. "You are a lovely boy, and I am a lucky woman to know you."

He couldn't help it, but tried to stop the tears.

He could smell the dog and the grass outside from her cardigan. The day was a terrible weight on him suddenly and he leaned against her, letting his cheek rest on her shoulder. She squeezed him—put two arms around him and squeezed the badness out.

"But you can't hurt people, Danny, *or my little animals,* for that matter . . ."

He pulled away at those words. Still shamed.

"I know people have hurt you, in lots of different ways, and I can understand you wanting to hurt back, but let me tell you . . . that road's only for *eejits.* I should know. There's *so* much more you can be."

Daniel sniffed and wiped his eyes and his nose with his sleeve.

"Did you have to cut him? You could have talked to him, or asked him to take you back if you had to. You didn't *need* to cut him."

Daniel nodded, chin so close to his chest that she was not sure whether or not she saw him agree.

"Why did you do it? Did you think he was going to hit you?"

"Maybe . . . I dunno . . . no." He shook his head, looking at her. Her eyes were turned down at the corners and there was a deep line between her eyebrows.

"Why then?"

He took a deep breath. He looked at his feet. His socks were hanging off. He twirled his foot and watched the sock dance for a moment.

"I want to stay here," he said, still watching his sock.

There was a pause. He watched her hands. They were loosely clasped. He was afraid to look at her eyes.

"You mean you did it so that they wouldn't want to adopt you?" she said finally. Her voice was quiet. He heard no criticism. It was as if she only wanted to understand.

He had a pain at the back of his throat. He remembered Tricia's words after he had said good-bye to his mother for the last time:

> *If nobody else wants me, do I get to stay here then?*
> *No, love. She's a foster parent. There'll be another little*
> *boy or girl needing to come here.*

"I want to stay here." It was all he could say. He made fists with his hands and waited for her to speak. It seemed like the longest time.

"Would you like *me* to adopt you? If you really want to stay, I'd like nothing better. I'd adopt you in a heartbeat if they let me. Matter of fact, I adopted you the minute I set eyes on you. Do you want to stay? I'll try for us? I can't promise, but I'll try."

She was looking him in the eye. She was holding his shoulders so that he had to look at her. He didn't want to say anything, because he knew he would cry again. He tried to nod, but he was wound up so tight that it must have looked like he was shaking his chin. She was frowning with one of her gray eyebrows raised.

"Want you . . . adopt me," he managed.

Her fingers were digging into his shoulders. "Know that I want that too, but it's a legal thing. I know you know more than anyone how that can go against you. The law works its own magic and I don't understand it, but I'll try for us. You mustn't get your hopes up until we actually sign. Understand?"

She hugged him and he swallowed, letting his tears again soak into the wool of her cardigan. He didn't make a sound, but his heart was breaking. He was flooded with joy, just then, because she wanted him.

"Mother of God," she said suddenly. "Your chips'll be cold and the bird'll be burned to a crisp."

He took a deep breath, looking forward to her cold chips. They were all he wanted to eat.

19

SEBASTIAN LOOKED DIFFERENT WHEN DANIEL RETURNED to the secure unit to meet with him. His cool, self-possession was unchanged, but he was heavier, bloated. The boy's face was fuller and there were dark circles under his eyes. His thin wrists had thickened and there were dimples on the backs of his hands. There was little exercise to be afforded at Parklands House and Daniel knew the diet of chips and pizzas would have been a shock after the organic Islington vegetables that he was sure Charlotte fed him.

"How's it going?" Daniel asked.

"All right," said Sebastian, a fist in his cheek pulling on his upper lip. "It's boring. And school here is worse than normal school. The teachers are stupid and the other children are stupider."

"Well, it's not long now until your trial. I just want to go through a few things with you today."

"Will I be chained up in the dock?"

"No. Before the trial, you'll be taken to see the court. A nice woman'll show you round. I know her. She'll tell you all about the procedures and what will happen. We already know that you'll be sitting beside me, your parents behind us, instead of in the dock. Will that be all right?"

Sebastian nodded. "Is that because they don't really think I did it?"

"No, it's because you're a child. They only put adults into the dock now."

"Will you tell the judge that I didn't do it?"

"You remember Irene Clarke, your QC?"

Sebastian nodded vigorously.

"Well, she'll put the case to the jury."

Daniel opened his pad and took the lid off his pen. Sebastian stood up and moved around the table to look at the papers in Daniel's folder. He leaned against Daniel and inspected again his business cards, his mobile phone, his ink pen, and the flash discs that Daniel kept inside his leather-bound folder. Daniel could smell the boy's clean hair and his strawberry breath. The gentle weight of the boy against his shoulder was poignant. Daniel remembered asking for love from strangers: leaning against them, for affection that was neither offered nor expected. And so Daniel did not shift away from the weight of the boy. He made notes on his pad, being careful not to turn and accidentally reject him. After a moment, Sebastian sighed and walked back around the desk, holding Daniel's iPhone in his hands. Daniel had turned it off when he entered Parklands House. Deftly, Sebastian turned the phone on.

Daniel reached out his hand, palm upward. The boy was smiling and their eyes met.

"Thank you," said Daniel, in expectation. He was not sure why he had allowed Sebastian to take his phone and now believed it would be returned without a fight.

"I get to play with my mum's phone."

"Great, sure, you can do that when she next comes to see you."

Sebastian ignored him, sitting back in the chair, scrolling through Daniel's address book.

Daniel tried to remember how Minnie had acted when he was being defiant. She would have given him her cold look, with the same eyes that could flood with warmth. He would be persuaded that she was stronger. Daniel felt his heartbeat increasing at the thought that he might not be able to control the boy. Finally Sebastian looked up and Daniel met his gaze. He remembered the steel in Minnie's eyes. She had never been afraid of him. He could not imagine that he could communicate as much strength as she had done, but Sebastian turned away as if stung and relinquished the phone into Daniel's palm.

"So," said Daniel, taking off his jacket and facing Sebastian. "The prosecution is going to put Ben's mum in the witness box, probably she'll be first, then your neighbors and one or two of the kids from the area and from school."

"Who?" asked Sebastian, his face alert again, his green eyes clear and focused.

Daniel flipped through his notes. "Poppy . . . Felix."

"They don't like me, they'll say I'm bad."

"That's why the prosecution is calling them. But we won't let them say you're bad. Legally, they are not allowed to introduce evidence about you being of bad character. It's irrelevant and not fair. Irene will put a stop to that. I just wanted to let you know about this, because I think Ben's mum and then the kids you know will be hard for us all to watch in court, but it's not the main part of their case. You need to try and not get upset by it, okay?"

Sebastian nodded.

"We're finalizing the details of your brief now. Are you sure there is nothing else you know that you want to tell me?"

Sebastian looked to the side for a moment, then shook his head fiercely.

"All right."

"Will I get to testify?"

"No. At the moment the plan is that you won't testify. It's not the nicest experience and I'm sure court will be hard enough just watching. But we'll need to wait and see how the case goes. Irene may decide at a later date that she wants you to testify, but we would talk to you about that if it came to it. Okay?"

"Okay."

"The main part of their case will be the forensic evidence, and that will probably go on for a long time. A lot of what happens in court is boring and scientific and it won't make much sense, but you need to try and stay alert. People will be watching you."

Sebastian sat up suddenly. It was as if the idea of being watched thrilled him. He clasped his hands and smiled at Daniel, his eyes sparkling.

"Really?" he said. "Watching me?"

Daniel stared at the boy and Sebastian met his gaze. There was no shame in the boy's eyes. No sense that what he had said was inappropriate. But he was a child, after all.

"Your mum and dad were here to see you yesterday, were they?"

Sebastian's shoulders fell. He nodded, looking at the table.

"I know it's hard. You must miss them."

"I think you're lucky," said Sebastian, looking Daniel in the eye.

"Why?"

"You didn't have a dad."

Daniel inhaled slowly. "Well, y'know, sometimes boyfriends can be just as bad," he said.

Sebastian nodded. Daniel was sure the boy understood.

"I want to get out soon to look after her. Sometimes I can make him stop."

"I know how you feel," said Daniel. "I used to want to protect my mum too, but you have to look after yourself. You have to remember that you're the little boy and she's the grown-up."

It was the kind of thing that Minnie might have said.

AFTER WORK, DANIEL WALKED TO THE CROWN, ON THE CORNER of his street, with his hands in his pockets and his chin down. It was late autumn now, and there was a chill in the air. Daniel almost turned back for his jacket, but couldn't face the stairs again.

Inside the bar was bright and warm, log fires crackling in the corner and the smell of pub food and damp wood in the air. Daniel ordered a pint and sat at the bar, turning the glass before

him, allowing it to settle. Usually he would read the paper, but
not tonight. He was sick of newspapers; each one he picked up
either featured Sebastian, unnamed but referred to as "Angel's
child murderer," or else he would be mentioned secondhand, in
opinion pieces about the "broken society." Ben Stokes was already immortalized, a martyr for goodness, for childhood itself.
He was never simply Benjamin Stokes, eight years old, but *Little
Ben*, or *Benny*, always depicted in the same way: a school photograph taken two years before his death, two front teeth missing
and the hair on the side of his head sticking up. He was the angel
of Angel, and so Sebastian had become the devil.

The constant media commentary was new to Daniel. The
teenagers he had defended in the past had not been much older
than Sebastian and had lived tougher lives, but they had been
almost invisible to the press. Their cases were given a few lines
on the side of the page, near the fold. *What did they matter?
They were just kids in gangs, controlling their own population. It was
the natural order.*

It was only three weeks now until Sebastian's trial. Just
thinking about it caused Daniel's mouth to become dry. He
took the first sip of his beer. Daniel was ready for trial, yet felt
futile before the will of the courts.

As Daniel stared at his pint, he remembered the boy's eyes
from earlier in the day, the intensity of them. His thrill at the
thought of going to court. The truth was that Daniel didn't
know what the boy was capable of doing. Despite the warm
bar, Daniel felt a chill.

"How's it goin', Danny?" said the barman. He was in his
fifties, with a belly that hung over his belt and a face that was
heavy with the stories he had heard. "You havin' a hard week?"

Daniel sighed and smiled, shaking his head. "Just the usual."

"Where's your good lady got to? Not seen her in ages."

"She moved out."

"I'm sorry, mate," the barman said, polishing a glass and placing it under the bar. "I thought you guys were tight."

"Some things aren't meant to be, eh?"

"Yeah, plenty of other fish, like they say."

The barman's gentle Cockney voice faded to the other side of the bar as he served a couple who had just come in, the woman shivering from the night air.

Daniel stared at the amber liquid in his glass. It was warm in his hands. Slowly, he took another sip, watching the sun set on Victoria Park, splitting the low clouds with a tawny pink light. The air in the bar was warm and comforting, sweet with the smell of cider and beer and hot food.

THINGS WERE CLEARER TO HIM NOW, SIMPLER, YET STILL HE felt driven. He wanted Sebastian's case to start and he wanted to find out more about Minnie's life. He wanted to understand her. It felt like that moment in a run when he found his pace and his breathing steadied. That time when he thought he could keep running forever. He had run the London Marathon like that in 2008.

His dinner was served and he ate his burger mechanically, then left, walking back to the flat with his hands in his pockets and his chin down.

He took the stairs slowly but ran the last few steps as he heard his telephone ringing.

"Hello?"

"Is that Danny?" the voice said. Daniel recognized the female voice but struggled to place it.

"Danny, it's Harriet."

He took a deep breath.

The hall was dark, but Daniel did not turn the light on. He slid down the wall and listened with the phone nestled between his shoulder and his ear. He rested his elbows on his knees.

"How are you?" he said. With his knees pressed against his chest, he could feel his heart beating. He wondered what she wanted to say, whether she still wanted to accuse him.

"I wanted to call you back. The more I thought about it, I was . . . unnecessarily rude. I've just been feeling so sad for her. I hope you understand that. She had a hard life, and I miss her now she's gone, but I know you must be feeling it too. No matter what went on between you, you were close once and it must be a terrible loss."

Daniel didn't know what to say. He cleared his throat and took a breath.

"I never approved of all that business of taking in all those children . . ."

"Of her fostering, you mean? Why not? She was good at it, wasn't she?"

"She was a good *mother*, but I suppose I couldn't see the point in it. I thought she was just torturing herself."

In the dark, Daniel frowned.

"Thanks for calling me back."

"Well, she wouldn't have liked me talking to you like that, anyway," Harriet's voice cracked and thickened for a moment, but then regained control. "I didn't wake you, did I?"

"No, I'm just in."

"You still working as hard? You always did work hard."

There was silence for a moment. Daniel could hear Harriet sniff, and the sound of the ten o'clock news.

"What was it you wanted to know about her, Danny?"

He stretched out his legs in the hall, and rubbed a hand across his eyes. He was not ready for this now. The week had left him bled, weakened. He took a deep breath before he replied.

"Well, I didn't blame you for not wanting to talk to me. You lost your sister. I didn't want to make all that harder for you. It's just . . . it's only now hit me that she's gone. Even at the funeral, I think I was still—angry with her. We never sorted all that out, but now she's gone, I suppose I really . . . miss her."

When he said the words *miss* and *her*, his voice thickened. He took a breath to catch himself.

"I went back to the house . . . the farm. I hadn't seen her— hadn't been back there for so long. It was . . . I don't know, it made me remember things. It was so many years ago, but it didn't seem like it. She left me a box of photographs too. I suppose I realized that there was so much I didn't know about her . . ."

"Tell me what you want to know, pet, and I'll tell you."

"Well, I want to know, why was she so sad?" He swallowed.

"Well, you know she lost her little one, and then her husband, pretty much one after the other."

"Yes, but she never talked about it, and I don't know the full story."

"Well, only a year after that she was taking in other people's children. I couldn't understand it. I *still don't* understand it. She was a good nurse, a good mother; I suppose she had to take care of people. She was one of those people who needed to care for others."

"I remember her telling me that was what happiness was . . . She never talked to me about Norman and Delia. Always avoided it—said it was too painful."

Harriet sighed. Daniel heard her husband asking if she wanted tea.

"What did you mean when you said she was punishing herself?" Daniel asked.

"Well, when your little girl is taken, you become a foster parent where they send you a new little girl every few months. But each one is never her . . ." Harriet's voice thickened again. "How could she stand it? And you know that until you came along they were *all girls,* every single one."

Daniel put a hand over his mouth.

"She said," Harriet's voice cracked again, and she allowed a single gasp of a sob, "that Delia had brought out so much love in her . . . she didn't know what else to do with herself, you see. She just had to keep on giving . . . it was that which killed her, believe you me! She died so alone, and it's not right when she loved half the world's unwanted."

"I never knew any of that," said Daniel. He pressed his back against the wall, his mind bright with memories in the darkened hall. "When I was little, when I first moved to stay with her, it was like she was the talk of the town. There were all these stories flying around about her. You wouldn't believe . . . "

"Aye, there would have been. Little towns like that're full of small-minded people, aren't they now, and she was such a character. She was a city girl. She loved London; she was happy there. It was Norman wanted her to move up to Cumbria. I mean . . . Cumbria . . . for the *love of God*. Minnie in Cumbria! After he died, I just couldn't understand why she stayed. She had no connection to that place. Move back to London, or move back here, I told her, anything but stay in that bloody place."

"She liked the farm, the animals."

"That was just an excuse."

"She raised a family there. She had a home . . ."

"Even if she'd come back to Ireland . . . but she was determined to stay, as if it was her penance."

"Penance for what?"

"Well, she blamed herself, didn't she? As if she would ever have knowingly harmed that little one. She loved her more than anything else in this world."

"What happened?" Daniel was whispering. "A car accident?"

"Yes, and can you imagine losing a child of six years? *And their only child*. And Delia was such a wee lamb. She was the brightest, funniest child you ever knew. She was the spit of Minnie when she was wee. Black curls and the brightest blue eyes you ever saw. She was a *darling*. I was working in England myself when it happened and I came as soon as I heard but the wee lamb was nearly gone by then . . ."

Daniel held his breath.

"She was still conscious, you see . . . drifting in and out. The worst injuries, and she was in such terrible pain. Minnie just couldn't take it. She was holding her hand and the little one was saying to her, '*Am I dying, Mammy?*' And, oh God, she was fighting it so hard, fighting to hang on. Minnie was suddenly so calm. I just remember her whispering to Delia: '*It's all right pet, you'll be my angel still . . .*'"

Harriet began to cry softly. Daniel stood up and put the hall light on. Its sudden brightness strained his eyes and he shielded them with his hand. He turned it off again.

"Minnie blamed herself because she was driving when it happened?"

"She was driving . . . but it wasn't just that." There was the sound of Harriet blowing her nose. "Delia had a party that night, you see. She was at one of her friends' houses for a birthday party and Minnie went to collect her. One of the other little ones wanted to go home then too and Minnie offered to give her a lift, so as to save her dad the trouble, you know . . .

"Good God, I remember like it was yesterday. Minnie told me that Delia was wearing her best dress, with the tiny daisies on it, and that she just looked so sweet. She told me Delia was carrying a bit of cake from the party in a blue napkin. I still remember—she said it was a *blue napkin*.

"Minnie, God forgive her, she gave Tildy, Delia's friend, I'm sure that was her name, the front seat with the seat belt and all. Delia was in the back, without a seat belt, you remember how it was back then, Danny, in the seventies . . . no such thing as safety. Hadn't even been invented yet . . .

"Minnie said that the little one was singing in her ear— Delia always loved to sing in the car. She had an elbow on each of the passenger seats, like, y'know how kids do, or did back then anyway, and Minnie told her *to sit back*, but then . . . that was it."

"What was it?" said Danny, his thumbnail between his teeth.

Harriet started to cry again. "They swerved. The roads were wet, you see. There had been so much rain and *those bloody country roads*, they were wet and slippery. Minnie said that Delia didn't make a sound, not even when she . . . hit the windshield . . . Oh, God! I'm sorry, Danny, I can't do this just now."

Harriet was now weeping. He heard her sharp intakes of breath.

"I just wanted to say that I was sorry," she cried, "for the other day."

"I'm sorry to have upset you." His chest was tight. "Thanks for calling back."

"She loved you, you know," said Harriet, sniffing. "She was proud of you. I'm glad you made it up for the funeral. She would have wanted you to be there."

Daniel hung up. The flat was cold. He had a pain at the back of his throat. He walked into the living room, which was also cast in darkness. The photo she had left him was like a black cutout against the white fireplace. Without turning on the light and picking it up, he could see her face. It must have been the late sixties, early seventies: the colors were brighter, happier than real-life colors, as if they had been painted, snatched from the imagination instead of life. Minnie was in a short skirt and Norman wore dark horn-rimmed spectacles. The child too was almost unreal: porcelain cheeks and white pearl teeth. She was like Ben Stokes: stolen from life when she was still perfect.

He walked in darkness into the kitchen, where he took a beer from the fridge. The brief light from the fridge taunted him. He felt cold and the chill bottle caused goose pimples to rise on his arms. He bit his lip and then drank deeply from the bottle, finishing half of it before letting it fall hard onto the kitchen work surface.

Daniel put one hand over his eyes. He was so cold, but his eyes were burning. He put the back of his hand to his lips, uncomprehending, as hot tears coursed down his cheeks. It had been so long since he had cried. He covered his face with the crook of his arm, remembering the comfort of her flesh wrapped in the rough wool of her cardigan. He swore, and bit his lip, but the dark was forgiving; it allowed it.

20

IT WAS SPRING. THE AIR WAS STRUNG WITH THE SCENT OF manure and brave new buds. Daniel's Wellington boots squelched in the mud of the backyard as he fed Hector and the chickens. The door of the coop was hanging off its hinge and some of the wire mesh was torn. Daniel knelt in the mud to repair the mesh and screw the lock back into place. Foxes had killed chickens at the farm next to Minnie's. Her own birds had only been startled, set clucking and fluttering against the mesh in the middle of the night until Minnie had gone out with Blitz to scare off the fox.

It was six thirty in the morning and Daniel's stomach yawned with hunger as he worked. It was still cold and his hands were pink to the cuff. He was growing out of his clothes again, and his shirts had begun to ride up his forearm. Minnie had promised to get him new ones at the end of the month, along with a football shirt. He was a forward now on the school team. But today was Saturday, and they had the market.

Daniel could see Minnie at the window, filling up the kettle and making the porridge. In the morning, her gray hair hung down, held up at the sides by two tortoiseshell clips. Only after she got dressed would she wind it up on top of her head. Daniel's mother's hair had been light brown and short, but she dyed it blond. As he emptied the last of the scraps into the chickens' pen, Daniel remembered the feeling of her hair between his fingertips. Her hair was thin and soft, unlike Minnie's heavy curls.

AFTER THE TROUBLE WITH THE THORNTONS, MINNIE HAD told Daniel that she would adopt him. They had done all the paperwork together, spreading the forms over the kitchen table. Now they were just waiting. The idea of being someone else's son, at the same time as being his mother's son, was strange to Daniel, yet he had agreed and felt a strange auspicious joy at the thought.

Minnie had asked him if he wanted to change his name to Flynn, but he had decided to keep his own name: Hunter. It was Daniel's mother's name, not his father's. He wanted to keep her name because he liked it. It was his name, but he also reasoned that when he was eighteen his mother might want to find him. If she ever looked for him, he wanted to be easy to find.

Inside, Daniel washed his hands in the bathroom, enjoying the feeling of the warm water on his cold fingers. When he was finished, he leaned on the sink and stared at his face in the mirror. He stared at his dark hair, which was almost black, and his dark brown eyes, which were so dark that you had to look really closely to distinguish the pupil from the iris. Daniel had often felt estranged from his own face. He looked so different from his mother. He did not know where his features came from.

He had never known his father. Several times, Daniel had asked for his father's name but each time his mother refused, or told him that she didn't know who he was. Daniel had seen his own birth certificate, but his father's details were blank.

Soon he was to have two mothers: one the state approved of and another who the state did not; one he had to care for and another who cared for him. But still no father.

Minnie had the radio on in the kitchen. She was stirring the porridge and moving her hips to the music. When she served it up, Daniel blew on his porridge before adding his milk and sugar. Minnie had taught him to pour the milk onto the back of the spoon so as not to pierce the skin of the porridge.

"Starving," he said as she poured him some orange juice.

"Well, you're a growing boy, so you are. Eat up."

"Minnie?" said Daniel, taking a mouthful of the sweet porridge.

"What, love?"

"Will it be this week we hear?"

"Should be. That's what they said. You're not to worry, mind. It'll happen. But when it does, we should celebrate."

"What'll we do?"

"We could go for a picnic. We could go to the beach . . ."

"Really? But you'd have to drive."

"Well, we could take it slow. Take our time."

Daniel smiled and ate the rest of his porridge. He had never been to the beach and the thought of it made his stomach flutter.

"Minnie?" he said, licking his spoon.

"After the papers come, will I call you Mam?"

She got up and started to clear the breakfast things. "As long as you're civil, you can call me whatever you like," she said, ruffling his hair.

Above her pink cheeks, her eyes were shining. Daniel watched—not sure if she was happy or sad.

It was still cold, and Minnie made him wear his parka as they set up the market stall. Daniel was now well practiced. He pinned the plastic cloth over the wooden table as Minnie took an inventory of the produce in the boot of her car. She was wearing two cardigans and gloves with no fingers.

Minnie arranged her table: eggs and three chickens she had slaughtered, plucked and gutted herself; new potatoes, spring onions, carrots, turnips, and cabbage all fresh from the earth. She had pots of her jam to sell as well: apricot and strawberry, and eight rhubarb tarts.

Daniel opened up the ice-cream tub that was her till, and counted the money. Anything to do with money was his job. He took the money from customers and counted the change. He counted their profits and his own wage as a percentage. When the car was emptied and the stall was ready, Minnie got out the flasks and the sandwiches: milky coffee for Daniel and sweet tea for her; boiled eggs and strawberry jam sandwiches. If it was busy they would probably not finish the sandwiches until they were packing up to go, but if the stall was quiet they would eat them all before eleven.

"Zip up your jacket."

"I'm not cold."

"Zip up your jacket."

"Zip up yourself," he said, doing as she asked.

"Don't be cheeky."

The stalls were arranged around Brampton's Moot Hall, which had stood in the center of town for nearly two hundred years. There were about eight other stalls besides Minnie's. Most sold either vegetables or meat, or homemade produce, but Minnie was one of the few who offered a range. Her farm was not big enough for specializing. She sold what she made for herself.

The first hour passed quickly, and Minnie sold the chickens but one, and several half dozen eggs. She knew that her chickens were the best and even those who disliked her would buy her eggs because of that.

Daniel's hands were pink from the cold. When Minnie saw him tucking his hands into the sleeves of his jacket, she rubbed his hands to warm them. She made him put both palms together, as if in prayer, and then she rubbed them between her own hands until the heat returned. She rubbed him vigorously, so hard that he shook.

As the blood returned to his fingers and his arms, Daniel remembered rubbing his mother's hands. She had always been cold: too thin and not enough clothes. He remembered the bones of her hands against his young palms. He wondered where she was now. He didn't feel the same need to find her, but still he wondered, and he wanted to know if she wondered about him. He wanted to tell her about the farm, and about Minnie, about counting the money and taking his cut. He remembered the touch of her thin hands, brushing the hair off his face. When he thought of it, he would feel a pain underneath his ribs. It was like an intense hunger—a yearning—to feel her sweep the hair off his face again.

"What are you thinking about?" Minnie asked.

Daniel took the plastic cup she handed him into his two hands, so that he could steal its warmth. He shrugged and took a mouthful of sweet tea.

"You were miles away!" Minnie reached out to him and Daniel twisted away. Again, she seemed to know what he needed. But it wasn't the same and it never could be.

A tight-lipped woman approached their stall. Daniel recognized her as Mrs. Wilkes from the sweets shop. She was his friend Derek's mother. Daniel knew she had called an ambulance for Minnie's dying husband. She had also reported two of his classmates to the principal for stealing gob-stoppers.

She worried her lips as she considered Minnie's jam, narrowing her eyes when Daniel caught her eye. He put his hands into the pockets of his parka.

"How much is the jam?" she asked, the corners of her mouth turning downward.

"Two pounds fifty," said Daniel, with one of his best smiles, although Minnie had priced the jam at one pound fifty.

"That's a disgrace," said Mrs. Wilkes, slamming the jam onto the table with a force that shook the eggs.

Minnie turned at the noise and frowned. She was holding a half-eaten tuna sandwich.

"Quality comes at a price, Mrs. Wilkes, you should know that," said Daniel, taking a hand out of his pocket to straighten the jam.

"So it would seem." Daniel was aware that Mrs. Wilkes had now lost interest in him and was addressing Minnie. Minnie had her mouth full and the wind was blowing her hair in her face, but she turned, her eyes giddy with mirth and crumbs on her chin.

"You all right, Margaret?"

"I'm just balking at the price here. That's daylight robbery." Mrs. Wilkes pushed a pot of jam gently, disturbing Daniel's display again.

"Take one, then," said Minnie.

Margaret Wilkes's mouth turned down at the corners.

"What do you mean?"

"I mean have one, a gift from me. It's good jam. Have it, enjoy it."

Daniel turned to look up at Minnie, but she was finishing her tuna sandwich, watching Margaret.

"I couldn't possibly. I'll give you what it's worth and not a penny more."

"Nonsense, take it. Enjoy. Thanks, Margaret."

Minnie turned her attention again to the flasks and the picnic that she had arranged in the trunk of her Renault. She helped herself to another sandwich.

"You're ridiculous, Minnie," said Margaret, thrusting three pounds into the ice-cream tub of money that Daniel guarded. "You ask for the world and then give it away. It's like these kids. Everyone knows you're just doing it to make yourself feel better. Can't care for your own and then all of a sudden you're mother to the world . . . But you're right, your jam is good." Margaret held the jar in the palm of her hand. Her tight mouth was pressed inward, as if to smile.

"What did you say?"

Daniel turned to Minnie's whisper. It raised the hairs on the back of his neck. "I said, despite it all, we all agree your jam is good." Daniel could see that Margaret Wilkes's teeth were brown and he wondered if it was all the sweets that had ruined them.

"No, before that." Minnie was still whispering but now she had her stomach pressed against the stall and was leaning toward Mrs. Wilkes. She was leaning hard on the table and Daniel could see the white marks forming on her pink hands from the strain. "Can't look after my own? Is that what you said?"

Margaret Wilkes was walking away.

Minnie stood up again and pushed the hair out of her face. Daniel noticed that her fingers were trembling. She opened a box of eggs and slipped her red, rough fingers inside.

Thwatt.

Daniel was still standing with his hands in his pockets, but he opened his mouth as Minnie took aim and hit Margaret Wilkes square between the shoulder blades with one of her own well-reared eggs.

Margaret turned, mouth turned down at the corners, but Minnie already had another egg in her hand. To Daniel's joy and amazement, Margaret Wilkes broke into a run, trotting crisscross in her navy heels in an effort to get out of Minnie's firing range.

Daniel pulled Minnie's elbow and punched a victory fist into the air. Minnie tutted at him and pulled her arm away.

"That was ace. You showed her."

"Enough!" Minnie said. Daniel did not understand why she was angry with him. Her cheeks were pink and her blue eyes were shot with rage. "Get tidied up. It's too cold and it's time to go anyway."

Daniel's fingers were almost numb with the cold, but he started to pack away the stall. She was working beside him, intent, slapdash. The flasks were thrown back into the bag. Usually she would have emptied them in the gutter then carefully packed them away.

"I'm sorry," Daniel said, but she didn't hear him.

She was pulling her cardigan around her and straightening the leftover boxes of eggs in the trunk of her car.

"I'm sorry," he said again, louder this time, reaching out to tug on her cardigan.

She turned to him finally, confused, angry little darts of light shot through her watery blue eyes.

"I didn't mean to set her off, like," he explained. "I told her it was two pounds fifty. The jam. Was just winding her up, like. Thought we might just make a bit extra out of her. Didn't mean for her to—"

"Never mind, love."

In the car on the way home, Daniel held the takings and looked out of the window. The small Brampton houses, the whiff of farms and the occasional sweep of undulating green were still surprising to him. Some part of his mind yet expected the tight redbrick of Newcastle, its estranged estates and urban muddle. Some part of him still felt out of place here. He wondered about Minnie and the fight with Mrs. Wilkes. He still didn't understand why so many of the locals disliked her. Some of them seemed to hate him too, because of her.

Minnie's hands were clenched on the wheel. She drove sitting forward, her stomach against the bottom of the steering wheel and her chin reaching over the top. Daniel watched her as she licked her lips and pressed them together.

Minnie had her window down and strands of her curly gray hair fluttered in her face. The few times that Daniel had been in the car with her, she had kept her window down, regardless of the weather. She said that she felt claustrophobic in the car.

Daniel took a deep breath before he said, "Not a lot of people like you around here, d'you know that?"

She didn't like talking in the car. She didn't take her eyes off the road, but Daniel could tell that she had heard him as her hands tightened their grip on the wheel.

"It doesn't matter though," he said. "Ah like y'."

Again, she said nothing, but she pursed her lips together in what Daniel knew was meant to be a smile.

IT WAS THE DAY OF THE COURT CASE. MINNIE HAD TOLD HIM that it was just a formality, that she would definitely be able to adopt him, but still he was nervous. He got up before the cock crowed and did his chores and was ready to go before she came downstairs for breakfast. He had put the porridge on already and fed the dog.

She rubbed his shoulder when she came into the kitchen, pushing a handkerchief into the pocket of her dressing gown. She made tea and put the radio on as Daniel set the table, putting out the butter and jars of her jam. She smiled at him as he milked and sugared their teas. Minnie liked three sugars and a lot of milk; Daniel liked one sugar and a little milk. He put her tea on the table by her bowl then stood in the middle of the kitchen, drinking his tea.

He looked around the kitchen as he sipped his tea. Blitz was asleep on a full stomach, his thin legs twitching in his dreams as he lay on the kitchen floor. Daniel watched the movement of Minnie's hips as she stirred the porridge, the spangle of light that the old windows spilled onto the spoons. He knew the song that was on the radio and tapped his foot to its beat. The room was warm with the smell of morning and Daniel held it in his mouth, as if to taste it. This was his home; this was going to be his home.

He watched as she yawned over the porridge pot, hand on the small of her back. After today, she would be his mam, and they would live in this house forever. Daniel almost could not believe it.

"WHY AREN'T YOU EATING YOUR PORRIDGE?" SHE SAID TO him, scraping her bowl clean.

"I am eatin' it, look . . ." He took a spoonful into his mouth.

"You're always first finished. What is it? Butterflies?"

"Bit, like," he said, letting his spoon rest with a clatter against the porcelain.

"You shouldn't be nervous. It's exciting." She reached across the table and tugged gently at his sleeve. "You do want this, don't you?"

"Aye."

"You know it's up to you."

"I want to, like."

"Me too. Today I get to be your mum, not just your foster mum, but . . . your real mum."

Daniel watched as her eyes filled, and her cheeks colored.

She gave him a big smile and it was only that, the rise of her cheekbones and the scrunching up of her eyes, which caused the tears to flash, instantaneous, thin, one down each cheek. Quickly, as if to brush away a crumb, she swept the palm of her hand across one cheek and the back of her hand across the other. The tears were gone and only her smile was left.

Real mam, Daniel remembered as he waited at the bottom of the stairs for her to get ready. *Real mam,* he reminded himself as he looked out of the bus window on the road from Brampton to Newcastle. They were getting the bus there and back so that Minnie didn't have to drive in Newcastle city center.

Daniel was wearing his school uniform and Minnie was wearing shoes. They weren't proper women's shoes. They were flat and brown and they laced up, but they weren't boots and Daniel stared at the strange sight of her feet in them. He hadn't seen her without her boots. She wore her gray skirt and green coat and a black top under it that was cleaner than some of her others.

Minnie had asked permission for Daniel to have a day off from school—for *family business.*

Family, Daniel thought, looking out of the window, feeling the press of her hip against his body. He wasn't sure if he had had a family before, or what that meant, but he was happy to go forward if it meant staying with her and being at the farm.

At the courthouse, Tricia was there. She was happy and restless, turning from side to side and asking if he wanted a can from the machine. She was holding files and telling them that the hearing would be quick.

"All this time, Danny," said Tricia. "When was the first time we met? Were you five years old or something?"

"Dunno."

"You were about that. You were four or five years old. All this time we've known each other and now you're getting adopted. I'm so happy. I never thought I'd see this day."

Their solicitor arrived. He was young, wearing a black suit and carrying a brown briefcase. He shook Minnie's hand and then bent to shake Daniel's hand too. Daniel looked at the open palm.

"Shake the man's hand, Danny, when he offers it," said Minnie.

Daniel reached out and felt his hand tugged by the warm, strong hand.

"I'm your solicitor," he said, and Daniel smiled at him.

He felt powerful for a moment, in his clean school uniform, with his own solicitor, waiting to see the judge and be adopted. He remembered what Minnie had told him about lawyers.

When it was time, they met in the judge's chambers. Daniel had imagined that the room would have stained-glass windows like a church, but it was just an office, with a large desk topped with leather and rows of bookcases.

The room smelled of pipe smoke and Daniel remembered his principal, Mr. Hart, but the judge wasn't like him. He had a long mustache that was white but yellowing at the ends and his eyebrows rose above his glasses when he smiled. Daniel, Minnie, Tricia, and the legal representatives were shown to the sofa area in front of the judge's desk. Daniel sat in one of the chairs, and Minnie sat in the other facing him. Tricia and the lawyers were on the sofa together and then the judge sat on his own sofa beside the clerk, who took a note of everything that was said. It felt different from the other times Daniel had been in court.

The judge wasn't wearing a gown. Daniel pushed his hands between his thighs and pressed his lips together as the judge began to speak. He liked the order of the processes and the way that his solicitor kept looking at him, both eyebrows raised, every time his name was mentioned.

"So," said the judge, "I suppose it comes down to you, young man. The most important thing is whether or not you want Mrs. Flynn to adopt you, making her your mother, and you . . . her son. Tell us what you think, Daniel."

There was a hush, and Daniel felt the room turn to him. Tricia was nodding at him to answer; the solicitor's forehead was wrinkled in expectation.

He looked up and Minnie was looking straight at him, smiling. She was nervous too, he realized. She was twisting her wedding ring, making her finger red and then white.

He cleared his throat and looked at the judge. He was smiling and it caused his yellowing mustache to turn up at the corners. "I want to be adopted," Daniel said. He said the words looking down at the table, but then grew more confident and looked at the judge and then the lawyer in turn.

Only when it was finalized, when formalities were over, and the judge handed Daniel a small white teddy bear to mark the day, did Daniel look at Minnie again. They stared at each other across the mahogany coffee table, lips apart, breathing hard from excitement, as if they had been running at full pace.

Leaving the chambers, Daniel felt his legs go weak. It felt like he had played football for too long. Minnie was ahead of him, with Tricia in between, and Daniel watched the movement of her hips in her gray skirt. Tricia was talking, smoothing back her hair and reaching into her bag. The solicitor was looking at his watch and putting his hand in his pocket.

"Well," Minnie said, hand on her hip, finally turning to him. "Give us a kiss, will you, gorgeous, 'cause I feel bloody great."

She lifted him off his feet and he laughed out loud as she pressed the air from his lungs and spun him. When she stopped he was dizzy and her smile was so big that he could see the tooth that was missing near the back. The sun was streaming into the atrium above and Daniel felt it on the skin of his hands and his face. It felt as if they were a prism, refracting their own joy.

"How old is it?" Daniel asked.

"Nearly two thousand years. Imagine all that time ago, before there were cars or trains or electricity, or anything like that, people were able to build a fortress like this."

"Why's it called Hadrian's Wall?"

"I think he was the Roman emperor who asked for it to be built."

"Why did he want to build it, like?"

"Maybe he wanted someone to remember him in two thousand years' time!" Minnie laughed. "That would be right. Bet he was an arrogant old bugger, excuse my language."

Daniel touched the stone bricks, stroking them with his fingertips. He clambered up on his hands and knees and pulled himself up on top. They were here to celebrate getting adopted and afterward Minnie was going to take him out for dinner.

"Careful, love," she called to him, one hand on her hip and another shielding her eyes. "Watch and not fall now."

"Come up."

"Don't be silly. I can barely climb the stairs."

They walked then, side by side, but Daniel high above. He turned and looked at the green hills that folded out before him. He opened his arms wide and spread his fingers. The space made him feel giddy.

"You get a great view from up here, like," said Daniel, teasing her.

"I'll take your word for it."

At the end of one section he stood with toes over the edge, bending his knees.

"Don't jump, Danny."

"You could catch me, like."

"You'll hurt your knees."

"I won't. I've jumped off higher walls than this."

"Okay, well, reach for my hands and it'll help break your fall."

He jumped and felt her strong rough hands squeeze his; he fell into her, breathing hard from the thrill of it.

They walked up the hill to find a cup of tea. Daniel glanced up at her, but she wasn't looking at him. She was smiling into the distance, her lips parted and her chest rising and falling.

Daniel swallowed then slipped his hand into hers. She looked down at him and smiled and he looked away, embarrassed but feeling a tightness in his abdomen, as if even his stomach was trying to smile. He liked the rough feel of her hand. As she walked she rubbed her thumb across the back of his fingers.

This is what happiness is, he thought: this clear day and the smell of grass, and the wall that had been there for centuries, and the feel of her hand and his lips wet in the expectation of a cup of hot, sweet tea.

He thought of his mother. He wanted her to know this moment. As his hand warmed inside Minnie's palm, so he imagined that his mother would come and take his other hand. The day was almost perfect, but that would complete it.

21

SEBASTIAN'S TRIAL WAS TO BE HELD IN THE OLD BAILEY.

Daniel woke up early for his run, but even after his shower his stomach was still tight with tension. He didn't know why the trial should make him feel so apprehensive. He was used to Old Bailey trials, and murder trials, but today he felt different: as if he himself would be on trial.

The entrance to the Old Bailey was now a throng of angry public and hungry press. He didn't expect the photographers would know who he was and expected Irene to get the attention, but as soon as he approached there was a cry of *"That's one of the solicitors"* and then a flash.

"Child killer," someone from the crowd screamed. "You're defending a child killer. The little bastard should fry. Go to hell!"

As a defense lawyer, he had become accustomed to enmity.

In the past he had been verbally abused in the street and sent hate mail threatening his life. Such things only made Daniel more determined to see the case through. Everyone deserved a defense, no matter what they had done. But the fury of the crowd here seemed exceptional. He understood anger at the loss of innocent life, but he could not understand why people seemed so ready to vilify a child. The loss of a child was cruel because it was promise stolen, but Daniel felt the criminalization of another child was just as cruel. Daniel remembered his foster father calling him evil. Even if Sebastian was guilty, he needed help, not condemnation. He watched the surge of the crowd—jeering faces asking for punishment. Protesters railed on the streets, waving placards that read LIFE FOR A LIFE. They screamed *bas-tard* whenever they saw someone related to Sebastian and jostled against a makeshift barrier and yellow-vested police officers.

A police officer pulled at his elbow, urging him forward, and Daniel jogged the last few steps until he was inside the court. Sebastian had been brought to court in a security van and was waiting in an observation cell downstairs.

When Daniel entered the cell, Sebastian was sitting on a concrete bunk covered with a blue plastic mat. He looked pale. He was wearing a navy suit that was a little big on the shoulders and a striped tie. The outfit made the boy seem even younger than his eleven years.

"How's it going, Seb?" Daniel asked.

"Okay, thanks," Sebastian said, looking away.

"Sharp suit."

"My dad wanted me to wear it."

It was nearly an hour before the trial would begin and Daniel felt sorry for Sebastian—the time he would have to spend in the harsh concrete cell, just waiting. It was hard enough on adults. Sebastian had been shown round the courtroom the day before and proceedings had been explained to him, but nothing could really prepare a child for this.

Daniel sat on the bunk beside Sebastian. They both looked straight ahead at the wall opposite, which was marked with graffiti: obscenities and devotions side by side. Daniel noticed one phrase that had been cut into the concrete with a knife: I LOVE YOU, MUM.

"Did you go for a run this morning?" Sebastian asked.

"I did. Did you get any breakfast?"

"Yeah," Sebastian sighed, looking away again, uninterested.

"I better go," said Daniel, standing up.

"Daniel?"

"Yeah?"

"I'm scared."

"You'll be all right. They showed you where you'll be sitting? You get to sit next to me, just like we said. Keep your chin up, eh?"

Sebastian nodded and Daniel knocked to be let out.

When the door was closed, Daniel placed a palm against it, and then made his way upstairs to the court.

THE JUDGE AND BARRISTERS WORE THEIR GOWNS, BUT NO wigs, as they were considered too intimidating for children. The public gallery was almost full of journalists and Daniel knew there were many more outside who had not been able to get in. Arrangements had been made to restrict the number of journalists allowed to ten. Daniel took his seat, where he would sit with Sebastian. Irene Clarke and Sebastian's junior counsel, Mark Gibbons, sat in front.

Sucking his lip, Sebastian was brought in by two police officers. Daniel leaned down and held his shoulder in reassurance. They were all a strange family then, waiting for it to begin.

Sebastian's mother and father were seated behind them. Charlotte was wearing a well-cut suit. Kenneth was leaning very far back in his seat, hands folded across his belly. He kept looking at his watch, while Charlotte examined her makeup in a small round mirror and reapplied her lipstick. There was a murmur from the press section of the gallery, but no one else seemed to be talking.

Daniel could hear Sebastian swallow.

The judge entered. Daniel nudged Sebastian's elbow, prompting him to stand. The court rose and then sat. The room hummed with anticipation.

Jurors were selected and then sworn in. The chosen ones stared without restraint at Sebastian from across the room. They had read so much about him, but now they could see his face, and would decide his fate.

Benjamin Stokes's parents were visible in the gallery too: Madeline and Paul. They sat side by side, still and heavy, neither offering each other comfort nor watching Sebastian. They also waited, laden with grief, for it to begin.

THE JUDGE LEANED ON THE PODIUM AND LOOKED OVER HIS glasses in the direction of the public gallery.

"Members of the press, I would like to remind you that

until further notice the defendant, Sebastian Croll, will not be referred to by name in all reporting of the trial."

The consonants in Sebastian's name seemed to assault the rapt room. Daniel frowned.

The judge slid his glasses farther down his nose and directed his gaze at Sebastian.

"Sebastian, I won't ask you to stand when I address you, as is our practice in court. You are also seated in the main courtroom, beside your solicitor and with your parents nearby, instead of the dock. Many of our court processes are protracted and may seem confusing to you. I remind you that you have your solicitors and barristers to talk to if there is anything you do not understand."

Sebastian looked up at Daniel, who put a hand on his back briefly to indicate that he should face the front. Sebastian had already been counseled on how to behave in court.

Irene Clarke stood up, hand on her hip underneath her gown.

"My Lord, there is a point of law I have to raise . . ."

She had an air of sheer authority, speaking the language of the court in received pronunciation.

The court waited as the jury shuffled out: eight men and four women; two were young, but the remainder, middle aged. Daniel watched them go.

"My Lord, we would like to make an application for a stay on the grounds that pretrial publicity has been prejudicial to my client's case. I present before the court a selection of newspaper cuttings which show the highly emotive language in which the case has been discussed in the press. The saturation coverage of this case has more than likely influenced the jury."

The judge sighed as he considered the bundle of articles that was passed to him. Daniel had seen this red judge before: Philip Baron was one of the oldest remaining on the bench. He had featured in the tabloids himself, following unpopular rulings. He had made headlines for his use of prejudicial language when delivering sentences in rape cases. He looked every bit his sixty-nine years.

The QC for the Crown, Gordon Jones, argued that the jury would not have been prejudiced by the coverage because the defendant had not been named and the main details of the case were not known to the press. The morning disappeared as the articles were considered and discussed. Daniel's stomach rumbled and he tightened his stomach muscles to suppress it. There was a sense that the whole room was fatigued now. So much anticipation stymied in the wake of bureaucracy. Daniel was used to it, but as Irene fought for him, he could see that Sebastian was already bored. He had been drawing pictures: tiny little conjoined wheels on the corner of the notepad. Daniel could hear him sighing and shifting in his chair.

The judge cleared his throat.

"Thank you, I have considered these points and will rule that the trial will proceed, but I will remind the jury of their duty to consider the facts of the case as presented here in court, only. I am, however, mindful of the time, and think this might be a convenient moment to adjourn. We'll resume after lunch. . . ."

The court session ended and Sebastian was taken back down to his cell.

Irene left court before Daniel could speak to her, so he went down to the cells to see Sebastian. The guard slid back the shutter on the observation window to check on Sebastian's position before Daniel was allowed in.

"You all right, Seb?" he asked. Sebastian was sitting on the edge of the bunk, looking down at his shoes, which were turned toe inward. "You'll get your lunch in a minute."

Sebastian nodded, not looking up at Daniel.

"I know it's boring . . . probably the worst thing about court."

"I wasn't bored. I just wish I didn't have to hear . . ."

"Hear what? What do you mean?"

"All the bad things about me."

Daniel took a deep breath, unsure how to respond, and settled down on the bunk next to him. "That'll get worse, you know, Seb," he said finally, leaning forward onto his elbows so that his head was level with the boy's.

"We lost the first argument," he said.

"True," said Daniel, "but it was an argument we expected to lose."

"Why argue if you know you're not going to win?"

"Well, for one thing because it's a valid argument, and in court, remember, even if one judge disagrees with you, on appeal another judge may think you're right."

Sebastian was silent again, looking at the floor. Daniel was not sure if he had understood. He thought about explaining more to him, but did not want to burden the boy. He imagined what he would have felt like, alone in this cell, as a boy of eleven. He had been close to it. The Thorntons could have easily reported him.

"Are you my friend?" said Sebastian.

"I'm your lawyer."

"People don't like me," said Sebastian. "I don't think the jury will like me either."

"The jury is there to consider the facts put before them. It doesn't matter if they like you or not," said Daniel. He wanted this to be true, but did not completely believe it.

"Do *you* like me?" said Sebastian, looking up. Daniel's first instinct was to look away from the green eyes that found his own, but he maintained eye contact.

"'Course," he said, feeling as if he were crossing a boundary again.

There was not much time left before court adjourned. Daniel bought a sandwich near St. Paul's and ate it looking out onto Cannon Street. Sebastian's low mood was upon him and the boy's questions turned in his mind.

He felt a sense of foreboding: he was not sure if it was fear of the outcome of the trial, or empathy for the boy and what he faced. He felt heavy with responsibility. A crow landed suddenly on the ledge outside the diner. Daniel stopped eating and watched as it choked back a chip it had snatched from the pavement. The bird cocked its head and looked at Daniel, its beak slick. Then the bird was gone, swooping up to the heights of the buildings where baroque fantasies had been cut from the Portland stone. Daniel watched the ascent until the bird was out of sight.

Flight: the control of opposing forces, weight versus lift, gravity and the pull of the great beyond.

Fight or flight: the body facilitates both at the same time; there is the choice to attack that which threatens, or to run from it.

It had been years since Daniel had felt the need to run, but he felt it now. He felt afraid of the outcome and responsible for his part in it.

IRENE WAS PACING OUTSIDE THE COURTROOM, MOBILE PRESSED to her ear, her gown trailing behind her when Daniel returned to the Old Bailey. Daniel winked at her as he passed and she raised her eyes at him.

Court 13 was nearly full. Sebastian was brought in and took his seat. He looked around for his mother. The Crolls were there behind, but not looking at their son. Charlotte was wearing sunglasses, which she kept pushing up onto her nose. She crossed and uncrossed her legs. Kenneth was looking at his watch and then at the prosecution's QC, Gordon Jones, who, Daniel thought—even without his wig—managed to look like a public school principal. Thin and always leaning forward slightly at the hip, Jones was one of those people of indeterminate age. He could easily be thirty-five, or he could be near retirement. The skin of Jones's face was pulled tight over his skull.

"What did you have for lunch?" said Sebastian.

"Sandwich. How 'bout you?"

"Spaghetti hoops, but they didn't taste right. They tasted plastic or something."

"That's not good"

"I only had a little. They were nasty."

"You'll be hungry. Do you want a sweet? You've got another while to go."

Sebastian popped one of Daniel's mints into his mouth. Daniel noticed one of the journalists pointing as he offered the sweets to Sebastian, then make notes in his pad.

Sebastian seemed pleased with himself. The judge entered. Irene was not yet back, so her junior was standing in. But this afternoon was for the Crown.

Gordon Jones stood up and supported himself with two fingers pressed against his lectern.

"Members of the jury, I appear on behalf of the Crown; the defendant is represented by my learned colleague Miss Clarke."

He took a deep breath and exhaled. It might have been a breath to calm him before he began, but Daniel knew it was meant as a sigh.

"William Butler Yeats once wrote that the 'innocent and the beautiful have no enemy but time.' Ben Stokes was innocent and he was beautiful. He was a beautiful eight-year-old little boy. He was just so tall . . ." Gordon Jones held up a flat hand to indicate Ben's height.

In the gallery, Ben Stokes's mother snorted suddenly. The whole court looked up at her as she was pressed into her husband. Jones waited for a few seconds until silence fell again.

"He should have had the world ahead of him: school, girlfriends, university, a career, and a family. But Ben unfortunately had another enemy, other than time itself. We will show that he was bludgeoned to death in a violent attack by someone he knew as a neighbor and a playmate, but who we will show was in fact a sadistic bully.

"Ben was just riding his bike near his home in Islington on Sunday the eighth of August this year. He was known as a quiet child, well behaved but shy. He liked riding his bicycle very much, as those of you with children in the family will appreciate, yet he left his bike abandoned in the road and the next day was found dead, having been beaten to death with a brick that lay in the corner of the playground where he was found.

"We will show that the defendant, Sebastian Croll, persuaded Ben to leave his home and his bicycle before taking him to Barnard Park where he was later witnessed bullying and physically assaulting the smaller and younger boy. Finally, when Ben refused to stay out and accept this abuse any longer, it is our contention that Sebastian became enraged and began a sustained and fatal attack on Ben in an area of the park playground that was hidden by trees.

"We will demonstrate that Sebastian Croll wielded the murder weapon, which he came upon in a savage manner.

"This is an unspeakable crime, but one which is still very rare. The newspapers would have you believe that our society is decaying and that grave violence by children against other children is more common than it was in the past. This is not the case. Murder of this kind is mercifully rare, but its rarity does not discount its gravity. The defendant's age should not deflect you from the facts of the case: that this small child, Ben Stokes, was robbed of his life before his ninth birthday.

"The task before the prosecution is straightforward—to show beyond a reasonable doubt that the defendant a) carried out the actions that killed the deceased, Ben Stokes; and b) that when he did this, he did so with the intention of killing him or seriously injuring him. We will show beyond a doubt that the defendant fought violently with Ben Stokes, choosing a secluded and leafy area of the park to launch a savage attack. We will show that the defendant sat on the deceased and wielded a brick at the face of the small boy with the clear intention of killing him. What followed . . . and let us be clear, this fact is in no way diminished by the prisoner's young age . . . What followed . . . was a premeditated act of murder.

"Ben Stokes was beautiful and innocent indeed, but we will show that the prisoner committed the ugliest of crimes, and is guilty beyond any reasonable doubt."

The whole room seemed to have suspended its breath and so Daniel held his. The oak panels and the green leather seemed to creak and rub with impatience in the lengthening silence. Daniel glanced behind at the Crolls. Charlotte sat upright, her mouth just turning down at the corners. Kenneth was frowning at Gordon Jones.

Sebastian was rapt. His boredom had passed. Daniel had watched him lean forward as he listened to Jones, as if it was a story created for his amusement with Sebastian as the protagonist.

Irene silently reentered the court.

When the Crown finished outlining the case for the prosecution, Daniel felt a chill. He himself did not know for a fact whether Sebastian was innocent or guilty; he only knew the boy was out of place here in the adult court—even with the tables rearranged and the wigs off and only ten reporters in the gallery.

Gordon Jones finally sat down, and Sebastian leaned into Daniel: "He's got it all wrong. Maybe I should tell them?" His clear, well-spoken voice was loud even in a whisper.

"Not now," Daniel said, aware of Irene clearing her throat and glancing in his direction. "We'll get our turn."

⊷

IT WAS THE SECOND DAY OF THE TRIAL AND DANIEL ARRIVED at court at nine thirty. He jogged past the rows of press photographers who were three deep behind the makeshift barriers. When he entered the Central Criminal Court it felt dark and humid. Each entrance to this court always felt daunting. It was like being swallowed: entering the rib cage of a beast. The marble statues reproached him.

Again, Daniel felt nervous, as if he was a younger, less experienced lawyer. He had been on countless criminal trials and at the Old Bailey more times than he could remember, but today his palms were moist, as if it was his own trial.

Before Sebastian arrived in the courtroom, Daniel took a deep breath and tried to calm down. Daniel knew what the day held and knew that it could only be hard on the boy.

"The Crown calls Mrs. Madeline Stokes."

Ben Stokes's mother entered and made her way to the witness box. She walked as if shackled. She wore her hair tied back. It was uneven, as if she had tied it back in a hurry. The hairstyle accentuated the hollows of her cheeks and her dark eyes. Daniel was at least twenty feet from her, and yet he was sure that he could see her tremble. She leaned on the witness box when she arrived and her breaths were audible in the microphone.

The heating made the room dry and hot. Daniel felt his armpits wet with sweat.

Seconds passed as Gordon Jones leafed through his notes. Everyone in the court was waiting for him to speak.

"Mrs. Stokes," he said after a long pause, "I know this is difficult for you, but I'd like to ask you to cast your mind back to the afternoon of Sunday August eighth . . . Can you tell the court about the last time that you saw your son alive?"

"Well . . . it was a nice day. He asked if he could go out to play on his bike, and I said that he could but that he had to . . . had to stay in the crescent."

She was obviously nervous, broken by a deep sadness, yet her voice was clear and genteel. It reminded Daniel of ice in a glass. When she became emotional, her voice deepened.

"Did you watch your son as he played outside?"

"Yes, I did for a while. I was washing the dishes in the kitchen and I could see him going back and forth across the pavement."

"What time was it, do you think, *the last time you saw him*?" Jones was softly spoken, deferential.

"It was about one. He had been outside for half an hour or so after lunch and I asked him if he wanted to put a jacket on or come inside. I thought it might rain. He said he was fine. I wish I'd made him now. I wish I had *insisted*. I wish . . ."

"So you allowed Ben to continue to play outside? At what time did you discover he was no longer playing in the crescent?"

"Not long after that. It was maybe fifteen, twenty minutes— that was all. I was working upstairs and I looked out of the window. I kept checking on him. I . . . You can pretty much see the whole of Richmond Crescent from up there but when I looked out . . . I just couldn't see him at all."

When she said *at all,* Madeline Stokes's eyes became very wide.

"What did you do?"

"I ran out into the street. I ran up and down the crescent and then found his bike, lying on its side, just abandoned around the corner. I knew right away something terrible had happened to him. I don't know why, but I did. At first I thought he might have been hit by a car, but everything was completely quiet. He had just . . . vanished."

Madeline Stokes was crying now. Daniel was moved by her, and he knew that the jury would be too. Her left hand was now red against the witness box, but her face was still white. When she cried she put a hand over her mouth. Daniel remembered what Harriet had said to him about Minnie losing her daughter. He remembered the day at the market with Minnie's hands cold on his and her sad, watery blue eyes begging him not to mention her little daughter. Like Minnie, Madeline Stokes had had only one child. She had lost everything that mattered and the world was now a dark place.

"I shouted for him down some of the other streets and stood at the gate near the park, but I couldn't see him in there. I called his friends, then his father and we . . . called the hospital and the police."

"Did you call your neighbors the Crolls?"

"No." She wiped her face with flat hands. Her eyes were rueful red pebbles; they turned and shone—watching the scene again, reliving the panic. "I didn't."

"Did Ben occasionally play with Sebastian?"

"Yes, not at school really, but sometimes at weekends. At first I had been fine about it, but then I found out that Sebastian was bullying Ben, getting him into trouble, and I stopped them seeing each other."

"Can you explain what you mean by 'bullying and getting him into trouble'?"

"Well, when we first moved to Richmond Crescent, Sebastian asked if Ben could come out to play. I was pleased that there was a little boy so close, even if he was a bit older, but then I decided he wasn't really . . . suitable."

"And why, may I ask, was that?"

"After playing with Sebastian, Ben started to use some *very vulgar* swear words—words that he didn't know before. I told him off and stopped him playing with Sebastian for a few days, but still at weekends they would occasionally play together. Then I noticed that Ben would have bruises after playing with Sebastian. Ben told me that Sebastian would hit him when he didn't do as he asked. I complained to Sebastian's mother and told Ben he was never to play with Sebastian again."

"When you complained to Sebastian's mother, did you receive a satisfactory response?"

"No, Sebastian is a law unto himself in that house, or so I gather. His own mother has no control over him and his father's away. I don't think she's well."

Mrs. Stokes wiped her nose and spoke down into her handkerchief. Daniel watched Charlotte out of the corner of his eye. She was impassive, but there was a shine on her makeup now. Neither woman looked at the other. Sebastian was sitting up straight, staring at Madeline. He blinked often.

"So, you didn't contact the Crolls about Ben's disappearance because you had forbidden your son to play with Sebastian and so did not suspect that the two boys would be together. But you think that Ben would have disobeyed you . . ."

Mrs. Stokes began to weep silently. Her shoulders shook and she pinched her nose with the tissue. Her voice was deeper when she spoke again.

"Ben was *in thrall* with Sebastian, I suppose. He was the

stronger, older boy. He hadn't played with Sebastian for months and I just didn't think. Now, it . . . it seems obvious."

"What happened after you called the hospital and the police?"

"My husband came home. The police were fantastic. I didn't expect them to do anything so soon, but they were right there taking details, and they helped us to look around the area and put out a description of Ben."

"Thank you, Mrs. Stokes," said Gordon Jones

Irene Clarke stood up. Daniel watched her as she smiled affirmatively and folded her hands on the lectern. She was somber, almost penitent before Mrs. Stokes.

"Mrs. Stokes, I am sorry for the great tragedy that you and your family have experienced. I only want to ask you a few brief questions. Please take your time."

Madeline gave a small strangled cough, and nodded.

"Had your son ever disappeared for a long period of time before?"

"No."

"You said that there was a time when he played regularly with Sebastian. On any of these occasions did the boys wander outside their normal play area or go missing for any period?"

Mrs. Stokes coughed and appeared to have some trouble regaining composure.

"Mrs. Stokes?"

"No."

"And is it not the case that until you knew that your neighbor's child had been arrested you did not suspect that Sebastian could have been involved in your son's disappearance?"

Madeline looked up into the corners of the court. Fraught in the witness box, she seemed exalted, and the room a hallowed space. Tears streamed silently down her cheeks.

"I didn't think of him," she said quietly.

"You testified that you had to stop Ben seeing Sebastian. Is it then true that Ben *enjoyed* playing with Sebastian?"

"No, he was a bully, he was . . ." Mrs. Stokes's fingers tightened on the lip of the witness box.

"You didn't like Sebastian, Mrs. Stokes, that much is apparent, but did your son not *ask* to play with him? You described him as being *in thrall* to Sebastian. Was it not the case that despite your disapproval, Ben and Sebastian were actually friends who enjoyed each other's company?"

Mrs. Stokes blew her nose and took small breaths. The judge asked if she wanted a glass of water. She shook her head and looked up at Irene.

"I'm sorry, Mrs. Stokes," said Irene, "I know this is very hard. Was this not the case?"

Madeline sighed and nodded.

"Mrs. Stokes, can I ask you to speak out your answers?"

"Maybe they were friends."

Irene glanced at Daniel and then sat down. She could have gone further, he knew, but the jury was tense with sympathy for the young boy's mother. This too Daniel respected about Irene; she could turn a witness when she had to, but she always remained kind.

The breaks were regular because of rules put in place since the Bulger trial. Daniel went to the men's room as soon as court adjourned. He felt heavy and tired. His heels sounded on the marble floors. The men's rooms were familiar to him, with their blue walls and gold taps, but they smelled of ingrained urine and futile bleach.

There was a free urinal in the far corner. Daniel exhaled as he urinated into its white porcelain.

"All right, Danny?"

It was Detective Superintendent McCrum. His shoulder nudged Daniel's slightly as he unzipped.

"Sometimes you wonder . . . ," McCrum said, his northern accent strangely warm and welcome in the cold Victorian toilet, "is there no other way? I can see this trial is going to be barbaric. It's wrong to put them through all this."

"I couldn't agree more," said Daniel. He shook and zipped and began to wash his hands. He didn't know how Sebastian would cope with the long days ahead and the worst still to come. "And we've only just started . . ."

"I know—that poor woman," said McCrum.

Daniel turned away. He left without saying another word to McCrum, nodding at him slightly as he passed. The older man watched him go.

22

ONE YEAR FOLDED INTO THE NEXT LIKE FURROWS OF TILLED earth. Minnie got the back windows fixed after the chickens pecked out all the putty. Some slates came off the roof in the wind and there was a leak that dripped slowly into a bucket on the stairs when it rained. She didn't have the money to fix it and it went on for more than a year. It was Daniel's job to empty the bucket in the morning.

Minnie's goat, Hector, died during Daniel's second winter at Brampton, but the following spring Minnie bought a doe and two kids to replace him. Daniel was allowed to do the morning milking: creaming her udders and then milking her patiently, methodically. Minnie taught him how. They made a new area for the goats and a special milking area that the other animals could not access. Minnie told Daniel that the milking area had to be kept very clean. At night they would separate kids from doe, to allow her udders to swell. The doe was called Barbara and Daniel named the kids Brock and Liam after Newcastle United football players, although they were both female.

At night, after his bath and his homework, he would play backgammon with Minnie as she swilled her gin and he sucked chocolate éclairs. She would marvel at his ability to count without tapping the numbers on the board. Or sometimes it would be cards: knockout whist or blackjack. She would play records while they played: Elvis and Ray Charles and Bobby Darin. Daniel would shimmy his shoulders as he sliced his cards down onto the table, and she would raise her eyebrows at him and toss a crisp at Blitz.

Daniel was thirteen years old and in the first year of the William Howard Secondary School on the Longtown Road. He was captain of the football team and had won two gold medals for long-distance running, but he was still smaller and thinner than the other boys in his class. He would start his GCSEs next year. He was good at English, history, and chemistry. There was a girl called Carol-Ann who was a year older than he was and she sometimes came to his house after school. She was a tomboy and he taught her how to do keepy-uppies with the football and how to look after the animals. Minnie would have her for tea if her mum was working late. Carol-Ann wasn't his girlfriend or anything, although he had seen her breasts when her bra came off while they were swimming in the Irving River last summer.

Daniel was popular at school. He had friends because of football and he hardly got into any fights anymore. But apart from Carol-Ann, no one came often to the farm. Danny was asked to birthday parties and went along to all the school dos.

He had a group of friends he hung about with at school, mainly from the football, but there was no one he played with regularly after school and no friend's home he visited more than a few times a year. After school, if there wasn't a game or a party, he would be home with Minnie, working with the animals, picking herbs for dinner, scrubbing potatoes, or kicking cans for Blitz in the backyard. And then there would be dinner and games and gin and music. Year in, year out. It was the symmetry of the days, the thankful realization of expectation, the structure of it all. It made Daniel feel safe.

Daniel learned how to hope. His desires had to be clipped to fit the confines of her home, like the chicken's wings she snipped in order that they didn't flee, but anything he could wish for in that house, Minnie gave to him.

It was Saturday and Daniel woke up before his alarm. He stretched out like a starfish, feeling the stretch all the way to his fingertips. Outside the thin pane of his window he could hear the cluck and fuss of the chickens and the irritated bleats of the goats. He lay in bed with his hands behind his head thinking, remembering.

Daniel tossed and yawned and then reached into his bedside table drawer. He took out his mother's necklace and stroked the gold *S*. It felt smoother than he remembered it being and he wondered if he had made it so, in the same way that the sea rubbed smooth the sharp edges of glass. Almost a year the necklace had been in the drawer wrapped in a tissue but he hadn't touched it. He had almost forgotten about it.

He lay back down, looking at the necklace. The memories that he chose when he stroked the necklace were not real memories, but rather photographs his mind had taken and then drenched in hope so that they could be strung in the dark, dripping with his own expectation. One of the photographs was his mother laughing in Minnie's kitchen, laughing so hard that you could see her two missing teeth, her eyes so tight shut with mirth that the laugh lines cut into her bones. Another was his mother feeding the chickens as Minnie waved from the window. In his mind, his mother's hands were always bony and slow: they let go of the feed in slow motion, as if her joints were stuck. In another photo they were playing cards together and his mother won; she rocked back on the sofa with her knees in the air and a screech of disbelief.

Daniel placed the necklace back in the drawer. He wondered what Minnie would think of his mother, were they to meet face-to-face. His mother would be so fragile before her: a sparrow before her stomping bear. Minnie would feed her and love her and set her to work, as she had done with Daniel. Faced with Minnie, Daniel's mother would be just another child. When he thought about it, it was that which made his heart break. His mother was a child to him, and every year he felt himself age beside her, while in his mind she stayed the same: young, thin, needing him.

Since Daniel had been adopted, the way he thought about his mother had changed. Before he had felt the panic of her loss, the rip and tear and sting of it. Now he wanted to comfort her. He remembered stroking her brow and pulling a cardigan over her as she slept on the sofa: black eyes and blue lips both smiling at him. He no longer wanted to run to her. He wanted the calm of his new life more than he wanted her chaos, but now he fantasized about bringing her into this new life. Minnie could adopt her too; she could sleep on the sofa listening to

Ray Charles as Daniel plucked umbrellas of rhubarb from the garden and pushed vegetables into the nimble lips of the goats.

Downstairs, Minnie had the porridge on. She was in her dressing gown, bare feet dirty on the kitchen floor. The soles of her feet were hard as leather. At night, she would watch television with her feet on a stool and Daniel would sometimes tap the inch-thick yellowed skin of her feet with his finger. She could stand on a drawing pin and realize a full week later, not because of the pain but because she heard the tap-tack of her foot on the floorboards. Then she would throw her ankle over her knee and remove the offending pin—but there would not be a drop of blood.

When she heard him she walked to the bottom of the stairs with the wooden spoon in her hand. She squeezed his cheeks and turned his face to the side to plant a kiss on his forehead.

"Good morning, gorgeous."

It was summer and although it was before seven, the day was bright, the sky a spotless blue. Daniel slipped his feet into his boots and went outside to feed the animals. His hands were cold and Barbara kicked and stamped when he placed them on her udders, and so he warmed them under his armpits before trying again.

Together again, the goats nuzzled and sniffed each other and Daniel carried the milk in to Minnie.

"You're a good lad," she said, placing his porridge in front of him with a hot cup of tea, which Daniel knew she would have already milked and sugared for him. "I'm going to get dressed."

When she came back, Danny was making toast. He asked her if she wanted some.

"Just half a slice, love. I'm fine with my tea."

Daniel gave her a whole slice, knowing that she would eat it anyway. She chattered to him about the garden and the leak in the roof and how she might get someone out to fix it next week. She had been saying that for months. She asked what he wanted to do today, since it was Saturday. If it stayed nice they might go for a walk, or if it rained they would watch afternoon films eating packets of crisps. Sometimes Minnie would cook or bake inside, while Danny kicked a ball about in the yard.

Daniel shrugged. "You know what I was thinking," he said, taking a tiny bite of his toast and watching her face.

She smiled—all blue eyes and red cheeks. "I'm sure you're going to tell me."

"Do you think the social worker would find out where me mam is now?"

The light in her eyes faded.

"Darlin', you know what they said. Eighteen and then you can have contact if you still want to. I know it's hard but that's the law and we have to obey it. You need to try and move past it."

"I can, I am, I just . . . I wanted to maybe show her the new goats, and my room now it's done. She'd like it. I just wanted to talk to her, like."

Minnie sighed. Her breasts rose up from the table and then fell again. "Danny, look at me."

"What?" he said, looking up at her, his mouth full of toast. She was frowning at him.

"You're not to run away again, you hear me?" She put a hand on her heart. "I just can't take it again, love."

"I'm not going to run away. I just wanted to tell her about

the new goats, like." He looked away, and finished his toast, putting too much into his mouth, daring a glance at her. She was sitting watching him, with her hands in her lap.

Daniel too looked away. "I thought it might be good if she came and lived with us," he said. Saying that out loud, it now seemed impossible, stupid, but still he turned to watch her response.

"You know that can't happen, Danny," she said, very quietly.

He nodded, feeling a pain at the back of his throat. "I just know she'd like it here. She needs looking after and I could look after her here."

Daniel felt her heavy hand in his. "You have to realize that it's not your job to look after her. It's my job to look after you."

Daniel nodded. His nose was stinging and he knew he would cry if he spoke again. He didn't want to hurt Minnie. He loved her and he wanted to stay. He only wanted to make her understand that his mum should come and live with them too. Then everything would be perfect.

"I'm not going to run away, like," he managed. "I just want to talk to her. I want to tell her about the farm 'n' stuff." He wiped his fingers over his left eye. "I just want to talk to her, like."

"I understand, my love," she said. "Let me talk to them. I'll see if they'll give me a telephone number or something."

"D'you mean it?" He leaned forward, smiling with relief, but she was frowning at him.

She nodded.

"D'you promise?"

"I said I would."

"Do you think they'll tell you?"

"I can only ask."

Daniel smiled and sat back in his chair. Minnie was clean-ing up: putting away the butter and the jam and wiping the half of the kitchen table that they ate off—the other half was piled with books and dog biscuits and old newspapers. Daniel felt a warmness spread inside him, up from his stomach to his ribs. It lifted him and he sat up straight and raised his shoulders.

LATER IN THE WEEK, DANIEL JOGGED HOME ACROSS THE Dandy. He found a tin can and dribbled it for a quarter of a mile or so, his school tie loose and his shirt hanging out and his schoolbag off his shoulders. The air was threaded with the smell of freshly cut grass. Daniel could hear his breath and feel the sweat forming at his temples as he tacked the can forward with his mud-specked school shoes. He enjoyed the bounce and spring in his muscles and his joints and the warm sunshine on his forearms and his face. He was happy he'd decided, happy to be here and running home to Minnie.

Home. He smacked the can hard and it rose in a glinting, sun-captured arc for at least ten yards before falling soundlessly into the long grass. *Home.* Daniel found it and kicked it again. It flew upward and he waited for it to fall before catching it on the side of his foot and then sending it flying again, down the hill toward Flynn Farm and Minnie, who would have mashed banana sandwiches waiting for him.

It was her predictability that he loved first. She had a gift of showing him her world and then repeating it day after day. Things happened when she said they would happen. She said that she would adopt him and she did. The judge's face had twisted in disbelief at the papers before him and Daniel's stomach had sunk, but sure enough he had decided in their favor and handed over the teddy bear and he had been made Minnie's son, just as she had promised.

Daniel looked at her differently now. He already loved her heavy body and the soft masses of her, but now he regarded her as having a new power. He trusted her. She was able to achieve the things she desired; they were within her reach. Even Daniel's fate she held in her grasp. When he thought of her, he would think of Blitz's ruff in her fist as she held him back, opening the door to strangers while he barked.

Daniel slowed to a walk. His breath was uneven. He took a deep breath and enjoyed the smell of warm summer grass. The sky was blue and so cloudless that he felt dizzied by its infinity.

He was aware of voices and then footsteps behind. He glanced over his shoulder and saw it was the three older boys who had beat him up before. He knew their names now: Liam, Peter, and Matt. They were in the year above him at school.

He felt tension creep into his muscles. He walked as if he was unaware of the boys, but exaggerated his stride and the swing of his shoulders. He could hear their conversation, although he guessed they were twenty feet behind him. They were talking about the football, but then they fell silent and Daniel felt the hairs on the back of his neck rise. He tried to listen for their movements.

"How's the old witch, Danny, eh?" one called. "She taught ye any spells yet, like?"

The voice was close.

Daniel ignored them, feeling the tension run from his shoulders down his spine. He pressed his teeth together and made fists with his hands.

"Fat witch like her. Like to see her trying to fly, like."

Daniel glanced over his shoulder again, and saw one of the boys mimicking a broomstick flight before he crashed and tumbled onto the grass. They all laughed then: dirty laughs. The voices were full throated and deep, newly broken voices oscillating in derision.

Daniel spun to face them. As soon as he turned, the boys squared up, feet spread apart and hands out of their pockets.

There was a pause, so that all Daniel heard was the rush in his ears.

"You got a problem?" It was Peter who spoke, jaw askew, eyes narrowed, willing Daniel to start something.

"Shut up about her, right!"

"Or you'll what?"

"Batter ye, like."

"Yeah, you and whose army?"

It was like before. Daniel charged at the boy, and hit him in the stomach with his head. He was bigger than Daniel still. He felt the older boy's fist pound his ribs and he inhaled with the pain. He could hear the other two jeering, calling: *Batter him, Pete. Batter him.*

Daniel remembered fighting his mother's boyfriend, the one who had pulled him off the floor by his hair. He felt rage snap, quick and bright and exquisite through his body. The jolt was strengthening, cleansing. He hit Peter and he went down and then he kicked him in the face until he turned away.

The other boys turned on Daniel then, but he was taut from

the attack and he did not feel their fists against his arms and chest. He hit Matt on the nose and felt the crack reverberate against his knuckle and then kicked Liam in the balls.

Daniel staggered away from them. His fist was stinging and he looked down and saw the knuckle cut, but when he touched it, he realized it was only Matt's blood. He spun round on the Dandy to face them one more time.

"I hear another word about her, y're dead."

The word *dead* came out of his mouth like a bullet. It echoed across the open Dandy. Birds scattered in its wake.

The boys, felled in the long grass, said nothing. Daniel walked away from them, still careful, but exaggerating his swagger all the same. There was a breeze and all the blades of grass bent toward him, as if in veneration.

Daniel knew that the boys might retaliate, but he felt good about himself as he walked toward the farm. His steps were light. They would think twice before slagging her again. She was his mother now; he would stand up for her.

When Daniel arrived at the farm, it was still. The hens were strutting and pecking, but quiet, and the kids were stealing a lick from the udder that would be denied them at nightfall. The daisies in the grass braced themselves against the wind.

Minnie was defrosting the freezer. Daniel went for a pee as soon as he came home. He washed his hand and looked in the mirror. He held up his T-shirt to look at his ribs. He had not a scratch. She would not guess that he had defended her earlier, fought for her and won.

He could not help squaring his shoulders as he walked into the kitchen.

She was in her wellies, hammering a wooden spatula against the impacted ice in the freezer.

"Mother of God, is that the time already?" she said when he walked in. "Sure and I thought it was just gone two. You'll be wanting your sandwiches and I haven't even got them ready."

Daniel wiped his nose and his forehead on his sleeve and waited as she pressed a banana onto fresh white bread and poured him a glass of orange squash. He downed the juice and ate half his sandwich before he spoke to her.

"What you doin' that for?" he asked, pointing at the open, weeping freezer.

"It's like all things in life, Danny. Every now and then you need to get out the hammer and start all over again."

Daniel was not sure what she meant. He started on the other half of his banana sandwich. The windows were open and the manure smell from the adjacent farm crept in. Minnie downed her tea in a gulp and then picked up the hammer and the spatula. She hacked against the ice in loud, hard thuds.

"I got an A in my history test today," he shouted at her. She stopped her assault on the freezer long enough to wink at him.

"Clever you. I told you. You're far too smart. You try even a little bit and you'll knock them all into next week . . . I told you so."

Blitz slunk into the next room to escape the noise of the battery. Ice slid across the kitchen floor, quiet and watery as repentance.

Daniel finished his sandwich and sat back in his chair, licking his fingers. He was aware of Minnie looking at him, hammer in hand. She wiped her brow with her bared forearm and put her tools to rest in the freezer. She sat down beside Daniel and laid a heavy red hand on his thigh.

"What?" said Daniel, wiping his nose with his sleeve.

"I spoke to Tricia."

The kitchen, strung with beads of light and toast smells and warmth, was suddenly taut as the strings of a violin. In the hall, the dog rested its nose on its paws. Daniel waited with his spine straight. Minnie still had her heavy hand on his leg. She began to rub his knee. He felt the friction of it, the warmth through his school trousers.

"I don't know how to tell you this, Danny. God knows I want to spare you more heartbreak, but you asked me to find out."

"What is it? Is she in the hospital again?"

"There's never a right time, so I'm just going to tell you. I found out today."

Minnie bit her lip.

"She is, isn't she? She's sick again."

"It was worse this time, pet." She looked at him without blinking, as if he would know without her having to say.

"What?"

"Darlin', your mum died."

The world was at once very quiet and very noisy. Everything seemed to stop and Daniel felt the pause, the hush. There was a ringing in his ears. It was like earlier, before the fight. It was as if he lost equilibrium for a moment or two. The noise in his ears made him distrust what he had heard and yet the dread that he could taste in his throat—sour, black—meant that he could not bear to hear it repeated.

Daniel stood up from the table, and felt at once Minnie's warm hands on his shoulders.

"It's all right, love," she said. "Don't run from this. I'll always be here for you."

In later years, when Daniel remembered these words, they would always make him run faster.

It was a shock, but a strange joy. He felt the jolt of it, as if shaken or punched, but then the smart and the strange thrill. His heart pounded, his tongue stuck to the roof of his mouth, his eyes were wide and dry.

Dead?

Air lapped in his mouth as if his throat was cut.

Dead.

He looked down and saw Minnie's hand on his arm; her warm fingers so much surer and stronger than his own mother's hands. They were strong, like a rope he could trust enough to leap off a rock, knowing it would hold him—poised in space and time—and take the weight as gravity pulled him down.

Dead.

Danny curled into Minnie. She didn't ask it of him. She didn't pull him into her, but he curled into her nonetheless, as a leaf curls in autumn because its energy is spent.

"There," she said. "There, there, my love, my precious child. You don't feel like it, but you're free—you're free now."

He didn't feel free, but he felt unattached and the fear of that made him press into Minnie again, for the first time really giving himself to her: asking her to love him.

LATER, SHE MADE HIM A CUP OF TEA, AND HE WAS FULL OF questions.

"How did she die?"

"It was another overdose, love. A big one."

He held the mug of tea in two hands and sipped it.

"Can I go to see her? Will she be buried somewhere?"

"No, love, it was a cremation. But you still have your necklace and you can think about her anytime you like."

"I should have been with her. I could've gotten the ambulance. I always get the ambulance to come in time."

"It's not your fault, Danny."

"It was because she was on her own."

"It's not your fault."

The thought of leaving Brampton came to him, of hitching a ride to Newcastle like before, but now that she was gone there was no point. Minnie was his mam now and he would try to make good.

23

THE PROSECUTION WERE NOW CLEARLY TRYING TO DEPICT Sebastian as an evil child. The witness list for the day included neighbors of the Crolls, children from Sebastian's school, and Sebastian's teacher. Out of the presence of the jury, Irene objected to the line of questioning as an attempt to elicit irrelevant evidence of bad character, but the judge allowed some leeway, particularly to do with Sebastian's reputation as a violent bully, seeing as it related to the offense.

Sebastian was alert today and focused on the trial. There had been no doodling, no swinging of his legs. His father was no longer in court. Daniel had spoken to Charlotte, who said that Kenneth had been called overseas, but would return in a few days. Charlotte seemed wrought: all tendon and sunken eyes and trembling fingertips. She was terrified to go outside for a cigarette, she told Daniel, in case she was set upon by the journalists. She couldn't bear the lies that people were writing about her son. Daniel had squeezed her elbow and told her to stay calm. *It'll get worse before it's our turn,* he told her. *You better prepare yourself.*

"*The Crown calls Mrs. Gillian Hodge.*"

Daniel watched her make her way to the witness box. The journalists in the gallery all scribbled furiously as she raised her right hand and swore to tell the truth. She was neighbor to both the Crolls and the Stokeses and a parent of two young girls. Daniel had spoken to Irene about her at the chambers party. Her voice was clear and strong, her gestures confident and composed. She was professional, yet maternal, with honest bright eyes and straight, prominent teeth. Daniel clasped his hands and waited, almost dreading her testimony. He felt Sebastian's small hand on his thigh and leaned down so that his ear was nearer to the boy's mouth.

"She hates me," was all he said.

"Just relax," said Daniel, almost to himself.

Gordon Jones swished his robe aside and assumed his stance by the lectern.

"Mrs. Hodge, could you tell us how you know the Crolls and their son, Sebastian?"

"I'm their neighbor, also neighbor to Madeline and Paul Stokes. I'm right between the two."

Daniel listened to her carefully. Her London public school voice was assertive and she almost didn't need the microphone in front of her.

"And their children," Jones prompted, "would you say you know them well?"

"My children used to play with both Ben and Sebastian, so I know the parents and their children well."

When she said *and their children,* Madeline turned distinctly toward Sebastian. Daniel straightened his spine as he felt her stern stare turn in their direction.

"You have two daughters, is that correct?"

"Yes."

"And how old are they?"

"One is eight and the other twelve."

"Your younger daughter is the same age as Ben Stokes?"

"Yes, they were in the same class at school." Gillian's large bright eyes sought out Madeline Stokes, who hung her head. Gillian cleared her throat.

"And your older daughter . . . similar age as Sebastian?"

"Yes, she's older, but doesn't play with the boys so much. My youngest is the tomboy. She liked playing with Ben . . ."

"Did you encounter any problems when your daughter played with either of the boys who lived near you?"

"Well, like I said, Poppy, my youngest, really did get on well with little Ben, but often Sebastian would try to join in, or else he would want to play with Poppy even when Ben wasn't there."

"Was this in any way problematic?"

Irene jumped to her feet and Daniel held his breath.

"With My Lordship's leave, I must object to this line, it really is hearsay . . ."

"Yes, but I'm going to allow it." Philip Baron's voice was deep and authoritative, although he sat slumped on the bench, corpulent in his robes. "I am satisfied that it is admissible in the interests of justice."

Irene sat down. She turned round to glance at Daniel. He nodded in support of her frustration.

"Sebastian could be very violent, very bullying . . ."

"In what way?"

"Once, when Poppy didn't want to play a game he wanted, he threatened her with a piece of broken glass. He was holding her hair so she couldn't get away and had the piece of glass right against her throat . . . I saw from the—"

Irene was on her feet again. "My Lord, I must protest this prejudicial line in front of the jury. My client has no opportunity to defend himself."

"Well," said Judge Baron, his fingers fluttering upward like an exalting Christ. "I see he has a more than adequate defense in you, Miss Clarke."

Irene opened her mouth to speak, but reluctantly sat down. Daniel scrawled a note and passed it to her junior, Mark. It read: *Ask her about domestic violence in Croll house?*

Irene turned when she read the note. Daniel met her gaze as she considered. The abuse brought context to Sebastian's behavior to the neighbor's children but Daniel understood that it was also risky. It could hint that Sebastian had learned to be violent, that he was driven to act out the scenes that he had witnessed in his family home.

"Poppy was quite terrified of him. She told me that she didn't like Sebastian, but I had encouraged her to try and get along. After seeing my daughter being threatened in that way, I forbade her to play with Sebastian again."

"Did you speak to Sebastian's parents about this incident?"

"I spoke to his mother, yes." Gillian stiffened, as if the memory was offensive to her. "She took no interest at all. She seemed utterly unconcerned. I just made sure that Poppy didn't play with him again."

"Thank you, Mrs. Hodge." Gordon Jones tidied his notes and sat down.

"Mrs. Hodge." Irene was composed.

Daniel leaned forward on the table, one hand under his chin. A second later, Sebastian did the same, mirroring Daniel's posture.

"Tell me, how long have you lived next door to the Crolls and the Stokeses?"

"I . . . don't remember, about three or four years."

"That's when you moved to Richmond Crescent?"

"Yes."

"The children played together. Did you spend time socially with any of the other parents?"

"Yes, of course, there was the odd glass of wine or cup of coffee—more with Madeline I would say—although I have been to visit . . . Charlotte once or twice."

"You told Charlotte Croll about Sebastian's behavior toward your daughter and you say she took no interest? A neighbor with whom you had socialized? Do you expect us to believe this?"

Gillian seemed to flush a little. Her large eyes searched the courtroom and then looked upward. "She was . . . understanding . . . but nothing changed. She didn't seem to have any control . . ."

"Mrs. Hodge, this incident to which you refer, where Sebastian purportedly threatened your daughter with a piece of glass, did you report this to anyone other than the boy's mother?"

Mrs. Hodge's eyes were wide. She looked up at Irene and shook her head.

"You're shaking your head. Did you not report the incident to the police or even the school—a social worker?"

Mrs. Hodge cleared her throat. "No."

"Why not?"

"I saw it happen and I told him off, severely, and then stopped Poppy playing with him again. That was the end of it. No harm was done."

"I see, *no harm was done*. When you told Sebastian off— *severely*—as you say, what was his reaction?"

"He was . . . apologetic. He is . . . very polite." Gillian cleared her throat. "He said sorry to Poppy when I asked him to."

At his side, Sebastian beamed up at Daniel, as if pleased by the praise.

"Mrs. Hodge, we have heard you say that Sebastian could be a little aggressive, that he sometimes used bad language. But did you *ever* have cause to report his behavior to the authorities in the nearly four years that you lived next door?"

Gillian Hodge reddened. "Not to the authorities, no."

"And as a good mother, if you had *ever* felt that Sebastian was any kind of real threat to your child or your neighbors' children, you would have done so immediately?"

"Well, yes . . ."

"You are the mother of two children, ages the same as the deceased and the defendant, is that correct?"

"Yes."

"Tell me, have either of your children ever acted in an aggressive way?"

Mrs. Hodge colored again.

Jones stood up, a hand held high in exasperation. "My Lord, I must question the relevance of this line of questioning."

"Yes, but I'll allow it," said Baron. "I have already ruled on the admissibility of this."

"Mrs. Hodge," Irene repeated, "have either of your children acted in an aggressive way?"

"Well, yes. All children can be aggressive."

"So they can," Irene returned.

She sat down.

The witness was excused.

"Very well, in view of the hour, I think this might be a convenient moment . . . " Baron twisted to face the jury. "Enjoy your lunch, but I'll remind you once again not to discuss the case unless all together."

There was a hush, a waterless wave, a rush of fabric and air in the stifled room as the court rose with the judge and then sat again in his absence. The clerk asked for the public gallery to be cleared and Daniel looked up to watch the reluctant faces turn away from the spectacle.

Daniel stood behind Sebastian's chair and squeezed both his shoulders gently.

"You okay, Sebastian?" Daniel asked, one eyebrow raised.

Sebastian started jumping up and down, nodding his head at Daniel as he did so; then he was touching his toes and spinning round. His suit was too big on the shoulders. The sharp edges of it rose up to his ears and down again as he jumped.

"Are you dancing, Seb?" the police officer asked. "It's time to go back downstairs."

"In a minute, Charlie," said Sebastian. "I've been sitting down so long."

"You can dance your way downstairs, then, Fred Astaire, okay?"

"Bye for now, Danny," said Sebastian, turning, the police officer's hand on his shoulder. "See you after lunch."

"See you later," said Daniel, shaking his head as he watched his young client go. Part of him wanted to laugh at the boy and his antics, but another part of him was deeply saddened.

Irene reached over and squeezed Daniel's elbow. "I just didn't feel it was right, Danny." Daniel smiled and looked her in the eye, thinking how pretty her eyes were. "It's a double-edged sword."

"Hey, I know, it's a judgment call," he said, smiling at her. "And honestly, it's probably the last thing Sebastian or his family wants to have revealed in open court."

She smiled at him.

"I trust your judgment," he said as they made their way out of court after Sebastian.

Daniel went down to the cell to speak to Sebastian. Charlotte was there too. As the guard let Daniel in, Sebastian kicked his mother in the thigh. She made no sound, but moved away, flat palm against her leg.

"Easy, Seb," said Daniel.

Sebastian was slumped against the wall, his lower lip pouting.

Charlotte seemed agitated after the evidence. "Why did they have to call her? She's always putting her nose in where it doesn't belong."

"She hates me," said Sebastian again.

"Gillian *hates us all*," said Charlotte.

"Can I talk to you outside, Charlotte?" Daniel asked.

She nodded in assent and turned from him to pick up her bag. Daniel could see her shoulder blades through her suit.

⌾

WHEN THE DOOR CLOSED, CHARLOTTE WANTED A CIGARETTE. Daniel begged permission from the security officer for her to go outside from the cells without going upstairs. Daniel was surprised that the guard allowed it, but it seemed that Charlotte had asked to be let out there to smoke before. The back door of the cells was isolated and free of reporters.

Her hands shook as she tried to light her cigarette. There was a slight breeze and so Daniel cupped his hand around it. When it was lit, she sucked hard before turning to him, deep frown lines cutting into her brow and her eyes turning down in distress.

"I know it's hard on you, Charlotte, but think how it is for Sebastian. Right now every single person who gives evidence is castigating him."

"He's my son. They're castigating me too."

"You have to be strong. This is just the beginning. It's only going to get worse."

"They shouldn't be allowed to say such things," she said. "That I can't control him, that I didn't care when he threatened other kids. I wasn't there when he tried to cut another child with a piece of glass."

Her voice was shrill, her face crumbling. She seemed so old suddenly.

"Try to remind yourself that when they stoop to things like this—bad character, hearsay—it's because they need to. Their evidence is mainly circumstantial. With his school reports showing a history of aggression this was going to come up, but try to remember that it doesn't prove—"

"*I'm* to blame—that's what they are trying to say. This is to be *my trial*. Find him guilty and say *it's all my fault?*"

Daniel reached out and squeezed Charlotte's shoulder. "Nobody's saying that . . ."

She turned away and when she turned back to take another drag from her cigarette, Daniel saw that she was crying. Her tears were black and they washed fragile white veins through her foundation.

"You're his mum," said Daniel. "He's eleven years old and on trial for murder. It could affect the rest of his life. He needs you to be strong for him."

The prison vans were huddled, dark and forbidding, in the courtyard. It reminded Daniel of the farm at night: the sheds where the animals were kept. There was a breeze and the emergency exit door they had slipped out of banged in the wind.

"Strong like you, you mean?" she said, knuckle to her lower lids, careful not to smudge. She placed her palm on Daniel's chest. Under his shirt, he felt his skin tingle at her touch. "*Feel* how strong you are."

"Charlotte," he whispered, taking a step back and feeling the building at his back. He smelled her heady perfume and then her cigarette breath. Her lips were an inch from his own. A column of ash trembled and fell onto the lapel of her jacket. Daniel stood up straight and let the back of his head touch the outside wall.

She let her hand fall slowly and he felt her long nails on his lower abdomen. He tightened his stomach muscles, and, under his shirt, the skin of his stomach withdrew from her.

There was something almost abhorrent about her, eye makeup smudged, foundation thick over her pores, but he felt a flush of empathy for her.

"Enough," he whispered. "Your son needs you."

Charlotte moved back, chastened. She seemed almost heart-broken, although Daniel knew that it was not just this rejection that had crushed her. Her eyes were smudges, her yellow fingers shaking the butt to her lips. "Sorry," she mouthed.

She let the cigarette fall to the ground. Daniel held the door.

"The Crown calls Geoffrey Rankine."

Daniel watched the man stand and walk to the witness box. He seemed too tall for the courtroom, trousers skirting the tops of his shoes. He had neatly trimmed, receding hair and eyebrows that were perpetually raised. When he swore to tell the truth before God he had a slight smile on his lips.

"Mr. Rankine, you reported to the police that you witnessed two boys fighting in Barnard Park on the afternoon of August the eighth. Is that correct?"

"That's correct. I've been watching the news since, and thinking if only I'd done something . . ." Rankine's voice was apathetic.

"You mention two sightings of the boys fighting in your statement of August the eighth; when did each of these occur?"

"It was about two in the afternoon the first time I saw them. I always take the dog out about then, just for a quick walk after lunch, let him do his business."

"Can you describe the two boys you saw fighting?"

"Well, it was like I said to the police; they both had short brown hair and there wasn't much of a difference between them in height, but one was slightly smaller. One was in a long-sleeved white top and the other in a red T-shirt."

"My Lord . . . if I may direct Your Lordship and the jury to page fifty-seven in your bundle, and the picture and description of Ben Stokes's clothing on the day that he died, particularly the red T-shirt," said Gordon Jones, allowing his glasses to balance on the end of his nose as he viewed his own bundle. "And on page fifty-eight the clothing recovered by forensics worn by the defendant on the date of the murder . . . Did you know either of the boys, Mr. Rankine?"

"No, not by name, but I had seen them both around. Their faces were familiar. We live not far from each other and I'm always out with the dog."

"Tell us about the first time you saw the boys that day."

"I was walking my dog, not in the park, but along the pavement that runs down Barnsbury Road. He's an old dog, you know, likes a good sniff around. I'm a keen walker and I get frustrated with him. That day was like all the others; he was possibly even slower than normal. It was sunny. The park was busy, I would say, and I knew some of the other dog walkers who I normally see, but then I became aware of two young boys fighting on the crest of the hill."

"How far away were you from the boys, would you say?"

"Maybe twenty, thirty feet—no more."

"What did you see?"

"Well, at first I wasn't much concerned. It was just two young boys having a bit of a scrap, but one of the boys began to get the upper hand. I remember he grabbed the smaller boy by the hair and forced him down onto his knees. He was punching him in the kidneys and the stomach. I have two sons, and boys will be boys, and normally I wouldn't interfere, but this seemed rather excessive, somewhat dangerous or . . . violent."

"Which of the boys you described seemed to be 'getting the upper hand'?"

"The slightly taller boy, the one in white."

"You spoke to the boys—what did you say?"

"Well, it just seemed they were getting a bit rough with each other, you know. I told them to cut it out."

"What happened?"

"Well, they stopped and one of the boys turned to me and smiled, and said they were only playing."

"Which boy was this?"

"The defendant. I wasn't entirely reassured, but boys will be boys as I say—I left them to it." Rankine's cheeks became suddenly gray. He hung his head. "I keep reliving it. I shouldn't have walked away, you see. I should have done something . . . if I had only guessed what would happen."

Rankine stood up straight suddenly. He looked up the center of the court in the direction of the Stokeses. "I'm sorry," he said.

Gordon Jones nodded understandingly, then continued: "You say they were being *rough with each other*? Did you regard it as rough play that was just getting out of hand, or would you say that one of the children was the aggressor?"

"Maybe, yes, I think so. It was a while ago, but I think the boy in the white top . . . He was the one the police asked me about, I think after they found the . . . body." Mr. Rankine shook his head and put a hand over his eyes.

"What did the boys do after you spoke to them?"

"Well, they went on their way and I went mine."

"Which way did they head?"

"Down the park toward the adventure playground . . . that youth club place."

"You described one of the boys as being 'in distress'?"

"Well, the police asked me about that, and I think that, yes, I think that was the case."

"Which boy did you perceive to be in distress?"

"Well, I think I said the one with the red top . . ."

"And you still remember that to be the case?"

"I think so, yes. Best I can recall."

"What features or aspects of the boy's behavior led you to think that he was distressed?"

"Well, I think the boy in the red top might have been crying."

"Might have been?"

"Well, I was a bit away by this time, several yards. It looked like it."

"By that do you mean wailing, a red face, tears?"

"Tears maybe, yes, maybe tears and a red face. I seem to recall him rubbing at his eyes."

Mr. Rankine looked into the distance, his own watery eyes trying to see again what he had seen months before, and ignored.

"The defendant in his interview confirmed that he did see you just after two that day, and that you called on him and the deceased to stop fighting. Did you see the boys fighting at another point that day?"

"Yes, much later on, it must have been about three thirty, or maybe even four o'clock. I was just going to the shop. I looked over at the park and in the adventure playground I saw the same boys fighting again. I remember because I considered crossing the road and telling them off again . . . I wish I had . . ."

"Describe this second sighting."

"I looked over at the park as I walked to the shop. I saw them—the same white shirt and red T-shirt. I saw the boy in white swinging his fists at the boy in red."

"But this time you did nothing?"

"No," said Rankine, seeming to crumple in the witness box. "I'm sorry. I'm so sorry." He put a hand to his mouth and pressed his eyes shut.

"What brought you to report the two sightings to the police, at the incident van set up on Barnsbury Road, shortly after Ben went missing?"

"Well, the next day there was the picture of Ben. He had been missing all night. I knew instantly when I saw it that he had been the little boy being beaten—the one in the red T-shirt."

SEBASTIAN HAD BEEN FOLLOWING THE EVIDENCE INTENTLY, watching Rankine with a thin frown between his two small eyebrows. Sometimes he leaned into Daniel, peering over the crook in his arm at the notes he was making on the testimony.

RANKINE SHIFTED RESTLESSLY IN THE WITNESS BOX AS IRENE stood up and placed her notes on the lectern. Journalists craned from the gallery.

"Listening to your testimony, Mr. Rankine, and comparing it with your police statement, it would appear that you are not terribly sure of what you saw on the afternoon of August the eighth. I refer you to page twenty-three in your bundle. This is your sworn statement, which you gave to the police. Please could you read from the second paragraph."

Rankine cleared his throat then began, "'*I saw two boys whom I recognized from the neighborhood fighting on the crest of the hill in Barnard Park. Both boys were white. One of the boys was smaller, possibly younger, and dressed in a red T-shirt and jeans. He was being attacked violently by a larger boy, who was wearing a white or pale blue shirt.*'"

"Thank you, Mr. Rankine. The fight between the two boys you describe as 'a violent attack' on one boy, and then again as 'a bit of rough fighting,' and note yourself that 'boys will be boys.' Which was it, Mr. Rankine? Did you witness a violent assault, or was it a bit of rough and tumble play between two young schoolboys?"

"It was quite violent. One of the boys definitely had the upper hand . . ."

"Quite violent? Was there any blood? Did either of the boys seem to be in any way injured as a result of the blows?"

"Well, like I said, there were a few hard punches. The younger boy did seem to be distressed . . ."

"What exact words did you use to stop the fight?"

"I think I said, 'Boys, stop that . . . that's enough of that.'"

"I see. Did you enter the park and try to pull them apart?"

"No, like I said, they stopped as soon as I called over."

"I see, and at this time neither boy was obviously injured."

"Well, no."

"And so you went on your way and they ran down the hill toward the adventure playground?"

"Yes."

"You didn't alert any authorities about the attack at this time?"

"No."

"What in fact did you do?"

"I went home."

"I see, and what did you do there?"

"I . . . watched some television."

"So it was fair to say that after witnessing this initial 'violent attack' you were unconcerned for the boys' safety?"

"Well, yes, but then, when I saw the boy was missing . . ."

"To summarize your initial sighting of the boys, considering both your police statement and your testimony here today, it would be fair to say that the fight, which you have described as *somewhat violent,* was in fact a bit of normal rough and tumble that did not merit reporting at the time, nor did it distract you from your other activities for the rest of the day, such as your afternoon television viewing. Would that be correct?"

"Well, I . . . I suppose."

"As my learned friend and colleague has reminded the court, my client stated on interview that he was play-fighting with the victim on the afternoon of his death and does remember an adult calling on them to stop. Let us now move to your supposed later sighting of the boys. You have testified that this second sighting was at about three thirty or four o'clock. Can you be more exact?"

"No, but it was about that time."

"I refer to page thirty-six in the jury bundle, a map of Barnard Park and Barnsbury Road."

Time was taken to locate Mr. Rankine's exact position on the far side of the Barnsbury Road at the time of the sighting. The witness agreed that he was probably fifty yards from the boys at the time of the second sighting. Mr. Rankine's optician records were placed into evidence, showing that he was short-sighted, with a prescription of -2.50. Rankine then gave evidence that he only wore glasses to watch television or to drive. After this was established, Irene launched her attack.

"The boy you saw in the white *or pale blue* top could have been any number of young people in the area. Is that not so . . . ?"

"I recognize him now to be the . . . defendant."

"Now, I see . . . *now*. Earlier you told us that the boys you saw were not 'noticeably different' in height, but your original statement to the police suggested a large and a small boy fighting. Which was it?"

"Well, one was slightly larger. There wasn't much in it, but one was discernibly larger—taller, as I said before."

"I see, and the clothing worn by the larger boy was 'white or blue' but now you seem sure that it was white?"

"I remember it being white now."

"*Now* you do, I see. Was that because the police specifically questioned you about a 'boy in a white shirt' whom they had already arrested?"

"I don't think so. I can't say for sure."

"Indeed, I don't think you are sure of much, Mr. Rankine, are you?"

Daniel tried not to smile. He felt a small swell of pride for her.

"Well, I . . . ,"

"Let us go back to your original statement to the police. I refer you to page thirty-nine, paragraph two in your bundle. Please could you read your statement, from '*sometime later that afternoon*' . . ."

Rankine cleared this throat and then began to read. "'. . . *sometime later that afternoon, I saw the boys again, this time fighting in the adventure playground. The smaller boy in red was being attacked by a larger person . . .*'"

"Let me stop you there, Mr. Rankine. *'A larger person'* . . . *'A larger person.'* Are you sure this was the defendant?"

"Yes, I had seen him earlier that day."

"Mr. Rankine, I remind you that you are under oath. You did see Sebastian earlier that day, but did you see him fighting in the adventure playground hours later? The Crown and the defense concur that there is no CCTV evidence of this sighting. We know that you were not wearing your glasses and that you were on the far side of the road, looking through the bushes and railings that surround the adventure playground. I suggest that you assumed the person you saw was my client, whom you had seen earlier that day—"

Judge Baron leaned forward. "Miss Clarke—will a question for the witness be coming anytime soon?"

"Yes, M'Lord."

"I am so pleased," the judge replied, mouth turned down.

"Mr. Rankine, is it not true that you had no way of identifying my client from the distance stated, particularly considering your shortsightedness?"

"I thought it was the boy from earlier."

"Really? What did you mean when you described the person you saw apparently attacking the deceased as *'a larger person'*? Can you tell us if you meant to indicate a person taller or heavier than the victim?"

"I thought it was the boy from earlier," Rankine stammered. He seemed confused, pulling at his earlobe. "He was a good bit taller, a little heavier than the little boy . . ."

"A good bit taller and heavier? We submit into evidence the height and weight of the victim, Benjamin Stokes, as four feet one inch and sixty-three pounds. The defendant was just

four feet three and sixty-five pounds when placed on remand.
I put it to you the boys were of similar height and weight and
one was not in fact 'a good bit taller and heavier.' I suggest, Mr.
Rankine, that who you saw later that afternoon was not Sebastian Croll, who you called to earlier, but was in fact someone
else entirely. Could that be so?"

"Well, I was sure at the time . . ."

"Mr. Rankine, you are under oath. We know your eye
prescription and we know the distance that you were from the
two people you claim to have witnessed at three thirty or four
o'clock that day. Could you not have seen someone else, possibly even an adult, with the victim?"

"Yes," Rankine said finally, seeming to slump in the witness box as he admitted. "It's possible."

"Thank you," said Irene. She was about to sit, but the witness stood, shaking his head.

"I'd be glad to be wrong," said Rankine. "If I never saw
him then I never could have stopped it happening. Glad to be
wrong."

"Thank you, no further questions, M'Lord." Irene swept
her gown under her before she sat.

"Irene's quite a good barrister," Sebastian whispered to
Daniel when the jury had been excused and he was about to
be taken back down to the cells. "He never saw me at the playground. He saw someone else."

Daniel felt a chill. He put a hand on Sebastian's shoulder as
he handed him over to the police officer. Daniel felt sure that
he fully comprehended everything that was going on.

Irene rolled her eyes at Daniel as she left the room.

⤙

Daniel worked late at the office and arrived home in Bow after eight. He closed the door of his flat and leaned his forehead against the frame. His home smelled unlived in. He turned the heating on and made a cup of tea, changed out of his work clothes into jeans and a T-shirt, and put a load of clothes into the washing machine.

He called Cunningham, Minnie's lawyer, to check on the progress on the house, but his cell phone was turned to answer phone. It was just then that there was a knock at the door. Daniel assumed it was a neighbor, as there was a buzzer entry system from the street. He opened the door to find a small, corpulent man with an iPhone held up like a microphone.

"Can I help you?" said Daniel, frowning, two fingers hooked into the back pocket of his jeans.

"You're Daniel Hunter, the Angel Killer's lawyer," the man said. "I wondered if you wanted to talk to me. I'm from the *Mail*."

Daniel felt anger flood his muscles, hot and quick. He laughed in a single syllable, then stepped onto the doorstep. "How dare you. How did you find me . . . ?"

"The electoral register," the man said blankly. Daniel noticed his crumpled shirt and nicotine-stained fingers.

"Get off my property right now before I call the police."

"It's a public stairwell . . ."

"It's *my* stairwell, *get out*," said Daniel, so loud that it echoed in the hall. He heard the northern lilt to his voice. His accent always thickened in anger.

"We're doing a story on you anyway. Might be better for you if you said something," said the man, again without expression, looking away to touch his phone and, Daniel presumed, record their conversation.

The action seemed to release something in Daniel. It had been years since he had hit anyone or been physical in that way. He took the man by the collar and slammed him against the wall of the stairwell. The phone fell to the ground with a crack.

"Do I have to tell you again?" said Daniel, his face leaning down close to the man's. He could smell damp raincoat and mentholated gum.

The man twisted from his grasp, bent in a hurry to pick up the phone and almost fell down the steps to the main door. Daniel waited on the landing until he heard the main door click shut.

Inside he paced in the hall, running his hand through his hair. He slammed the wall with his open palm.

He walked into the living room, cursing under his breath. He saw Minnie's photograph on his mantelpiece and imagined what she would say to him now. *What's a bright boy like you needing to use your fists for anyway?* He smiled despite himself.

He tried to imagine her coming to visit him: struggling up the stairs, asking why he couldn't find something on the ground floor. She would cook for him and they would drink gin together and laugh about the fights they had had.

But she was dead and now he would never know what it would be like to be an adult with her. She had taken him in as a child and he had left her as a child—older but still a child—angry and embittered. He had missed the chance to share a gin and hear her story—hear it as an equal, not as someone who had saved him. It was that more than anything that he regretted now, the sense that he had missed out on knowing her properly.

Daniel got up and went into the kitchen in search of gin.

He kept his spirits in a box in a cupboard. There were all sorts left over from parties: Madeira, Advocat, Malibu rum, and Daniel rarely touched them. He lifted the box down and searched until he found a half-full bottle of Bombay Sapphire. It was better than she would have allowed herself, yet Daniel took care to make it up the way that she would have liked: a tall glass, ice in first and then the lemon (when she had them) squeezed over the top. He was sure she added the ice first so as to fool herself that the measure was not as large as it seemed. Tonic fizzed over the ice and gin and lemon and Daniel stirred it with the end of a fork. He sipped in the kitchen, remembering her pink fist gripping the glass and her twinkling eyes.

The football was on, but he muted the sound and picked up her address book, turning again to the page with Jane Flynn's number and Hounslow address. He looked at his watch. It was just after nine—not too late for a call, he reasoned.

Daniel dialed the number, which Minnie had written carefully in blue ballpoint pen. He did not remember Minnie being in contact with Jane, and so he reasoned that this number may have been recorded while Norman was still alive.

Daniel listened to the ring as he sipped his drink. The very smell of the drink reminded him of Minnie.

"Hello?" The voice sounded echoey, lonely, as if spoken in a dark hall.

"Hello, I wanted to talk to . . . Jane Flynn?"

"Speaking. Who is this?"

"My name's Daniel Hunter. I was . . . Minnie Flynn was my . . . If I'm right she was your brother's wife?"

"You know Minnie?"

"Yes, can you talk right now?"

"Yes, but . . . how can I help you? How is Minnie? I often think of her."

"Well, she . . . died this year."

"Oh, I'm sorry. That's awful. How did you say you knew her . . . ?"

"I'm her . . . son . . . she adopted me." The words took the breath from him and he leaned back against the sofa, winded.

"How awful," she said again. "God . . . thank you so much for letting me know. What did you say your name was?"

"Danny . . ."

"Danny," Jane repeated. Daniel could hear children screaming with laughter in the background, above the sound of the television.

"Did you know her well?" he asked.

"Well, we all used to go out in London when we were young. She and Norman met down here. We would go dancing together, have fish and chips. After she and Norman moved back to Cumbria—not so much."

"You and Norman were from up there originally?"

"Yes, but I rarely went back. Norman missed it, missed the life, but I've always liked the city. When is the funeral?"

"It was a few months ago. I'm late in calling round . . ." Daniel colored slightly: assuming the guise of the dutiful son. "She left me her address book and I saw your number in it. I thought I'd ring, just in case you were still there . . . in case you wanted to know."

"I appreciate it. Such sad news, but . . . God bless her, she didn't have an easy life, did she?"

"Do you know what happened to them—Delia and Norman?" Daniel could still feel his cheeks burning.

"It took me years to get over it. Part of me was always angry with Minnie . . . that must sound awful to you, I'm sorry, but of course now I realize that was wrong of me. It's just how you feel when something like that happens. You want to blame someone, and you can't blame your brother. I think that was why we didn't keep in touch. I know you must think I'm awful . . ."

"I understand," said Daniel, quietly. "What happened to Norman?"

"Well, when Delia died, Norman took a shotgun into the garden and . . . put it into his mouth. Minnie wasn't home. The neighbors found him. It was in all the papers. I understood him being . . . He loved that little one, but it wasn't his fault . . . Their marriage was ruined, you see. I think they went through a really black period. He blamed Minnie for it. . . ."

"I think Minnie blamed herself."

"She was driving, after all . . . He made it to the hospital to see her one last time: he was with the little one when she died but he . . . he never recovered. It was just a few months after she died that he killed himself.

"I hope you never have to go through that, Danny. I was up in Cumbria for my niece's funeral, then back three months later for my brother's. Is it any wonder I don't care to go back there now?"

"What was Minnie like, at Delia's funeral, I mean?"

"She did well. She had us all back to the house and she'd made a spread. She didn't shed a tear. We were all in bits, but the pair of them had it together. I remember something though . . ."

"What was that?"

"We were done. The priest had said his bit. The gravediggers were filling in the hole, but then Minnie twisted away from Norman and ran back and threw herself down in the mud by the grave. She was wearing a pale gray flowery dress. She threw herself down on her knees by Delia's grave and reached in over the edge. We had to pull her back. Norman had to pull her back. She would have gone into that grave with her. That was the only sign, really, that she was, that she was . . . when we were back at the house she had made fresh sponge cakes. Fresh sponge cakes, not bought, her own. She must have been up baking the night before. And I remember her passing them around with a smile on her face and her eyes dry . . . but with those two brown circles of mud on her dress."

Daniel didn't know what to say. There was silence as he imagined the scene that Jane described.

"When Norman died, she didn't try to throw herself into his grave. She hadn't even changed her clothes from what I could see. She was in her housecoat. She wasn't even wearing stockings. There were no sponges at Norman's funeral. Minnie just waited until it was over and then left. At the time I didn't think kindly of her, but now I don't blame her. She had reached her limit. We all have our limits, you know. She was very angry with him. God, I was too, after I got over the shock."

Silence again.

"I'm so sorry," said Daniel.

"I know—it's a terrible business. Minnie and I didn't keep in touch because I blamed her for causing Norman's death, but the truth is . . . and I tell you, it's only recently I've managed to admit this to myself . . . it was his choice, not hers, and it was a cowardly choice. We all die, after all. Nothing surer. He just couldn't bear it. I knew Minnie, she would have hated that . . .

cowardice . . . especially since she braved it out, and her loss must have been even harder to bear."

"Why do you say that?"

"Why, because she was driving. She must've thought, what if the little one had been in the front with the seat belt on . . . what if she'd swerved in a slightly different direction. It would drive you mad. She did well to remain sane. I trust she did . . . ?"

"Very sane," said Daniel, allowing himself a small smile. "Saner than most."

He exhaled: half sigh and half laugh.

"What do you do now, Danny? Where are you calling from?"

"I'm a lawyer, I'm in London too. In the East End."

"I'm sorry for your loss, pet."

"Thanks for talking to me. I just—"

"No, thanks for letting me know. I would've come to the funeral if I'd known. She was a good woman. All the best . . ."

Daniel hung up.

A good woman.

He finished his gin, knowing that the story of the mud on her dress would be true.

24

MINNIE WAS ON HER KNEES IN THE DIRT, PLANTING FLOW-ers in the front garden. She pressed the cuttings down and then knuckled the earth around them. She sat up when Carol-Ann and Daniel walked past, schoolbags hanging off their shoulders, school shirts hanging out of their trousers.

"A'right, Min'?" said Carol-Ann.

Minnie got up and walked toward them, dusting the dirt from her hands on her skirt.

"How did it go then?"

"A'right," said Danny, throwing his schoolbag down on the grass. "Another five next week though."

"But these went well," Minnie prompted, taking Blitz by the scruff of his neck to stop him sniffing at Carol-Ann. "You feel confident . . ."

"Who knows," said Daniel. He was taller than she was now,

but even though she looked up at him when he spoke somehow he still felt smaller. "It was okay. We'll know soon enough."

"Okay is good. Carol-Ann, are you staying for your tea, pet? It's Friday, I bought some fish."

"Aye," she said. "That'd be great, like, Min'."

The pair fell onto the grass beside Minnie, chatting and teasing each other, as she continued with her planting. Daniel had changed out of his school clothes. Carol-Ann screamed as Daniel tickled her, and Minnie looked over at them both, smiling. The pair flopped back onto the grass. Carol-Ann rolled over and then threw her leg over Daniel. She leaned over his face, pinning each of his wrists to the grass.

"Prisoner?" he asked.

"That's right," she said, trying to tickle him as he pinned his arms to his sides and swatted her hands away.

A white butterfly floated, blind and charming, over Daniel's face. He watched its dizzy flight.

"Hold still," cried Carol-Ann suddenly. "It's on your hair. I want to catch it. I'll give it to you as a present."

Daniel lay still, watching as Carol-Ann reached above his head and cupped her hands around the butterfly.

"Enough!" Minnie was standing above them, her voice raised.

Daniel was confused. He raised himself up on his elbows, and Carol-Ann, still astride him with her hands cupped around the butterfly, turned.

"Let it go *right now*," said Minnie.

Carol-Ann opened her hands immediately. She climbed to her feet and put a hand on Minnie's arm.

"I'm sorry, Min," she said. "I didn't mean to upset you, like."

"I'm sorry too," said Minnie, turning away, a hand on her forehead. "It's just if you hold them, you can take the powder off their wings. They won't be able to fly and they'll die."

CAROL-ANN RUBBED BREAD CRUMBS ONTO THE HADDOCK, while Daniel cut the potatoes into thick chips, dropped them into the wire sieve and lowered them into the deep-fat fryer. Minnie fed the animals and then they sat at the kitchen table, three spaces cleared amid the old newspapers and spaghetti jars. Daniel had just turned sixteen.

Carol-Ann would stay for dinner two or three nights a week. It was time for their GCSEs and Minnie had been fraught for weeks: asking him if he shouldn't study first before going out to play football, buying him a new desk for his bedroom and telling him to take long baths to relax and go to bed early.

"You don't realize it and it won't feel like it," she kept saying to him, biting her top lip between sentences, "but this is an important time. You're at the doorway between one life and another. I don't care what you do, but I want you to go to university. I want you to have choices. I want you to see just what's on offer."

She helped him with his biology and chemistry and told him to eat more because it would feed his brain.

"This is good, Minnie," said Carol-Ann, squeezing a spot of ketchup onto the corner of her plate. Blitz watched them intently, a thin string of saliva stretching from his lower jaw toward the floor.

"Eat up then, love." She passed a chip to Blitz, who snapped it from her fingers hungrily.

Daniel was eating with one elbow on the table.

"So, basically, what you're telling me is that it was no problem. There was nothing that you couldn't do, and you had time to check it all through before you left?"

"Aye, it were fine," he said, his mouth full and his gaze on the fresh flakes of fish on his fork.

"What's that, love?" she said, brushing the hair out of his eyes with her left hand.

He sat up and pulled away from her gently. He didn't like it when she touched him like that when his friends were here. When they were on their own, he would allow it.

"I said it were fine," he said, not loud, but meeting her eyes this time.

"Don't look at me like that with your baby browns." She raised her eyes at Carol-Ann. "I was only asking, so I was." She smiled at him defiantly and gave another chip to the dog.

Later, after Carol-Ann had gone home, he got his books out again and sat at the big oak desk she had bought for him. She brought him hot chocolate and homemade scones thick with butter for his supper.

"Don't work too much longer, love," she said, rubbing the space between his shoulder blades. "You don't want to get overtired."

"I'm fine."

"Will I run your bath now? Get a good soak and then come and talk to me."

"All right."

"I know you did well today."

"How do you know?"

"I just know. My Irish sixth sense. This is going to be the start of something great for you. You had some rough luck when you were little, but this is you on your way." She made a fist and held it up to her face, smiling. "I can see you in a sharp suit one day. Maybe you'll be in London, or maybe Paris or something, earning the big bucks. And I'll come and visit you . . . will you take me out for lunch?"

"Aye, I suppose so. A slap-up lunch, anything you fancy."

Minnie threw back her head and laughed. He liked her laugh. It bubbled up from her stomach. She put a hand on the desk to steady herself.

"You're a card, so you are, but I'll hold you to it."

Again she wiped the hair back from his face and planted a wet kiss on his forehead. He smiled and pulled away from her again.

"Your bath'll be ready in ten minutes. You be sure and get finished by then, or it'll get cold."

Daniel listened as she made her way downstairs, the floorboards and banister protesting under her weight. Blitz barked once as she neared the foot of the stairs, irked that she should think to leave him for so long. He heard the living room door creak shut and the muffled sound of the television making its way up through the floorboards. Outside it was still light and early summer birds were springing from tree to tree. He still didn't like this place: wanted the city with all its distrust and unassumed freedom. But at the same time, he felt at home with her.

It had been more than three years since she had adopted him, and yes, he did feel different. He felt looked after. It was this which was perhaps most strange to him. When he stopped fighting her, she had lavished him with care and attention. Even when she embarrassed him, kissing him in front of Carol-Ann or praising him to the other stall holders at the market, he felt warmed by her. She told him that she loved him, and he believed her.

In the bath, he let himself sink down so that his shoulders were underwater. He was now five feet ten and a half, over half a foot taller than Minnie. He could no longer stretch out in the bath. He was too thin, though. He made a fist and pulled his forearm toward his face so that he could inspect his bicep. In addition to his football training, he had started to do weights. The television became louder when the living room door opened. He heard Minnie pad back and forth to the kitchen. The bathroom was steamy, although he had the window opened three inches—enough for him to see out into the yard. The rowan was like a tendonous, skeletal hand stretching out of the earth at the night sky.

On the shelf in the bathroom was the butterfly, placed just to the side the way Minnie liked it. He wiped sweat off his face and watched the butterfly, imagining the small child placing it on the shelf. Daniel swallowed and then looked away.

He dried himself and dressed in tracksuit bottoms and T-shirt. He toweled his hair dry and pushed it off his face. It was getting long on the front. He wiped a hand across his jaw, inspecting it for signs of a beard. It was smooth and clean and hairless.

In the kitchen he made himself toast and poured a glass of milk, then went into the living room to sit with her.

"Do you want some toast? I'll make you some."

"No, love, I'm grand. Are you hungry again? You have a bottomless pit for a stomach, so you do. I wish I could eat like you."

She tried to put her elbow on the edge of the armchair but missed and spilled some of her drink onto the floor.

"There I go again," she said, dabbing the spill with the heel of her sock.

Daniel gave Blitz the last of his toast, then finished his milk as he listened to Minnie rant at the news. The prime minister, John Major, was talking about the potential for economic recovery.

"Yer arse in parsley," Minnie railed at the screen. "They'll not be satisfied till they have this country on its knees . . . God I hated that woman, but he's not much better."

She wasn't expecting an answer from Daniel and so he said nothing. He put a piece of coal on the fire.

"How was your bath, love?" she asked him, her cheeks wet, as if with fresh tears. She leaned over the arm of her chair, a smile on her face and her eyes merry. "Did you get your work finished?"

"Aye."

"That's good."

"Are you all right?" he asked her, seeing her wipe her face again.

"I'm grand, love. I'm just incensed by the sight of that bloody man. Change the channel or turn it off. I can't even stomach the sight of him."

Daniel got up and changed the channel. It was sports and he glanced at her to see if she would allow it. Usually she would ask him to watch it on the black and white in the kitchen, or she would say yes, but then lose patience. Tonight her eyes wavered before the screen, then closed for a long blink.

As Daniel sat down to watch the game, her eyes closed and her head twice bobbed down sharply, waking her. When her eyes began to close again, he got up and gently took the glass from her hand and carried it through to the kitchen. The dog wanted out and so he opened the back door. He washed up the dishes from dinner and wiped the portion of the kitchen table from which they had eaten.

When Blitz came back inside, Daniel locked up, closing the windows and bolting the back door. The dog settled into its basket as the house warmed to Minnie's snores.

In the living room her head was thrown back in the chair, the fingers of her right hand still reaching out to grasp the glass that Daniel had removed.

Daniel stood with his hands on his hips for a moment and sighed. He turned off the television and put the guard across the fire. He turned out the light beside her chair then took her hand and helped her forward until he could get an arm underneath her shoulder.

"No, leave me, love, leave me," she protested.

But he lifted her up, put her arm over his shoulder and walked her, a hand by her waist, out of the living room door and upstairs. Twice he had to stop and steady himself, a foot behind him on the lower step, when she leaned back into him, but he got her upstairs and then lowered her onto her bed, where she lay with her lips parted and her torso twisted so that her feet were on the floor.

Daniel knelt and unlaced her boots, slipped them off and

then her big wool socks. He was always amazed by the small-
ness of her feet. He loosened her blouse and peeled the cardigan
from her, then took the clasp from her hair, allowing her long
gray curls to spill over the pillow.

He took her feet and slipped them under the covers, lifted
her shoulders a little and centered her on the pillow before
pulling the quilt over her.

"You're a good lad," she whispered to him, when he was
still leaning over her. Always she would do this: surprise him
with her consciousness. "I love you, so I do."

He tucked her in, and turned off the night.

"G'night, Mam," he whispered in the near dark.

25

IT WAS THE SECOND WEEK OF SEBASTIAN'S TRIAL. DANIEL was deliberately not reading the newspapers, but he was distracted by a story he saw when he glanced over someone's shoulder on the tube. When he reached St. Paul's he ran into a newsagent's where he picked up a copy of the *Mail* and flicked through it. On page six there was his photograph. He was frowning; it was a shot taken at the entrance to the Old Bailey. The headline read: "The Man Who Wants to Free the Angel Killer." The report also mentioned Irene.

Daniel put the paper back on the rack. When he arrived at court, it was just before nine. The crowds down the Old Bailey road had not lessened since the trial began. A policeman shielded Daniel as he tried to enter the court, a cup of coffee in one hand and his briefcase in the other.

"Mr. Hunter, what's the defense going to be?" a journalist

shouted, and Daniel turned in case he recognized the man, but it was not the journalist who had called at his flat. "Would you say the Crown's winning?"

The crowd jostled around the reporter.

Inside the Old Bailey, Daniel straightened his shoulders and walked toward Court 13 looking up at the ornate, painted walls. He saw Irene minutes before the judge came in. She tapped his shoulder as she passed, and bent down to whisper: "Bastards," so close that her voice tickled his ear. He knew she had seen the article.

"They don't know how they pervert justice," she said. "How dare they be judge and jury?"

"Don't worry about it," Daniel whispered back. "Good luck."

"The Crown calls John Cairns."

John Cairns was a man uncomfortable in a suit. Daniel could see from the way the suit pulled at the shoulders that Cairns felt constricted. Cairns stepped into the witness box and took a sip of water before looking at the jury, at the judge, and then at Gordon Jones, who was addressing him in long silk robes with a sharp upturned jaw.

"Mr. Cairns, you work at the Barnard Park Adventure Playground, is that correct?"

"Yes."

"Please can you state your role, and how long you have been employed there?"

"I am one of the play managers, and I've worked there for the last three years." His voice was thick, as if he was nervous or recovering from a cold.

The court was freshly convened and rapt.

"Mr. Cairns, can you tell us about the morning of Monday, August ninth, of this year?"

Mr. Cairns sniffed, and leaned on the witness box for support. "I was first in. I'm always first. I opened up as usual and then made a cup of coffee. I always check the yard on Monday, in case any of the ropes are loose or . . . usually I need to tidy up some litter, so I did that next. It was while I was doing that, that I found . . . the child's body."

"The body was later identified to be the body of the victim, Benjamin Stokes. Can you confirm for us the exact location of the body when you found it?"

"It was partially hidden under the small wooden house that we have in the corner of the playground, so in the far corner of the playground near Barnsbury Road and Copenhagen Street."

"At this point I would direct you to page fifty-three in the jury bundle. You will see here a map of the playground with the areas identified by numbered and lettered squares. Please can you tell us the approximate location on this map?"

"E three."

"Thank you. Was the body immediately obvious to you?"

"No, not at all. I saw there was something there, but to be honest I just thought it was a plastic carrier bag or something, litter that had gotten caught by the trees near the fence. . . ."

There was a gasp from the gallery. Daniel glanced up to see Mrs. Stokes lean forward, a hand over her mouth. Her husband pulled her into him, but she was now inconsolable and had to be taken out. Sebastian sat up straight with his hands folded in his lap. He seemed interested in the testimony of the play man-

ager and also strangely pleased by Mrs. Stokes's breakdown.
Daniel put a hand on his back to ask him to turn around when
he turned to watch Mrs. Stokes go.

Kenneth Croll was in court, and he leaned forward then,
rising out of his seat to do so, and poked Sebastian in the back.
The thick finger was enough to send Sebastian jolting forward
in his seat. Daniel glanced at Croll out of the corner of his
eye. Sebastian began scrunching up his eyes again, and rocking
slightly, back and forth.

The scribblers in the gallery had noticed. As had the jury.

"Please continue, Mr. Cairns," Jones prompted.

"Well, as I drew nearer, I saw the boy's trainers, and again . . .
my first thought was that they were discarded shoes and trousers
that had possibly been thrown over the fence . . . you get that
kind of thing . . . but as I drew near . . ."

"We have photographs of the body as it was when you discovered it. If the jury could refer to page three in their bundle."

Daniel watched as the jury viewed the photograph, hands
over their mouths in distaste, although there was worse to
come. Sebastian watched their faces. At the same time he was
drawing in ballpoint pen—a picture of trees.

"Mr. Cairns, I am sorry to press you on this, I know it must
be disturbing for you to recall, but if you could continue telling
us what you saw."

"Well, as I drew near, I saw that it wasn't a pile of clothes,
but rather a small boy, underneath the wooden house."

"Immediately you could see that it was a boy?"

"No, I could see his legs sticking out. His face was well
hidden, in the trees and under the house, but I realized it was
a child."

"What did you do?"

"I crawled through the trees and then down on my belly to pull him out from under the wooden house, but as I drew near I realized . . ."

"Yes, Mr. Cairns?"

"Well, I realized that he was dead and so I daren't touch him. I went inside immediately and called the police."

"Were you aware that a little boy had gone missing?"

"Well, I don't live in the area, but when I came to work in the morning, I saw the pictures and I saw the incident van. I hadn't watched the news. I didn't know what it was all about . . ."

"You just described to us how you accessed the body," Jones placed his glasses over his nose and held his notes at arm's length to read: "Crawling . . . on your belly." He removed his glasses and leaned forward on his lectern: "So would it be correct to say that the area where the body was found was difficult to access for an adult?"

"Very much so, it's totally grown over. I think that's why the body wasn't spotted. I'm only glad it was me and not one of the kids who found him."

"Indeed."

"When the little boy was identified, did you recognize him?"

"No. He wasn't a regular at the playground."

"Thank you, Mr. Cairns."

There was the usual hush as Gordon Jones turned toward Irene Clarke. Daniel bit his lip as he waited for her question. He watched her consulting her notes, noticing the tendon defining her long neck.

Jones looked pleased with himself. He had preempted the

defense's assertion that the injuries inflicted on Ben required strength difficult to attribute to a child. The jury was not aware of it, but Jones was trying to show that the murder site was accessible only to a child and to cast doubt on the defense's theory that the force needed to kill Ben was an adult force.

Irene leaned on the lectern with both hands and smiled at Mr. Cairns with closed lips. Daniel admired her poise.

"Mr. Cairns, you describe the structure under which the victim was found as a wooden house; could you describe it and its purpose for us, please?"

"Well, it's a small hut or house, raised off the ground on stilts . . . I suppose you might call it a tree house, but . . . it's only a couple of feet off the ground. It's still surrounded by trees, so it gives the kids that kind of feeling. I suppose that's the idea."

"Is this a popular part of the playground for children to play?"

"Well, sometimes they do play there, but I wouldn't say it's popular, no. Because it's so overgrown, it's a bit too wild for some of the kids. Quite often there are insects and nettles and such . . ."

"My goodness, it sounds to me like a difficult area to reach, even if you were a child?"

"To some extent. You have to push branches out of the way, maybe get yourself a bit dirty. Most kids don't mind that though."

"So would you say it took you, what . . . ten minutes to reach the tree house and the victim's body?"

"No, less than a minute."

"Less than a minute? For a grown man to push through all this greenery?"

"Yes, I would say so."

"So it is *not the case* that this area of the park is accessible only to children?"

"No, we couldn't have that. We supervise all the play and so we want to be able to get into all the corners, in case kids are in trouble."

"Might it even be the case that some children would have difficulty reaching the house, possibly if they lacked the strength to hold the branches back?"

"Well, yes, that might be the case, but most of the children just crawl in under the trees. An adult would have to push the trees back."

"Thank you, Mr. Cairns, nothing further."

After the break, Daniel noted Kenneth Croll sitting far back in his chair, glaring at Sebastian. The boy turned from his father, looking down at the table, as if shamed. Daniel had found a word search in one of the newspapers that had been left in the common room. He placed it in front of Sebastian, turning to glance and nod at Croll.

Sebastian dipped his head and took the lid off his pen and began to circle the words, intent. Daniel observed the boy's fragile neck, the nape with its tapering baby hairs. He had watched grown men weep at their trials and wondered what strength allowed Sebastian to maintain such concentration and composure.

The video screens were being checked. Madeline Stokes was in tears. Her face was white and twisted, and Daniel had to look away. Daniel had seen their family liaison officer explaining something to them during the break. Mr. Stokes had been nodding, his face dark. Daniel could guess what they were being told. The pathologist, police witnesses, and forensic scientists were next to be called. The solicitor would have explained that the photographs of the body were all necessary and that they needed to be projected in order to highlight details, but that they did not need to stay. Possibly Mr. Stokes had identified his son's body: confirming a birthmark on the shoulder, or the shape of Ben's feet.

Now he did not turn to comfort his wife as she cried, nor pass her a handkerchief when she opened her handbag in search of a tissue. Only his eyes belied his pain; they searched the courtroom, every corner, every face, as if silently asking *why.*

"Are they going to show a movie?" asked Sebastian.

"No, they'll be showing some pictures of—" Daniel stopped from saying *the body,* remembering Sebastian's fascination. "The other side's lawyers will have some experts to explain what they think happened to the victim. I expect they'll want to point things out on the screen . . ."

Sebastian smiled and nodded, put the lid on his pen and clasped his hands. It was as if a show was about to begin.

The afternoon began with police evidence: photographs of the child's body, found flat on his back, arms at his sides. Sergeant Turner, who had interviewed Sebastian, went into the witness box. Footage was shown of Sebastian being questioned—refusing to admit that he had hurt Ben in any way. Jones took the rest of the afternoon to question Sergeant Turner, while playing footage of Sebastian talking about the blood on his clothes, and breaking down in tears. Jones also lingered over Sebastian's bravado in the face of questioning and his clever, logical explanations for the forensic evidence being on his person. The jury seemed to be left with the impression that Sebastian was clever and manipulative beyond his years.

It was the next morning before Irene was able to properly
cross-examine the police sergeant. The court seemed heavier
and quieter than usual, as if everyone was still shocked by the
sight of the young boy sobbing in police custody from the day
before. He had seemed so small on the tapes.

"Sergeant, I'd like to ask you a few questions about Mr.
Rankine's statement if that's okay?" Irene began.

"Of course," said the sergeant. Under the bright courtroom
lighting, his face seemed red, almost angry, yet he smiled at
Irene.

"We have heard from the pathologist that the victim could
have been assaulted anytime on the afternoon of August the
eighth—four, five, even after six o'clock, nearer the time of
his death. Mr. Rankine stated that he saw a person in a pale
blue or white top seemingly attacking the victim around three
thirty or four in the afternoon. What did you do to confirm
the identity of this white attacker?"

"A white top belonging to the defendant has been submit-
ted into evidence. The witness seemed confident that he saw
a boy matching the description of the defendant earlier in the
day—which the defendant admits—and then later on."

"I see," said Irene, turning and raising her hand to the jury.
"But of course!" She turned to face the sergeant. "Your defendant had a white top and admits squabbling with the victim
around two. No need for you to do anything further. No need
to investigate whether or not there was another attacker, possibly an adult in a *pale blue top* . . ."

"Miss Clarke," said Baron, with another crumpled smile,
"do you intend to pose a question to the witness?"

"Yes, M'Lord . . . Sergeant, did the witness become convinced he saw a child in a white top because your colleagues suggested that you had someone of that description in custody?"

"Certainly not!"

"Miss Clarke, I would have expected better from a young QC," chastised the judge.

Daniel glanced at Irene but she was undaunted. She had a tilt to her chin, as if in challenge.

"Sergeant Turner," she continued, "Mr. Rankine has admitted in court that he may in fact have seen an adult, wearing a blue or white top. Regardless of whether the defendant owned a white top, can you tell us what you did to trace this sighting of someone attacking the victim late in the afternoon at a time when my client has an alibi?"

"We did examine CCTV footage, but could not confirm anyone in the playground at the time . . . in fact, for the entire afternoon and early evening."

"Does that mean that a pale blue–shirted adult did not attack the victim that afternoon?"

"No, nor does it prove that your client did not attack the victim that afternoon."

"And why is that?"

Sergeant Turner coughed. "Well, the TV cameras were mainly aimed at the surrounding streets during the afternoon and not turned on the park for sufficient time to allow a sighting . . . basically the attack was not on camera, neither was the fight the boys had earlier, to which the defendant has already admitted."

"How convenient." Again Irene turned to the jury. "The

cameras were not pointed at the park in the afternoon, a witness spots a white- or pale blue–shirted person attacking the
victim, you have a child in custody who owns a white shirt, so
that's that—"

"A white shirt marked with the victim's blood," said Sergeant Turner, interrupting her, raising his voice.

Daniel felt the courtroom bristle as Irene again tilted her
chin to the attack.

"When the CCTV footage proved useless, what else did
you do to find the late-afternoon attacker?"

"As I said, forensic evidence convinced us that we had our
man."

Turner paused and seemed to blush, as if in recognition of
the inappropriateness of his language.

"*You had your man,*" repeated Irene. "I see. You had a very
small boy in custody, and a witness who told you that he saw
someone in a pale blue or white top attacking the victim around
four o'clock—"

Again Turner interrupted Irene. "The witness said he saw *a*
boy . . . the same boy from the afternoon."

Daniel could sense that the jury was displeased by the sergeant shouting at Irene.

"I see, so you had a fit . . ." Irene turned to the witness and
paused.

"We didn't fit him up, he fit the description." Turner's face
was now very red.

"What if I were to tell you that Mr. Rankine testified to
being myopic, and that he now considers he may have seen an
adult that afternoon, would you still consider that you had a fit?"

"Yes, the forensic evidence speaks for itself."

"I would say your lack of police work speaks for itself. If there is *a chance* that the witness did see an adult attack the victim, do you not consider it reasonable to do everything in your powers to locate this person?"

"We conducted a thorough investigation. The defendant matched the description given by the witness, and was later found to have the victim's blood matter on his clothes."

"Job done, I see," said Irene, raising her eyes to the jury and sitting down.

Baron lowered his glasses on his nose to stare critically at Irene before excusing the witness but said nothing.

Daniel noticed that she was breathing hard when she sat down. He watched the gentle swell of her chest. He stared at her for a few moments, hoping that she would turn to him, but she did not.

In the afternoon, scenes of crime officers then testified to the evidence that had been recovered from the crime scene: the brick and blood-soaked foliage.

"Let us be *very* clear," Irene said in cross-examination. "You did not find *a single fingerprint* at the crime scene?"

"Well, we found some partial prints, but these were not identifiable."

"To clarify, you did not find a single viable fingerprint at the crime scene?"

"Correct."

"What about on the murder weapon? Did you get a print from the brick?"

"No, but that is not surprising considering the nature of the surface . . ."

"I will thank you to answer yes or no."

"No."

After the scenes of crime officer left the stand, there was a break and then the Crown's expert forensic scientist was called: Harry Watson.

Jones stood up and asked Watson to confirm his name and title and state why he was qualified as an expert. Watson listed his qualifications: bachelor of arts from Nottingham, a chartered biologist, and a member of the Institute of Biology. He had attended basic and advanced bloodstain pattern analysis courses held in the United States of America and was a member of the International Association of Bloodstain Pattern Analysts. Watson stated his experience as being mainly in the area of biological aspects of forensic science, such as body fluids, hairs, and fibers.

Daniel could sense that Sebastian was bored. It had been a long afternoon, but this evidence was key to the Crown's case and Daniel was hoping that Irene would be able to undermine it.

"Which particular items did you analyze?" Jones asked.

"Mainly the clothes of the victim and the clothes of the defendant." Watson was about fifty and tightly packed inside his suit. He sat rigid, with tight lips as he waited for the next question.

"And what did you find?"

"The defendant's jeans taken into evidence on a search of the home. A concentration of fibers was found on the inner thigh area of the jeans. The fibers were positively matched with fibers from the trousers of the victim. Blood spatter was also identified on the defendant's shoes, jeans, and T-shirt. This blood was positively identified as belonging to the victim."

"How would you describe the blood pattern found on the defendant's clothes?"

"The stains found on the T-shirt were expirated blood— that's blood blown out of the nose, mouth, or a wound as a result of air pressure that is the propelling force."

"What sort of injuries to a victim would cause this kind of blood spatter on the defendant?"

"The blood spatter is consistent with facial trauma—a violent assault to the face or nose, with the victim then blowing blood onto the attacker."

Shocked murmurs rippled through the courtroom.

"So Sebastian Croll was spattered with the victim's expirated blood. Was there anything else about the blood on the defendant's clothes that indicated he had been involved in a violent incident with the deceased?"

"In addition to the expirated blood found on the defendant's T-shirt there was contact staining on the jeans and shoes, which suggested that the defendant had been in close proximity to the deceased at the time of the fatal assault. There was also a small amount of blood on the sole of the defendant's shoe."

"What might the blood on the shoe sole indicate?"

"Well, this may have occurred as a result of standing in the victim's blood, after the assault had taken place."

"Was there anything any forensic evidence suggested that the violent incident had taken place where the body was discovered?"

"Yes, the knees of the jeans of the defendant and the bottom area of the trousers belonging to the victim were consistent with the leaves and dirt found at the crime scene."

"Was any other biological material from the victim recovered from the defendant?"

"Well, yes, the defendant's skin was found under the victim's fingernails and there were scratches on the defendant's arms and neck."

"So Ben had tried to fight Sebastian off and scratched him in the process?"

"That is how it appeared."

Gordon Jones took his seat as Irene Clarke rose.

"Mr. Watson," said Irene, not looking at the witness but instead consulting her notes, "when did you join the Home Office Forensic Science Service?"

Mr. Watson straightened his tie then replied: "Just over thirty years ago."

"Thirty years. My! Quite a wealth of experience. You joined in 1979, is that correct?"

"Yes."

"And in those thirty-one years of service, can you tell us how many cases you worked on?"

"I have no way to tell without checking my records."

"Estimate for us—what would it be: thirty, a hundred, more than five hundred—how many, roughly."

Irene was leaning forward on her lectern, shoulders near her ears. Daniel thought she looked like a girl leaning out of a window watching a parade.

"In thirty-one years, I would say I have been directly involved in hundreds of cases, maybe less but maybe more than five hundred."

"And at how many trials have you given evidence in your thirty-one years of service?"

"Over a hundred I'm sure."

"Two hundred and seventy-three, to be exact. You are indeed an expert witness. Tell me, in those two hundred and seventy-three cases, how many times have you given evidence for the defense?"

"My evidence is impartial and I have no bias toward defense or prosecution."

"Of course, let me clarify; in how many of your two hundred and seventy-three trials have you given evidence as a witness called by the prosecution?"

"Most."

"Most . . . would you hazard a guess at how many?"

"Maybe two-thirds?"

"Not quite, Mr. Watson. In two hundred and seventy-three trials you have been cited as a witness for the defense only three times. Three times in thirty years. Do you find that surprising?"

"A little; I would have expected a few more."

"I see. A few more. Regarding your qualifications, I see that you have a bachelor of arts from Nottingham . . . economics . . . do you find economics useful in your current field?"

"I have since become a chartered biologist."

"I see. You have testified that there were fibers from Ben Stokes's jeans on the defendant's clothing. Tell me, would we not expect that two boys—neighbors—who played together might have fibers of each other's clothes on their person as a result of normal play?"

"It is possible, yes."

"Similarly, the defensive scratches on the defendant and the skin under the victim's nails—these could have been the result of a normal rough and tumble fight between two schoolboys, could it not?"

"It is possible."

"And you have also stated that the blood on Sebastian's clothing was expired. You testified that this was consistent with a blow to the nose or the face. Correct?"

"Yes."

"The defendant made a statement to the effect that the victim fell and hit his nose while they were together, causing it to bleed severely. My client has stated that he leaned over the victim to inspect the injury. Tell us, is it possible that transfer of the identified expired blood would have been possible under these, more benign, circumstances?"

"The blood spatter is consistent with force, and I consider this to be the more likely cause, but it is possible that the expirated blood transfer could have been the result of the accidental injury you describe."

"One more thing," said Irene. "The blood on the defendant's clothing—expired, contact staining, and otherwise—is minimal, would you say?"

"There is not a significant amount of blood on the clothes."

"The blood transfer was clearly evident on forensic examination—but referring to the photographs on page twenty-three of the bundle, they are not clearly apparent to the naked eye."

Sebastian watched, eyes wide. Daniel remembered watching friends' children viewing video games, their stillness unnatural in ones so young. Now Sebastian's attention was also unnatural. He pored over the photographs of the blood spatter on the soiled clothing.

"The blood spots were apparent to the naked eye, but they were not so large or significant as to be clearly identified as blood."

"I see. Thank you for that clarification, Mr. Watson. . . . With a severe injury of this type—blunt-force trauma to the face—obviously carried out with the assailant in close proximity to the victim, would we not expect that the attacker would be somewhat . . . covered in blood?"

Watson shifted in his seat. Daniel watched him. His ruddy facial coloring suggested that he was quick to anger.

Watson cleared his throat. "The type of injury would be consistent with significant loss of blood and we would expect significant transfer of blood onto the attacker."

"Typically, with this type of blunt-force trauma, would you have expected that the expired blood and contact staining would have been significantly more than the localized staining found on the defendant's clothing?"

"We have to remember the position of the body and the fact that most of the damage was done by internal bleeding . . ."

"I see," said Irene. "But you did just say that you would expect significant transfer of blood nevertheless?"

Again Watson cleared his throat. He looked around the courtroom as if for help. Jones was staring at him, his chin pinched between two fingers.

"Mr. Watson, is it not the case that we would have expected the attacker's clothes to be covered in blood with this type of injury?"

"Typically, we *would* have expected a greater amount of contact staining, or airborne transfer of blood."

"Thank you, Mr. Watson."

The cross-examination went so well that Irene decided not to call the defense's forensic scientist when the defense began. This turning of the Crown scientist to the defense's benefit was more powerful.

THE WEEK CLOSED WITH THE CROWN'S PATHOLOGIST, JILL Gault. When she took the witness box, she was as warm and reassuring as she had seemed to Daniel in her office overlooking St. James's Park. She was tall, in boots and a gray suit. She looked like the kind of person who went rowing on weekends, untroubled by the knowledge of how—exactly—a child's skull had been crushed.

"Dr. Gault, you conducted a postmortem on the victim, Benjamin Stokes?" Jones began.

"Yes, that's correct."

"Can you tell us the conclusion that you came to about the cause of death?"

"Cause of death was acute subdural hematoma, consistent with blunt-force trauma—caused by a blow to the front-right side of the skull."

"And, in layman's terms, Dr. Gault, how would you describe a subdural hematoma?"

"Well, it is basically bleeding in the brain, causing increasing pressure on the brain and which, if not treated, will result in brain death."

A model of the brain and the injury described was projected for the jury, to show the exact location of the wound. There was a photograph in the jury bundle of Ben Stokes's face. Sebastian studied it, then leaned to whisper into Daniel's ear:

"Why is his other eye not shut? When you're dead, don't your eyes close?" Daniel felt the boy's balmy fingers on his hand. He leaned down to hush him.

"Dr. Gault, did you determine what the instrument was that caused this fatal blow to the head?"

"The injury was consistent with blunt force—the murder weapon would therefore have been a blunt, heavy object. A brick was recovered from the scene and small pieces of brick were retrieved from the facial injury."

The clerk brought an exhibit bag, and a brick enclosed in cellophane was shown to the jury.

"This brick was found at the crime scene and we have heard testimony to confirm that the victim's blood, brain matter, skin, and hair were identified on its surface. Did you find the shape and size of this brick consistent with the injuries sustained by the victim?"

"Yes, the contours of the brick match those of the wound exactly."

Again, a model was used to show the fit of the brick in the wound.

Sebastian turned to Daniel and smiled. "That's the *actual* brick," he whispered with honeyed breath.

Daniel nodded, a hand held out to hush him.

The pictures of Ben Stokes's mutilated face flashed on the screens, which were provided for judge, jurors, and counsel, but invisible to the gallery. The child's right eye was open—as Sebastian had noted—white and clear; the left reminded Daniel of a smashed bird's egg. Jurors recoiled. Judge Philip Baron considered his screen impassively. Daniel studied the older man's face, the weight of his skin pulling his mouth down. Jill Gault used a laser to indicate the point of impact and spoke of the force necessary to create the damage to skull and cheekbone.

"And were you able to approximate the time of death, Dr. Gault?" Gordon Jones continued, his pen stabbing into his folder.

"Yes, approximately six forty-five in the evening on Monday the eighth of August."

"And would that rule out an attack earlier in the day, for example, in the afternoon at either two, or even four o'clock, when the defendant was last seen fighting with the victim?"

"Not at all. With acute subdural hematoma, it is possible only to approximate the time of death, not the time of injury. The nature of this injury is such that death may occur shortly after injury, or following a period of hours. Hemorrhaging causes pressure on the brain but it can be anything from minutes to hours before it becomes fatal."

"So, Ben may have died some hours after he was struck in the face with the brick, is that correct?"

"Yes, that is correct."

"May he have been conscious during this period?"

"It is highly unlikely . . . but possible."

"Possible. Thank you, Dr. Gault."

Judge Baron cleared his throat noisily and leaned into his microphone.

"In view of the hour, I think this may be a convenient time for a break." He turned at the hip, swiveling his robes and jowly face toward the jury. "Time to slope off and get a cup of coffee. I remind you not to discuss this case outside your number."

All rise.

Daniel stayed until Sebastian was escorted downstairs, then stepped outside. He put his hands in his pockets as he watched the people who reeled in the ornate, painted hallways of Central Criminal Court: shoals of lost souls shuffling with grief and poverty and ill fortune. Happiness and misery were decided here, not found. He felt desolate, another of the lost souls who reeled in its spaces, and took his phone out and called Cunningham. He was with a client, so Daniel left a message asking for information on the sale of Minnie's house.

He felt a touch on his shoulder. It was Irene.

"Everything okay?"

"Sure—why do you ask?"

"Every time I looked at you in there, you were frowning."

"Looking at me a lot, were you?" he flirted, although he realized the mood wasn't right.

She tapped him punitively on the arm with her pen. "What's worrying you?"

"Did you see the jury's faces when those pictures were shown?"

"I know, but we're going to prove that Sebastian is not responsible."

"And Jones asking if he had still been conscious for the possible hours before he died. God." Daniel shook his head but Irene placed a hand on his forearm. He felt the warmth of her.

"Don't lose faith," she whispered.

"Not in you," he said as she turned from him and headed back to court.

"DR. GAULT, YOU DESCRIBED SUBDURAL HEMATOMA AS 'bleeding in the brain,'" Irene said in cross-examination. "So we expect that blood loss would be substantial?"

"Well, blood collects in the brain as a result of trauma. With any subdural hematoma, tiny veins between the surface of the brain and its outer covering, the dura, stretch and tear, allowing blood to collect. It is this pressure that causes death."

"Thank you for that clarification, Doctor. But tell us, with this type of blunt-force facial trauma, would you expect that an attacker would be . . . splattered in the blood of the victim as a result of the assault?"

"Yes, it is likely that a facial trauma of this nature would have caused significant blood spatter onto the perpetrator."

Irene paused and nodded. Daniel watched her melon-seed face tilt, considering.

"One final question—how much does a brick weigh, Dr. Gault?"

"Excuse me?"

"A brick, your average brick, like the brick in evidence, how much does it weigh?"

"I would say about four pounds."

"So tell us, Doctor, in your opinion what kind of strength or force would be needed in order to inflict the injuries that Benjamin Stokes sustained, bearing in mind the weight of the murder weapon?"

"Quite significant force."

"Would you imagine that the necessary force could have been produced by an eleven-year-old boy—particularly one of the defendant's small stature?"

Dr. Gault shifted in her seat. She glanced in Sebastian's direction and Daniel noticed that Sebastian met her gaze.

"No, I would have imagined that the necessary force was more consistent with an adult assailant . . . but having said that . . . If someone of smaller stature, or indeed a child, had inflicted these injuries, this might have been possible if the victim was below the assailant, allowing the force of gravity to compensate for the lack of physical force."

"It is your expert medical opinion, Dr. Gault, that a child would have difficulty in inflicting these injuries because of the weight of the murder weapon?"

"The witness has been asked and has answered, Miss Clarke," said Baron. Irene sat down, a brief flush on her cheeks. "Mr. Jones?"

"If I may, My Lord, a point of clarification . . ."

Judge Baron fluttered his fingers in agreement. Irene shot a glance at Daniel.

Gordon Jones once more assumed the lectern. "Dr. Gault, very briefly, if the fatal blow was delivered with the aid of gravity, would this be consistent with the position of the body when it was found—faceup, hands by the side?"

"Yes," said Dr. Gault, with some hesitation. "Several positions may have been possible, but certainly if the victim had been somewhat stunned or afraid, it might have been possible to deliver the blow while he was on the ground, either from a standing position, or sitting . . . astride, as it were. This would have been easier for a . . . weaker assailant."

"Thank you, Dr. Gault."

DANIEL BROUGHT HOME SEVERAL NEWSPAPERS AND FLICKED through each until he found reports from the trial. Several of the stories focused on his and Sebastian's relationship: *"the boy huddled into his solicitor."* One wrote of Dr. Gault's testimony: *"The Crown pathologist, Dr. Jillian Gault, speculated that the Angel Killer may have sat astride his victim in order to wield sufficient force to bludgeon him to death, face-to-face."*

Daniel washed a hand across his face. The flat was dark, but he could not bear to turn on the lights. The kitchen table was covered in his work files. He stood at the window and watched the park in the vacillating moonlight. The lake turned like a penny in the changing light. He felt tired but it was a restless weariness and he knew he would not be able to sleep.

He noticed the answer phone flashing. Cunningham had left a message. The line was bad and Daniel could not hear every word: "Danny, hi, I got your message . . . the house is cleared and I have a buyer lined up. Young couple from the city who've been looking for a small farm like this for a while. I sent you an e-mail. It's a good offer, so give me a call and let me know if we can proceed to sale."

Daniel exhaled. Automatically, he deleted the message. He wasn't ready for this now. He needed time to prepare. He lay down fully clothed on the bed and stared at the ceiling, unblinking. He remembered going to Minnie's house for the first time as a child. He remembered his tantrums and his rage. But after all that had happened between them and all that she had done for him, what he remembered most clearly was the last words that he had said to her face: *I wish you were dead.*

Now that she was dead, he wanted to say he was sorry. He

turned onto his side. The trial of the boy only forced him to think about her more. The trial made him realize how close he had been to being in Sebastian's position. She had hurt him, but she had saved him too.

He ran the palm of his hand across his chest, feeling the bones of his rib cage. He remembered Charlotte's inappropriate advances at the back door of the cells. He was uncertain why he so pitied her. Daniel felt cheated on Sebastian's behalf for Charlotte's weakness and desperation.

He put a hand underneath his head. He could understand Sebastian's passion for his mother. As a child he had been willing to die to protect his own. He remembered standing barefoot, in his pajamas, between her and the boyfriend. He remembered feeling the slow, hot vein of his urine down his leg, and yet still being prepared to take what was coming, if it would save her.

After that he had been taken into foster care.

He thought of his mother now: the marks on her arms and her mood swings, the unclean smell of her breath. He pitied her now, as he pitied Charlotte. His desperate, childish love for her had been eclipsed long ago. He had been a grown man before he realized the harm that she had done him.

Daniel sat up and ran a hand across his jaw. He changed out of his work clothes and then picked up the phone in the hall. He stood with the receiver in his hand, undecided, before dialing the number. It was Harriet's husband who answered the telephone this time. Daniel stammered slightly, explaining who he was.

"Oh, yes, of course," said the man, "I'll just get her."

Daniel ran a hand through his hair and stood with a palm pressed against the wall as he waited. There was the sound of the television in the background, and the older man clearing his throat. Daniel bit his lip.

"Hello again." Her voice was tired. "Lovely, but I'm surprised to hear from you again so soon."

"I know, it was just something that you said the other day. I've been thinking about it. Do you have time right now?"

"Of course, love, what is it?"

The sound of her voice reminded him of Minnie. He closed his eyes.

"I spoke to Norman's sister. She told me more about the crash . . ."

Harriet said nothing, but he could hear her breathing.

"It's just that I don't think I ever fully understood what Minnie went through, and now I do and . . . I was thinking about something that you said . . ."

He could feel his heart beating. He paused to allow her to speak but still she remained silent. He wondered if he had angered her again.

"What, love?" she said finally. "What did I say?"

He took a deep breath. "About her torturing herself by taking in all the foster kids."

"I know, God love her."

Daniel made a fist with his hand and punched it lightly into the wall. "Why me, do you think? Why did she adopt *me*, and none of the others?"

Harriet sighed.

"Was it because I asked her to? Or . . . because I was scared of being sent away? Had she considered adopting one of the others?"

He waited for Harriet to speak but she did not. The silence lingered gravely, like the low note of the piano with the pedal pressed.

"Don't you know, pet?" she said, finally. "She loved you like her own. You were special to her, so you were. I remember the first year you went to stay with her. She had a lot of *trouble* with you, at first, I remember. You were a wild one. But she saw something in you . . ."

"I mean, she wanted the best for you, of course. She would have given you up for your own good, like she gave up the others. She was on her own and she kept telling me how children needed families—brothers and sisters . . . a man around. I remember her trying to find a proper home for you, all the while desperate to have you stay."

"She was family enough for anyone . . . for me anyway."

"That day she adopted you, she called me after you were asleep. I hadn't heard her so happy since before Delia died."

Daniel cleared his throat. Harriet began to cough: a rasping cough so severe that she had to put down the phone for a second. Daniel waited.

"Are you all right?"

"I can't shift this cough. Mother of God . . . But you have to know, Danny . . . She wanted nothing more than for you to be her son. You were so important to her."

"Thanks," he said, almost whispering.

"Don't think of these things now, son. It does nobody any good. Put it behind you."

Harriet began to cough again.

"You should go to a doctor," he said.

"I'll be grand. Are you all right? I thought that I saw you on the news the other day. Are you on that Angel Killer case, now? What a terrible business that is."

"I am," said Daniel. He stood up straight; mention of the case shook him from the morose claw of his memory.

"What is the world coming to? Have you ever heard the like—children killing each other like that?"

Daniel slipped a hand into his pocket and said that he would need to go.

"Right you are, love. You always did work so hard. You go and put your feet up now. Stop thinking about all this."

Daniel hung up. He went to bed, regret chiming inside him.

WHEN HE WOKE, IT WAS SIX THIRTY AND HE WAS LATE FOR his run. A dream was still fresh in his mind. He had dreamed of the house in Brampton. The walls of the house had been open, like a model nativity scene or a doll's house. The animals had walked freely inside and out. Daniel was grown in the dream, but still living there, caring for the animals. Minnie was outside somewhere, but he couldn't see or hear her.

In her kitchen, he had found a lamb: asleep, breathing audible contented snores, its abdomen rising and falling, and a gentle smile on its lips. Daniel had bent and carried the lamb outside, where bright sunshine was splitting the trees.

Sitting on the edge of the bed, Daniel could still remember the tangible weight of the lamb in his hands and the warmth of its thin fleece.

After breakfast he checked his e-mails, then returned Cunningham's call and agreed that the farm could be sold. Daniel spoke very quietly when he said the words, in case he changed his mind. It was time to sell the house, he decided. He needed to move on. Perhaps when the house was gone, he would be free of regret. He would think about her no more.

26

MINNIE HAD WANTED TO DRIVE HIM TO UNIVERSITY, BUT Daniel knew that she was anxious about it. In the end he got the train to Sheffield, allowing Minnie to drive him only as far as Carlisle. Blitz had whimpered all the way in the car, and then Minnie's eyes glassed over with tears when they reached the platform.

"Mam, I'll be back in ten weeks. Christmas is in *ten weeks*."

"I know, love," she'd said, reaching up to hold his face in both hands. "It seems like such a long time, and the time I've had with you now seems too short. I can't quite believe it."

It was a warm day. Blitz was straining on his lead, turning to the sounds of people and trains. Daniel smelled the diesel and felt a brief frightened thrill at the thought of leaving Brampton and living in a city again. He watched Minnie putting a knuckle to her eye.

"Are you going to be okay?" he asked.

She heaved a sigh and beamed at him, her cheeks pink. "I'll be just grand. You make sure and enjoy yourself. Call me once in a while so I know you're alive and not taken to drink or drugs." She laughed, but Daniel could see the sheen come to her eyes again.

"Will you call me?" he asked.

"Try and stop me."

He smiled, chin down to his chest. He wanted to leave now, but it was a few minutes until his train. Leaving her was harder than he had imagined and now he wished that he had said good-bye at the farm. Part of him worried that she would be lonely, part of him was filled with apprehension for himself. Some childish part of him did not want to go. He didn't know anyone who had been to a university: he didn't know what to expect.

"And don't start thinking you're not worthy," she said, as if she had been reading his mind again. Her eyes split with mirth and wisdom. "All you needed was this one chance. Take it and show them all just what you're made of."

He held her, bending down to squeeze her, feeling her body yield to him. Blitz yelped and jumped on them, trying to break them up.

"You're nothing but a jealous fool," she derided Blitz, roughly patting his head.

Then it was time. Daniel had smiled, kissed her wet cheek, stroked Blitz's wary ear, and then he was gone.

AT SHEFFIELD UNIVERSITY, ALTHOUGH MOST OF THE STU-dents he became friends with were a year older than he was, having had gap years abroad, Daniel still felt strangely older than they were. He joined the football team and also a running club and would go out drinking with friends from both. Carol-Ann stayed in Brampton and he saw her occasionally during term and during the holidays when he went back to the farm, but he slept with other girls at university and said nothing to Carol-Ann, who knew him well enough not to ask.

One of the girls he slept with got pregnant and then had an abortion, early in his second year. He was living in a shared flat on the Ecclesall Road at the time, and had gone along with her to Danum Lodge in Doncaster to get the procedure done. They had both been frightened and afterward she had bled and been in pain. He had looked after her, but after a few weeks it was as if it had never happened.

Daniel was not sure if it was this which caused him to begin thinking about his mother again—his real mother—but shortly before his second-year law exams, he called Newcastle Social Work Department and asked to speak to Tricia. He was told that she had left the department in 1989.

Daniel remembered being told that he would have the right to trace his mother when he was eighteen. Although she was dead, he still wanted to know how she died and if there was a memorial. He decided he would visit Newcastle again, to see what he could find out about his mother's death. Some part of him wanted to return. He didn't tell Minnie what he was doing—knowing that it would upset her too much. He didn't want to hurt Minnie, but away from Brampton he felt more able to make the call. He called social services back three times before he managed to speak to someone who could help him.

"Daniel Hunter, did you say?"

"That's right."

"And you say your birth mother was Samantha. You were adopted in 1988 by Minnie Florence Flynn?"

"Mmm-hmm."

The social worker was called Margaret Bentley. She sounded exhausted, as if the very words she spoke cost her precious energy.

"All I can find on your mother is notes from the drug team, but nothing recent . . ."

"It's all right. I know she's dead. I just want to know how she died, 'n' maybe find out if there's a memorial. I know she was cremated."

"I'm sorry, we don't keep that information, but you could ask at the register office in Newcastle. They'd have her death certificate. The council would tell you where she was cremated and if there's a memorial . . ."

"Well . . . the last report from the drug team, was it bad?"

"We're not really supposed to give out that kind of information."

"You're not tellin' me anything I don't know, like," Daniel said. "I knew me mam took drugs. It's just . . ."

"Well, this last report was very good. She was clean."

"Really, when was that?"

"1988, same year you were adopted."

"Thank you," said Daniel and hung up.

He thought about his last meeting with his mother, the way she had struggled to face what was happening. He wondered if she had tried to get clean for him; if losing him had scared her away from the drugs. But if she hadn't overdosed, Daniel wondered why she had died so young. He thought of the men in her life and pressed his teeth together.

He had revisions to do, but he got up the next morning and took the train to Newcastle. Returning was a strange joy. As the train pulled in, he looked north toward the Cowgate estates. The city still seemed to be under his fingernails and in between his toes. He walked differently when he was here: he kept his head down and his hands in his pockets, but he knew instinctively where to go. He had not been in Newcastle since the day that Minnie adopted him. He felt a delicious, conflicted thrill, as if he was trespassing, but at home.

He didn't know where the register office was, but he asked at the central library. It was on Surrey Street and he went straight there. He had written down his mother's full name and date of birth as he remembered it.

The register office was a Victorian building of pale, unblasted sandstone. It seemed to have shouldered the grime of decades with appropriate resignation. The hallways were institutional, civic, minimally clean. Daniel felt slightly inhibited as he walked to the desk. It reminded him of his first visit to the university library; his first tutorial, before he learned that he *did* know enough and had a right to be there. He was wearing a long-sleeved football shirt and jeans. He stopped on the steps to smooth back his hair, which was getting long on the front and starting to fall into his eyes. Inside he went to the men's room where he tucked it in, then untucked his shirt. While he waited in line, he wondered at the source of his anxiety: whether it was because he was about to query the dead, or because he had been disowned by the dead.

Disowned.

When it was his turn, Daniel stepped up to the desk. Suddenly he felt abandoned, abnegated, cast. He remembered his mother's long nails, tack, tack, tack on the table.

"Yes, can I help you?"

The registrar was young. She leaned on the desk with both her elbows and smiled up at Daniel.

"Yes, I wanted to get a copy of my mother's death certificate."

Forms were filled in and Daniel had to wait, but then he was given the certificate, folded into a clean white envelope. He thanked the young registrar and left, not daring to open the envelope until he was outside, and even then he felt inhibited as people pushed by him on the busy street.

There was an old-fashioned tea shop off Pinstone Street and Daniel slipped inside and ordered a coffee and a bacon roll. There was an overweight man with purpled cheeks eating a pie and beans and two women with the same dyed-blond spiky hairstyle sharing a cigarette.

Daniel carefully opened the folds of the paper. He could taste the smoke from the women's cigarettes in his mouth. His heart was beating but he didn't know why. He knew she was dead and he could guess how, but still there was a feeling that he was uncovering something hidden. The typeface swarmed at him. His fingers were trembling and so the paper shook.

She *had* died of a drug overdose, as Minnie had told him. Daniel stared at the paper imagining the syringe rising valiantly from his mother's arm and her blue rubber tourniquet releasing, as one hand releases another over a cliff.

His eyes scanned and then rescanned the dates: born 1956, died 1993, age 37 years.

He pushed his roll away, left his coffee, and ran back to the register office where he skipped up the steps just as they were closing for lunch.

He pushed his way to the desk. The young woman who had served him called over. "I'm sorry, we close for lunch. If you can come back later?"

"I just wanted to ask . . . one question, just one, I swear."

She smiled and came to the desk again. "I'll get in trouble," she said, her eyes sparkling at him.

Daniel did his best to play along, although he wanted to shake her. "Thanks so much; you're great." The registrar's lids lowered and lifted. "I just wanted to check, like . . . this certificate says 1993 on it, but me mam died in 1989 at the latest."

"Right? That's strange."

"Could you have made a mistake?" Daniel asked, feeling his eyes wide from the panic, but still trying to relax in front of her.

"Well no, I mean . . . that's your mother's official death certificate. Are you sure she died in 1989?"

"Yeah . . . ," he said, and then, "No . . ."

"Well, I expect it's right then."

"How do I find out if she's got a memorial . . . ?"

"You need to talk to the council, remember?"

The girl smiled, pursing her lips in apology. Daniel turned and left. When he was outside, the certificate was creased in his hand, although he hadn't meant to crush it.

Daniel waited for the council offices to open. His stomach

rumbled and cramped, but he paid no attention to it. He sat on the steps for ten minutes then walked around the block before returning. Three times he read the sign that said it was closed between one and two o'clock.

When it opened, he was directed to Bereavement Services, where he had to wait for twenty minutes despite being the first person in line.

"I want to find out if my mother has a memorial—I think she was cremated . . . I have her death certificate."

"What's her name?"

Daniel waited in a plastic chair, with his stomach muscles so tight that they began to ache. He had forgotten about university. This was all he cared about.

He expected to have to fill in more forms, to show his identification or to part with money. The woman returned within a few minutes. She told him that his mother's name was not on any of the cremation lists. She had double-checked and found that his mother had been buried at the Jesmond Road Cemetery.

Daniel thought that he had thanked her, but then she asked him loudly if he was all right. He was standing with his fingers holding on to the desk and the death certificate crushed in his hand.

Off the Jesmond Road, Daniel saw the graveyard. He had bought carnations as an afterthought and carried them in a plastic bag, petals facing the ground.

The entrance reared up in front of him: a red sandstone arch that was at once beautiful and terrifying. He stood outside for a moment, kicking small stones out of his path. He found himself drawn into the red arch and once inside, the need to go deeper was powerful. He didn't know where she was laid or if he would find her, but as soon as he entered he felt a hard peace fall on him. His heart was quiet. He moved from grave to grave looking for her name. He searched methodically, carefully, without frustration when another row of graves passed without finding her name inscribed, and without preemptive relief when he found graves on which were carved similar names.

Finally, just after four o'clock, he found her: SAMANTHA GERALDINE HUNTER 1956–1993. MAY YOU REST IN PEACE.

Already, the black-painted letters were beginning to flake. Daniel tried to imagine her, with her thin shoulders and her long nails. She was a child in his imagination. He thought how young she had been when he saw her last.

He stood for a moment, and then knelt, letting the grass wet through his jeans. He wiped some new raindrops from the marble, imagining her small bones beneath. He laid the carnations at the foot of the cross.

1993. She had died only months before. He would have been less than an hour from her, when her time came. He could have come to her, he could have helped her, but she had died without knowing that he was near. She had been clean the year that she lost him. He wondered if she had been getting clean so that she could have him back. His eighteenth birthday had come and gone. Maybe she had lost hope. Maybe she had thought he had another family and no longer thought of her.

Someone must have paid for her headstone; someone must have chosen the white marble and decided on the words. He remembered the name on the death certificate: *Informant— Michael Parsons.* Daniel recalled all the names and faces that had surrounded his mother's life. He hung his head. The breath was uneven in his throat yet he couldn't weep. The grief he felt for her was small and fragile. It was grief confused with so much else. Invisible birds sang with a noise that seemed deafening.

Daniel stood up. He was aware of a sharp pain in his head. He turned and walked out of the graveyard, his feet crunching on the red chips with purpose after his slow and patient discovery. The sun was bright and in his eyes. His muscles were tight and he could feel a cold tear of sweat making its way between his shoulder blades.

He remembered the day Minnie told him his mother was dead and pressed his lips together. His jaw ached.

He was going back to Brampton, and he was going to kill her.

27

DANIEL FLASHED HIS PASS TO THE OLD BAILEY GUARDS AS he entered the courthouse. Today was the first day of the defense. He held his chin up as he walked to Court 13, reminding himself of the reprieve implicit in reasonable doubt. He realized that this was the first time in his career he had actually felt real fear about the prospect of losing. He hated Sebastian's family and worried about the child returning to that world of material privilege and emotional deprivation, but the thought of Sebastian inside, in the system, was worse. Bright as the child was, he didn't realize how the press had already demonized him and how difficult it would be for him, for the rest of his life, if he was ever found guilty. Daniel tried not to think about it. He believed in Irene's abilities. She had not lost a single case since their defeat together on Tyrel's case last year.

"My Lord, I call Dr. Alexander Baird."

Baird seemed as nervous as when Daniel had visited the psychologist in his office. He leaned in too close to the microphone as he was sworn and was startled by the feedback. Irene was matter-of-fact beginning her examination in chief. She smiled broadly at Baird, making large sweeping gestures to the court, as she asked him to share his thoughts on Sebastian.

"Dr. Baird, you examined Sebastian Croll twice in September 2010. Is that correct?"

"Correct."

"I would ask you to summarize for the court how you found Sebastian."

Baird moved close in to the microphone, his smooth hands loosely gripping the lip of the witness box. "In terms of intellectual function, I found him to be highly intelligent. His IQ was measured at 140, which certainly suggests very superior intelligence, or indeed borderline genius—but certainly highly gifted."

"What did you find about Sebastian's emotional maturity and his understanding of complex processes, for example, court proceedings?"

"Well, Sebastian seems to have quite a short attention span, which may in itself be due to his high intelligence, but I did find him prone to emotional outbursts more typical of a younger child."

"You questioned him about the alleged offense; what was your opinion about Sebastian in relation to the charge?"

"Sebastian knew the difference between right and wrong. He understood the nature of the alleged offense and stated convincingly that he believed himself to be innocent."

"Did you discuss the happenings on the day of the alleged offense?"

"Yes, we did and we attempted some role play around the day. On the whole I found him to be entirely consistent. His concept of morality was clear and he stated several times that he was innocent."

"Considering his intellectual ability, did you feel he understood the gravity of the crime he was charged with?"

"Without a doubt. He was clear that he understood the penalties for such a crime, but felt he had been misunderstood. We discussed the events of August eighth several times in a variety of different ways: telling a story, using dolls, and revealed through question and answer, but each time he was entirely consistent."

"Thank you, Dr. Baird."

Irene nodded at Daniel before she sat down. Gordon Jones rose and stood for a moment as the court watched him opening ring binders and balancing them on his lectern. The room was airless and Daniel loosened his tie slightly. The defense had begun well and Irene seemed relaxed, but Daniel had a feeling of unease about the testimony to come, which he could not account for. Sebastian was losing interest. He was swinging his feet and occasionally making contact with Daniel's legs.

"Just a few questions, Dr. Baird," said Jones, on cross-examination. "I note from your report that you mention Sebastian's earlier diagnosis, by his school educational psychologist, of Asperger's?"

Sebastian leaned in to whisper something but Daniel held out a hand to silence him.

"Yes, Sebastian's school reports show an earlier diagnosis by an educational psychologist. I disagreed with the diagnosis."

"But you do consider him as having . . ." Jones made a show of pushing his glasses to the end of his nose, wrinkling his nose, and turning down his lips as he read: " 'pervasive developmental disorder not otherwise specified'?"

Baird smiled and nodded. "Indeed, otherwise known as PDD-NOS—essentially a catch-all diagnosis for those who demonstrate atypical symptomatology for Asperger's, or indeed autism."

"I see. Well, in layman's terms please . . . what is this exactly, this, eh . . . PDD-NOS and how does it relate to the earlier diagnosis?"

"Well, it simply means that Sebastian does show a range of Asperger's traits, but not all . . . and indeed is highly functional in areas we would expect him to have trouble with, if he had Asperger's syndrome proper."

"I see. Asperger's is a kind of high-functioning autism, is that correct?"

"That's correct."

"And what symptoms are typical of a child with Asperger's syndrome?"

"Well, typically they will display problems in three main areas: social communication, social interaction, and social imagination."

Irene stood up. "My Lord, I question the relevance of this. Does my learned colleague have a point to this questioning?"

Baron leaned forward and raised his eyebrows at Jones in expectation of a response.

"My Lord, we are legitimately exploring the implications of disorders the boy may suffer from that may be related to the offense."

"Continue," said Baron. "I consider this to be relevant."

"You just listed three areas which typical Asperger's sufferers would have difficulty with—can you elaborate on this?" Jones prompted Baird.

"Well, typical sufferers will display a range of behaviors—difficulty in social situations—that often manifest in a desire for friendships but a difficulty maintaining them. Often there is a hyperfocused interest in a single topic . . . they tend to have difficulty in reading emotional responses in others . . . another thing is that they often have problems with sensory integration—they can overreact to loud noises, for example."

Irene stood up again. "My Lord, I really must protest. The witness has stated my client *does not have* Asperger's, so again I question the relevance of exploring the typical symptomatology."

"Miss Clarke, the witness has stated that the defendant shows a range of Asperger's traits, so we will hear this out as an explanation of the traits in question."

Irene sat down. Daniel watched her. Her shoulders were raised with tension.

"Thank you, M'Lord," said Jones. "So, tell us, Dr. Baird, does Sebastian display *any* of these typical Asperger's behaviors and problems?"

"Yes, he displays some, but not all."

"What about hyperfocus on one topic. Did you find Sebastian to be deeply interested in a particular subject . . . ?"

Baird flushed. He glanced at Irene.

"Dr. Baird?"

"Well, I did note a preoccupation . . . but I was not sure if this qualified as hyperfocused interest . . . I would need to study him over a longer period."

"I see . . . what, exactly, did you find preoccupies Sebastian?"

Hearing his name in such an auspicious tone, Sebastian sat up. He looked at Daniel and smiled.

"He has what one might call a morbid curiosity."

"In what way . . . what things, exactly, is he morbidly curious about?"

"He seemed very interested in blood, death, and injury . . . on this, again, I cannot be sure, I would have to study his behavior further, but I would cite a discussion that we had about his mother's miscarriage."

"Why did this alarm you?"

Irene was on her feet. "My Lord, I really must protest: My learned colleague is putting words into the witness's mouth. He has not stated that he was *alarmed* in any way."

Jones nodded at Irene and then rephrased: "Tell us what the conversation relating to his mother's miscarriage revealed, Dr. Baird."

"Well, I considered his knowledge to be more detailed than one would have expected and also somewhat inappropriate, particularly for a child of his age . . . but again, this is in no way definitive."

Daniel watched Irene furiously scribbling notes on her pad. He knew she would return to this subject on cross-examination.

"I see, *not definitive.* Tell us about Sebastian's ability to handle social communication."

"Yes, he does seem to have problems with social communication and social interaction . . ."

"Yet you failed to diagnose Asperger's, preferring . . ." Again Jones twisted his face to read from his notes, "PDD-

NOS. In my layman's view he is sounding like a model example of a child with Asperger's syndrome. Why is that not so?"

"Well . . . Sebastian did show an ability for social *imagination* . . . not only an ability but indeed an aptitude for it. This became very apparent in the role play that we did. It was this lack of . . . one of the key symptoms of Asperger's that led me to disagree with the earlier diagnosis. But on reflection I did consider that he may demonstrate PDD-NOS."

"And what exactly is social imagination?"

"Essentially, it is being able to imagine a range of possible outcomes to a situation—particularly a social situation. Many people with Asperger's can be creative, but a typical symptom of the condition is the inability to imagine different outcomes to situations presented, or to . . . predict what will happen next . . . often they will have trouble working out what other people know."

"I see." Jones was standing tall now, flourishing his robes and looking straight at the jury. "Tell me, Dr. Baird, is social imagination important to be a good liar?"

Daniel held his breath. Jones had raised his voice as he said the last word. Daniel looked up. The courtroom shuffles and murmurs had stopped. Baird swallowed. Daniel watched as his eyes flicked toward Irene.

"Dr. Baird?" Jones prompted.

"Well, certainly, if a lie is complex and involves visualization of certain outcomes, then social imagination will be very important . . . but it should be noted that people with Asperger's often find it impossible to lie."

"But, Dr. Baird," said Jones, a predatory smile on his lips. "You just told us that Sebastian did not have Asperger's, for the very reason that he showed an ability . . . indeed *an aptitude* . . .

for social imagination, something that may have allowed him to lie convincingly about the murder of young Ben Stokes. Is that not the case?"

"I . . . think that PDD-NOS is a more appropriate diagnosis, yes . . . I cannot speak about—"

"Dr. Baird. Would you say that children with Asperger's and indeed those diagnosed with the lesser condition of PDD-NOS often tend toward violence?"

"Well, I—"

Irene stood up. Daniel clasped his hands.

"My Lord, again I question the relevance . . . the witness is giving his expert opinion of *my client's* psychological state. We have no time for generalizations . . ."

"That may be, Miss Clarke, but the witness may answer . . . As an expert he is entitled to show how your client's psychological state pertains to . . . more general conditions."

"Well . . . ," Baird stumbled, "children who display symptoms of PDD-NOS and Asperger's may become frustrated more easily and as a result are more prone to temper tantrums, meltdowns, intense anger, and violent behaviors."

"I see . . . *intense anger and violent meltdowns*," Jones repeated, turning in the jury's direction. "Would children displaying such symptoms also lack . . . empathy?"

"Again, the disorder has a wide spectrum, but . . . and this is true of aggressive children in general . . . they quite often do not feel, or indeed understand, the suffering of others . . ."

"Thank you, Dr. Baird," said Jones.

Jones seemed pleased with himself.

"If I may, My Lord," said Irene, standing up again.

Judge Baron fluttered his fingers in consent.

"Dr. Baird . . . focusing now on *Sebastian,* and moving away from previous generalizations, is it your expert opinion that he was aggressive or indeed duplicitous when you met with him—twice?"

"That was not my experience of him, and we should not assume that he would be capable of these things."

"I see. You have testified that you consider that Sebastian may have a disorder on the Asperger's spectrum, PDD-NOS. Is this common?"

"Very much so."

"Is it therefore likely that a large number of otherwise healthy and sane adults in society would show these mild Asperger's spectrum traits?"

"Yes, of course, although there would be no way to tell how common, as even now it largely goes undiagnosed."

"So people in this courtroom, other than the defendant, may also have PDD-NOS?"

"It is entirely possible."

"People in the jury could have PDD-NOS, or even the barristers, solicitors, and judge in court today?"

Her words were shocking and Daniel glanced at Baron. The old man was scowling, but said nothing.

"Again, it is . . . possible."

"And is this not worrying? Is PDD-NOS indicative of criminality or violence?"

"Not at all, it is just that the limitations of the disorder can increase frustration and occasionally result in outbursts in certain individuals."

"Thank you for that clarification." Daniel watched as Irene consulted the notes she had made during Jones's questioning.

"Now in relation to the defendant's supposed *morbid fascination,* you have cited his description of his mother's miscarriage as an example. Page sixty-three, paragraph four in your bundle notes the transcript of the conversation to which you refer. What exactly did Sebastian say that you considered morbid or *inappropriate to his age?*"

"The biological details he noted were startling—the exact age of the fetus, his awareness of trauma to the womb, and the consequences for his mother's fertility. He vividly described the hemorrhaging . . ."

"I fail to understand why this is attributable to a disorder, Dr. Baird. My client was expecting a little brother. The pregnancy was third trimester, and he had, as you would expect, felt his sibling move through his mother's stomach—in fact he spoke of this event. I am sure you are aware of the questions this experience will prompt in a child, about the specifics of biology. You are aware that the baby was lost as a result of a household accident . . ." Irene paused. Daniel wondered at her choice of phrase. "Do you not consider it wholly understandable that a child who witnessed the fall and such a late-term miscarriage in his own home may have been somewhat justified in becoming . . . morbidly preoccupied, as you put it? Would this not represent a significant trauma for the boy and his family?"

"Indeed that is a reasonable explanation. Previously I answered questions on general aspects of the condition—not specific to Sebastian's case."

"Thank you," said Irene, triumphant. "Now once again, according to your assessment of the defendant, do you think that Sebastian is capable of the alleged offense?"

Baird paused, almost tasting the words before he spoke. "No, I do not consider him capable of murder."

"Thank you, Dr. Baird."

The court adjourned for lunch and Sebastian was taken downstairs. Daniel walked alone through the Old Bailey halls, running a hand through his hair. He felt angry with himself. He had been wary of Baird's testimony and now castigated himself for not thinking it through more fully. Their first witness had been turned, but he was glad that Irene had been able to bring him back. He'd tried to catch her leaving court—he wanted to congratulate her for her recovery—but she had to speak to her pupil about another case.

Daniel wasn't hungry. He slotted coins into the drink machine, choosing a coffee instead of lunch. While he was waiting, he felt fingernails dig into his upper arm and turned to find Charlotte almost in tears. She was Sebastian's alibi from three P.M. and later on the day of the murder, and was due to testify after lunch.

"Daniel, I don't know if I can do this," she said. "It's *that man* I'm afraid of—I watch him *ripping* people apart. I'm scared I'll trip up . . ." Daniel knew that she meant Jones.

"You'll be fine," said Daniel. He heard his tone as deep, almost severe, but he didn't want her to fall apart and instinct told him not to indulge her. "Keep your answers short, like we discussed with Irene. Talk about what you know and nothing else. You're not on trial, remember."

"But my son is. I see the way they're all looking at me, like I'm the mother of some kind of . . . devil."

"Don't even think that. He's innocent and we're going to prove he is, but you're an important part of that. *We need you* to win this. You're his mother and he needs you to stand up for him."

Twice he had said these words to Charlotte. He wanted to shake her. He knew what it was like to have a mother who was dependent as a child, who had been unable to protect him.

Charlotte looked upward at the high vault of the Central Criminal Court. She searched its expanse as if for answers; when she looked down again, a black tear spilled, which she wiped away quickly with an already blackened tissue. He remembered the touch of her nails on his abdomen. Looking at her he felt again a wave of disgust and pity so strong that he had to look away.

"You can do this, Charlotte," he said. "Sebastian's counting on you."

When Charlotte was called, she was composed, but Daniel still held his breath as he watched her make her way to the witness box. The bones of her elbows protruded through the sleeves of her jacket. Sebastian leaned forward, hands stretched out in front of him on the table, as if trying to reach out to her. Charlotte cleared her throat and took a sip of water. From a distance she seemed fragile but strikingly beautiful, her features even and her eyes huge.

Irene was warm and conversational when she began her examination in chief. She had one elbow on her lectern and addressed Charlotte in a familiar, gentle way although the two women had only spoken briefly.

"Just a few short questions . . . Can you tell us what you remember about the day of August eighth this year?"

"Yes," said Charlotte, at first quietly, but soon gaining confidence. "I wasn't feeling very well that day. My husband was overseas and after I made Sebastian's lunch I decided to have a lie-down."

"What did Sebastian do on that day?"

"Well, he went out to play while I was lying down."

"Did you know where he went to play?"

"Well, normally he just plays in the crescent, sometimes with the neighbors' children, but even if he goes to the park, I can often still see him from the top bedroom window, it's so close."

"Did you watch him as he played on that day?"

"No, I just had a lie-down. I had a headache."

"When did Sebastian return home?"

"It was just before three P.M."

"You're quite sure."

"Quite sure."

"And when he returned home, did he appear different, for example, very dirty—were his clothes visibly marked?"

"No more than usual." Charlotte allowed a small smile. "He's a little boy. He often comes home in a bit of a mess, but no, there was nothing unusual."

"What about his behavior, did he seem troubled or upset?"

"No, not at all. We had a snack together and watched some television."

"Thank you." Irene nodded and sat down.

Daniel exhaled and leaned in toward Sebastian. "You okay?" he whispered to the boy.

"Don't let him be mean to her," Sebastian whispered back, not turning to Daniel as he spoke.

"Don't worry," Daniel assured him, although he too was

concerned about Jones's cross-examination. He knew Charlotte could not take a lot of pressure.

Jones managed a toothless smile before he began. Charlotte was rubbing her neck, her eyes flicking anxiously in the direction of the public gallery.

"Mrs. Croll, does your doctor prescribe any medication that you take on a regular basis?"

Charlotte cleared her throat and then said, "Yes . . . I have trouble sleeping and I have problems with . . . anxiety, so I take . . . um . . . diazepam, beta blockers, fairly frequently, and on nights when I can't sleep . . . tamazepam."

"I see, quite a cocktail. And on the day of August eighth, did you take any . . . diazepam, for example?"

"I don't remember exactly, but most likely I would have. Most days I need to take one, to calm me down."

"I see, so you admit taking sedatives on August eighth while your son went out to play, but you are now testifying under oath that you are certain he returned at three P.M. sharp?"

"Yes, I lay down, but I didn't actually sleep that day. I was not feeling well and just needed to calm down. I heard Sebastian come in at three o'clock and then I made us something to eat. I didn't sleep. I know I didn't sleep. I was too . . . tense. I know what time he came home."

"Do you love your son, Mrs. Croll?"

"Yes, of course."

Sebastian reached over the table again when his mother spoke. Daniel noticed that he was smiling at his mother across the courtroom.

"And you would do anything to protect him?"

"Anything I could." Charlotte was looking straight at Sebastian. "Except, of course, to cover up a murder," she concluded, turning back to Jones.

"When the police came to the house on Monday, you were reportedly home but fast asleep. So . . . *out of it*, that you didn't even realize that your son had been taken to the police station, is that correct?"

"Yes, on that day I was asleep. The anxiety often builds up and on Monday I was exhausted. But on Sunday, I was awake and *I know* the time that he came home."

"A witness has testified that he saw Sebastian in the Barnard Park Adventure Playground fighting with the deceased much later that afternoon. In fact you have *no idea* what time your son came home. You were drugged up and oblivious that day."

"That's not true. I heard the witness testify earlier. He might not have seen Sebastian. It could have been someone else. I know I was awake that day. I was sick with nerves. I couldn't have slept if I'd tried. He came home at three o'clock, of that I am *certain*."

"Sick with nerves. I am sure you are, Mrs. Croll, sick with nerves. How many milligrams of Valium did you take on August eighth?"

Charlotte coughed. "Ten. I only have ten-milligram tablets, sometimes I bite half, but that day I had a full one."

"And we are to believe that you were still conscious let alone aware of the hour after ten milligrams of Valium?"

"I have been taking antianxiety drugs for some time. Ten milligrams has a sedative effect on me, but no more. You can ask my doctor, smaller amounts don't even calm me. I know my son was home at three P.M."

Daniel smiled and exhaled. Jones finished his questioning

and Charlotte made her way back to her seat. Her elbows still protruded, like sharp wings. She glanced briefly at Sebastian and Daniel before she sat. Daniel turned to her and mouthed: *You did well.*

AFTER A SHORT BREAK, IT WAS TIME FOR THE DEFENSE'S PAthologist. The defense had not started well, with Baird's testimony and the Crown's assertion that Sebastian had a disorder on the Asperger's spectrum, but Daniel thought that Charlotte had been a good witness. It had been dangerous to ask her to testify. As an alibi she was important but her volatile emotional state and her lack of attention had worried both Irene and Daniel. Yet Charlotte had excelled. She had been honest about her drug taking and about her anxiety and Daniel felt that her alibi's evidence was more credible than Rankine's later sighting of the fighting boys, after the time when Sebastian claimed he had returned home.

Irene seemed less confident when he met her and Mark afterward. She was stripped of her gown, pacing in the robing room where there were lockers for the barristers.

"I just don't think it's strong enough, Danny," she said. "That bloody psychologist hurt us." The bone-clean cuff of her collar flapped in emphasis as she spoke, hand on hip, two neat lines between her brows. "We need something more."

"We still have our forensic scientist to call, but I assume you're not going to call her now," said Daniel.

"No need since we turned Watson. His capitulation is stronger than anything she could say."

"There is one person who they're still waiting to hear from," said Daniel.

Irene spun round to face him. Her eyes were intense. "You mean put Sebastian on the stand? It wouldn't be allowed at this stage. The defense is under way."

"Could you not make a formal application to the judge?" Daniel asked.

"I could, but he's not certain to allow it. Do you really think he's up to it?"

"He might be."

"Do you really think this will help us? I had wondered as much myself. By not letting him testify we could be harming his chances. We need the jury to understand him, especially with the Crown throwing in Asperger's and his mother's drug addiction and the morbid fascination. He's saying nothing and the jury's imaginations are running riot . . ."

"I agree—they're all waiting to hear his side of the story. His silence now is implicating him," Daniel said.

She exhaled. "God, let's all go and get a drink. I think we need it. We can talk about it then. We'd need reports from the psychologist and then I would need to apply to Baron."

By eight o'clock they were on their third pint at the Bridge Bar in Gray's Inn, giggling in the corner behind Judge Baron's back. The judge was on the other side of the bar with a small sherry.

"You all right, Danny boy, eh?" said Irene, leaning forward and sweeping back the hair from Daniel's face. He allowed it, letting his head fall back gently against the wood paneling. "You seem really heavy lately. You're not like you were at the last trial. I wonder if it's all getting to you, and I see our little client likes you . . . a lot."

"He *hates* me," said Mark, Irene's junior.

Daniel gave him a sideways smile. Mark was an awkward lad, never seeming to find a shirt to fit.

Daniel pounded his fist gently on the table, making the head on his beer vibrate.

"I didn't see all that Asperger's stuff coming. He'd ruled it out—he'd specifically ruled it out."

"None of us saw it coming, Danny, let it go . . . Hopefully we did a good recovery. I think the way to deal with it is just to acknowledge it from now on. I think I might even mention it in closing, but we have to reiterate the point we have already made, that . . . even if he does have the nondiagnosed Asperger's—whatever he called it—Sebastian is not a *murderer*."

Daniel and Mark nodded in agreement.

"The bigger question," Irene said, crossing her legs and leaning back in her seat, "is whether we take your suggestion and call him."

"I know he can do it," said Daniel. "I wouldn't suggest it otherwise. He's not like a lot of little boys. He could handle it."

"What's your opinion, Mark?" Irene asked.

Daniel could tell from her tone and the way that she looked at Mark that she was not really asking him for his opinion, but testing him, teaching him.

"I think it's dangerous. There's no real precedent for it. Venables and Thomson didn't testify at the Bulger trial because they were said to be suffering from posttraumatic stress. Mary

Bell testified, but that was in the sixties and does not draw a true parallel. . . ."

"I think Danny's right that the jury needs to hear from Seb, and I also think he'll surprise us with his ability to perform. What is not certain is whether the psychologist will agree the boy's up to it, and ultimately if Baron will accept the application."

"I think you should go for it," said Daniel.

"Let me sleep on it. What I find disarming," Irene continued, "but . . . nevertheless helpful for his defense . . . is that he is quite a charming child—Asperger's or not. He's weird, he's unsettling, but he's charming nevertheless. And he's very mature, very good in adult company." She let her hand fall onto Daniel's knee. "I think you might be right. We *can* put him on the stand."

Daniel wished that Mark was no longer there. He leaned back, resisting the urge to take her hand.

"He doesn't like *my* adult company," said Mark. Daniel smiled again; Mark seemed genuinely offended to have been rejected by the child.

"You're being paranoid," said Irene. "Why does he like you so much, Danny?"

Daniel shrugged. "Just generally likable, I suppose."

"Do *you* like *him*?" asked Mark.

"That's funny, he asked me that same thing the other day."

"What did you say?"

"I said I did like him . . . I'm not sure *like* is the right word, though. Some part of me . . . understands him, or I think I do. Whether he murdered Ben Stokes or not, we all know he's a very disturbed little boy. He needs looking after."

Mark was looking at Daniel in a strange way, as if he had said something he disagreed with but was afraid to challenge.

"It does make you wonder," said Irene. "When I think of the things I got up to as a child . . . God, it doesn't bear thinking about . . ."

"Like what?" said Danny, one eyebrow raised.

She smiled at him and let her head fall to one side. "I set fire to Maddie Houghton's dress because she said I looked like Laura Ingalls."

"Set fire to her?" Daniel leaned forward.

"Yes, we had a big open fire in the kitchen and I was furious with her. I got a little piece of kindling and set the frill of her dress alight. It could've been a terrible accident. I could've found myself in Sebastian's position."

"What happened?" said Mark and Daniel together.

"Miraculous. She just patted the flames and they died. Just patted them away. Of course she told on me . . . and her dress was ruined."

"I knew you'd've been a little hell-raiser."

"I'm a fire starter," mimed Irene, shooing Mark off to get more drinks.

"What were you like when you were little?" said Irene coyly. "Bet you were *adorable*."

"I was a tearaway," said Daniel, meeting her gaze.

"Yes," she said. "I can see that too."

DANIEL MET WITH THE CROLLS AT PARKLANDS HOUSE. THE psychologist had stated that Sebastian would be able to testify under certain conditions. Irene was preparing her application to Judge Philip Baron to ask if Sebastian could testify.

The rain was hard and the day was black outside. King

Kong was heavy in the meeting room, Sebastian waiting on his own upstairs. The plastic secured chair strained under King Kong's weight.

"Are you saying that you've fucked this up? That is what you're saying, isn't it? Why should he give evidence? Is he not in danger of incriminating himself?"

"There is an argument that by *not* testifying he's incriminating himself, and he held up really well in the police interviews. He's been so bright . . ."

"Don't patronize me. I know my son is intelligent, he wouldn't be my son if he wasn't. Of course he'll be better than your average stupid little kid in the dock. What I want is the strategy. Why is this the best move?"

"Because we think the jury needs to hear from him. The evidence about Asperger's, the later sighting, and the issue over the alibi all seem to ask for Sebastian's comment. We think his testimony could be very important. Essentially it's important at this stage for the jury to hear that he didn't do it. We have already shown that there is reasonable doubt—but we feel that the jury needs to hear it from him."

Kenneth's right eye twitched as he listened to Daniel.

"If Sebastian handles it well, it could make the difference."

"If? . . . I don't deal in *ifs*. I'm surprised that you do."

Daniel took a deep breath.

"We could ask Sebastian what he thinks," said Charlotte.

"For God's sake—he's a child—what would he know?" Kenneth turned to Charlotte in contempt. A fine spray of his spit landed on the table.

"A lot will depend on how well he comes across," said Daniel, loosening his tie. The Parklands House interview room felt claustrophobic. Winter rain was thrust against the small ceiling windows in gusts, so that it fell like handfuls of grit. Daniel was not sure why, but it reminded him of Minnie's funeral. "If he performs well, we might still be able to win. If he performs badly, if Jones manages to rattle him or confuse him, then it could hurt us again." Daniel exhaled, and looked Kenneth and then Charlotte in the eye. "It's a risk, but I think it's worth taking to let the jury hear his point of view."

Charlotte glanced at her husband then asked, "And what if he doesn't testify?" She looked at the table instead of meeting Daniel's gaze. "Will he be found guilty for sure?"

"Not at all."

"But you think he should give evidence?"

"Yes, I think Sebastian should go into the witness box," said Daniel.

Kenneth pouted, exaggerating his already full lips. Daniel watched his eyes, which were at once intelligent and cruel.

"I think we all know he's up to this," said Kenneth slowly. "And I think this madness has to come to an end. We want him home. If he wants to do it, and you think it might help, we'll let him."

SEBASTIAN WAS CALLED. HE ENTERED THE ROOM SLOWLY, A small smile on his white face and his green eyes twinkling with auspicious excitement. He sat at the top of the table, with his parents to his left and Daniel to his right. Charlotte put a palm to his cheek and Sebastian leaned into it.

King Kong snapped his fingers. "Sit up, please, we have something quite serious to discuss."

Sebastian did as he was told, not looking at his father. Once again, Daniel thought that he looked *so* young, his feet still not touching the floor when he sat in the chair, his large head balanced on a thin neck and two dimples on his right cheek when he smiled.

"What do you think about testifying, Sebastian?" said his father. "You going into the witness box to give evidence?"

"Well, you wouldn't actually have to do that," corrected Daniel. "You would most likely be in a room near court. They'd set up a video link. You would have a social worker with you."

"Couldn't you sit with me?" said Sebastian, addressing Daniel. "That would be best."

"What is this ridiculous infatuation?" boomed Croll suddenly. "There are more important things at stake. Testifying might be a way to keep you out of jail. Do you understand?"

Sebastian was cowed suddenly, his green eyes darkening and his rosebud mouth tightening. Daniel glanced at him in time to see the glint of the boy's lower teeth.

"I would probably have to stay in court," said Daniel. "But I could come and see you at the breaks. We can work all this out later. We want people to hear your story. We'll give you lots of practice before . . . but it's up to you."

"I want to testify," said Sebastian, looking at Daniel. "I want to tell the jury what actually happened."

Kenneth Croll took a deep intake of breath and then sighed. "Well, that's that decided then." He nodded at Daniel, as if they had just cut a deal.

28

WHEN DANIEL GOT OFF THE BUS, THE SUN WAS SHINING. The air was still, and the flowering nettles were alert as he walked toward Minnie's farm.

As he walked through the town, people he vaguely recognized stepped out of his way. He walked past the butcher's, which he knew sold a stock of Flynn chickens and eggs, past the sweet shop where mean old Mrs. Wilkes had worked. It was boarded up now—victim of the times. He walked past the police station, which was always closed. He saw the telephone in its doorway, which Daniel knew would connect to Carlisle police.

By the time that he reached the farm, he was out of breath. His hands were relaxed and heavy but he felt his fingers tremble. Sweat beaded at his hairline and he ran a hand through his hair, wiped his palm on his T-shirt, and hooked his forefinger into his back pocket. He stood on the crest of the hill, watching the house until his breathing returned to normal. The stillness of the day was disarming. He walked up to the front door.

He turned the handle and the door yielded with a short creak. Blitz was getting older and no longer ran to greet guests, but Daniel could hear the dog's nails on the linoleum as he stepped into the hall.

The dog turned its head with ears raised, then came to him, head down and tail wagging. Daniel did not kneel to pet the dog, as he would have normally, but he bent to feel the velvet ears and scratch, momentarily, Blitz's white chin.

"Hello, boy," he whispered.

He looked in the direction of the kitchen, feeling his heart beating harder now, in anticipation of the confrontation. The sun streamed through the windowpanes.

He saw her outside, backside in the air, brown skirt riding up to reveal her unlaced brown tackety boots. She was fixing part of the chicken coop and pulling stray weeds out of the yard as she did so, tossing them onto the compost heap.

She was standing in the yard with a metal pail and a brush in hand when Daniel opened the latch on the back door and stepped outside. He watched her from the door, some part of him still pleased to see her after the months apart. The yard was beautiful to him suddenly, with its whiff of dung and the grass bitten to bowling green neatness by the goats. The kids were grown and one of them was now even larger than the doe. He felt a pain in his throat to acknowledge that this was his first real home, and his last.

Still she didn't see him and Daniel considered waiting until she turned and saw him in the doorway. Blitz sat down on the doorstep beside him.

"Minnie," he called out.

Minnie, not *Mam.*

She turned and dropped the pail and the brush and put both hands to her cheeks, as if surrendering, relinquishing her arms.

"Oh, my, love . . . what a surprise," she shouted.

Hand on her bad hip she made her way to him, with a smile so broad that her blue eyes almost disappeared. She walked toward him with a hand up in front of her face to shield it from the sun. He knew she was not able to see the expression on his face. He imagined himself, a dark cutout in the doorway.

She laughed, and Daniel inhaled. Her laughter had been so important to him, and he was conditioned to appreciate it. She dusted off her dirty hands on her skirt.

"To what do we owe this honor?"

She stepped near him, took her hand away from her eyes and stepped into the cool shade where he stood. Her hands were stretched out to take his, but then their eyes met.

"Are you all right, love? Is everything all right?"—She placed a hand on his arm in comfort. She was frowning with concern, her worried lips dimpling her cheeks.

"No, not really," he whispered, twisting his arm away from her, walking past her into the middle of the yard. One of the goats nibbled at the hem of his T-shirt and he snatched it away, stamping the ground once, twice, until the animal started.

She walked toward him. Blitz was at her heels, skipping to and fro, standing in front of her, looking up at her face to see what was wrong. He whimpered a little, scratched the ground with his feet. Minnie put out her fingers to touch the dog's head, but did not take her eyes off Daniel.

"What is it, love?" she asked again. "What's happened?"

Daniel's heart was beating hard now and his palms were moist. He tried to find the breath to say it to her quietly, but his mouth was too dry. He meant to tell her about the thinking he'd been doing, about his urge to find out what had happened to his real mother, now that he was over eighteen. He had planned to tell her about the register office, the death certificate, and the graveyard with the white marble cross, and the paint already flaking off the letters in her name. He had planned to tell her that his mother had been clean when Minnie told him that she had died. She had been getting clean for him, and only overdosed when she thought he would never come looking, that he had forgotten her. It was too much for him, and so he screamed at her:

"My mother died last year!"

He was surprised that tears sprang suddenly to his eyes. He could feel the vein at his temple swelling and the pain at the back of his throat. It was the tears that angered him most. He didn't want them. He hadn't planned on them.

"Last year," he shouted, picking up the metal bucket. He aimed it at Minnie and thrust it forward in a fake throw, to try to scare her, but she didn't flinch. He hurled it then, one yard to her right, so that it crashed onto the doorstep in a clatter that sent the goats to the corners of the yard and set Blitz onto his haunches. He picked up the broom and threw that too, then took a spade that was leaning against the chicken coop. He brandished it, feeling the tears spill, enjoying the easy weight of the spade in his hands.

He bit his lip. "You lied to me," he whispered.

She stood before him, hands at her sides and a look on her

face that he remembered from his childhood: calm, determined.

He tossed the spade in his hand, watching her. "What do you have to say to me? What do you have to say to me, eh?"

The rage bit again.

"Eh?" he shouted.

He took the spade and raised it above his head, took a step forward then smashed it hard into the corner of the chicken coop. He stabbed and swung with the spade until the coop buckled. Chickens fussed in his wake. He swung the spade around and knocked over a bucket with feed and a collection of bedding pots she had stacked near the shed. Blitz was at first startled, then positioned himself next to Minnie, crouched on his forepaws barking and growling at Daniel, running forward and then back as if to nip—disciplining him as he would a wayward sheep.

"I have her . . . death certificate. I saw her *grave*. She died last year. I could've seen her. Could've . . ."

The tears were hot on his cheeks. He didn't wipe them away. He wasn't looking at her face. The backyard was a whirling mass of images: the broken coop, Minnie before him, one hand in another, the frightened goats, and the dog protecting her with teeth bared.

"Let's go into the house," she said. "Let's sit down and talk about it."

"I don't want to go into the house. I don't want to talk about it. I wish you were dead!"

He dropped the spade. The dog jumped back and then resumed snarling. Daniel covered his face with his hands. He could taste salt on his tongue. He felt her hand on his arm.

"There, love," she was saying. "C'mon, let's get you a cup of tea."

He pulled his arm away from her with such force that she lost her balance and fell, hard on her side in the yard. Blitz skipped forward and back, snarling and then whimpering. Minnie looked up at Daniel. He thought she seemed frightened for a moment, but then the look washed away and she wore the look she always had, as if she could see right through him. He remembered watching her through the living room door, watching her tears drip from her chin onto the ivory keys, her bare feet on the pedals, and wanting to understand her in the same way that she seemed to understand him.

"Get on your feet," he shouted. His tears had evaporated, the sun had vanished behind the house and the yard was in shade. "Get up." He kicked at her boot, which caused Blitz to snap at him then back away. Minnie rolled over onto her knees, got one knee up and then slowly rose to her feet.

He stood looking at her, hands on hips, breathing hard, as if he had run to Brampton from Newcastle. She turned and walked slowly into the house. He thought of hitting her with the spade, of knocking her to her feet again, of taking a fistful of her gray curls and smashing her face against the side of the crumbling farmhouse. The dog followed her, standing at the door when she entered it, as if to warn Daniel not to follow.

Daniel took a deep breath and a look around the yard. The goats returned to nibble at his pockets for treats. The chickens stopped fussing and returned to peck at the weeds. He followed her into the house.

She was not in the kitchen. The bathroom door was open and Daniel looked inside, at its long thin sunlit stretch, and the porcelain butterfly still on the shelf, in full wing. Daniel looked away.

She was standing in the living room with one hand on the piano and another on her hip. She was still frowning.

Daniel looked around the room, as if he was seeing it for the first time. On the fireplace was the picture of herself as a young woman, with her husband and daughter. Beside that were three pictures of Daniel, two in his school uniform and one which had been taken at market.

Daniel stood with his hands in his pockets. It felt strangely familiar to be enraged again before her. It reminded him of all the other times as a boy. He felt too tall, too broad now for such anger, taking up the doorway while she stood by the piano. He remembered feeling like this so many years before: angry, distrustful, alone. He had been so much smaller then. She could pin him to the floor with her weight, but no longer. Now he was stronger.

"Do you want a drink?" he asked her.

Minnie said nothing but shook her head.

"Why not, 'bout time, isn't it?"

"Obviously you have something that you want to discuss."

She had the voice on, the one she used at market for people she didn't like.

"Aye, like why you lied to me."

He felt the tears in his throat again. The dog was between them, confused, looking from one to the other, tail wagging one moment then between its legs the next.

"You were a young boy. You needed stability. You needed the chance to settle, to love and to trust. I just gave you a chance not to run for a year or two. I gave you a chance to be . . ." She was whispering. Daniel had to strain to hear her.

"Be with you?"

"To be, to just be you . . ."

"You make me sick."

She shrugged. Her hand swept the surface of the piano, as if to remove dust.

"What was I? Just a fucking replacement for her?"

Minnie turned to him. Her chest swelled but she said nothing.

"You were no replacement. You are my son. You *are my son*."

"So you wanted me so bad that you had to kill my mother off five years before her time? I could have seen her one more time. I could've . . ."

He put the back of his hand to his nose. She was still looking at him.

"What you needed was space not to think about her. To . . ."

"What? So I could think about you, *Mam*?"

"So you could think about yourself for once, be a boy, not have to look after anyone."

"Why was putting you to bed any different from putting her to bed?"

That riled her. She put the guard over the fire and picked up papers that were scattered on the sofa.

"Just stop it," she said. She sounded tired, as if there was no fight left in her anymore, but she raised her chin and spoke in a calm voice. The firm gentleness of it leeched his violence, as it always had. "I know you're hurt. I understand that. Maybe

I should have told you when you went away to the university, but I didn't think that was the time to distract you either. I'm sorry she's dead. I thought maybe when you were older, I would explain. You've no idea the change in you when you didn't have her to worry about. Just look at you now. God willing you'll be a lawyer soon. Your mother would have been proud of you. You were a good, kind boy, but you needed to be free of her so that you could choose for yourself for once."

Daniel spoke to her through his teeth:

"I came all the way here to tell you, to your face, that I will never see you, never talk to you again. I don't want a penny from you. I don't want to hear anything about you. I hate you."

MINNIE STOOD UP STRAIGHT, ONE HAND ON THE ARM OF THE sofa. Her face was washed with grief. Daniel remembered nights when she had been crying and that same look in her eye. She swallowed, her lips parted.

"Son, please. Let's talk about this again when you've calmed down. You're upset. I want you to understand why I did it. It wasn't for me. You don't understand how she was ruining you. Your mind was torn with thoughts of her, and once she was gone, it was as if you could concentrate. Look where you are now, and it was all because of those years of peace knowing that you didn't need to run to her."

"But *I did* need to run to her, don't you understand? She's dead and now it's too late."

Daniel took a step toward Minnie. She raised her chin as if she expected him to hit her. Daniel shivered, the muscles in his neck were tight with the tension.

"I'm sorry, then," she said. "Maybe it was wrong of me. I was doing it for your own good, but you're right that I shouldn't have lied to you. I'm sorry."

Daniel's throat was aching from holding back the tears. He bit his lip and pulled the cuff of his sweatshirt over his hand. With one sweep of his hand, he knocked the pictures off the fireplace. They fell onto the hearth and the dog jumped back and barked when the glass smashed.

Minnie was covering her mouth with both hands.

"No, you shouldn't have lied to me, but what's done is done." He walked toward her, arms at his sides. "This is the last you'll ever see of me. I wish you were dead."

He left, tears hot again on his cheeks as he opened the door and walked down the hill. *Please come back*, he thought he heard her call.

His legs felt weak as he walked down the hill. He staggered, as if wounded, but the sun was warm and reassuring at his back. He wiped a palm over his face to dry it, knowing that all the warmth and the love he had known in the world was also behind him. And he was leaving it behind.

29

BACK FROM HIS RUN, DANIEL SHOWERED AND STOOD WITH a towel around his waist, shaving. Normally he would be in a rush, and would smooth the shaver over his jaw before eating breakfast standing up in the kitchen. This morning he had plenty of time, and so he soaped up. Irene's application to the judge had been successful. Today Sebastian would give evidence. It was possible that by the end of the week there would be a verdict.

Daniel finished shaving and wiped his face dry. He stood with his hands on the sink staring at his reflection. He saw the line of muscle on his upper arms and, when he held his breath and tensed, the rows of muscle on his abdomen appeared. His chest was hairless apart from one or two hairs around his breastbone, and a sparse triangle below his navel. He ran a hand over his now-smooth jawline. He felt relaxed after his run, but his mind was still troubled.

Cunningham was proceeding with the sale of the farmhouse. Daniel didn't want the farm, yet whenever he thought of it, he felt a sharp pang of grief. It was like Minnie's butterfly, he realized—a tangible reminder of something lost.

He stared at his face again. He remembered Minnie taking his chin between her forefinger and thumb and telling him he was good looking. He remembered sweeping all her photographs off the fireplace. He remembered her face, twisted with the pain of thinking that she would lose him after all that they had been through together. He missed her, he admitted now. He had missed her even as he stood before her promising that she would never see him again. He had taken out loans and worked in bars in Sheffield at night, determined to finish at the university without her; determined to prove that he didn't need her. He had missed her then and he missed her now.

She had wanted to come to his graduation, but he wouldn't let her. He had never admitted it to himself before, but he had missed her that day too. He remembered looking anxiously around in case she had come nevertheless. All the other parents were there, brothers, sisters. He had drunk champagne on his own and then snogged one of the waitresses.

And then he had been working, and Minnie was off his mind. Success came quickly and he paid off his loans and bought the flat in Bow.

He put both hands on the edge of the sink and leaned forward until his brown eyes came into focus. It seemed incomprehensible to him now that he had sustained so much anger toward her, for so long. He had always wanted more from her—repentance had never been enough. He didn't consider what she had already lost before he forced her to lose him too.

Daniel took a deep breath. With regret so heavy on his mind, he didn't want to face the day, but he was ready for it.

In the cell, Sebastian was playing rock, paper, scissors with the police officer. He was kneeling on his bunk in his jacket and tie, giggling. The jury should see this, Daniel thought: no monster, but a child who still takes delight from childish things.

"Do you want to play, Danny?" Sebastian asked.

"No, we need to go soon."

The judge agreed that Sebastian could give evidence, but there was no question that this would be via video link. There was no way to gauge how the child would perform on the day, plus there were practical considerations, such as his stature being too short for the witness box, and the necessity of the court seeing his facial expressions. The criminal justice system had been criticized enough over the years for its indifference to young people accused of serious crimes and Justice Baron would not open the proceedings to further criticism. The video would be shown in open court but out of view of the gallery.

Walking to Court 13, Daniel checked his phone. There was a text from Cunningham:

> House contracts to be exchanged end of week. Call me later.

Daniel stopped on the flag-stoned hallway, the stone arches of the old court stretched overhead. *Not now. Not now.* He breathed out and pressed his lips together. Irene appeared at his side.

Daniel switched off his phone and put it in his pocket.

"Listen, I want you to keep a close eye on him this morning. If you get any feeling that he's not coping, we can stop it. He seems to talk to you," she said.

"I'm not with him. They have a social worker . . ."

"I know, but we'll take regular breaks. Check on him."

"Will do. . . . Good luck," said Daniel.

"My Lord, I now call . . . Sebastian Croll."

The screen flickered and then Sebastian's face appeared. He was sitting up straight and wore a thin smile.

"Sebastian?" said Philip Baron, turning himself round to face the screen.

"Yes, sir?"

Daniel sat back in his chair. *Yes, sir.* During rehearsal, Sebastian had not been told to address the judge that way. Daniel glanced up at the gallery. It was full today, but restless. Daniel could see the journalists' frustration at being unable to see the screen: necks craned and fingers appeared on the edge of the balcony.

"I want to ask you a question. Do you know what it means to tell the truth?"

"Yes, sir, it means you don't tell any lies."

"And do you know the difference between the truth and a lie?"

"Yes, the truth is what really happened and a lie is what didn't."

"And if you promise today to tell the truth, what do you think that means?"

"I *must* tell the truth."

"Very well," said Baron, to the court. "He may be sworn."

IRENE STOOD UP. "I WANT YOU TO TELL US, FIRST OF ALL, about your relationship with Ben Stokes. How long had you known Ben?"

"For about three or four years."

"And how would you describe Ben, would you describe him as a friend?"

"He was my friend and my neighbor and my schoolmate," said Sebastian clearly.

"And did you play with him regularly?"

"I played with him sometimes."

"How often would you say that was?"

The projected image of Sebastian was pensive, the large green eyes, turned up to one side, considering the question. "Probably about three times a month."

"And what kind of things would you do together?"

"Well, if we were at school, we might play with a ball or play tag. If we were at home, sometimes he would come to my house or I would go to his, but normally we would play outside."

"On the day that Ben went missing, Sebastian, did you see Ben?"

"Yes."

"Can you tell us what happened?"

"Well, like I told the police, he was out playing on his bike and I asked him if he wanted to play. We played by our houses for a while, but then we decided to go to the adventure playground."

"Whose decision was that?"

"Well, it was really a joint decision, I suppose."

The judge interrupted, his heavy cheeks coloring with temper: "You must *slow down*, Miss Clarke. You forget I have to note this down!"

"Yes, My Lord, getting somewhat carried away . . ."

"Well . . . ," Baron muttered. "Just bring yourself back down to earth!"

"Yes, My Lord," said Irene. "Now, Sebastian, a little slower, did you tell either of your parents where you were going?"

"No."

"Why was that?"

"Well, we were just going to the park. It's only over there, and we would be back before they knew it."

Daniel exhaled down his nose. Sebastian had suddenly changed the pace of his speech, pausing after every phrase to allow the judge to take notes.

"What happened when you got to the park?"

"Well, we were running about and chasing each other and then we started to have a play fight, which turned into a bit of a real fight . . . Ben started calling me names and shoving me . . . at first I told him to stop it, but he wouldn't stop at all. So I pushed him back. It was then that the tall man with the dog called over . . . Mr. Rankine."

Irene faltered for a moment. Sebastian had remembered the name of the witness.

"He told us to cut it out, and so we did for a little bit—we ran over the crest of the hill."

"What happened then?" prompted Irene, clearing her throat.

"Well, we ran into the playground. It was closed, but there's still a way in. When we got there, we climbed up to the highest part of the climbing frame, but then I started to wonder about my mum. She was having a lie-down 'cause she had a headache. I thought I would go back and check on her . . ."

Daniel saw Irene's shoulders relax. Sebastian was on track.

"But . . . Ben didn't want me to go home. He started pushing and shoving me again. I was scared that he was going to shove me off the climbing frame. He was punching me in the stomach and pulling my hair and wrestling me. I told him to stop, but he wouldn't, so after a while I told him it wasn't fun anymore and I was definitely going home."

"And then?" prompted Irene.

"Well, I was about to climb down, but Ben seemed really sad that I was going home. He wanted to stay out. He told me he was going to jump off the climbing frame. I told him to go on then, but I didn't really think he would do it. I think he wanted to impress me. I'm *older* than he is," Sebastian informed her, smiling. "He wanted to stop me going home . . ."

"Did Ben jump off?"

"Yes, he jumped down and landed in a bad way. He hit his nose and his forehead and there was some blood. He rolled over onto his back, and I climbed down to help him."

"How did you help him?"

"Well, I didn't really. I know a bit of first aid, but not much. I leaned over him, and I tried to stop the blood. His nose was bleeding *a lot*. It was making his face red. . . . But he was angry with me. He was calling me names again. I didn't know why because it had been his idea to jump off."

"What happened then?"

"I left him in the playground. I told him I was going to tell his mum that he had hit me and called me names, but I didn't. I thought I might get into trouble for hitting him back while we were in the park. I feel bad now for leaving him there. I don't know who hurt him, but sometimes I wish I hadn't left him like that. I think that I could've done something . . ."

"Why is that?" asked Irene. Daniel could tell from the tone of her voice that she was almost afraid of hearing the answer.

He's using the evidence he has heard, thought Daniel. He wants to explain the expirated blood on his shirt. Daniel also wondered if the boy was copying the other witnesses, who had expressed regret at doing nothing that day—like Rankine.

"I didn't know someone would hurt him. If we'd made up and gone home together, maybe he would still be all right."

Once again Sebastian looked straight into the camera. Daniel held his breath. The tiny smile had gone, and the green eyes seemed to brim with tears.

"And what time was it when you left Ben in the playground and returned home?"

"I was home about three o'clock."

"Thank you, Sebastian," said Irene.

When she took her seat, she gave a reassuring look to Mark, her junior, who sat behind, and then raised an eyebrow at Daniel.

After the break, Gordon Jones stood up to question Sebastian. The boy's thin smile returned. Daniel leaned forward, transfixed.

"Sebastian, did you hear the police recordings that were played earlier in the trial—recordings of your interviews while you were in custody?"

"Yes, sir."

"I read now from your statement: '*We went to the adventure playground and climbed up to the highest parts, but then I had to get home. I thought I would check on my mum, see if she needed her head rubbed.*' Do you remember telling the police that?"

On the big screen, Sebastian nodded, unblinking.

"Sebastian?" said Judge Baron, interrupting again. "I know it is probably strange for you to be . . . on television, so to speak . . . but if you could annunciate your answers, that would help us greatly . . . by that I mean—"

"It's all right, I understand. I can't nod, I have to say yes."

"That's correct," said Baron. The judge gave a small, crumpled smile of appreciation, which he directed at his notes.

"You do remember making that statement to the police, Sebastian?" prompted Jones.

"Yes."

"And it was only later, when the police advised you that they had found Ben Stokes's blood on your clothes and shoes, and also advised you that this was expirated blood, that you changed your story to incorporate the fall and the nosebleed. Is that not correct?"

"I was *very* frightened at the police station," said Sebastian. His eyes were huge, and Daniel stared into them. "They took away all my clothes and put me in a white paper suit . . . They said I couldn't see my mum—they wouldn't tell her to come back in—until I had answered all their questions. I got very confused. I just felt really scared." Again, the magnified eyes seemed to mist with tears.

Daniel smiled again to himself. He had great faith in Sebastian to overcome Gordon Jones. The darts of accusation would wound, but they would not take him down. Sebastian had remembered Daniel's anger when the detectives would not allow his mother to return to the interview room, and was using it to his advantage now in court. Damage had been done by Baird, the psychologist who had been turned by the Crown, but Sebastian was turning his own case around. Daniel had defended adults who lacked the boy's adroitness.

"Scared or not, you do appreciate that you told the police one thing and then when you realized your story wasn't holding up, you *changed* your story . . . you *lied* . . . is that not true, Sebastian?"

"I don't think I was *actually* lying. I was just scared and confused and got things a bit mixed up and forgot some things. I just wanted to see my mum."

"Sebastian," Gordon Jones continued, "Benjamin Stokes's blood was found on your T-shirt, jeans, and trainers; your skin was found underneath Ben Stokes's fingernails and fibers from your jeans were found on the waistband of Ben's trousers, as if—and I am sure you have heard the pathologist suggest just that—you had straddled him. I ask you, did you strike Ben Stokes in the face with a brick at the playground?"

"No, sir."

"Did you hit him in the face, causing his eye socket to fracture and causing a severe head injury that would result in his death?"

"No, sir," Sebastian's voice was louder now, insistent. His eyes were wide and round.

"I think you are a *liar*. You admit lying to the police?"

"I was confused. I didn't lie."

"And you are lying to us now, are you not?"

"No, sir, *no*," said Sebastian. His head bowed. The tiny hand covered his face. He pushed the knuckle of his forefinger into his eye, as if to stop a tear.

The court listened for a few moments as the boy sniffed, before the judge addressed the social worker, who was sitting with Sebastian, to ask if a break would be required.

Daniel watched as the social worker leaned into Sebastian, face close to his. Sebastian shook his head and drew away from her.

Jones continued. He leafed through his ring binder and Daniel wondered if he was going to produce more police transcripts.

He paused longer than seemed necessary. He was an actor: poised, holding the moment in the spotlight for as long as possible, drawing all the attention toward him.

"Are you a clever boy, Sebastian?"

"I think so."

"Do a lot of people think so?"

"Maybe."

"Do your teachers think so?"

"I suppose."

"Your parents?"

"Yes."

"I think you're clever too, Sebastian. I think you're a *very* clever little boy . . ."

Sebastian smiled at the praise, with lips closed.

Jones's voice was sinister.

"You understand very well what's going on in court here today, don't you? You understood the doctor talking about Benjamin Stokes's injuries and about the blood and DNA that was found on your clothes, did you not?"

Sebastian nodded, carefully, and then said, "Yes."

"Do you watch television, Sebastian?"

"Yes."

"Every day?"

"Almost every day, yes."

"How many hours of television do you watch every day?"

"I don't know. Maybe two or three."

"What kind of things do you like to watch?"

"Most things."

"Do you like watching police dramas?"

"Sometimes."

"Crime programs where they try to find the murderer?"

"Sometimes."

"I see. Are you interested in murder, Sebastian?"

"Everyone's interested in murder," said Sebastian. Daniel held his breath. "I mean, there are a lot of TV programs about it. There wouldn't be so many if people weren't interested in it."

Daniel exhaled.

"Did you hear the doctor earlier, saying that you had an *unhealthy* interest . . . a morbid curiosity, in fact . . . about blood, death, and injury?"

Jones said each of the words slowly, enjoying the drama as their vowels bludgeoned the room.

"Yes, I did hear, but I didn't think he knew anything about me. He met me just twice. He doesn't know what I'm interested in, or what I like or don't like, or anything."

"I see," said Jones, almost to himself. "The expert witness didn't know anything . . . yet he did comment on your previous diagnosis of Asperger's syndrome. Do you have Asperger's, Sebastian?"

"No!" A scowl appeared on the small boy's face. The green eyes darkened as his brows lowered.

"Do you know what Asperger's is?"

Sebastian sat dumb, frowning, as Irene jumped to her feet. "My Lord, with your leave, the expert witness did assert that Sebastian *did not* have Asperger's syndrome, as previously diagnosed."

Baron shrugged and turned his mouth downward. "Yes, Mr. Jones, if you could rephrase."

"Let me ask you, Sebastian, is it true that you have *no* friends?"

"I do have friends."

"I see. Not according to your teachers. Who are your friends . . . Ben Stokes?"

"I have friends."

"I see. We have your school records here. They tell us that you are a bully, that nobody wants to be your friend because you're mean to them."

"That's *not true*."

Sebastian spat quiet but distinct rage into *not* and *true*. Under his breath, Daniel began to whisper, *It's all right, calm down. You're all right, just calm down.*

Irene turned round in her seat slightly and shot a look at Daniel. He nodded at her to assure her that things would be okay. Inside, he was no longer sure.

"Is it true that when you do make friends it is only for a *very* short time?"

"No."

"Other children don't want to be with you, Sebastian, is that not correct?"

"No." The boy was not shouting, but his lower teeth appeared. They were tiny and white, like the teeth of a pike.

"Is it not true that as soon as other children get to know you, they do not want to be friends with you?"

"No!"

The court was spellbound. On the screen, Sebastian's cheeks were pink with rage.

"I have here notes from the secure unit where you are currently on remand. The warden has specifically mentioned your inability to get on with the other children and to form friendships . . ."

Irene stood up. "My Lord, I must protest. My client is an innocent boy on remand in a secure unit where he is by far the youngest child among a number of severely disturbed teenagers. I should think it obvious, and to my client's credit, that he has found it difficult to form friendships in these circumstances."

There was a small pause and Daniel relaxed as both Jones and Baron conceded Irene's point.

"Let's get back to the subject of Ben's murder . . . murder, after all, is what interests you. You had Ben Stokes's blood on your clothes and your shoes: how did that feel?"

"What do you mean?" Sebastian's temper left him for a moment as he was drawn into Jones's abstraction.

"Well, when Ben supposedly burst his nose and his blood got onto your clothes and your shoes, how did it feel?"

"All right. It's just blood. Everybody has blood."

"I see, so you felt quite good with Ben's blood on you when you walked home?"

"I felt okay. It was just a natural thing." Sebastian was looking up in the corner of the screen, as if remembering. His thin smile had returned.

"What about when Ben was hurt, how did you feel then?"

"Well, *he* was hurting. I wasn't. I didn't feel anything."

"What do you suppose Ben was feeling?"

"Well, he fell down and he was bleeding, but that is sometimes what happens when your nose gets banged. Sometimes . . . you don't have to hit someone very hard . . . sometimes they can just get slapped and their nose starts bleeding. Noses are quite sensitive."

Daniel felt pain in his diaphragm. Sebastian seemed so far away. Behind the screen, it was as if he was in another dimension, lost to all their efforts to save him. He was irreclaimable, gone. The court heard a boy who lacked empathy discussing random violence, but Daniel knew that Sebastian was specifically referring to King Kong hitting his mother.

"Did you hit Ben, Sebastian, to make his nose bleed?" Gordon Jones was almost whispering.

Daniel was surprised that Sebastian could hear. If it had been in open court, Jones would have had to speak louder.

Sebastian shook his head. "No."

"Blood . . . is natural," repeated Jones. "Everyone has

blood . . . When you had Ben's blood on you, you felt fine. Had you ever had anyone else's blood on you, Sebastian?"

"Well . . . my own . . . if I got hurt."

"I see, anyone else?"

Sebastian was pensive for a moment, green eyes to the side and looking upward, remembering. "My mum's blood . . . I don't mean when I was born, because being born there is a lot of blood, and it gets onto the baby, but afterward if she got hurt and she touched me, sometimes it would get onto me."

"I see. Have you ever caused another to bleed?"

Irene rose to her feet. "My Lord, I must question the relevance of this line of questioning."

Baron nodded and cleared his throat loudly. "Yes, Mr. Jones, if you could try to stick to the point."

"Very well, My Lord. Sebastian—did you tell the police—and I read now from the transcripts of your interview:

> *Do you know whose blood might have been on your shirt?*
> *A bird's.*
> *Why, did you hurt a bird?*
> *No, but I saw a dead one once and I picked it up. It was still warm and its blood was all sticky.*

Again Irene rose to her feet. "My Lord," she began, but Baron silenced her with a hand.

"I will hear the answer," he said. "But, Mr. Jones, Miss Clarke is correct, you must make your question clear."

"Yes, M'Lord." Irene sat down.

"You remember telling the police that, Sebastian?" said Jones.

"Yes."

"Why did you think the blood on your clothes belonged to the bird and not to Ben?"

"I got confused. The bird was another day."

"I see, another day. Did you hurt this bird?"

"No," said Sebastian, but then he paused. His eyes turned up and to the left of the screen as he considered. Daniel thought he looked like a young boy saint, persecuted. He pulled his lower lip into his mouth and sucked it. He released it with a sound that was almost like a kiss. "I helped it . . ."

"Tell me about the bird, Sebastian. What did you do to it, to cause its blood to transfer onto your clothes?"

Again, Sebastian's eyes rolled upward as he remembered. The eyes of the boy seemed enormous on the big screen.

"Well . . . there was a bird I found in the park one day. It had a broken wing. It was a pigeon or something. It was turning round and round because it couldn't fly. It was going to die, you see. It would get eaten by a fox or a dog or a cat, or it would just starve to death . . ."

"I see, so what did you do?" Jones had his body turned toward the jury, but each time he addressed Sebastian, he would look in the direction of the camera.

"I stamped on its head; I had to put it out of its misery, but it didn't die. Its claws were still moving." As if the words were not enough, Sebastian raised both hands up before his face. He held his hands like claws and made them twitch. "So I had to end it."

"What did you do?" asked Jones.

"I pulled its head away from its body, and then . . . it was still." Again Sebastian looked upward and to the left, remembering. "But I had the bird's blood on me then." Sebastian turned to look into the camera again. He rubbed his hands together, as if washing them.

Daniel clasped his hands tightly together, under the table. They were damp with sweat.

"Why did you decide you needed to kill the bird, Sebastian?" whispered Gordon Jones, still turned from the boy.

"I told you. It would have died anyway. I had to put it out of its misery."

"You could have taken it to the vet. Why did you not want to help the bird? Why did you decide to murder it?"

"I don't think vets help pigeons with broken wings," said Sebastian. His tone was authoritative, condescending. "The vet would only have killed it too, just with a needle."

The word, *needle,* seemed to pierce the skin of silence in the room. There was a rustle, as the people in the court shifted in their seats.

"How did you feel when the bird was dead?" asked Jones.

"Well, it was only little and it had to die, so that was a shame. But it was better that it didn't suffer."

"Ben Stokes was only little. Were you upset when he died?"

Sebastian blinked, twice or maybe three times; he turned his head to the side, as if in anticipation of Charlotte's fingers coursing through his hair.

"Well . . . *I'm* only little too," he said. "Why is everyone so interested in Ben? He's dead now, but I'm still here."

The room was unnaturally silent.

"No more questions for this witness, M'Lord," said Jones.

"Miss Clarke?" Baron asked.

Daniel almost could not breathe, but he watched Irene stand up. Despite the evidence, she seemed strong, valiant.

"Sebastian," Irene called.

Her voice was clear and awakened the room. Sebastian turned anew to the camera, blinking.

"Ben Stokes was your friend. What did you like about him?"

"He was funny and . . . He could do very good backward rolls. I can't do them. They hurt my neck."

"You had known Ben for nearly four years. In all that time had you fought physically, so that either of you had to visit the hospital or even have first aid?"

"No, but we sometimes played wrestling and we had a few fights, but we didn't really get hurt."

"I see. Did you kill Ben Stokes on August eighth of this year?"

"No." Sebastian was quiet, chin down to his chest.

"Did you hit your friend Ben Stokes in the face with a brick in the adventure playground on August eighth?"

"No!" Sebastian's mouth was round, his eyes turned down in distress.

Daniel could feel the energy in the room change. The jury, even the gallery, seemed shocked that Irene should confront the child in this way. But Daniel was proud of her for it. The bird might now be forgotten.

"No further questions, M'Lord."

Without voice, the video buzzed. Sebastian stared at the camera, his eyes shining and a slight smile on his still-pink lips. Sebastian wiped each eye in turn and then looked upward.

His white face captivated the court one last time, and then the monitor was switched off.

Daniel stepped outside the court because he needed air. He would need to go down and see the child before court convened again.

It had been hard for Daniel to watch Sebastian testify. He turned up his collar and looked at the clouds that pressed down on the buildings. His mind was a confusion of recent and distant memories. He saw Sebastian's face enlarged on the screen; heard the clatter of the pail and the spade in Minnie's yard; he watched Minnie fall again—losing her footing and falling on her bad hip when he pulled away from her.

He had hurt her, he saw that now.

His own pain over the lie she had told now seemed less important than the pain that he had caused to her. She had always known what was best for him. He had not understood it at the time, but she had protected him. He thought of her dying, wanting to see him one more time, but knowing that he would not come. She was the only person who he truly believed had loved him. He closed his eyes, remembering the warm weight of her hand on his head when she said good night. Even during the years of anger, he had not doubted that she loved him. He hoped she had known that he had loved her too. Years he had denied her, but now he acknowledged all that she had done for him.

Daniel went to check on Sebastian, who was again playing games with the police officer in his cell. He was talkative and energetic, standing up on his bunk and reaching for the ceiling. He seemed unaffected by cross-examination, unaware of how he had done badly and how he had done well.

"Did I do okay?" asked Sebastian, eyes blinking up at Daniel.

Daniel put his hands in his pockets. "You did fine."

Upstairs, Daniel called Cunningham.

"You'll be relieved this is all over," Cunningham said. "I know you thought it would take ages to sell, but this is quicker than I ever thought it would be. Will you come up, or do you want me to handle it?"

"You handle it," said Daniel quickly. He ran a hand through his hair and turned in the corridor. "Or . . . can you wait? I might come up at the weekend. I want to see the place one more time—I just . . . Can you just wait, actually?"

"Of course. I'm sorry this has happened at a . . . difficult time for you."

"What d'you mean?"

"I saw you on TV. The Angel Killer. You're on the case."

Daniel took a breath. Everyone else had made up their mind about Sebastian. He wondered what the jury would decide.

30

JONES LOOKED TRIUMPHANT AS HE GLANCED OVER HIS notes. Closing speeches were scheduled for the morning, with the judge's summing up to follow that afternoon. The judge arrived and the gallery filled up. Daniel tried not to look up into the journalists' faces.

Jones placed his papers on the podium and turned toward the jury, hands in his pockets, rocking back on his heels. Daniel thought he looked pleased with himself.

"Cast your mind back to everything you have heard relating to the events of August eighth this year . . . You have heard the defendant admit that he was playing with little Ben Stokes on that day. A witness saw the defendant fighting with Ben in the open park and then later identified him fighting in the adventure playground where Ben was found dead.

"The type of injury that Ben sustained means that we

cannot pinpoint the time of the attack, only the time of death, around six P.M. in the evening. This means that Ben could have sustained his fatal wounds at any point that afternoon and evening, since he was last seen alive about two P.M. The defendant claims to have an alibi—his mother—from three P.M. onward, but you have heard the cocktail of drugs that the boy's mother ingested that day and you are therefore correct to wonder if she is reliable. You are also correct to wonder what story a mother would concoct to protect her son.

"You have heard from forensic scientists who explained to you how the victim's blood was transferred onto his attacker's clothing. I remind you that the defendant had defensive scratches on his arms and also fibers from the victim's clothes on his jeans, suggesting that he had straddled the victim. From this position, it would have been possible for the defendant to use the force of gravity to help him cause the significant, brutal facial injuries that resulted in young Ben literally bleeding to death.

"You heard the forensic expert attest to the fact that the bloodstains on the defendant's clothes were a result of a violent assault to the face or nose, with the victim then blowing blood onto the attacker.

"Make no mistake." Jones paused and stabbed the lectern with his forefinger. He leaned forward onto his finger for emphasis, staring unblinking at the jury. "This was not an easy murder to carry out. There was no accident here, no sleight of hand or loss of footing. This was violent, bloody murder, carried out face-to-face.

"You have heard the defendant himself tell of his fascination with murder and death. You have heard experts testify that the defendant has a mild disorder on the Asperger's spectrum, a disorder that makes him prone to violence, which makes it difficult for him to form friendships, but a disorder which would not prevent him from *lying* about his actions. And lie he has done, when, testifying, he told you that he did not murder the victim. We have heard from neighbors of the victim, whose children were terrorized by the defendant before he took this one stage further, when he brutally murdered Benjamin Stokes. The defendant threatened a neighbor's children with broken glass, and indeed bullied and physically injured the victim before he finally murdered him on August eighth.

"Boys may be boys, but this boy was a known danger in the neighborhood. He is proven to be capable of this ghastly crime. Forensic evidence puts him at the scene of the crime. We know that the defendant and the victim fought, and the victim's blood was transferred onto the defendant's clothing.

"Sebastian Croll is a proven bully with a sick interest in murder, and murder he did on August eighth this year.

"I know when you stop to consider the facts of the case, you will find the defendant, Sebastian Croll . . . guilty."

Daniel could see the headlines already: "A Bully with a Sick Interest in Murder." He thought of Tyrel's trial and how the verdict had seemed another violence.

At the break Daniel followed the Crolls out of the courtroom. Even the skin on Charlotte's face was trembling. He accompanied the family to the public waiting room. Kenneth Croll maneuvered his wife by her elbow into the room. He demanded coffee but Charlotte was shaking too much to get the coins into the slot. Daniel helped her and carried the cups over to where Kenneth had reclined in a chair, legs akimbo and hands clasped behind his head.

"We can appeal?" said Kenneth.

"We talk about appeals if he's found guilty," returned Daniel.

Croll's eyes seemed to flash with anger. Daniel met his gaze.

Back in court, Daniel thought that Irene looked nervous. He had never seen her nervous before. She was fidgety, twirling her watch on her wrist. He had not had a chance to speak to her, but she looked over at him before she stood up. Daniel mouthed *Good luck*. She smiled and looked away.

When called, Irene stood up and rested her open notebook on the lectern. There was silence as she glanced at her notes and reminded herself of her arguments. When they were defending Tyrel, Irene had rehearsed her closing arguments to Daniel the night before. He remembered her pacing back and forth before him, in her stocking feet.

Now she turned to face the jury. So much rested on her speech.

"Sebastian . . . is a little boy," she began. She no longer looked nervous: shoulders back, chin raised. "Sebastian . . . is eleven years old. If he were eighteen months younger, he would not be before you today. Sebastian is a child on trial for murder. He is accused of killing another little boy, a child even younger than he is now.

"That Ben was murdered is a tragedy and something that we should all feel devastated by . . . but we won't get justice for little Ben by convicting the wrong person, and certainly not by convicting another innocent little boy.

"The papers all love a good story, and I know you read about this case in the newspapers before you even got to court, before you knew that you would sit on this trial. The papers have talked about societal decay, about the failure of the family . . . the papers have used words like evil, wicked, and depraved.

"But, ladies and gentlemen, I have to remind you that this . . . is not a story. This trial is not about societal decay and it is not your task to address it. *It is* your job to consider the facts, as they have been presented to you *in this courtroom*, and not in the press. It is your job to consider the evidence and *only the evidence* before you decide if the defendant is guilty or not guilty.

"You've seen some terrible images and heard some disturbing evidence during this trial. It's natural when presented with shocking acts of violence to want to blame, to want to find . . . someone responsible. But this little boy is not responsible for the violence that you have had described to you in the course of this trial.

"So what is the evidence?

"There were no witnesses to this terrible crime. No one saw Ben being harmed. A witness did claim to see Sebastian and Ben fighting late on the afternoon of the murder but the witness's account was unreliable. There is a murder weapon in evidence, but it cannot be tied to any one suspect. No fingerprint or DNA was found on the brick that was used to kill little Ben Stokes. He suffered a cerebral hematoma, which means that we know approximately what time he died—around six o'clock in the evening—but we don't know when he was attacked and suffered the fatal blow. Sebastian was home in his house from three o'clock in the afternoon, well before Ben was reported missing.

"Sebastian admits fighting with Ben earlier that day and he told us how Ben jumped from the climbing frame, causing his nose to bleed. Spots of Ben's blood and fibers from his clothes were transferred onto Sebastian's clothing, but no more than you might expect in the course of a few hours of play outside where there was a childish disagreement and an accident. The prosecution's own scientists told you that they would have expected much more blood to be on Sebastian's clothes if he had in fact killed Ben in this very violent way. Those of you with children will know that the small amounts of fibers and blood found on Sebastian's clothing are entirely consistent with normal rough and tumble play.

"Ben's murder was brutal, but it also required considerable strength, and I know that you will question the ludicrousness of the prosecution's suggestion that the small boy before you today would have been able to wield such force. We know that the witness, Mr. Rankine, is shortsighted. He didn't see Sebastian with Ben that afternoon, but did he see someone else trying to hurt that little boy? He has told you that it was possible he saw a small adult attacking Ben."

Irene turned a page in her notebook. She took a deep breath and swallowed, nodding gently at the jury. Daniel watched them. They were rapt, watching Irene, believing her.

"You have heard that Sebastian suffers from a very mild disorder known as PDD-NOS—a disorder on the Asperger's spectrum—and this may make Sebastian seem more . . . *intense* than other eleven-year-olds you may know, but . . . however unusual you may find him, you must not let that distract you from the evidence of the case. Sebastian . . . was brave enough to tell you his story. He didn't need to, but he wanted to speak so that you could hear the truth about what happened that day, in his own words. Sebastian may be intense, but he is not a murderer. He may be a bully at school, but he is not a murderer.

"The facts: If Sebastian had killed Ben, he would have gone home that day *covered* in blood. He would not have arrived home at three o'clock and watched television with his mum. Sebastian is a small boy and could never have wielded the murder weapon with the force required to kill Ben. But more significantly there is no evidence tying the brick to Sebastian, and no one saw Sebastian hurt Ben. He was seen chasing and fighting Ben in the park, but this fight was of so little concern to the man who witnessed it that he did not even feel the need to physically separate the boys, or to report the incident to the police. The prosecution's witness went home and watched television because what he had seen was not an act of violence preceding murder but a very normal argument between two little boys, and the boys, when called on by an adult to stop, did exactly that.

"More important, what role have the police played in insuring justice was done in this case? Mr. Rankine admitted that he may have seen an adult in a pale blue or white top attacking Ben. What did the police do about this? They checked the council's CCTV tapes and found nothing, so what else did they do . . . ?"

Irene raised both hands up to the jury, as if asking them to contribute.

"Not a thing," she shrugged her shoulders and leaned on the lectern, as if resigned to such faineance.

"By all accounts there could be an adult assailant—someone who had a white or pale blue top, who attacked and killed Benjamin after Sebastian left the playground. This important possibility, highlighted to us by the Crown's witness, was not properly followed up, as it should have been. Are we sure that this boy committed this crime, or is there indeed the chance that someone else did?

"And so you must ask yourself, is it safe to convict this boy on this evidence? Once you set aside the newspapers, the terrible images you have seen, and the things you have heard; once you consider that there is absolutely no evidence that directly proves Sebastian killed Ben, no forensic evidence consistent with an injury of this type, no fingerprints on the murder weapon, no witnesses to the actual attack—you have to come to the only rational conclusion that is left.

"The prosecution has to prove beyond *all reasonable doubt* that the defendant is guilty. The burden of proof lies with the prosecution, not on the defense. You must now consider whether that has been achieved, or if you indeed doubt the circumstantial evidence that has been presented to you. This is no hardened criminal who stands before you, with a string of convictions in his past. This . . . is a little boy.

"When you come back from your jury room, I want you to be very sure . . . *very sure* that you have made the right decision. I know that you will see the facts as they are and realize that Sebastian . . . is not guilty.

"If you believe that Sebastian is innocent, you must acquit. If you believe that Sebastian is probably innocent you must acquit. Even if you think that Sebastian *might be* innocent, you must acquit."

Irene gathered up her notes. "Thank you for listening."

THE JUDGE'S SUMMING UP LASTED ALL AFTERNOON, AS EXpected, and then the jury were excused to consider the verdict.

Daniel worked late at the office and then went to the Crown for last orders. He texted Irene when he was halfway through his pint: "Thinking about tomorrow. Not sure I am ready for it. Hope u r ok." There was no reply.

THE NEXT DAY WAS FRIDAY, AND DANIEL WORKED IN THE morning before he got the call to say that the jury had reached a verdict.

In the courtroom, everyone assembled again: lawyers, family, journalists, and public. Sebastian sat beside Daniel waiting for the decision that would define the rest of his life.

Daniel looked around when court was in session. Minutes passed dizzily, a flutter of processes. He glanced down at the small boy beside him, noticing again the valiant tilt of his chin, the young green eyes expectant, wary.

He put a hand on Sebastian's back. The little boy seemed so smart today in a fresh shirt that was too big in the collar and a striped tie. He looked up at Daniel and smiled.

Baron raised himself in his chair, and peered over his glasses at Sebastian and Daniel. "The child need not stand."

The clerk stood up and addressed the jury. "Will the foreman please stand?"

The foreman was a woman. She rose to her feet and folded her hands in front of her.

"Have you reached a verdict on which you are all agreed?"

"Yes," said the woman, who was middle aged, clearly spoken.

"Do you find the defendant, Sebastian Croll, guilty or not guilty of the murder of Benjamin Stokes?"

Daniel couldn't breathe. The air was thick. Each pair of eyes in the crowded court was focused on the woman's lips, waiting for her to speak. Daniel could feel the tension emanating from the young boy beside him, as his past was considered and the rest of his life was decided.

When Tyrel had been in the dock, Daniel had felt separate from him and powerless. Yet now it felt worse having Sebastian at his side, feeling the brush of the boy's arm, watching the almost imperceptible rock of his body, smelling his clean hair. With his little client right beside him, he was no more able to protect Sebastian than he had been Tyrel.

If Sebastian was convicted of murder, a lengthy period of incarceration was inevitable. Although politicians no longer determined the length of the sentence—as had previously been the case for convicted children—judges were given guidelines on life tariffs, which advised a minimum of twelve years' imprisonment even for a child Sebastian's age. Daniel knew that if Sebastian was found guilty, it would mean he would be an adult before he was eligible for parole.

Daniel thought about the years the child would spend in secure units and then adult prisons; the drugs he would be introduced to, the relationships he would form and learn to lose; the estrangement he would feel from society and from the future itself. The future would always imply some kind of imprisonment. The leader of the jury raised her eyes to look at the clerk who had addressed her.

Sebastian exhaled and at the same time slipped his hand into Daniel's. Daniel coursed his thumb across the back of the boy's hand, as Minnie might have done. Daniel remembered the roughness of her thumb on his young skin. It was an instinct of care and, after all, she had taught him to care.

Irene's spine was completely straight. Daniel wished he could take her hand too.

"Not guilty."

"And is that the verdict of you all?"

"Yes."

There were no cries of rapture. The courtroom reeled in shock. There was a gulf of silence before the voices came, hushed and insistent, like a wave crashing onto shore. The silence was broken with a choke of sobs from the victim's family, angry voices of protest.

Baron silenced the courtroom. "I will remind you that this is not a football ground."

"WHAT DOES IT MEAN?" SAID SEBASTIAN WHEN COURT HAD closed and the jury had been relieved. He was still holding on to Daniel's hand.

"It means you can come home, darling," said Charlotte, turning her son toward her. Her eyelids trembled as she raised them above her large eyes. Sebastian leaned, weary and willowy, into his mother. She curled around him and tousled his hair.

The court began to clear. Daniel followed Irene and Mark out into the great hall of the Old Bailey.

As he made his way toward the exit, Daniel felt a strong hand grasp his shoulder and turn him round. Before he could say a word Kenneth King Croll was shaking his hand and slapping him on the back. Kenneth then reached out to Mark and shook his hand before taking Irene by the shoulders and shaking her lightly before planting a kiss on each cheek.

Released from Kenneth's grasp, Irene turned to Daniel and smiled. Daniel wanted to hold her, but felt inhibited with their clients nearby.

"Where are you going now?" Daniel said, looking down at her, trying to find her eyes.

"Back to the office, I suppose. I don't know. I'm exhausted. Go home, maybe. What about you? You'll have to meet the great British press."

"Face the music."

"Shall I wait for you, then?" she said.

"Yeah, wait and we can go get a drink or something. I might be a little while. I'll be done as soon as I can."

When Irene left, Daniel turned back toward the court to see Ben Stokes's parents leaving with the family liaison officer. Paul was holding Madeline by the shoulders. He seemed to be half-carrying her. Her feet moved with tiny steps, her head down, hair over her face. Just before she reached Daniel she pushed her hair back and Daniel saw the red eyes and nose, the sunken cheeks. Her eyes flashed for a moment and she pulled away from her husband. Daniel stood back, sure that she was going to attack him. But it was Charlotte who Madeline targeted. The vast hall echoed as Madeline screamed and reached out—fingers like claws—toward Charlotte's shoulder.

"*He's a monster,*" Madeline Stokes screamed. "*He killed my little boy . . .*"

Daniel was about to call security, but Paul Stokes pulled his wife away. As she passed she became passive again, allowing her husband to lead her away.

"Are you all right, Charlotte?" said Daniel.

Charlotte had opened up her handbag. She was searching through it fervently. Objects fell out and onto the floor: a hairbrush, a compact mirror, eyeliners and pens. Deftly, bending at the knees each time, Sebastian bent to pick them up.

"I need, I need . . . ," she said.

"For God's sake, woman, calm down," Kenneth hissed.

Daniel reached out to her, but it was too late, Charlotte's knees buckled and she fell onto the court floor, letting her handbag fall open. The pills she had been searching for rolled out. Sebastian held them up to his father.

"Here," the boy said, presenting them.

Kenneth's face was almost purple, and Daniel was not sure if it was embarrassment or the strain as he helped Charlotte onto her feet.

A security officer came up and asked them if they needed assistance.

"Look, we're fine," Croll boomed. He turned to Daniel. "Could I ask you to watch Seb for a moment? I need to calm her down before we go out."

Daniel nodded, watching them go. Sebastian looked up at him, hands by his sides, chin tilted, so that the child's entire round face was turned toward Daniel.

"We'll be in that conference room," Daniel shouted after Croll.

"Give us twenty minutes."

Daniel looked at his watch. The boy was still staring at him.

"She's having a panic attack. She can't breathe and her face goes all white and she starts to breathe like this . . ." Sebastian began to mime hyperventilation until Daniel put a hand on his shoulder. Already the boy was red and coughing.

"Come on," said Daniel, opening the door to one of the conference rooms and saluting the security guard who stood nearby. "Let's go in here and sit for a while until your mum's feeling better."

The door closed behind them, sealing them in its insulated space. There were no windows in this room. Daniel was reminded of the funeral parlor where Minnie had been cremated. The sound of the Old Bailey: heels on the flagstones, lawyers talking over each other into cell phones, solicitors whispering to clients—were all forbidden.

There was a warm, germinating silence. The boy's eyes were dry and his pale face pensive. It reminded Daniel of the first time they'd met, in the police station in Islington.

"Do you think most people are sad that I was found not guilty?" said Sebastian, looking up at Daniel.

"It doesn't matter what other people think; you had a good defense and the jury found you not guilty. You can go back to your life now."

Sebastian got up and walked around the table to Daniel. He stood by the side of Daniel's chair.

"I didn't want to go back to Parklands House."

"No," said Daniel. He was leaning forward on his elbows, so that his face was level with the boy's. "I didn't want you to have to go back there either."

The little boy sighed and then leaned into Daniel. He rested his head on Daniel's shoulder. Daniel had watched the boy comforted by his mother enough and knew what to do. After a moment's pause, he raised his hand and ran his fingers through the boy's hair.

"It'll be okay," Daniel whispered. "It's all over now."

"Do you think I'll go to hell?"

"No, Seb."

"How do you know?"

"Because hell doesn't exist. I don't believe in it, anyway."

"But you don't actually know. Nobody *actually* knows. Believe means you just *think* something is so."

"Well, call me stubborn but I think I do know. All sounds like rubbish to me."

"Will Ben be in heaven? Everyone says he's an angel."

"Seb, listen, I know this has been really hard on you—the case's been on TV and in the papers and all the other kids at Parklands House have been talking about you, but you have to try not to pay attention to all the newspapers and stuff. They only do that to sell papers, not because there's a shred of truth. . . ."

"Truth," said Sebastian, calmly. "Do you like me, Daniel?"

"Yes," said Daniel, exhaling.

"If I tell you something, will you still like me?"

Daniel considered, then nodded.

"I put the brick on Ben's face."

Daniel held his breath and watched the small boy. The light was catching his green eyes. He had an almost imperceptible smile on his lips.

"You told me you just went home . . ."

"It's all right," said Sebastian, smiling properly now. "I'll be okay. You don't need to worry about me."

Daniel nodded. He felt his stomach muscles tighten.

"I like you too," said Sebastian. "I think you're my friend. I'm glad you were my lawyer . . ."

Daniel nodded again. His collar was tight at his throat.

"What do you mean . . . you put the . . . brick on Ben's face?"

"I didn't like Ben's face. I just wanted to cover it up, so I wouldn't see it anymore. He was all crybaby and snot and wanting to go home. I told him he had to *stop crying.* I told him that if he tried to go, I'd *give him something to cry about* . . . and then after I put the brick on his face, he didn't cry at all. He didn't make a sound. Not anymore."

Daniel let his shoulders fall. He exhaled and loosened his tie. He leaned forward and put both hands through his hair.

"You should've told me, Sebastian." His voice was loud in the room. "You should've told me at the beginning. We would have done things differently."

Sebastian smiled, and sat down again, opposite Daniel. He was all innocence: all eyelashes and freckles and neatly parted hair. "I thought you wouldn't like me if I told you. I wanted you to like me."

"It's not about *like*, Sebastian. I told you at the beginning, you needed to tell me everything, the truth, pure and simple. I'm your *lawyer* . . . you should have *told* me."

"Well, you know now," said Sebastian. He tilted his head to one side.

Daniel felt sick, a chill sweat on his back. He pressed his tongue to the roof of his mouth, controlling himself.

"I have to go now," said Daniel. "Let's . . . find your parents." The boy looked up at him, and Daniel took a deep breath. He didn't know what to say to the child.

Outside, Charlotte was on her feet again, wavering like a sunflower, large black shades over her eyes. Ken was still holding on to her elbow.

"Thanks, Dan," said Kenneth as he returned the boy to their care. Daniel winced at Croll's out-of-place informality.

"All right, young man?" Kenneth boomed at his son.

Sebastian slipped between his parents and took their hands. The sight of the family like this sickened Daniel. He wanted to look away.

But then they were gone, all hand in hand, walking out the doors of the Old Bailey, Sebastian looking over his shoulder at Daniel as he was tugged gently outside.

Daniel undid the top button of his shirt, pulled his tie off, and put it in his pocket. His legs felt unsteady. It felt like walking away from Minnie for the last time. It wasn't the first time a client had lied to him. Daniel didn't understand why, this time, he felt so shorn.

He stood in the ornate hall of Central Criminal Court and looked around him. His loss was draped in a strange relief. One way or another, it was all over now.

Daniel walked out into the swarm of journalists. It was cold and threatening rain, but he felt the heat of the camera flashes. He was blinded by them and couldn't see the faces that addressed him, only the foam-encased microphones that were thrust toward him.

"We are pleased with the outcome of the trial; my client and his family are looking forward to the return of normal family life. Our thoughts are with the family of the victim at this difficult time."

Daniel pushed his way through the crowd as one of the

journalists shouted: "How did it feel when you won? Were you surprised?"

Daniel turned and faced the man who'd addressed him, knowing that he was now too close to the camera. The emotion apparent in his face would be broadcast, and commented on, in news feeds later: "Nobody won today. A little boy lost his life, but we are grateful that justice has been done for my client."

There were more questions, but then the Stokeses came out. Madeline was recovered but brittle, Paul had a resolute turn to his lips. Daniel and the CPS solicitor were abandoned in favor of the parents of the victim.

Daniel looked around for Irene but couldn't see her. He started to walk toward the tube, then saw her ahead of him. She seemed dejected, eyes to the ground.

"I thought you said you were going to wait for me," he called, running to catch up with her.

"God, there you are. I didn't know where you'd gotten to." She brushed a strand of hair from her face. "I thought you might be lost in that scrum of press."

"Are you all right?" Daniel asked as he looked into her tired eyes.

"I dunno," she said with a strange smile. "I feel weird. Probably just exhausted."

"You won," he said.

"We won," she said, putting a hand on his lapel. He enjoyed the weight of her hand on his chest. For a second he thought about pulling her to him, kissing her.

He inhaled, preparing to tell her what Sebastian had told him, but stopped himself. She was the only person he wanted to tell, the only person who would understand. He would tell her, but not now; they had both been through enough for one day.

"How did you get on?" she said, motioning toward the crowd of journalists in the distance.

"Fine. You know how it is—they've moved on to the Stokeses already."

Irene looked away. "My heart breaks for them. They have absolutely no resolution now. Their son's dead and no one has been blamed."

Daniel remembered Sebastian whispering that he had put the brick on Ben's face. He shuddered in the damp cold, trying to shake off the memory. He put his hands in his pockets and looked up at the dark sky, which promised rain.

"We're a good team, though," she said.

He met her eye and nodded. She put a hand on his lapel again.

Suddenly he felt the weight of her tilt toward him. She stood on her tiptoes and kissed his lips.

Her lips were cold. He felt the first drops of rain on his head. He was too jolted to return the kiss, but he stayed close to her until she backed away.

"I'm sorry," she said, turning from him, a flush on her cheeks, allowing her hair to fall over her eyes.

He ran his hand up her neck and his thumb across her chin. He didn't know what would happen now, but it felt significant.

EPILOGUE

THE RAIN HAD JUST STOPPED WHEN DANIEL PULLED INTO Brampton. He felt a rare calm settle on him. Until he'd reached Cumbria, the trial had been on his mind.

He was not sure if he had ever thought Sebastian innocent. It had never mattered to him beyond the case. But now that the little boy was free and had admitted his guilt, Daniel felt responsible. The child needed help, but Daniel's role in that was now over. He could only hope that the case conference and the professionals who had been involved with Sebastian so far would realize what he needed.

If the verdict had been different, Daniel knew that he would not feel better. His experience of secure units, juvenile detention centers, and prisons had shown him that however damaged juveniles had been in the past, however desperate their

problems, they would only be made worse in the places they
would be sent for punishment and rehabilitation.

Now that he was in Brampton, Sebastian seemed far away:
painfully faint, like a note he had to strain to hear. It was nearly
winter, and Brampton's trees had been blown free of their
leaves. The naked trees stood stark against the sky, like lungs.
He heard the rain splash against the tires of his car as he drove
into the village. He took a breath and held it, wondering what
rare change would have been possible if Sebastian had known
a Minnie.

He tried to push aside thoughts of the boy. He remembered
the taste of Irene's lips from the evening before and smiled.

He pulled up outside the farm. The yard had been tidied
and the old coop had been removed. The garden had been dug
and the grass at the front cut. Daniel inhaled the clean smell
of the earth. The air was cold and so he took out his key and
stepped inside the farmhouse, for the last time.

It was different from before. There was almost no trace of
her now. The floors were spotlessly clean and the bathroom
and kitchen smelled of bleach. He had never seen the old elec-
tric cooker shining so white. He ran his forefinger along it, remembering the meals she had cooked for him there: shepherd's
pie, fish and chips, roast beef and Yorkshire puddings.

The putty around the windows had been replaced and the
windows painted. The table was clear and the fridge open and
clean. He would meet Cunningham later to exchange the con-
tracts and hand over the keys. He remembered coming to the
empty house a few months before, still angry with her, aching
but not acknowledging her loss—asking for all her things to be

thrown away, professionally cleared. Now he wished to see the
newspaper she had been reading, her jars of odd buttons, her
old clothes, her vinyl records that had not to be marked with
fingerprints, the animals that had shared her life while he had
scorned her.

Daniel's throat hurt. He opened the door to the living room.
It was empty: gone her old couch, gone her old-fashioned television and video recorder, gone her photographs and pictures,
gone the footstool on which she would rest her thick-skinned,
hard-nailed feet.

The floorboards were scuffed from the feet of the piano, the
wood darker where the body of the instrument had shaded the
floor from the light. Daniel covered his eyes with both hands.
I'm sorry, Mam, he whispered in the quiet, empty farmhouse,
his throat tight as hot tears flashed across his cheeks. *I never once
thanked you . . . Forgive me. Please forgive me.*

HER BARE FEET PUMPED THE PEDALS, HER KNEES APART AND
the material of her skirt falling in between her thighs. She
straightened her shoulders and leaned back with a laugh as she
struck the keys.

"When did you learn to play the piano?" he asked her. He
was lying on the couch watching her with his hands behind
his head.

"When I was a child. My father liked to play and he taught
both us girls . . . and he would take us to concerts . . . and make
us sit still with our fingers on our lips listening to his records.
Some of those records in there belonged to him, and I listened
to them when I was a little girl." Minnie leaned toward Daniel

as she spoke, right hand tinkling up the keys, her left forefinger pressed against her lips. "Would you like me to teach you?"

He shook his head. "Did your daughter play piano?"

She didn't answer.

He still didn't understand about the little girl whose butterfly he had tried to steal, but each time he saw the butterfly he thought of her.

"She could play a little," was all she said, and then she started to play again, loudly, so that he could feel the vibrations through the couch. It made his scalp itch. He watched her, as her cheeks reddened and her eyes misted with tears. But then, like always, she threw back her head and laughed. She looked out of the window, her strong hands heavy on the keys.

"Ach, *come on,* will you now, Danny. Sit down here beside me and let me see what you can do."

Again he shook his head.

"I heard you playing the other week, you know. You thought I was outside but I heard you try. It won't break, you know. I can teach you how to play a tune, or you can do your own thing. It doesn't matter. It just feels nice to make a noise sometimes. It stops the noise in your head. You'll see. Come and sit beside me . . . "

She moved over on the long piano stool, and patted the spot beside her. It was only a fortnight since he had been beaten up and run away to his mother's. His nose still felt funny and he sniffed as he sat down beside her and looked at the keys. He could smell the damp wool of her and feel the soft cushion of her hip against his.

"Do you want me to teach you a wee easy song, or do you just want to make a noise? Both are fine with me."

"Teach me something, then," he said quietly, letting his fingers fall on the keys. He listened to the lonely, hollow notes that sounded.

"Right, well, if you look at the keyboard, you have your black and you have your white keys. What do you notice about the way the black keys are grouped?"

Daniel stroked a finger across the black keys. "Some are in twos, some are in threes."

"God, you're a smarty-pants, aren't you now. Why don't you teach me to play the bloody piano?" She laughed and Daniel turned to smile up at her. From this angle he could see the space in her teeth: her missing tooth was on the top, near the molar.

"And now listen to this." She reached to the right side of the piano, stretching across him so that her face was close to his. She struck the keys and then ran her fingers down the keyboard and struck the keys at the very left of the piano. "What do you notice about the difference in the sound?" she said, leaning close to him, so that he could see the dark blue rings around her pale blue eyes. They were like marbles, hard and clear.

"That's low and that's high," he said, pointing at either end of the piano.

"Right you are, high on the right and low on the left—sure but you're a natural. Now, we'll try *a duet*."

She took time to show him the high keys of the piano, numbering them one, two, and three, in the order that she wanted him to play them, and then she started to play a tune at the low end of the piano. She showed him when to push down on the keys, trying to get him to use a three-finger action, but he preferred to stab with his forefinger, enjoying the chill note that he produced.

They did that for a few minutes, with her playing the song on the left of the keyboard and elbowing him in the ribs and shouting *now, now,* with her strange Irish vowels, when she wanted him to play the notes she had taught him at his end. She told him the song was called "Heart and Soul."

But he tired of it, and slammed the keys with his palms. *Tring tring tring,* up and down. He expected anger from her. He still didn't know her well. He looked up into her eyes, but they were wide with glee. She slammed her own palms down on the low keys, so that the grave noise chimed with his high-pitched squeals and yelps. It was a duet all the same. The noise chased Blitz from the room, and she started singing at the top of her voice, any old words and so did he, until he was hoarse and until they were half deaf and tears ran down both their cheeks with laughter.

Then they were still, and she pressed him into her. He was tired and he allowed it. As the ringing subsided in his ears, a thought came to him, sharp and clear as the high note on the piano. He liked her, and he wanted to stay. The thought resonated slowly in his head and it made him quiet. He smoothed the ivory-coated wood of the piano, his fingers still tingling from the bashing he had given the keys.

ACKNOWLEDGMENTS

I WOULD FIRST LIKE TO SAY A BIG THANK YOU TO MY UK editor, Emma Beswetherick, for her creativity and support, and to Amanda Bergeron and to all at William Morrow in the U.S. for their tireless enthusiasm.

Several people have given their time to help my research for this book, and this was crucial in helping to make the worlds the characters inhabit more believable. I would particularly like to thank Kate Barrie, Tony Beswetherick, Iain Cockbain, Jason Cubbon, Jacinta Jones, Eileen Leyden, John Leyden, Sarah Long, Alastair and Juliette MacDonald, Sandra Morrison, Laura Stuart, Sarah Stuart, and Scott A. Ware for their various help on everything from the legal world to regional accents, music, and locations. Very special thanks to Gerry Considine for allowing me insight into the work of a criminal solicitor, and to Liz and Alan Paterson for their advice on social work issues.

Writing involves spending a lot of time by yourself, but

ACKNOWLEDGMENTS 453

I doubt that this creative solitude would have been possible without my many friends, family, and colleagues who all believed that someday this would happen even though I doubted it. I would particularly like to thank Paul Ballantyne; Russell Ballantyne; the Darroch sisters, Mairi, Jane, and Val; Marie Kobine; Helen Leyden; Allan MacLean; Erin MacLean; Jennifer Markey; Julie Ramsay; Ian Thomson; Gordon Webb.

But it is readers who complete writers, and my greatest debt is to my own early readers, without whose positive criticism I may never have written another word: Kent and Mary Ballantyne, Rita Balneaves, Mary Fitzgerald-Peltier, Mark Kobine, Phil Mason, and Elizabeth McCrone. This book would not exist without you.

While researching the novel, I read *As If,* by Blake Morrison, and *The Case of Mary Bell,* by Gitta Sereny. I would like to thank both writers for their very different but equally insightful portraits of children on trial.

Last, but certainly not least, a great many thanks to my wonderful agent, Nicola Barr, for her astuteness, her faith, and her encouragement.

About the author

About the book

Insights,
Interviews
& More . . .

Read on

Meet Lisa Ballantyne

LISA BALLANTYNE was born in Scotland and is a graduate of the University of St. Andrews. She spent most of her twenties working and living in China, before returning to the UK in 2002 to work in higher education, most recently at the University of Glasgow. She lives in Glasgow, Scotland. This is her first novel. ∿

Reading Group Guide

- Who do you think is "the guilty one" in the story?
- How do the two strands of the story complement each other? Do they work together successfully?
- Who is your favorite character and why?
- Do you think it was right for Minnie to lie to Daniel?
- Can you discuss Daniel's resentment toward Minnie?
- How well does the story explore the subject of foster care and/or children in the criminal justice system?
- What connections can you draw between Daniel as a child and then as an adult?
- Can you comment on the way in which the story explores the relationship between mothers and sons/adults and children?
- Before the truth was revealed, did you believe Sebastian to be guilty or innocent?
- What have you taken away from the story? What do you think the author was trying to say? ❧

Write What You Know?

by Lisa Ballantyne

THE FIRST COPYEDITOR who read *The Guilty One* contacted my UK editor to ask if it was written by someone working in social work, psychiatry, or law. It is a terrible admission, but I actually have no experience in any of these fields. I literally did make it all up and am therefore not a good example of the adage, "write what you know."

My own experience is vastly different from the world of this book. I studied literature at university, and I have worked in the charity sector, international development, and higher education. I spent six years of my life in China and have traveled all over the world . . . but I have *never* visited Cumbria where one narrative of the book is set.

To make the world of the book believable, therefore, I had to undertake *a lot* of research, which included visiting the infamous Old Bailey courthouse in London. I scouted out the location for the murder and the area where Daniel lived. I researched farming and the Cumbria area where Minnie Flynn lives. I consulted social workers and criminal solicitors to learn more about the worlds of my characters.

Once my notes were complete and the characters were fully formed, it was just a case of getting it out, writing it, and trying to make some sense of the story. When I was writing, I could never have imagined that I would be able to get published; I just felt very driven to tell the story.

So why did I write this book? For me, writing is very much an act of discovery and I am often more surprised than anyone else about where it takes me. In this case, I began to have a clear image of the book's two main characters: Daniel as a child, and his foster mother, Minnie. I could see them and I could smell them. In the same way you might dig something out of the sand, I discovered the story from working through that essential relationship.

I knew that Daniel was telling us the story as an adult. I could see him in a suit in London, but it was later that I pictured him as a lawyer, and a criminal defense solicitor. Similarly, I knew that Minnie was drinking too much because she was in terrible emotional pain, and it was after a while that I realized she had lost her daughter and her husband.

When I was working on the beginning of this book, there were a number of stories in the UK press about two young boys who had nearly killed another two children. The ▶

newspapers were vociferous, demonizing the boys, and invoking other famous children who had killed.

At the time, reading those newspaper stories, I felt appalled by the crime but also very frustrated. There seemed to be an issue that few were discussing: *Why* the children had committed this terrible crime, and, now that it had happened, what they needed to help them realize what they had done and move past it.

I then became interested in juxtaposing Daniel's troubled childhood—which was heading for a similar life of violent crime before Minnie's intervention—with that of a young client accused of murder.

This book is very much Daniel's story—of being a young, damaged, and violent child, but someone who grew to become a largely functional, caring adult. Sebastian, the young boy on trial in the book, is there to throw Daniel's story into relief. There is a quote at the beginning of the book from Victor Hugo's *Les Misérables*, which reads, "The soul in darkness sins, but the real sinner is he who caused the darkness."

For me, this draws out one of the main themes of the book: The causes of crime, and our responsibility to the people who commit crime, particularly the children. The question of Sebastian's guilt or innocence is really irrelevant, as everyone in the book is guilty.

So perhaps the adage should not be write what you know, but write what interests you. Certainly, the journey that I undertook in writing this book was very satisfying. I can only hope that readers will share my fascination with these characters and their struggle. ∽

Author Q&A

Have you always wanted to be a writer?

Yes, but not always a novelist. For many years I wrote poetry, which, as a pastime, is somewhat more sociable. I felt compelled to write long fiction because characters and their lives began to inhabit me.

Can you tell us a little about what inspired you to write The Guilty One *and whether the writing process was an easy one?*

I am always drawn to characters, and I was "visited" by the characters of Minnie and Daniel. The other characters and the story of *The Guilty One* evolved as a result of trying to understand this fundamental relationship.

How did it feel to find a publisher for your debut novel?

I can't describe it. Even now, months after the fact, I have trouble believing it has happened.

After your book deal in the UK, The Guilty One *then sold here in the U.S. and around the world. How did you react to this?*

Luckily I was very busy at work while all this was happening, and it helped me to distance myself from it. I still wonder if I somehow slipped into a parallel universe.

New writers are often advised to write about what they know. Do you know a lot about criminal law and foster care in order to have written about it so authentically?

I don't write about what I know, but I do write about what interests me, and my commitment to the characters fuels my research. In wishing to make my characters believable, I want to make the worlds they inhabit believable, too—however, I am still reticent to call my representations of these worlds authentic. At best I would hope they are believable. There are few things more fun than researching fictional characters. It is like stalking your own imagination.

Did your characters appear in your head fully formed or did they transform as the book evolved? Who is your favorite character?

Daniel and Minnie were very vivid— right down to the smell of them— from early on. Other characters, but also the adult Daniel, evolved as the story progressed. ▶

Daniel is the most intriguing, and I wonder what he is up to now, but I admire Minnie's bravery.

Daniel has a very strong view about the ways in which society should deal with juvenile criminals. Do Daniel's views mirror your own?

The character of Sebastian developed almost as a construct to elucidate Daniel's struggle with nature and nurture. The story suggests that criminals are made not born but the adult Daniel also highlights how out of step the UK is with much of Europe when it comes to children and criminal justice.

Do you think Minnie did the right thing in lying to Daniel?

I think when we love people we often make choices that can be difficult to justify afterward.

In your opinion, who is most guilty in the story?

Almost everyone in the story is guilty. They are all guilty in different and almost incomparable ways.

What are you working on now?

A story about obedience and rebellion. ᔐ

The Top Ten Things Lisa Ballantyne Has Learned About Writing a Novel

1. Write if you feel driven to, then you will always find it satisfying.

2. Once it's written, it exists—don't think too much, write it down. It is easier to revise a finished piece of work.

3. A writer writes.

4. Spend time perfecting your work, but show your work to others.

5. Read, read, read.

6. Research is for background and for confidence. You don't have to squeeze it all in.

7. Live life, or you won't have anything to write about.

8. Write about what interests you, then it is more likely others will be interested.

9. Exercise before sitting down to write.

10. Delete as little as possible and keep all your drafts. ᶜᵛ

What Is on Lisa Ballantyne's Bookshelf?

Jean-Paul Sartre—*Being and Nothingness*
Simone de Beauvoir—*The Ethics of Ambiguity*
Poems of Norman McCaig
Toni Morrison—*Beloved*
Richard Holloway—*Godless Morality*
Margaret Atwood—*Cat's Eye*
Michael Ondaatje—*In the Skin of a Lion*
Joyce Carol Oates—*We Were the Mulvaneys*
Germaine Greer—*The Beautiful Boy*
Milan Kundera—*The Unbearable Lightness of Being*
Robert M. Pirsig—*Zen and the Art of Motorcycle Maintenance*
John Irving—*The World According to Garp*
Olive Schreiner—*The Story of an African Farm* ❧

Don't miss the next book by your favorite author. Sign up now for AuthorTracker by visiting www.AuthorTracker.com.